I0721606

# WINDS OF COURAGE

# A MAGE'S APPRENTICE SERIES

Winds of Courage

Storms of Allegiance

Tempests of Truth

*And set in the same world:*

# A MAGE'S INFLUENCE SERIES

Seeds of Glory and Ruin

Vines of Promise and Deceit

Thorns of Hope and Betrayal

Forests of Grandeur and Malice

# WINDS OF COURAGE

## A MAGE'S APPRENTICE BOOK 1

MELANIE CELLIER

LUMINANT PUBLICATIONS

WINDS OF COURAGE

Copyright © 2023 by Melanie Cellier

A Mage's Apprentice Book 1
First edition published in 2021 (v1.1)
by Luminant Publications

All rights reserved. Without limiting the rights under copyright reserved above, no part of this publication may be reproduced, distributed, transmitted, stored in, or introduced into a database or retrieval system, in any form, or by any means, without the prior written permission of both the copyright owner and the above publisher of this book.

The characters and events portrayed in this book are fictitious. Any similarity to real persons, living or dead, is coincidental and not intended by the author.

ISBN 978-1-922636-94-2

Luminant Publications
PO Box 305
Greenacres, South Australia 5086

melanie@melaniecellier.com
http://www.melaniecellier.com

Cover Design by Karri Klawiter
Editing by Mary Novak
Proofreading by James Packer
Map Illustration by Rebecca E Paavo

*For everyone who has ever had the courage to face their own
weakness*

HIDDEN CITY
NOMAD LANDS
KINGDOM of CALISTA
VIRIDIAN RIVER
CELADON RIVER
CALINARA
NOMAD LANDS
LAKE ATERRA
CADENCE'S HOUSE
HUNTING LODGE
CELADON RIVER
KINGDOM of TARTORA
TARONA
VIRIDIAN RIVER
N
W
E
S

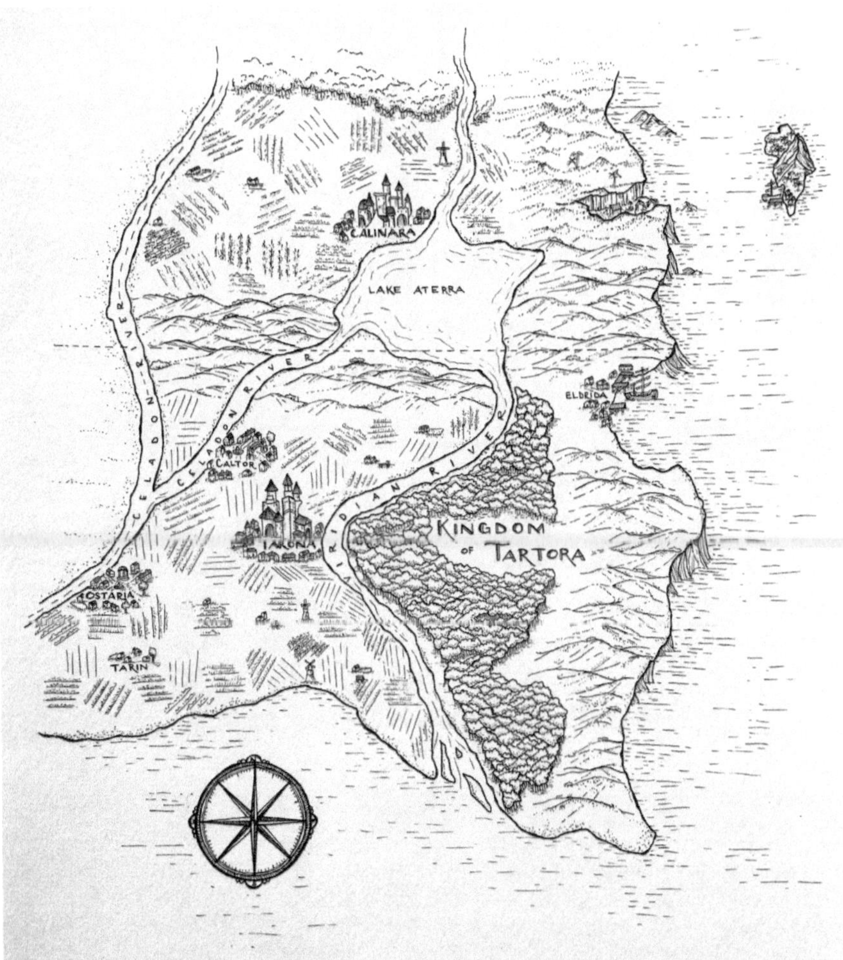

CALINARA
LAKE ATERRA
ELDRIDA
CELADON RIVER
CEVADON RIVER
VIRIDIAN RIVER
CALTOR
IRONA
Kingdom of TARTORA
HOSTARIA
TARIN

CHAPTER

# ONE

Rocky ran past, his lean, black legs flying as he joyfully circled the meadow. He would have made a fine sheep-dog, but Father had been too fond of him, even as a puppy. When he took him into the house as a pet, he had claimed it was for my benefit. I had spent years begging for a dog who could live inside with us instead of outside as a working animal. But, given the way he doted on the tiny ball of fur, he didn't fool either Mother or me.

And Rocky responded to my father's love with a brightness that made us all smile. His unswerving loyalty would rouse affection in the coldest heart. Rocky might belong to Father first and foremost, but I always let him come for a run when I came out to inspect the fields.

A high yip made me freeze, my eyes skimming the fields as I looked for Rocky's moving body. He had disappeared.

Picking up my skirts, I ran for the spot I had last seen him. My heart contracted when I called his name and heard nothing in reply. The fields were bare and ready for planting, so there was no chance his lean body was hidden within the tall green stalks that usually covered the brown dirt. Where could he have gone?

I was moving so fast, I almost pitched headlong into a large crack in the ground that cut off the far corner of the field. The unexpected drop was hard to see from a distance, and Rocky had been running much faster than me.

I ignored the problem of the ditch's appearance—the earth in this area did shift occasionally, and it always meant days of work to restore the field. All I cared about in this moment was the missing animal.

I dropped to my knees in the rough dirt and peered over the unstable edge. Rocky gave a pitiful whine at sight of me, mustering the energy to thump his tail slightly against the ground beneath him. The effort made my heart twist. Even when injured and in danger, Rocky responded to the presence of one of his family.

"Good boy," I murmured, even as my mind raced.

He had survived the fall, which was my first worry, but it wasn't like him to just lie there. He would have risen if he was able to do so.

If I jumped in after him, would I be able to hoist him out and then scramble out myself? The trench was deep, but I might be able to manage it.

I leaned further over, trying to get a better look at Rocky's state. My eyes fell on one of his back legs which was bent at an unnatural angle.

As soon as I saw it, the blood rushed from my head, a roaring sound filling my ears. I fell back, gasping for breath and trying to suppress the light-headedness that was threatening to send me into unconsciousness. Forcing myself not to think of Rocky's injuries, I knelt in the dirt, my head hanging low as I debated whether I needed to lie down. The worst thing I could do right now was faint. Rocky was relying on me.

As the seconds passed, the feeling slowly faded, replaced by tears that welled in my eyes, stopping just short of falling.

There was no way I could go into that trench to rescue Rocky. I was useless to him, just as I always was in this sort of crisis.

After several more ragged breaths, I risked standing. When my head and stomach remained settled, I called down to Rocky, keeping my eyes carefully averted as I did.

"I'm sorry, boy." I hoped my voice conveyed some reassurance. "I'm going to have to go for help. You just lie still until I get back."

His tail thumped again, and it took everything I had to turn and leave him. As I ran, making for the farmhouse by the most direct route, I could barely suppress more tears. Why was I so useless? Surely eighteen years should have been enough to overcome such a foolish weakness. Why did I never get any better? Just the thought—let alone the sight—of illness, injury, or the inner workings of the body was enough to set me off and make me more useless than a newborn baby.

I sped through dark brown fields which lay ready for spring planting, moving faster than was probably wise. But the thought of Rocky lying alone in the ditch drove me on.

By the time I arrived in the clear space between the front of the farmhouse and the barn, I was ready to collapse. But a distant bark reached me from across the fields, sending a shot of energy coursing through my limbs.

"Father!" I called between my gasps. "Come quick!"

He appeared from inside the barn, his steps quick and his brow drawn.

"Delphine! What's wrong?"

I didn't usually make a fuss, so just the sound of my anxious tone had him worried. When he saw my expression, the lines of his face deepened.

"What is it, lass?" he barked. "What's happened?"

"It's Rocky." My breath had finally calmed enough for normal speech. "The earth shifted in the northeast field. There's a trench there now, and Rocky fell into it. I think he's injured, and..." I hesitated. "I couldn't get him out on my own," I finally finished in a defeated voice.

Father sent me a sharp look, glancing toward the farmhouse although there was no sign of my mother anywhere nearby. I knew better than to even allude to my weakness in her presence. Father had been with me the first time I encountered an injured animal as a child, and he had sworn me to utter secrecy, even from Mother.

I had instantly grasped the shame I brought to the family by being so weak, so I had been careful ever since, although it hurt to keep a secret from my mother. But I didn't want to see her wounded by my impediment—not when she had already grieved so much at only being granted one child.

Even back then, I had known that I carried the future of our farm on my shoulders. And how many times had Father said that farms required strength of both body and mind?

"He's too far down," I added. "We need rope."

I finally noticed the coil of rope slung over my father's shoulder, and affection rushed through me. Despite my unexpected arrival, and his anxiety, my father had kept a level head, grabbing a potentially useful tool on his way out. If Father expected strength from me, he expected even more from himself, exemplifying the kind of person who kept a farm thriving and prosperous.

"Let's go then," he said gruffly, clearly trying to hide his emotion over his beloved pet being alone and in danger.

I nodded, trying to hide my exhaustion as I hurried to his side. He set out across the fields, and I followed close behind. But within a short distance, I realized he was holding back his pace for my sake, aware of the fatigue weighing down my limbs.

"You go on ahead," I said. "I don't like the idea of Rocky lying there alone. Just don't try anything on your own. I don't think I could pull both of you out of there, even with a rope."

He paused, looking back at me with uncertainty.

"Go! Go!" I flapped my hands at him, and he nodded once before increasing his pace.

I followed as fast as I could push myself, the distance between us widening. Despite my warning, I doubted Father would wait for my arrival to begin the rescue process. I would likely find him in the trench with Rocky when I arrived.

Sure enough, when I finally reached the spot, there was no sign of my father. Peering carefully over the edge, I saw him easing the rope around Rocky's middle, murmuring reassurances as he did so.

I kept my eyes averted from Rocky's back legs, focusing on my father instead.

"Really, Father?" I put my hands on my hips. "Do my words mean nothing to you?"

He laughed gruffly. "I'll be fine, lass. You know that." He grinned up at me. "You get more like your mother every day. But worrying won't run a farm."

I rolled my eyes at his oft-repeated pronouncement.

"Neither will getting stuck in a ditch," I muttered but without heat. My father was stronger than I was in more ways than one, and there wasn't a ditch that could keep him contained. I was only quibbling out of the wish to be useful in some way.

It didn't take him long to finish securing Rocky. Despite the dog's injuries, he submitted to my father's actions without complaint, making my heart squeeze again.

Looping the loose end of the rope over his shoulder several times, my father prepared to climb back out. I leaned over, reaching down an arm, but he waved me away.

Frowning at the wall of dirt in front of him, he remained still for several moments. Curious, I leaned back over, trying to see what was happening.

At first I could see nothing, but then slight movement drew

my eye. Pushing slowly from the rough dirt like a thick worm, the tip of a root appeared. There must have been trees in this area once, before it was cleared for planting, leaving behind this long-buried trace of their presence.

Another root appeared, pushing out of the dirt higher up the trench wall. It was followed by a third and a fourth before my father's shoulders slumped in fatigue, his face relaxing.

"That should be enough," he said.

I examined their placement. "You'll use them to climb out?"

He answered with his actions, placing his foot on the first of the roots and reaching up to grasp the highest one with his hand. With the help of the perfectly placed foot and hand holds, he was back up at ground level within seconds.

Frustration churned in my gut at this reminder of yet another way I was weaker than my father. His plants power might be considered barely middle strength, but it was endlessly helpful on a farm. Whereas I was entirely useless, unable to use any power at all.

Father didn't speak any criticism, though. Instead he handed me the rope.

"You pull from back here, and I'll pull from beside the trench so I'm on hand to help him over the edge."

He knelt in the dirt, gesturing for me to back up. As usual, he was silently protecting me from triggering my squeamishness, finding ways not to draw attention to it, although we were alone out here.

Blinking back tears again, I stumbled several steps backward. Father looked my way, checking I was in position as his hands tightened around the length of rope.

I planted my feet and leaned slightly back, bracing myself as I began the first pull.

"Stop!" The shout rang across the fields, making me start so violently I nearly dropped the rope.

Swinging around, I stared at the person hurrying in our

direction. Who could it be? I could see at a glance it wasn't my mother, but there was no one else on the farm. When I was young, Father had a farm hand to help him, but our land was small enough that we had been making do with just Mother, Father, and me since I turned fourteen. We did occasionally have visitors from Tarin, the closest town, but they came via the road, not across the fields.

The figure was moving at speed, quickly becoming clearer. It was a woman—not old, but not young either. At a guess she might have had fifteen years on me. She appeared to be entirely alone, but she showed neither discomfort nor concern at approaching two strangers.

Her steps finally slowed as she reached me. Caution replaced my surprise as I took in the simple but expensive material of her clothes. Even their cut spoke of wealth, the design giving her an air of elegance even as she stooped to kneel in a dirt field. Lone travelers—especially women—were unusual, and even more unusual was a lone affluent traveler. I could only think of one group in society who would behave in such a manner.

Mages.

Churning anxiety, previously held at bay by the urgency of the situation, flooded through me. What was a Guild mage doing in Tarin, let alone on our farm?

I threw a frantic glance at my father. His hard expression showed he'd come to the same conclusion. I tried to think of what I could do to mitigate the situation, unsure if I should be shielding Father from the mage or the woman from my father.

But it was hard to process past the question being shouted silently inside my mind. Had she come for me?

Surely she hadn't come for me.

The woman seemed to confirm my conclusion when she didn't glance in my direction. Instead she was focused on Rocky inside the trench, my father's frozen, furious look doing nothing to put her off.

"If you pull that animal up, you'll cause him great pain and likely considerable further damage."

My father's hands relaxed around the rope, new concern showing in his eyes as he glanced at the trench. But when he looked back at the woman, his face hardened again.

"And how would you know anything about the matter?"

"I sensed his distress from all the way over on the road. His injuries must be significant."

My father frowned, so I forced myself to find my voice. "You have a healing affinity, then?"

It would have been remarkable good fortune if a healing mage happened to be passing by just as Rocky was injured. Mages of any affinity never passed our remote farm, let alone the specific one we needed.

Father shot her a look, and I knew him well enough to read the struggle behind it. The last thing he wanted to do was accept help from a mage, but if this woman could really heal Rocky, how could he refuse her services?

But the woman gave a regretful grimace. "I'm afraid I don't. But my influencer did." When neither of us spoke in response to this astonishing disclosure, she continued. "I'm an elements mage."

"You're elements cross healing, and yet you sensed Rocky from the road?" I gaped at her. "You must be very strong!"

Only those with a healing affinity had a connection with animals. Not even the strongest elements mage would be able to sense a dog's distress. And while it was true that someone with a cross influence had traces of their influencer's affinity clinging to their power, for that hint to be enough for such a thing...I shook my head. It was hard to fathom that sort of strength.

The woman smiled slightly, turning her attention toward

Rocky in an obvious dismissal of the subject. Her lack of response shook loose the rock in my stomach. If she'd come for me, surely she would have taken the opportunity to boast of her strength. From what I had heard about Guild mages, that was their usual style.

"So you can't tell how injured he is?" I leaned forward to peer down at Rocky, concern at his unusually subdued demeanor overriding my worry about my own reaction.

"Not in any detail." The woman sat back on her heels with a sigh. "Even a healer would need physical contact with him to make a full assessment." She shot a quick glance at me. "But don't be too concerned. I heard him bark from the road, so he has some spark left."

I nodded briefly in response to her sympathetic smile before turning my attention to my father. His silence was uncharacteristic, but I could see he was still wrestling with his internal conundrum. Hoping to take the weight of interacting with a mage off his shoulders, I turned back to the woman.

"We need to get him out. You said not to pull him up, but we can't just leave him in there."

The woman turned to look at me, her eyes focused on me in a way they hadn't been previously.

"My name is Amara, by the way," she said.

I hesitated, unsure if I should attempt a curtsy despite my personal distaste for mages. If she could save Rocky, I was willing to put aside my pride. But a curtsy seemed out of place in the middle of a muddy field, so after an awkward pause, I settled on bowing my head respectfully.

It was less difficult to do than I had expected. Despite her background, something in Amara's gaze and bearing commanded instinctive respect. And I couldn't even hate her for the effect since her eyes held not only strength but also a warm spark that softened the overall effect.

Something about her made me think she would be a

dangerous woman to cross—but that if you found yourself in need, she would help without thought of return. I shook my head to dislodge the fanciful idea. Our family knew well how alluring mages could be, but they didn't help unless there was something in it for them.

Amara gave me a pointed look, and I cleared my throat. "I'm Delphine."

She waited as if expecting more, but I said nothing. After a moment, she turned back to the trench.

"My influencer was unusual in that he specialized in both humans and animals," she said, referring to the mage she had apprenticed under. "I've seen many injured creatures, and from observing Rocky, I suspect he has injured both of his back legs."

"Both?" I squeaked, horrified.

I had seen one but since I'd looked away immediately, I hadn't registered the injury to the other. It would be impossible to hoist him out of the trench without jarring his legs repeatedly. If we damaged them enough, they might end up injured beyond the capacity of the single animal healer in Tarin. And if Halmir couldn't save the legs, Rocky would have no chance. A dog could survive with only one back leg, but not without both —not a dog like Rocky, anyway.

"I acknowledge it would be more helpful if I had a healing affinity," Amara said with unabated calm. "But my elements ability is not without its use here. I'll bring him up, protecting his legs in a cushion of air. I can make sure they aren't jostled or moved."

She looked at my father. "Tarin must be the closest town. Is there an animal healer there?"

"Aye." My father nodded, breaking his silence. "Just the one, but he has enough strength for a simple break, and he should be able to set a more complex one on the path to healing." Obviously his concern for Rocky had won out over his hatred of Guild mages.

Amara smiled in satisfaction. "Excellent. I suspect they're clean breaks, so he should do well. As long as we can avoid causing further damage. Unless..." Her voice lingered on the word.

"Unless?" I asked, my anxiety for Rocky making the word come out sharper than I'd intended.

"Unless you think you've learned enough to heal him where he lies?" She turned to me. "That would be the best solution, and if the breaks are simple enough it shouldn't take much skill. As long as you have the strength, it could be accomplished, I suspect."

"What?" I stared at her, the earlier anxiety rushing back through me in a wave strong enough to make my knees waver. I drew in a deep breath, forcing my legs to lock and my back to straighten.

"I'm not a healer." I faced the woman, excess energy coursing through me. I had to grip my hands into fists to stop them shaking.

She raised her eyebrows, looking me slowly up and down. "I heard that the daughter of this house was born with a powerful healing seed. And you look as if you must be seventeen already. Are you not her?"

I looked away, unable to meet her eyes. So she had come here on purpose to see me, after all? If so, was she just pretending not to know that I hadn't had the seed of my power activated at seventeen according to the usual custom?

"Delphine is our only daughter," my father said. The pride in his voice made my eyes sting.

"I'm a simple farmer like my parents." I let my eyes roam over our barn and surrounding fields before returning to the mage. "Whatever you've heard, I'm no healer."

Amara continued to assess me, her gaze cool and curious.

"Interesting. You say you're no healer, and yet you don't claim an elements or plants affinity instead. So does that mean you do have a healing seed, but you resent your affinity? You wouldn't be the first. Since the foolish in the capital view the elements affinity as the strongest, some children wish for an elements seed. But healing is usually well-regarded also. Don't you find joy in knowing you can ensure the health and safety of your family and loved ones? Most people value that."

I met her eyes, my chin lifting. "I don't need to be a healer to keep my family safe. My parents are hardworking, and ours is a prosperous farm. I intend to make it even more so. I will earn the gold necessary to hire any healer our family might need."

The woman glanced at Rocky, not needing words to make her point.

I hated how quickly this mage had seen through to my hidden weakness. My healing seed was a horrible mistake since I would clearly never be a healer. I couldn't even help Rocky with my own two hands without almost losing consciousness. My parents used their plants power to aid our farm, but since I had been saddled with a healing seed, I could never follow in their footsteps in that way.

My fists tightened, and I carefully avoided looking at my father. He must be furious at the turn of the conversation, although he was clearly holding in his thoughts out of concern for Rocky.

"If you're trying to suggest that I should be activated so that I can provide healing in the case of future accidents," I said, "then you must know less of the world than I thought. My seed has been assessed as strong enough to qualify as a mage, and everyone knows mages don't live on remote farms. They go away to the Guild for their apprenticeships, and if they ever return from the capital, it's only to run healing clinics in cities and town centers or to pass through briefly at planting time or harvest. A healing mage will never be on hand in our fields. But I will be here. As I said, I'm no healer."

The woman's face shifted slightly, but I didn't know her well enough to read the emotion.

"It sounds as if it's the strength of your seed you resent, rather than your affinity," she said calmly. "It's a rare thing for a strong seed to be born to two weak parents—most families count it a great blessing."

My father muttered something under his breath that I hoped Amara hadn't caught.

"That is their business." I glared at her. "I will keep my eyes on my own business, and I request you to do the same."

I expected Amara to take offense at my words, but she didn't respond at all beyond a slight tightening around her eyes. After a silent moment, she turned back to the trench.

A whimper from within its depths dispelled my nervous energy and sent me to my knees so I could peer over the edge to check on Rocky. A gasp escaped when I felt a cross breeze on my face and saw Rocky rising slowly into the air. I turned my head to stare at Amara. She was already bringing him up?

Her attention was focused on the moving animal, but otherwise she gave no indication of being in the middle of a difficult task.

I wasn't sure what I had expected. Mages were merely people with a stronger seed than the seeds of normal folk. They didn't use their power in a different way, they just had the ability to do more. And when the adults I knew used their power in their daily lives, I never felt it. I wasn't sure why I had expected Amara to be any different. Had I thought the strength of her power would make it palpable?

A momentary curiosity brushed against my thoughts. If my seed was activated, and I could access my own power, would that give me the ability to feel others using their power?

I shook my head at my foolishness. Sensing power itself was the province of those with a power affinity—a seed so rare that no one I knew had ever met someone who possessed it. I had no time for fairy stories—my attention was needed in the daily toil of reality.

I leaned away from the trench as Rocky floated high enough to appear above its edge. Now that he was so close, I realized the breeze from earlier had only been the outer stirrings of a much more concentrated movement of air. A tight circle of wind moved impossibly fast, its speed and density creating a platform that lifted Rocky upward.

I shook my head in wonder. I had never seen a feat that required so much strength. I snuck an admiring glance at the woman next to me. Despite her lack of boasting, she must be strong indeed.

Amara followed Rocky's progress with her eyes, still using neither words nor gestures to direct the unnatural mass of air. My parents never needed outer movement to use their power, but then they had only the weak seeds of regular folk. Despite knowing mages were no different at base—merely stronger—I had always imagined them grandiloquently waving their arms in the air.

"Hold out your arms," Amara directed my father, and he obeyed without question.

The air carrying Rocky gently deposited him into my father's waiting arms. Rocky whimpered again, reaching up as if he intended to lick my father's face, but one stern word was enough to make him meekly settle back down.

"I have a small cart." Amara pointed toward the road. "It's not large, but I can take Rocky and one of you into town in it."

Father hesitated, his body rigid but his eyes glued to Rocky. I winced and hurried to his side.

"I'll go," I said softly, resting a hand on his arm. "I'll take Rocky."

He looked from me to Amara, and I could once again see him wrestling with himself. He wanted to stay with his beloved animal, but sitting beside a mage for all that way would strain him beyond bearing.

"Please let me go," I repeated, desperate to be of use in some small way. "I want to be the one to take him."

I saw the moment he capitulated, giving a single nod of his head before striding toward the cart. I hurried behind him, the two of us reaching it several steps before Amara.

"Watch yourself," Father muttered, shooting Amara a suspicious look. "She'll probably have all sorts of tales about a life of luxury at the Guild, but—"

"Do you have so little faith in me?" I hissed. "I'm not enough of a fool to be taken in by such things. I'm not like my uncle. I won't abandon you and Mother so easily."

Father's face softened as he nestled Rocky among the bags and parcels secured in the back of the cart.

"You're a good lass, Delphine, and you always have been. I trust you." His eyes narrowed again. "I just don't trust her."

Amara arrived, and he fell silent, jerking his head in a movement that could possibly be interpreted as a respectful nod.

"Don't worry about a thing," Amara said kindly, as if Father had protested about imposing on her. "I was already on my way to Tarin, and I won't rest until I see poor Rocky healed. You may be assured I'll take excellent care of both him and your daughter."

Father hesitated, as if that was exactly what he most feared, but I made a shooing motion from behind Amara, and he relented enough to make a small bow.

My eyes lingered on his retreating form as he headed back across the fields toward our farmhouse. When I finally turned back around, Amara was watching me, open curiosity in her gaze.

Uncomfortable, I moved forward to greet the horse harnessed to the cart. The mare had barely moved at all during the rescue process, merely positioning herself where she could graze on the grass that grew on the fringes of the road.

"She's a good girl," Amara said as I ran a hand down her neck.

The horse shook her head slightly in response, making her mane toss. I couldn't help but smile at how much the effect reminded me of Serena, one of the stronger apprentices in town—a girl as well aware of her own worth as this horse was.

With a final pat for the lovely mare, I pulled myself up onto the wooden bench at the front of the cart that served as a seat. As soon as I was settled, I wondered if I should have checked with Amara before climbing up. Perhaps she wanted me in the back with Rocky.

I hated the idea of bowing and scraping to someone just because they were a mage, but it wasn't her status pushing me to show respect for Amara. She had gone out of her way to help us when she was under no obligation to do so, and so far she had asked for nothing in return.

I cleared my throat as Amara climbed up beside me.

"Thank you for helping us."

She smiled across at me. "Of course. I couldn't just ride past an animal in pain. If it makes you feel more comfortable, you can think of it as something I'm doing for Rocky."

I nodded, feeling inside my pocket for the small pouch my father had slipped to me. Its leather was worn and soft beneath my fingers, its weight reassuring. It had the necessary gold to pay for the healing, so at least we weren't imposing on the mage for more than a ride.

But even as I was grateful for the coins, I wished we didn't have to part with our funds so unnecessarily. If only I wasn't so useless, I could have healed Rocky myself. A mage might have to leave home, but I could have activated my power at a lower level if only I wasn't crippled by my weakness.

What sort of useless person was born with both a healing

seed and unconquerable squeamishness? It was a wasteful combination, and I understood my father's instinct for secrecy. Why would I want to advertise my shame?

"Don't worry," Amara added, perhaps seeing the discomfort on my face and misunderstanding the cause. "If the healing takes too long, I'll see you have a safe place to stay for the night."

I tried to smile although the expression felt false. Was she flaunting her wealth and philanthropy? Or did she think I would be eager to spend time around her?

Nothing could be less true. While I knew my heart was safe, my parents would worry the whole time I was gone. A lone mage wasn't the Guild, but it was a close enough connection to make them uncomfortable. My uncle had left and never returned, so I could understand their anxiety. I could only hope the healer would work quickly, leaving enough time for Rocky and me to make it home before darkness fell.

# TWO

Our farm wasn't too far out of town, but the road felt interminable when every bump and swerve made the passenger in the back whine in pain. Rocky's obvious efforts to suppress his response only made it worse. Several times I had to restrain myself from urging Amara to go faster.

"You know this area better than me," she said after a particularly loud whimper from Rocky. "Is Tarin much further?"

"No, we should arrive soon. And it's not an especially large town. It won't take us long to reach Halmir."

"Halmir is the animal healer, I presume. In which case, I'm guessing he's located on the outskirts of the town. Is he on this side or the other?"

"He's on this side," I replied, impressed with her knowledge.

She gave me a look that held a suspicious hint of amusement. "For all the differences between towns, some things are always the same. Most townsfolk don't want a parade of injured animals being led into the house next door. Even in smaller villages, the animal healers live on the edges."

"That makes sense." I hesitated, frowning over her words.

"You said *healers*, plural. Do some small villages have more than one?"

She shrugged. "It completely depends on the region and town." She hesitated, casting a speculative glance in my direction. "Are you younger than you look? How old are you, Delphine?"

I gave her a wary look, but she merely watched me in silence, waiting. After a moment, I sighed and answered.

"I'll be eighteen in the summer."

"Interesting." She turned her gaze back to the road ahead, so I couldn't see her expression.

After the tension roused by her question, her silence got under my skin.

"That's it?" I blurted, even as I scolded myself for not remaining quiet. "You're not going to lecture me about how I need to be activated?"

"It sounds like you've had enough lectures already." She cast me a quick glance, a slight smile curving her mouth. "Besides, I've been told to mind my own business."

I looked away, warmth creeping into my cheeks. It had been rude of me, given she was not only my senior but a stranger who had gone out of her way to help my family.

"I apologize," I said stiffly, and she chuckled.

"No, no, you mustn't backtrack now! I might think you're weak and an easy target."

The warmth in my face flared hotter. "You're mocking me."

She surveyed me for a moment before inclining her head. "It's ungracious of me, is it not? Now I'm the one who owes an apology."

I looked swiftly back at her, but there was only sincerity on her face. After an awkward moment, I cleared my throat.

"No, indeed," I said. "There's no need."

"Have you always lived with your parents on their farm?"

she asked, her voice surprisingly gentle. "I think, perhaps, that you haven't spent much time around other youngsters."

I couldn't prevent a momentary grimace, but I banished it swiftly, loyalty to my parents flaring. When I was younger, I had longed to spend time with the other children in Tarin and had often complained to my mother. But despite my complaints, I had known she would never even raise the issue with my father.

Usually a loving, supportive figure in my life, any talk of leaving the farm would turn him silent and moody, sometimes for days at a time. When my mother finally explained why, I had become as careful about the topic as she was.

My father had always been prone to the occasional unexplained angry outburst, but it was only after the town healer tested my seed that the days of silent withdrawal started. And after my mother's explanation, it all made sense.

My father had an older brother who I had never met, and as boys they had been very close. My uncle had also been assessed as having an unexpectedly strong seed—although not as strong as mine. He had fallen just short of qualifying for a Guild apprenticeship.

Even so, the family had been elated, sure he was the key to turning around their fortunes. Even after my grandparents' sudden death, the two brothers had worked hard to keep the farm profitable, running it alone while they were barely more than children, and saving every coin they could. Every scrap of their savings had been pooled and used to send my uncle to the capital where he intended to seek training from the mages. Even if he couldn't be apprenticed to one of them, in Tarona he could find someone of a similar strength to his own to activate him. And with gold, he could purchase additional training from actual mages.

The brothers had been convinced my uncle's ability would ensure their future prosperity. And my father had been willing to work back-breakingly hard to keep the farm afloat alone for the two years of his brother's apprenticeship.

But my uncle had never returned.

Given he was alone, my father couldn't leave the farm himself, but eventually he had scraped together yet more coin and used it to seek information on his brother, who he feared must have died. He discovered his brother had abandoned Tarin, their family farm, and my father himself and had used their shared savings to establish a life for himself in the capital.

Instead of learning from the mages of the Guild and returning, my uncle had instead been seduced by the Guild's position and power—and by his own resentment at not being strong enough to join their ranks. Rather than accepting the reality of his lesser place, he had used the family savings to buy himself the lifestyle he thought he deserved.

My father was the strongest man I knew, and he hadn't been broken by the betrayal. He had found my mother and built himself a life. But working the farm alone had meant always working hard, without breaks. My father had once dreamed of a farm bustling with family, but that dream had been twice stolen from him—first by his brother and then by my parents' inability to have more children.

So I could understand how shattering my seed assessment had been for him. I was not only strong like his brother, but even stronger—actual mage material. And that meant that, just like my uncle, I would leave our farm and go to the Guild.

My father knew from bitter experience that if I left, I would be lost to him forever. Once again, he and my mother would be alone on their farm, and even the small family he had built would evaporate.

But I wasn't like my uncle, and I refused to go. There was no point in my being activated anyway. Not given my secret.

I wasn't sure who my birth had been a joke against, but it must have been against someone. The squeamish heir to a remote farm had no business with a powerful healing seed. I refused to be activated and not only make my life a misery but lose my family as well.

And here was a stranger criticizing the choices my parents had been forced into.

"I had no need to go into Tarin to school," I said coldly. "My mother taught me everything I needed to learn. And we always came into town for the festivals and celebrations. I don't need anyone's pity."

"No, I'm sure you don't—especially if the rumors are true." Amara spoke with an unexpected note of bright cheerfulness. "I assume you do, indeed, have a powerful seed? And it's a personal choice of some kind that you haven't been activated yet?"

Reluctantly, I nodded. Amara had already admitted to having heard of me. But she had been heading toward Tarin when she passed our farm, not away from it. So how was that possible? Halmir was always pestering me to go to the Guild and take up a mage apprenticeship. Had he sent word to the Guild of my existence? Surely they didn't care enough to send someone to fetch me?

I stiffened at the idea, giving Amara a sideways look. I had resolved back in the field that she wasn't after me, but the more I saw of her, the more I realized I couldn't trust my judgment on such matters. Amara was nothing like the mental image I had built of a mage.

"You do know you have mage level strength, don't you?" Amara asked into the silence, sounding concerned. "The local healer explained it to you, and all about seeds and activation? Sometimes parents have their own reasons for keeping things from their children."

My hands balled into fists as I leaped to my mother's defense.

"Of course my mother explained it all! And my parents had

me assessed as a young child, just like all the other children in and around Tarin. The mage running the healing clinic at the time was clear about the results."

Amara nodded.

It was always the healers who tested children to determine the strength and affinity of their seed. A healing ability allowed someone to connect with living bodies in a way other affinities couldn't. All it took was physical contact.

Of course, any parents with a healing seed could take a guess at the affinity of their own children's seeds, as well as any other children they touched, but it was still common practice to have a formal assessment by the local healer. A certain level of strength and experience was needed to accurately gauge a seed's level, and no one wanted to raise false hope.

"So you knew of both your healing affinity and your unusual strength from childhood," Amara said. "You weren't kept in the dark, as I feared."

I sighed at her unpleasant assumption, restraining myself from launching to my parents' defense yet again. Instead I was swamped with memories. The shocking moment of my testing at the forefront, followed by the subsequent confusion. Everyone had heaped attention and praise on me after my testing—as if I had done something to earn my strong seed. But my father had gone silent, and without my mother's explanation, I had assumed his anger was directed toward me, although I couldn't work out what I had done wrong.

The inhabitants of Tarin had all assumed I would leave as soon as I turned seventeen, traveling to the distant Mage's Guild to start an apprenticeship that would make me a mage. No one had doubted I would be excited to leave my family and my whole life behind.

"It's not fair," I said, my frustration leaking into the words.

Amara laughed, a low, velvety sound. "No, who gets a

strong seed isn't fair at all. But usually it's others making the complaint, not someone in your position."

I folded my arms across my chest. "I didn't ask to be born this way, and I don't want it."

Even without turning to look at Amara, my peripheral vision caught the crease between her eyes as she examined my face.

"I meant it earlier when I said most people hope and dream of a situation like yours," she said softly. "It's not a common thing to have a child whose seed far surpasses their parents. Most people follow the normal pattern of heredity in their ability as in everything else."

"It happens," I said quickly. "The current Master of the Elements was born to blacksmiths."

Amara nodded. "Of course. I wasn't denying the phenomenon, just saying that most people view it favorably. And most people see value in having a range of affinities within one family as well. Affinities often skip generations, and everyone has all three of the main affinities in their heritage somewhere, so it's fairly common."

I sighed, trying not to think how much easier everything would be if I had been born with a normal, weak plants seed, like both my parents. If that had been the case—as I had expected when I arrived for my testing—then I would already be activated by now and would have begun my apprenticeship under my father.

I pushed away the appealing image. It did no good to dwell on it. I didn't have a plants seed, I had a healing one. Even if I bound my strength by choosing a weak activator, I couldn't risk unleashing my healing ability. If I was constantly drawn to connect with the bodies of those around me, I would be fainting or vomiting more often than I was well.

"I don't mean to pry," Amara said, a statement I found less than believable given her number of questions so far, "but I just want to be completely sure both you and I understand the situation."

She paused briefly, and when I didn't protest—already resigned to allowing the conversation to go its course—she continued.

"You are aware that your seed will lie dormant and unusable until it is activated by someone else's power? It doesn't matter how old you get, you'll never come into your power on your own."

"Of course," I said, impatient. "Seeds might become ripe for activation sometime around your seventeenth birthday, but they don't change after that without activation. Believe me, I could hardly be unaware given how many times Halmir and the local healer have badgered me since my seed ripened four months before my last birthday."

"Four months?" Amara gave me a speculative look. "If you were ready for activation that early, you really must be strong."

"You can't tell?" I asked, the petulant note in my voice embarrassing me.

She smiled. "No, my healing cross-influence doesn't extend to anything that subtle. I'm as much in the dark on such matters as you are. But your local healer must have run those sorts of tests hundreds of times. He or she would know what they're doing."

I shrugged. "I don't know why they bothered checking. It didn't matter when I was ready—as I kept telling them. Four months before my birthday, or four months after, I had no intention of abandoning my home and family to go to the Mage's Guild."

My tone colored my final two words with more emotion than I had intended to reveal, so I fell silent. Amara's eyes were on the road again, but her face had a false stillness that told me she was purposely hiding her thoughts.

"Don't you care about sacrificing your potential?" she asked eventually. "Your seed gives you the possibility of great strength, but it's only a possibility. You'll also be limited by the strength of your activator. With a seed as strong as yours, only a mage influencer will allow you to realize your full potential. From what you're saying, you must have been told that a hundred times. And yet you truly don't care?"

I sighed, disliking hearing the familiar lecture on the lips of a stranger—and a mage at that. "If I could give my seed away, I would do so happily. I have no interest in becoming a mage." My voice dropped to an irritated mutter. "And you're right that I've heard it a hundred times. Even the mayor herself lectures me every time she sees me. I really don't need to hear it again from you."

"Apologies," Amara said lightly. "I have a particular reason for wanting to fully understand your situation."

A particular reason? I gave her a suspicious sideways glance. Was she really sent by the Guild then? I reviewed everything I'd said, a hint of uneasiness appearing. I hadn't spoken flatteringly of mages or the Guild. Was I risking harm to my family by speaking so openly?

"I have to ask, though," Amara added after a moment of heavy silence. "The mayor?"

I sighed. "It's been a long time since Tarin sent anyone to the Mage's Guild for an apprenticeship. They seem to think it will boost our town's status to ship me away."

*Not that it did Tarin any good when my uncle sought out the Guild,* I added silently.

"Perhaps they're thinking of your return rather than your departure," Amara said gently. "Smaller towns can find it difficult to secure a senior healer to run their healing clinic, so having one of their own as a qualified mage is an appealing prospect."

"Who's to say I'd ever return?" I said shortly.

"You fear the Guild would keep you prisoner?"

Was that amusement in her tone? I shifted uncomfortably, remembering my earlier concerns.

After a moment, Amara gave a light chuckle. "While there are those in the Guild who would be astonished to hear me utter any defense of it, I can assure you they're not in the habit of taking their students prisoner. Healers, especially, are encouraged to return to their home regions once they've received their qualifications. There's always a shortage of healers in the more remote parts of Tartora."

I shot her a surprised look. Her words made it sound like she was no supporter of the Guild. But that was impossible. As a mage, she was bound to the Guild. It wasn't an optional connection.

"So you know that in your case, realizing your potential means going to the Mage's Guild in search of a mage influencer," Amara said thoughtfully. "But you're refusing to do so."

She frowned, although she looked more intrigued than unhappy. "For some reason, you don't want to be a mage."

Silence fell in the wake of her statement.

I couldn't deny any part of what she'd said. But neither did I want to explain my reasons.

"I've never encountered anyone like you before," she said when I didn't speak. "I've never even heard of a similar situation."

Again she waited, as if expecting me to say something, and again I stayed silent.

In truth, I didn't have an aversion to being a mage, but to the Guild itself and the lifestyle of the capital. But the two were inextricably linked.

Mage wasn't an official rank but rather a general honorific for anyone who had completed an apprenticeship with a member of the Guild. Since Guild members only activated young people of similar or equal strength to themselves, completing such an apprenticeship was sufficient to earn you the title. And completing such an apprenticeship also made you a member of the Guild—bound to both its privileges and its control.

Once again, I surreptitiously examined Amara. Despite my initial aversion, I was already starting to warm to her. She was nothing like I'd imagined a Guild mage to be. And she clearly had strength that would distinguish her, even among other mages. It was even possible she was a master, although she didn't act like a member of our kingdom's top elite.

Every mage began as an apprentice and after two years graduated to become a proficient. The majority of mages remained proficients for their whole lives, the cachet of their magehood enough to carry them through life. But those with sufficient power and control to pass the mastery exams were permitted to take the title of master, beyond which rank there was only affinity head.

Since the affinity heads generally held their position for many years, few masters ever reached such heights. Given the political nature of the role, I wasn't sure all masters even desired such a promotion.

The three affinity heads not only ruled the Mage's Guild, under the collective title of the Triumvirate, but they also joined with the king to govern the kingdom. The king was prohibited from passing laws without their input, with the Royal Mage standing between them as liaison. It was a system designed to allow the people a voice within the kingdom's governance—a fallacy that had always made me angry.

What ancient authorities had thought the strongest of all mages were representative of the people? It was clearly a system designed by those who had never known anything but power. To them it must have seemed logical that a society dominated by various guilds should be represented by the guild at the top of that hierarchy.

When I had raged about it in my lessons as a child, my

mother had always tried to defend the thinking. But while I could acknowledge her words, I could never truly embrace them. Mages might be essential to the smooth running of the kingdom—ensuring everything from our health and our defense to our weather—but they didn't understand the life of the common Tartoran citizen. It would benefit no one for the crown and Guild to be at odds, but it didn't necessarily follow that their unity always benefited the common people either.

I finally spoke into the silence, curiosity getting the better of me. "Are you a proficient or a master?"

Amara laughed, and it occurred to me that perhaps it was a rude question—like asking a farmer if they owned their own fields or only rented them. But she smiled at me easily enough.

"I passed my mastery exam many years ago."

As I had suspected, she was a master. Given her actions back on the farm, it was no great surprise.

I twisted to look back at Rocky who thumped his tail enthusiastically in response to my attention, although the movement made him whimper. Awareness of his presence and his pain pressed against my back, and I struggled to refocus on Amara.

"We were fortunate you happened to be passing by at that moment," I said, my concern for the dog making my words genuine.

Amara hesitated. "Good fortune, indeed," she said eventually, and I frowned.

"What is it?" I asked.

She laughed again. "You're not slow, despite this foolishness over your seed."

"It's not foolishness," I said, bristling.

"Oh?" Her eyebrows arched, her face settling into a thoughtful expression. "You're very confident in your opinions on this topic. Can I assume, then, that your parents support you in this matter?"

I hesitated. My father backed me wholeheartedly, but my

mother had always disagreed, arguing that I had a responsibility to use the gifts I'd been given. It was why she had never suggested activating me herself, even though she didn't know about my squeamishness.

Amara clearly picked up on my hesitation, her perception stronger than I would have liked.

"I'll admit I half expected to arrive and find you already activated," she said. "While I've never met someone who resented their strong seed, my old master once encountered a family who didn't want their child to leave home. In that case, one of the parents activated the boy the moment he was ready, thus locking him to their own level for life. It was a sad waste, but there's no way to undo an activation."

"You mean you *were* looking for me!" I exclaimed, latching onto the important part of her speech. "The Guild sent you after me?"

When I shifted in my seat, inching away from her, she launched into speech.

"Halmir did send word of your existence and unique reluctance to the Guild, and it happened to reach my ears. But given all the recent upheaval and unrest, the Guild is too busy to track down unwilling potential members. I came entirely on my own initiative." Her mouth twisted into a self-deprecating smile. "It was curiosity that drove me mostly, if I'm honest."

I relaxed slightly, although I couldn't entirely regain my former ease. How far did Amara's curiosity go, and what was she willing to do to satisfy it?

Amara smiled at me, either not noticing or choosing to ignore my discomfort.

"I must admit, having met you, my curiosity has only increased."

I stared straight ahead, my jaw clenched.

"Relax, child." Amara chuckled. "I don't intend to pry into

your life, and I certainly don't intend to report anything back to the Guild."

Her words surprised me enough to make me look at her. As soon as our eyes met, her smile widened.

"I hope you'll let me satisfy my curiosity on another matter, though. I'm curious to know the thoughts of such an unusual thinker on cross influencing."

"Cross influencing?" I stared at her, trying to keep up with the abrupt change of topic. How had she known I held unpopular opinions on that matter as well?

"Well?" she asked, readjusting the reins and looking entirely at ease. "Don't tell me you have no thoughts on the topic because I won't believe you."

Reluctantly I grinned. She really was perceptive.

"I think everyone is too obsessed with strength," I said.

Amara laughed. "They are a little, aren't they." She gave me a conspiratorial smile. "It's always nice to meet someone who thinks differently."

I shook my head, amazed. Could Amara really be a Guild master? Given the way she talked, I wouldn't have believed it if I hadn't seen her power for myself.

Your affinity allowed you to connect with those aspects of the world around you that aligned with your seed, and having an influencer who was of the same affinity consolidated and strengthened those connections. So traditional thinking held that you should be activated by someone with the same affinity wherever possible. But my argument had always been that while doing so increased your power, it also limited it.

Did Amara—a master mage from the Guild—agree with me?

She had admitted to being cross-influenced herself. Her seed was elements, making her an elements mage, but she had chosen to be activated by someone with a healing affinity. Why?

Had the healing mage in question merely been the strongest available option? Or was it just a sign of Amara's own strength? Was she so powerful she didn't need to worry about further shoring up her strength? Or was there some other reason behind her decision?

"Why did you choose to be cross-influenced?" I asked.

I knew why I had always had an interest in the other affinities and the possibilities of cross-influencing, but Amara was different from me. She didn't have a reason to desperately hope another affinity could overpower her own.

How often had I wished that being activated by one of my parents—who could connect with the crops of our farm as well as the earth itself—was enough to cancel out my healing ability.

"I know it's not the popular choice," Amara replied, "but I see cross-influence as a positive thing. It's incredible, the way we're never entirely free of our activator. Just that one small moment of activation leaves our power forever tangled with traces of theirs—that's why their strength and affinity influence us so strongly. By allowing your power to be colored with traces of a different affinity, you expand the reaches of your power and open up the possibility for all sorts of different abilities. I've spent considerable time researching how it was used in the past, and I firmly believe that the popularity of cross-influencing will eventually rise again."

I grinned slowly. "You sound like you're on a one-woman mission to spread word of its benefits."

Seeing the light in her eyes was almost enough to make me reconsider the idea that cross-influencing might be the answer to my problems after all.

Amara smiled back. "I do feel strongly on the matter. Although I admit cross-influencing can cause minor complications in the training process."

I nodded slowly. Training was one of the reasons for the

lack of popularity of cross-influencing. The law stated that anyone who activated another person was required to take on their apprenticeship. It ensured everyone received training in the use of their power and that the training came from someone with a similar level of strength. But the requirement could become awkward when the teacher and student didn't share the same affinity.

"I believe the answer is for mages to form small training groups," Amara said, clearly warming to a favorite topic. "That way an influencer is still responsible for their apprentices' training, but the apprentices can also benefit from training sessions given by a mage of their same primary affinity."

"Is that how they do it at the Guild?" I asked, curious in spite of myself.

Contempt flashed across her face. "Of course not. The Guild is hidebound and rigid. And almost all apprentices choose an influencer of their own affinity anyway."

"Oh." I wasn't sure what else to say, but my interest in the woman sitting next to me had just risen dramatically.

I had thought she would be horrified if she realized the extent of my feelings about the Guild. But it was almost as if she shared my aversion to the institution.

But how could that be true of a master mage? Who exactly was Amara, and what was she doing traveling alone through this out-of-the-way part of the kingdom? She couldn't possibly have come all this way just for me.

"You must be wondering why I brought up cross-influencing." Amara's voice startled me out of my thoughts.

I remained silent, not willing to admit to my extreme curiosity and completely at a loss as to what might come next.

"I wanted to be sure I understood your situation before I extended my offer," she continued. "Especially since it's not one I've ever made before." She took a breath. "Delphine, you obviously have a reason for not wanting to be a mage, but I get the impression some of your dislike of the idea is directed at the Guild itself. Given that, I wonder if you would consider an apprenticeship offer from me?"

"An apprenticeship?" I asked blankly. "With you?"

She laughed. "I can't offer you one with anyone else."

"I..." I tried to think of a polite way to turn her down. Was this why she had offered to transport Rocky into town? If I told her I wasn't interested, would she abandon us both by the side of the road?

"I can consult with your local healer, if you like," she offered. "But I'm confident my strength is great enough that I wouldn't limit you in any way. I don't have a healing affinity myself, of course, but you've already heard my opinion on that matter."

"I'm not interested in a Guild apprenticeship," I said stiffly, concerned about her reaction but also irritated that she would suggest I be activated after I'd already expressed my opinion on the matter so clearly.

"I understand you don't want to go to the Guild," she said. "That's largely why I made the offer. I am a Guild member, of course, but are you aware there's more than one kind of Guild apprenticeship?"

"I...what?" I stared at her.

"Officially, every graduate of a Guild apprenticeship is a member of the Guild—whether they want to be or not. It's the Guild's way of controlling those of us with strength." She sounded resentful, but she brushed off the emotion to continue. "And, therefore, every apprenticeship completed under a qualified mage is a Guild apprenticeship. There's no rule that says the apprentice ever needs to step a single foot inside the Guild itself. They don't run classes, remember. And some of us Guild mages choose to occupy ourselves outside of the capital."

"You mean you don't normally live at the Guild?" I asked, latching onto the least confusing part of her speech.

She grimaced. "I spend as little time as possible there. I'm what's called a traveling master."

"A traveling master?" I stared at her. I had never heard of such a person.

She sighed. "There's all too few of us, unfortunately, so I'm not surprised you haven't heard the term. But some of us care about the kingdom beyond the capital and major cities, and we believe our power should be of use to all." She smiled. "Don't worry, I pay my way easily enough and can afford to take on an apprentice. Tarona might hold much of the kingdom's wealth, but there is still gold to be found elsewhere. The rest of the kingdom is far from destitute, and my abilities are often in demand."

"You're saying that if I apprenticed to you, I wouldn't need to go to the Guild or the capital?" I asked, so shocked it was hard to think. "You want me to travel with you? For two whole years?"

Amara nodded. "You have a gift, Delphine, and I don't believe gifts should be wasted."

Her words sounded so much like my mother's that it was hard to dismiss them.

"I don't have a healing affinity like yours," she continued, "and I don't even have a plants affinity, like you wish you had. But an elements affinity can be very useful—for farmers as much as anyone else."

"You want to activate me?" I repeated. "Yourself?"

"I believe I've already mentioned that I'm not qualified to offer on behalf of anyone else," she said with a chuckle.

"I'm sorry," I said, unsure how polite I needed to be given the unexpected turn of the conversation. "But I'm not interested in leaving my fam—"

"My offer has come as a surprise, of course," she said, calmly cutting me off. "Take some time to consider it."

"I don't need ti—" I tried to say, but she cut me off again.

"Take some time to consider it."

I opened my mouth only to close it. I would look foolish if I kept insisting. I could just as easily wait before refusing her offer for a second time.

I could even admit there was a certain intrigue to the idea. She wasn't insisting I travel to Tarona—most likely never to return—like everyone else did. But she still wanted me to activate my healing seed which made the idea untenable. I just hoped I could get away with not telling her why.

"I'll talk to your parents, of course," Amara added, and my heart sank.

Maybe I should make more of an effort to convince her immediately, after all. My mother would love the idea, while my father would almost certainly resent both it and Amara herself. The last thing I wanted was to introduce tension into our home.

But I couldn't find the right words to convince her—not without revealing the weakness my father had sworn me to secrecy over. So instead I just kept sneaking glances at the mage beside me. The master mage.

A traveling master, apparently.

I might not want to accept her offer, but that didn't mean I wasn't intrigued by Amara herself. The more she spoke, the more mysterious she grew.

She said she'd never taken an apprentice before, so why did she suddenly want to start now? Why, exactly, did this woman want to activate me of all people? And how far was she going to go in her attempts to convince me?

CHAPTER

# THREE

"Is that the animal healer's house?" Amara pointed ahead at a comfortably sized home that stood out among the smaller dwellings on the fringe of the town. Her words jerked me back to the pressing matter at hand, and I nodded confirmation. When I turned to look at Rocky, he couldn't even muster the energy to acknowledge me, sending my concern spiking.

As soon as Amara pulled her horse to a stop, I leaped down, running forward to pound on the house's front door.

"Halmir!" I shouted. "Hurry!"

The door was yanked open in seconds, but the older animal healer wasn't on the other side.

"Delphine!" The girl in the doorway sounded surprised and pleased to see me. She peered over my shoulder. "What's wrong? Has something happened to one of the cows again? Do you need Father back on the farm?"

I shook my head. "It's Rocky. He fell into a hole and has badly hurt his legs. We brought him here."

"Rocky?" The girl's ready sympathy flared, her face falling.

Miranda always found an excuse to tag along when her

father was called out to our farm, and no one who had met the friendly dog failed to fall for him.

"You cannot be the healer," Amara said from behind me, her light tone taking any sting from her words.

Miranda gasped when she saw the limp form in Amara's arms. Stepping back to clear the doorway, she let the woman and dog inside. I peered back toward the cart, checking the horse's reins were secured to the hitching post before I followed them inside.

Miranda had darted ahead, calling loudly for her father, and Amara was already halfway through the house in the girl's wake. I hurried to catch up with her and direct her the rest of the way. I had visited often enough to know how to find the treatment room at the back of the house with its attached fenced yard.

By the time we reached the room, Halmir had appeared, joining us at the large table in the center of the space. Amara briefly outlined the accident that had befallen Rocky, while I tried not to focus on either her words or the room itself. Being here always made me uncomfortable. The air was heavy with past treatments and the weight of future expectation. Halmir had long hoped that I might assist his daughter in the future running of his clinic.

My heart rate picked up slightly—a natural response to the pressure, no doubt. I ignored a heady, breathless feeling that didn't quite fit. That hint of hopeful excitement had nothing to do with Amara's proposal. It was only relief that Rocky was finally receiving the help he needed.

Since Amara's assistance had prevented further injury, Halmir should be able to restore Rocky to his previous strength. The animal healer's seed hadn't been strong enough to qualify as a mage, but he had been close. I had often heard him tell the story of nearly being chosen for a Guild apprenticeship. We were fortunate to have him in Tarin.

As soon as Amara gently deposited Rocky on the table, Halmir leaned over him. I tried to look away, knowing the danger and telling myself I wasn't interested in the process anyway. But I couldn't keep my eyes from sliding across the room to latch onto Halmir's hands as they gently cupped the dog's heaving sides.

My fascination warred with the churning in my stomach and lost.

"I'm going for a walk," I announced abruptly.

Halmir was too absorbed in his task to acknowledge me, although none of the rest of us could see any outward sign of the connection he had forged with Rocky. Amara gave me a sharp look, however, and I turned away from the mix of censure and speculation in her gaze.

Miranda, who had been standing close beside her father, bounded to my side with a sunny smile. "I'll come with you."

I shrugged and hurried from the room. I didn't mind if I had company or not, I just wanted to get away from the stifling atmosphere of the healing room.

Outside, I headed up the street toward the center of town, not really seeing the houses on either side of me as they grew larger and more prosperous looking. Night had started to fall, but the lingering hints of daylight were bolstered by the moon, which was already hanging in the sky, nearly full. I had no issue seeing the road in front of me.

"It's always distressing when someone you love is in pain." Miranda placed a gentle hand on my arm, her face full of sympathy. "But you don't need to worry. It sounded like a straightforward healing, and my father has never failed at one of those." She hesitated before continuing. "And I'm sure he won't charge too much. You came to us, after all, so it's not as if he had to spend a long time traveling out to the farm. And he likes Rocky, you know." Her voice brightened by the end of her speech, as if she'd succeeded in convincing herself.

I smiled back weakly, wishing my discomfort stemmed from something as simple as payment. What was wrong with me that I couldn't even spend a few minutes in Halmir's healing room? And yet neither could I overcome the fascination that made me want to try.

Miranda linked her arm through mine and smiled brightly up at me. The younger girl had always followed me around ever since we were little. Having her appear every time my family visited town had annoyed me when we were younger—back when I'd wanted friends my own age. But my perspective had changed after my testing. Everyone in town was interested in me after that, but only because of my seed. Miranda was the only one who had liked me from the beginning. I even began to imagine that if I'd had my longed-for younger sister, she might have been something like Miranda.

"If you wait just a little longer," she said, "then we can get activated together. I know Father would be delighted to take you on." She squeezed my arm. "Wouldn't it be the best fun to be apprentices together!"

I managed a pained smile. It wasn't the first time Miranda had made the suggestion, and my refusals never seemed to make an impression on her. The longer I remained unactivated, the more convinced she became that we would be trained together.

Despite my irritation, part of me couldn't help amusement over her definition of *a little longer*. She wasn't even sixteen yet, despite already being taller than me, and her seed wasn't mage strength, which meant she would likely have to wait for her seventeenth birthday for activation. All the adults in Tarin seemed to think every month I delayed was a wasteful crime, but apparently well over a year was nothing to my friend.

"Miranda," I said wearily, but she cut me off, her tone as cheerful as ever. I suspected she knew what I was going to say and didn't want reality intruding on her happy fantasy.

"Oh, look!" She pointed toward two figures ahead of us.

I squinted through the half-light, trying to identify them. I didn't know everyone in Tarin—we didn't spend enough time in the town for that—but I knew the more prominent adults as well as all the other young people around Miranda's and my ages.

I didn't recognize the people loitering down the side road, though. They were tall, their bearing confident and shoulders broad. These weren't the youths I was used to seeing in town.

I frowned back at Miranda. What was she doing spending time with men who must be nearly ten years her senior? Other than her inexplicable devotion to me, she had never been one to chase after the older children or want to hurry into adulthood.

A young woman appeared from the other direction. She joined the men, a friendly greeting on her lips as she looked at the taller and more confident of them. I relaxed slightly at sight of her. Serena was a year older than me—already nearly finished with her plants apprenticeship—so she wasn't a particular friend of Miranda's, but at least she was familiar.

"Friends of yours?" I asked, trying to sound more relaxed than I felt. It seemed darker now than it had before, although I hadn't noticed the last of the daylight slipping away.

"Oh yes!" Miranda smiled happily. "Shall I introduce you?" At my look of uncertainty, her nose wrinkled. "I know they're a bit old, but you shouldn't mind that. They're only passing through Tarin, and they have the funniest ideas. They've completely broken the monotony around here, so all the young people hang around them. See."

She pointed toward the small group where the arrival of yet another person seemed to confirm her words. The new arrival was another familiar face, a gangly youth a little younger than me who liked to complain loudly about his father, Tarin's black-smith. I usually avoided him, so it took me a moment to recall his name—Stefan.

I frowned, although I understood the situation now. Many of the youths in Tarin found life in a small town monotonous. They couldn't understand why I didn't leap at the chance to run off to the capital. Naturally they weren't close friends of mine, but I still understood their perspective somewhat. Even I would have found remote town life constricting if it hadn't been for the wide-open fields of our farm and the unswerving love of my parents.

The newcomers, however, were another story.

"What kind of grown men spend their time roaming the kingdom with a bunch of youths? Are they trying to make themselves feel important or something?"

Miranda's face fell, and I immediately felt bad for repaying her friendliness with harsh judgment.

"I'm not saying I want to go following them off to the new land they're always talking about," she said hurriedly. "I just find them amusing." Her lips twisted. "There isn't much else of interest happening around here."

I forced a smile. If the men were recruiters for Calista, then their presence made more sense, although I was surprised they'd made it as far as Tarin.

"Sorry, don't mind me," I said. "I'm just in a crotchety mood because of worrying about Rocky."

Her expression lightened, and she gripped my arm in sympathy. "Of course! I'm the one who was thoughtless. You'll be wanting to get back to him." But even as she said it, her eyes glanced wistfully toward the group of four down the side street.

"Yes, I should be getting back." I removed her hand from my arm, giving it a squeeze. "But you don't need to come with me. Like you said, it's a simple healing and your father will have everything well in hand. Just because I need to return doesn't mean you have to."

She glanced at the small group again before giving me an

uncertain look. "You really don't mind walking back on your own?"

I laughed. "Of course I don't. I'm not exactly a stranger in Tarin. I won't lose my way."

She brightened further. "No, of course not. I'm being silly again. I'll be off, then."

She sped away from me, throwing a smile and a farewell wave over her shoulder. I watched her go with a smile of my own. No matter how many times I had tried to shake Miranda loose when we were children, I'd never been able to do it. She always managed to win me over.

Shaking my head at my own foolishness, I turned back toward Halmir's house. But something made me pause, glancing back. I had told Miranda to go, but I was suddenly having second thoughts about leaving her behind.

Tartora's northern neighbor of Calista had been nothing but dangerous, poisoned land for generations, its surviving population scattered into Tartora and the nomad lands. Now that the land itself had been restored, it was understandable that its new rulers were recruiting subjects from among the descendants of the refugees. From what I'd heard, you didn't even have to have Calistan blood to be accepted in the newly reformed kingdom. A willingness to do the work of rebuilding was all that was needed, although a strong seed was appreciated. But surely the Calistan recruiters weren't encouraging underage children to leave their homes?

I tried to reassure myself with Miranda's own words. She had said she wasn't interested in Calista, that she just found the men's tales amusing. And the gatherings themselves must have been safe enough. If they were raucous or dangerous, the town mayor would have put a stop to them before now.

But still I hesitated.

Without forming any real plan, I faced back toward the men and their cluster of attendant youths. The group was on the move now, and I found myself trailing them, staying just far enough back not to attract attention. If Miranda saw me, she would find it odd, but none of them looked in my direction.

As they moved toward the end of the street, I began to berate myself. What exactly was I doing? Halmir would be finished by now, and Amara must be wondering what had happened to me. Why was I following this group? I wasn't even close enough to hear their conversation, although they were talking animatedly. What did I think was going to happen?

I couldn't answer the question, and my progress slowed. Just as I was about to turn back, a sharper tone ahead caught my attention. The voice had lifted enough to reach my ears, although the exact words still weren't clear. I frowned, peering into the shadows that enveloped this section of the street. The houses here were closer together, less of the moonlight making it between their hulking shapes.

The anger seemed to be coming from the blacksmith's son, and dismay filled me when I saw he was facing Miranda, clearly berating her for something. She shrank back, and I increased my pace again.

Before I could make any progress, however, several things happened at once. Stefan and Serena took off toward the edge of town at a half-run. The two men followed, each of them gripping one of Miranda's arms as they hustled her along with them. Before I could even shout a protest, a shadow detached from the darkness of one of the houses between me and the running group, forming into the shape of a man.

His height and the breadth of his shoulders immediately called to mind the fleeing strangers. Apparently there were three strange men in Tarin, not two. And this one carried an exposed sword in his right hand.

Were the others dragging Miranda somewhere more secluded so that he could dispose of her?

My concern transformed into full panic, and I threw myself

at the man's back with a guttural scream. My fear lent me strength, and I leaped high enough to get my arms around his neck, wrapping my legs around his middle as my weight cut off his airway.

He gave a strangled grunt and thrashed violently, nearly dislodging me. I clung on tighter as he dropped the sword, his hands coming up to claw at mine. I held on as tightly as I could, but I couldn't resist his strength as he pried my grip apart. As soon as my hands were loosened, he gripped the top of my arms, flinging me over his shoulder and onto the ground in front of him.

I landed hard on my back, the breath pushed from my lungs as I stared up at a terrifying face.

The darkness clung to him, his inky hair and the black leather of his clothes blending with the night behind him. Only the light skin of his face and hands stood out, an unnatural contrast of light against his shadowy form.

The expression on his face was as black as the deepest shadows, however, his features twisted with anger. He stooped to retrieve his blade, and I cowered away, my hands coming up in an instinctive gesture of defense.

Instead of attacking, however, he merely stepped over me, disdain in his eyes as his attention returned to the empty street where the others had previously been. He clearly intended to follow after them, so I rolled to the side, my hands flashing out and catching at his ankles.

He stumbled, only just catching himself before he joined me on the ground. Cursing, he spun to glare at me again.

"I won't let you hurt my friend," I said breathlessly, pushing myself up to my knees.

"Grey isn't your friend," he said in a deep, rough voice.

I stilled, surprise making me pause in my attempt to grab at his legs.

"Who?"

He also stilled, throwing me a look of equal surprise.

"I don't know who you are," I said, recovering my determination and my voice, "but I won't let you hurt Miranda."

"Miranda?" He glanced from the empty street to me, letting out a low groan.

"I won't let you hurt her," I repeated, lunging forward in an attempt to grab him around the knees and trip him up.

He stepped easily out of reach, and I barely kept my balance, scrambling inelegantly back to my feet. Racing around him, I blocked his passage down the street. He let out another mumbled curse, shouldering his way roughly past me.

I darted around to cut him off again, this time grabbing both his arms to hold him in place.

"What do you want with her?" I asked, breathless.

"Want with her?" He sounded incredulous. "What could I want with a girl too foolish for her own good?" It was obvious he wasn't just talking about Miranda. "If you're really her friend, you shouldn't have gotten in my way."

"I..." My words stuttered to a stop as I registered his piercing blue gaze which seemed to cut all the way through me, judging everything he saw.

Hadn't his eyes been black before? It must have been a trick of the shadows because there was no denying the brightness of the blue now. And how had I mistaken his age? Despite the breadth of his shoulders, he wasn't as old as the other men had been. At a guess I would put him within reach of my own age, perhaps a year or two older, although he carried himself with a confidence and assurance far beyond mine.

With the full force of his attention on my face, I could barely breathe. How could someone so attractive be so menacing? He must turn heads wherever he went, but I couldn't decide what stood out more—the handsome lines of his face and bright color of his eyes or the thrill of warning and fear that coursed through me as a result of his attention. Every nerve in my body was telling me to run from this man.

Gritting my teeth, I held my ground. It didn't matter what he looked like or how well he could wield his sword. Miranda was what mattered, and I wasn't going to turn tail and flee.

"What are you talking about?" I asked, proud of how steady my voice sounded.

He ripped his arms from my grasp. Moving too fast for me to block, he flipped our places, grabbing both my wrists in a crushing grip.

I gasped and tried to pull away, but he held me in place, leaning forward until he took up all the air around me, making it hard to find my breath.

"If your so-called friend is never seen again, you can blame yourself." His low words were sharp and cutting.

"What?" I gasped. "What do you mean never seen again? What are you going to do to her?"

Impatience twisted his features. "Me? What am *I* going to do to her?" He flung me away from him, looking down the empty street before whirling back to glare at me. "If you're really so clueless, you should never have gotten involved. Thanks to you, I've just wasted weeks of effort. And who knows when I'll get this chance again."

I faltered back a step, feeling my certainty draining away. None of his words made sense.

"What are you talking about?" A creeping dread filled me. "Are you...are you not with those men?"

He shot me a contemptuous look, his face answering my question as the situation crystallized in my mind. I had thought I was protecting Miranda, but I had actually been barring a potential rescuer. Heat rushed through me, and my legs trembled.

"You said she might never be seen again. What did you

mean by that? Who are those men? Where have they taken Miranda?"

His eyes were lidded now, the storm of emotion gone from his face, although the tense lines of his body told me he was eager to be on the move.

"That is something I would very much like to know," he said. "But they're experts at covering their tracks. Now that we've lost them, I won't find them again. Not unless I can work out which town they'll be appearing in next."

"Next town?" I asked, still dazed.

He half turned to go. "Your friend won't be with them then, though. She'll be long gone."

# FOUR

"Wait!" I lunged forward and gripped his closest arm with both hands, holding on firmly when he tried to shake me loose. "What do you mean? Where will she be? Are you saying they'll kill her? If those men have just kidnapped Miranda, we have to go after them before they get too far away."

"Did they just kidnap her?" His words made me freeze. "Is that what you saw? Are you sure?"

"I—" My rushed assurance faltered as I replayed the scene in my mind. Was that what I'd seen? Now that I considered the matter closely, I wasn't entirely certain.

It had been Stefan who had yelled at her, not either of the men. My instincts had been shouting about danger, but it was possible the strangers had been supporting her after the confrontation rather than dragging her away.

But if that was true, why were we talking about never seeing her again? Nothing about the situation made sense.

"If you're completely certain she didn't go with them willingly, we can turn the town out to join the search." The stranger's eyes were locked on me, and I could feel the tension of his muscles beneath my hands, as if he was ready to launch into action at a word from me. "There might be some slim hope of finding them if we have everyone helping. But if we do find them, and she denies being taken by force..."

I hesitated—only a matter of seconds—but when my hands fell away from his arm, the tension drained out of him, replaced with the earlier frustration.

"When you say go with them..." I asked, still trying to make sense of the situation.

"Willingly or unwillingly, your friend is gone," the stranger said shortly. "And she won't be back. I knew they were making their move tonight, which is why I haven't let them out of my sight for hours."

He gave me an accusing look, but I was too horrified to take any notice.

"You can't mean you think she's run off with those people? Miranda would never abandon her father like that! If that's what you meant, then of course I'm sure she didn't go willingly."

He shook his head. "Unless you're willing to swear you saw her forcibly dragged away, it won't be enough. This isn't the first town they've visited."

"Not the first town? Who are they?"

"That is what I've been trying to find out for a long time. And thanks to you I have to start all over again." He began to stride away from me, but I raced after him.

"Wait," I said again, and he paused, although I could easily read his desire to be gone. "What am I supposed to tell Miranda's father?"

He shrugged. "Tell him what you like. That's not my problem."

His callous attitude made me stiffen and glare at him. "How can I possibly explain where Miranda's gone when I don't understand myself?"

For a moment I thought he was going to stride off without an answer, but with a sigh he remained in place.

"I think you'll find he's not as surprised as you seem to think he'll be."

"What?" I stared at him.

"Not even the most advanced concealment skills could have protected Grey for so long if he was openly taking people by force. There's a reason he targets youths—there's always a few who are willing to abandon everything in search of adventure and riches."

"Not Miranda," I said with certainty. "She's not like that."

"Did I say they all left with him willingly? I wouldn't be following him if I believed that."

"Then how come—"

"Grey is persuasive, and he targets his victims with care. If you have some proof I'm not aware of, by all means, please come forward with it."

His superior look made me want to smack him, but I kept my distance. My body was still shaking with leftover tremors from our earlier proximity.

"Today was my chance, but I lost it," he said. "Thanks to you."

"I was trying to help." My voice sounded weak even in my own ears. I cleared my throat. "Maybe it's not too late. Maybe together we can find—"

"Don't even think about it." The stranger's eyes narrowed, his face transforming instantly as the earlier menace returned. "I don't want help from anyone, let alone you."

I shrank back before I could stop myself, but I forced out words anyway. "I won't just abandon Miranda. Of course I have to try to help."

"You would be a hindrance, not a help. If you really want to help your friend, then stay out of my way next time. If I never see you again, it will be too soon."

He strode away without a backward glance, and this time I didn't try to stop him. I still didn't properly understand what had just happened, but anger had consumed my earlier instinctive fear.

How could I possibly have known he was trying to stop this Grey and rescue Miranda? I hadn't meant to get in his way, and yet he dismissed me without knowing a single thing about me. How did he know I couldn't help? Who was he to reject assistance so confidently?

I forced my trembling legs back toward the main street. I had to tell Halmir what had happened. Perhaps he would be able to rouse the town, even if the stranger wasn't willing to do it.

My legs didn't cooperate, moving more slowly than I asked them to. I kept replaying what had happened in my mind, but my encounter with the dark stranger already seemed more dream than reality. Would anyone even believe my account? What if he had been nothing more than a madman, and I would find Miranda already back home, having bid her friends goodnight while I fought with a stranger in the street?

That hopeful thought made me pick up my pace, but I couldn't truly believe in it. The stranger might have seemed dreamlike, but he had never seemed mad.

As I approached the edge of town, I massaged my left wrist which ached after his tight hold. What power did he have to give him such confidence?

Fiery defiance rose inside me. He had dismissed me as weak and worthless, but if he'd known about my seed—if I'd been activated—he wouldn't have dared grab me like that. He wouldn't have dared to even let his skin brush against mine.

Healers needed skin to skin contact to send their power into someone else's body, but once they had that contact, there was nothing stopping them using their power to still a heart as easily as start one. Elements mages might have the flashiest power, but the most feared assassins had a healing affinity.

I swiped angrily at the tears that had appeared on my cheeks. If I had access to my power, I wouldn't have killed anyone, of course, but I could have taken down the stranger and stopped Grey—or whatever his name was—from taking Miranda. I could have helped my friend.

But only if I was activated. I had been convinced for so long that I could never activate my power. I had been so set and sure on my course. But then Amara turned up out of nowhere with a path I had never considered and suddenly everything around me seemed less sure. What if it was possible to find a way around my squeamishness after all? What if I could fully access my power without ever going to the Guild?

Halmir's house loomed in front of me, and I pushed the door open without pausing to knock. Light and sounds from the back of the house led me to the treatment room.

I didn't have time to absorb who was present before a furry blur launched himself at me, tongue out.

I cried out in protest, telling Rocky to stop even as I dropped to my knees and wrapped my arms around him. It was the sort of confusing mixed signal Father would never have allowed— even toward an animal who was a pet rather than a working dog—but I was too relieved to see him healthy to care.

"He's been pacing ever since I got him down." Halmir's amused voice came from over near the table. "I think he was wondering where you were."

I dredged up a small smile as I considered how best to broach the more important topic of Miranda. I came up blank, realizing there was no easy way to say it.

"Does Miranda know someone named Grey?" I blurted out, standing and finding Halmir with my eyes.

He immediately stiffened. "Don't tell me she's gone off with him again! And at this hour!" He sounded annoyed rather than worried, and I relaxed slightly.

"She's gone off with him before?" I asked. "And she came back?"

"Came back?" This time there was a trace of concern in Halmir's tone. "I only meant she spends more time hanging around him than I'd like. All the local youths are enamored of his stories about faraway wealth and luxury." He snorted. "A waste of time and energy, but I can't keep her trapped at home all day every day."

I could hear his fondness beneath the words. Halmir had always been a doting father, perhaps because his wife had passed away while Miranda was young.

"She went off with Grey and another man," I said reluctantly. "Along with the blacksmith's son and Serena."

Halmir sighed. "I never liked her hanging around with the older youths, but she's become good friends with that Serena in the last year. She even stays out late some nights, which she never did before." He hesitated. "The ladies of the town tell me it's normal for a daughter to start to rebel around this age."

"Miranda? Rebelling?" I frowned at him. "She's never seemed the rebellious type."

I tried to remember if she'd made any particular mention of Serena on my more recent visits to town, but I couldn't recall her doing so. But then, she might have avoided the topic on purpose. Serena was no fan of mine. Before my assessment, hers had been the strongest seed in our generation, and she wasn't one to appreciate competition. Miranda knew we didn't get on.

Halmir looked away, rubbing at his jaw. "Miranda's seed is similar to mine. She wouldn't have been accepted into the Guild ten years ago, but times are changing. Tarona and the Guild are different now. If she travels to the capital, she might be able to secure an apprenticeship with the help of one of those new power mages."

Amara made a politely skeptical noise that alerted me to her presence. I kept my focus on Halmir, though.

"She doesn't want to go," I guessed.

He sighed. "She kept saying she didn't want to leave me. And then suddenly she was barely speaking to me and instead spending her time with those newcomers and all the others who hang around them. I tried telling her that her behavior just proves she doesn't want to be stuck here with me forever, but that wasn't received well."

Amara chuckled quietly. "I can imagine. It's a difficult age. But she doesn't have to make an immediate decision. You said she's only fifteen, didn't you?"

Halmir nodded while I tried to order my thoughts. The stranger had seemed certain Grey was hurrying Miranda out of the town, but it was possible they'd merely been moving somewhere else within the town limits. If I made a big fuss now, and Halmir tore the town apart searching for Miranda, I might just deepen the current wedge between them.

"They met on a side street," I said slowly. "And then they all disappeared off in the other direction to me. I was just worried that..."

Halmir sighed. "I apologize, Delphine. Miranda shouldn't have abandoned you like that."

"Oh no, no." I waved my hand to dismiss his words. "I told her not to worry about me. I know my way back well enough."

I smiled, but even as I did, my heart sank further. It was true I'd told her to go to her friends. If she really had been kidnapped, I could have prevented it by insisting she return with me.

"The thing is," I said, "I met a stranger—a different stranger, I mean. He seemed to believe they were all on their way out of town."

Halmir's lips thinned, pressing together. "If she's gone

jaunting out of town, then she's taken things too far this time. And so I'll tell her next time I see her."

I cleared my throat. "This other stranger seemed concerned they weren't going to return. That they were gone for good." I looked at Halmir hopefully. "That's nonsense, surely?"

To my surprise, Halmir gave me a smile, moving over to pat me reassuringly on the shoulder.

"It's kind of you to worry about Miranda, Delphine. You've always been kind to her, and I appreciate it. Don't be too concerned. This is only a phase, and I'm sure it will pass soon."

I hesitated, but I couldn't think of anything to say. The stranger's words of challenge kept echoing in my mind, making me question my memory more and more. I could no longer be sure I'd seen Miranda hustled away at all.

"I may only be a new acquaintance," Amara said with a smile, "but I already have the impression that Delphine is too responsible by nature to have experienced that particular phase. You needn't worry." She directed the last words to me. "Halmir is right that it's a perfectly normal phase many young people go through. Your friend will return to her usual self soon, I'm sure."

Halmir returned her smile, nodding his agreement, and I fell silent.

"We should leave Halmir to his evening," Amara added. "It's past time for us to be moving to the inn." She thanked him, sweeping me from the room before I could protest.

"The inn?" I tried to gather my scattered thoughts. "I don't need to go to the inn. Now that Rocky's been healed, he and I will head straight back to the farm."

I stepped outside, the excited dog on my heels. Breathing in the cool evening air, I tried to reassure myself with Halmir's words. Miranda would be back at any moment.

"Don't be ridiculous," Amara said briskly, capturing my full attention. "It doesn't matter if you're going to be my apprentice or not. I was the one to bring you into town, and I can't allow a child to go wandering off into the night alone."

I rolled my eyes. "I'm hardly a child."

She gave me an impatient look. "You've already told me you're only seventeen, so don't claim you're of age now."

She sounded so sincere that I subsided, accepting the inevitable. It was ridiculous, of course, to treat me as if I were a child. The official age of majority might be nineteen—since activation happened at seventeen, and official apprenticeships lasted two years—but no one considered seventeen- and eighteen-year-olds to be children. They might not have legal status, but everyone was treated as an adult once their seed was activated.

At least, that was the case among normal folk. Perhaps it was different in the capital, among the upper class members of the court and Guild? Not for the first time, I felt a swell of sympathy for the poor children born into those families.

An image flashed through my mind of the young man I had tackled in the street. I was willing to bet my whole farm that no one treated him like a child. Did his arrogant assurance come from a powerful seed? If I could wield my own power, would it give me confidence like his?

My steps slowed as I realized what I was considering.

Amara slowed as well, matching my pace and regarding me with patient curiosity. She wasn't going to ask me anything, instead waiting for me to speak.

I drew a deep breath. "What exactly would being your apprentice involve?"

# FIVE

Amara's brows rose almost to her hairline. "This is an abrupt change," she said lightly. "What exactly happened with your friend?"

I ignored the question, my dislodged thoughts now moving at fever pace. I couldn't shake the lingering feeling of weakness or the clamoring thoughts that told me I had to make sure I was never helpless again. I had thought the best way to be strong was to avoid my power setting off my squeamishness. But when confronted with a true threat, it was my lack of power that had made me weak.

If I had been activated, I could have protected myself and helped Miranda. And there hadn't been any injuries or illness involved, so I wouldn't even have fainted while doing it.

If my power was activated, I didn't have to do anything with it that I didn't want to do. At least, I wouldn't have to once my apprenticeship was complete. I could return to my farm and continue with my life as normal, but I would have a powerful weapon ready at my disposal. Surely I could endure for just two years?

My stomach tried to rebel at the thought of what might be involved in my apprenticeship, but I clamped down on the feelings, suppressing them with all the force of my will. The next time I encountered that arrogant man, I wouldn't be the useless villager he clearly thought me.

I drew a steadying breath. *If* I ever encountered him again. The odds were against it. The stranger had given the impression he was following Grey all over the kingdom—and that he intended to continue doing so. He wouldn't be staying in Tarin now that Grey was supposedly gone.

I shot a glance at the woman beside me. Amara had claimed to always be on the move herself. Had she encountered Grey before? Would she perhaps encounter him again?

If I accompanied her, would I have the chance to get to the bottom of whatever was going on? An image of the dark stranger rose in front of my eyes. He'd told me to stay away from the whole situation, but how was it any more his business than mine?

Did he think he was at the center of everything, just because he wasn't some weak villager from a remote corner of the kingdom?

I had seen firsthand how differently you were treated when you had a powerful seed, and I resented it on Miranda's behalf. I doubted youths from the capital had started disappearing. If Miranda had been snatched, it was because she came from a remote part of the kingdom and didn't have important relatives or a strong ability. Was Grey just getting away with his villainy because no one cared?

*No one except that stranger,* an unwelcome voice said, and I pushed it away. Whatever that man's motivations, I hadn't seen any traces of compassion in his manner. He didn't care about Miranda or any of the other people he claimed had been taken. If I had to guess, perhaps he had some rivalry with Grey.

As my anger rose, my determination rose with it. Everyone had been telling me for years that my strong seed came with a responsibility to make use of that power. I had been doing my best to ignore them, but this was a situation I couldn't ignore.

I drew a deep breath and turned to Amara. She was watching me in silence, giving me the space to sort through my thoughts. Her consideration made it easier to speak my new resolution.

"I've changed my mind. I want you to activate me. I'll be your apprentice for the next two years if you'll take me with you on your travels."

She stopped, cocking her head and assessing me with her eyes. "I thought it was going to take longer to persuade you."

I brushed off the flare of resentment at her certainty of eventual success. After all, she'd been proven right.

Something else made me hesitate, though.

"You said it won't be a traditional healing apprenticeship, right? Since you aren't a healer. You'll just teach me to control my power?"

Amara resumed her progress toward the inn, and I hurried to keep up.

"There certainly won't be anything traditional about the apprenticeship. But, of course, I'll take the responsibility of being your influencer seriously. I'll arrange training from healers whenever I'm able."

I drew a slow breath, not meeting her eyes. If we were traveling constantly, how deep could the healing training go? Surely not very. I would be fine.

"When will you activate me?"

She chuckled. "Why the hurry?"

I just shrugged, unwilling to explain my reasoning to her.

"Don't you think we should discuss the situation with your parents? You're under age, after all."

Uneasiness stirred inside me at the thought of telling my father about my decision. Mother would be delighted, and I hoped Father would accept this solution since it would keep me away from the Guild. But his dislike of mages went far deeper than mine.

"The law is clear on the matter of activation," I said, hoping she hadn't noticed my hesitation. "I might not officially be of age for well over a year, but everyone has the right to choose their influencer for themselves. My parents have no legal say in the matter."

Her brows knit, her eyes searching my face. "No legal say, perhaps, but I had the impression you're close with them. Don't you want to talk to them about it?"

I shrugged again. Whatever my parents' reactions, I had no intention of telling them the true reason for my change of mind. Telling them about Grey or the stranger who was following him would only make them worry for no purpose.

"I would still feel more comfortable if we spoke to them first," Amara said as we arrived at the inn door. "We can ride back to your farm first thing in the morning."

I hesitated again before nodding agreement. The churning emotions in my middle were giving the situation a false urgency. Tomorrow would do just as well as today.

Rocky barked, attracting the attention of the innkeeper who shooed him back outside.

"You can't bring animals inside!"

"But he's just been healed." I glared at the man. "He needs to rest."

"He can rest in the stable easily enough." The man's expression left no room for argument. "If you feel the need to be with him, you're welcome to sleep there yourself."

"Very well, I will." I stalked off in the direction of the stable doors, Rocky frisking around me in an excited manner that undermined my words about rest and recuperation.

Inside the stables, I found an empty stall with a layer of fresh hay that would make a comfortable enough bed. I had just plopped down into it when Amara appeared.

"You won't convince me to go inside," I said before she could speak.

She smiled slightly, dropping a pack into the corner of the stall. "Did I try to do so?"

I gaped at her. "You're going to sleep out here, too?"

"A master has no business sleeping in a proper bed if her apprentice is in a haystack. This is my promise to you. If you become my apprentice, I can't guarantee two years of ease—in fact, I can almost certainly guarantee the opposite—but I can guarantee that whatever you go through, I'll be there by your side."

"I—"

Her promise, solemnly delivered, made me feel like my decision had been hastily made—but also that my instincts had served me well. Amara was the sort of master I could not only follow but also respect.

"Thank you," I said at last.

She smiled and lowered herself into the hay with a sigh. "My own horse and cart have been attended to by the inn's staff. In the future, we'll often have to do it ourselves. Do you have experience with a vehicle like mine? I can only assume you're familiar enough with horses."

I filled her in on my years spent caring for the various farm animals as well as driving our own simple cart. She listened and asked respectful questions, the conversation only finishing when I yawned widely, setting her to yawning as well.

"Enough for now," she said. "We'll talk to your parents in the morning, and if they're in agreement, I'll activate you."

*And we'll stop off to see Halmir on our way out of town,* I thought as I drifted into sleep. Surely Miranda would be back home by then.

nfortunately, our morning's visit to Halmir proved my hope unfounded. Miranda had not returned, and the animal healer had lost his relaxed attitude from the evening before.

"To tell you the truth," he told us, "it seems you may have been right. Word in the market is that Grey fellow left town last night, taking some of our youths with him."

"Let me guess," I said, my heart sinking. "The youths are Stefan and Serena."

He grimaced. "That's right. And my Miranda apparently. But she's not the type to run off." He didn't sound entirely convinced of his own words, though, and I remembered the way he had talked about his daughter the night before.

"You mustn't doubt her," I said quickly. "I don't think she's really changed, not underneath. Nothing she said to me gave the impression she was about to run off."

"Then what am I meant to believe?" he asked. "That she was kidnapped?"

The fear in his eyes was enough to explain why he preferred to think his daughter had left willingly.

"The other parents don't seem surprised," he said in a heavy voice. "It sounds like their children have been more open about their dissatisfaction and desire to leave Tarin."

"I don't—" I stopped, not sure what to say. If only I was confident I'd seen her abducted, I would be able to speak up freely. But I couldn't be sure of what I'd seen. "Is anyone looking for them?"

"They've been traced out of town, heading north, of course, but we don't know the exact route," Halmir said heavily. "And no one in Tarin has a strong enough ability to track them. We would need someone from the capital for that."

I bit my lip. I could keep insisting that I didn't think Miranda left willingly, but what would it achieve? I had no evidence to convince the town with—I didn't even have a strong eyewitness account—and Halmir was right that he had no hope of finding them on his own.

But it wasn't true that we had no one with a strong ability in Tarin right now. I glanced at Amara, and she caught my look, raising her eyebrows before turning to Halmir.

"North, *of course*? What makes you so confident they're heading north?"

"Because Calista is north. I never paid much attention to those fellows—I'm too busy for nonsense—but according to Miranda and the others, they were always going on about the glories of a new land. From the way some of the youths talked, that man had them convinced it's some sort of paradise up there."

Amara frowned. "Those men were Calistan?"

"Who else could they be?" Halmir asked dismissively. There aren't any other new kingdoms sprung from the rocks. And everyone knows the Calistan crown is scouring Tartora and the nomad lands for recruits to repopulate their new kingdom."

Amara continued to frown, obviously bothered by his words although they made sense to me. After a moment of silence, Amara spoke.

"I was intending to continue on my journey imminently," she said to Halmir. "I'm not an expert tracker, by any means, and I'll be heading northwest to Ostaria initially. But after that I'll be turning north more directly, and I'd be more than happy to keep an eye out for any sign of the runaways."

"Yes," I cried, leaping in. "Of course we'll look for Miranda! Don't worry, Halmir. One way or another, we'll find her."

"We?" He looked back and forth between us. "Are you leaving, Delphine?"

"Delphine has agreed to become my apprentice," Amara said calmly.

Halmir whistled. "I was starting to think I would never see Delphine activated."

I glowered at him, but my emotions softened when he grasped my left hand in both of his.

"Thank you, Delphine. You've always been kind to my Miranda, and she's always admired you. If anyone can convince her to come home, it's you."

"I—" Once again I swallowed my words. I didn't think it was a matter of convincing Miranda, but that didn't change my intentions. I would rescue her and bring her home safely.

"Of course," I said. "Try not to worry."

The weight of responsibility sat heavily as we extracted ourselves, and it kept me silent all the way home in the cart, Rocky behind us among the bags. When we pulled up in front of the familiar farmhouse, Amara didn't immediately get down.

"Are you having second thoughts?" she asked.

"What?" I started and turned to her, trying to shake loose my lingering concerns. "No, no, not at all. Sorry."

She smiled. "That's good." She paused, examining me with a creased brow. "Is it your friend, then?"

I bit my lip, wondering how open I should be with Amara. She'd said she was willing to help look for Miranda.

"Yes, I'm worried about her," I said.

"Is that why you've accepted my offer?" she asked slowly. "Because you want to look for your friend?"

I considered, wanting to give her an honest answer. It seemed the least I could do if we were going to bind ourselves to each other for the next two years.

"No," I said slowly. "At least, it's not the whole reason. But I do want to be able to help people like her. I don't know why I have this seed, but my mother is right—I don't want to waste it."

She nodded, looking pleased rather than upset with my mixed answer.

I climbed down slowly, more nervous than I'd expected now that it was actually time to face my father. My earlier thought that he would see this apprenticeship as a satisfactory work-around now seemed less and less likely. Would he think I was betraying him, just like his brother had done?

My breath quickened, as both my parents emerged from the house. Rocky had alerted them to our arrival with a series of excited yips. He had already leaped down from the cart and was racing around the yard, sniffing everything as if he suspected it had changed in his short absence.

As soon as my father appeared, Rocky raced to him, pressing against his legs and happily receiving pats and words of praise.

"You're back," my mother looked torn—clearly relieved at my return but also uncomfortable at the presence of a mage on our farm. "I'm pleased to meet you, ma'am," she finally added with a respectful nod of her head.

"The pleasure is all mine, I assure you." Amara gave a friendly smile and held out her hand.

My mother looked from the hand to Amara's face, clearly taken by surprise by her humble attitude. As Mother took Amara's hand to shake it, her manner warmed noticeably.

"We're so grateful for your assistance with Rocky. And for bringing our daughter back safely. I understand Rocky might have been in real danger without your intervention."

Amara smiled and demurred, probably thinking that my father had reported positively on her assistance. I knew it was far more likely he had been enraged at being forced to accept the help of a mage.

"I'm sorry for any worry we caused you by not making it back last night," Amara said. "I generally try to avoid traveling after dark, so we stayed at the inn. Your daughter was very devoted to Rocky's care. I was impressed."

My mother glowed with pride, and I moved forward to give her a hug. She had always been supportive of me, the only tension between us my refusal to take an apprenticeship with Halmir.

Praise of me had been the only thing needed for Mother to warm to Amara, despite her mage status. She beamed at the other woman, one of her arms wrapped around my shoulders.

"Thank you for taking our Delphine under your wing."

"Actually, about that…" Amara glanced at me as if she wasn't sure if I wanted to tell them myself or have her do it.

A sharp twist in my gut made me want to delay, but there was nothing to be gained by doing so.

"I've agreed to be Amara's apprentice," I blurted out.

"What?" my mother cried, her voice halfway between shock and delight.

Usually my parents agreed on everything, and my mother had never shown anything but understanding and compassion for my father's occasional outbursts and silent withdrawals. But on the matter of my activation, she had always stood firm in opposition to the two of us. Father might support my not being activated, but Mother had always held out hope.

But it was my father who drew my attention, his silence louder than my mother's exclamation. Every line of his body was stiff and taut, his face frozen in a mask of disapproval.

I slipped out of my mother's grip and hurried over to him, my words falling over themselves.

"Amara is a traveling master. She doesn't live at the Guild, or even spend time in the capital at all. She travels around to small towns like Tarin. As her apprentice, I'll travel with her. Apparently I don't ever need to go to the Guild at all. I can graduate without them."

My father's stance relaxed slightly, although his expression remained displeased. I pressed on, slowing down as I chose my words more carefully.

"Amara's an elements mage, as you know. So she won't be teaching me healing. But we both believe there's value in cross-influencing, and she'll still be able to teach me the necessary control."

I glanced briefly at Amara to find her watching me with a hint of confusion on her face. I fell silent, my face flushing. Did Amara think I was insulting her teaching before she'd even begun? I couldn't backtrack my comments though since they were intended to convey a message to my father that neither Amara nor my mother would understand.

My father finally moved, swinging his head to look me in the eyes.

"You want to leave us?"

I swallowed. "Just for the two years of my apprenticeship. I'll have a chance to see the latest farming techniques from across the kingdom, and then I'll return to help put them into practice here. I can't do anything about not having a plants seed, but at least I should be able to use my power to help us a little. It would be better than being completely powerless."

"Would it?" he asked gruffly, not breaking his gaze.

I took a step closer, lowering my voice to plead with him.

"Please, Father. I don't want to always be weak and power-less and vulnerable."

A shadow crossed his face, and he shot a look at Amara, clearly wondering what had happened during my absence. He wasn't entirely wrong, but I didn't want him to blame Amara.

"It's not her," I whispered, even more quietly. "But I want to be able to protect myself. I want to be able to protect all of us."

I could hear the fierce note in my voice, despite the quiet volume, and apparently my father could too. The skin around his eyes tightened, but he slowly nodded.

I couldn't be sure if he actually agreed or if he had simply accepted that there was nothing he could do to reverse the momentum that had already begun.

"You'll really be all right?" he murmured, and I knew what he was referring to.

"I'll find a way to be all right," I said. "I have to. I'll overcome *all* my weaknesses, and then I'll return."

He nodded again and turned to Amara.

"It seems the mages are to steal away my daughter, after all."

"Father!" I hissed, but I couldn't help a slow smile spreading across my face.

His agreement might be reluctant and halfhearted, but it was still agreement. He didn't intend to disown me for aligning myself with a mage.

"I'm grateful to you for loaning Delphine to me," Amara said, cautious but polite. She clearly knew there was something going on here she didn't understand, but she didn't press for answers. "I waited to activate her until we'd talked to you, but I can do it now if you're both in agreement."

"It seems like a dream!" Mother turned to me with a smile. "Have you truly agreed to this, Delphie?"

I grimaced. "Is it so hard to believe?" But even as I said the words, I realized it was. I had always been so set against activation, with my father as my staunch supporter. "You know that means I'll be leaving for two whole years, right?" I added, wondering how she could be so happy about the prospect.

My mother's arms wrapped around me in a tight hug. "I'll miss you every day, of course I will. But loving your children means wanting them to have a full life and to fulfill every bit of their potential—even if that means they have to spread their wings and leave for a time. Your father and I have each other. We'll survive just fine."

My brow creased as I considered the practicalities. "Will you, though? You'll need help for the farm."

"Then we'll get it," she said firmly. "We've done so in the past. It's not as if we have to pay for your apprenticeship." She looked to Amara for confirmation, and the mage nodded.

"That's correct. I will fund my apprentice for the entirety of her training, including food and board. In return, I will receive any earnings from our combined efforts in those two years."

"That's fair." My mother looked at my father, as if daring him to protest. He remained silent.

"It won't be a life of luxury," Amara warned, looking a little concerned. "The life of a traveling master isn't as glamorous as life at the Guild. We'll be sleeping by the road rather than in a castle. But if Delphine assists me with any particularly high-paying tasks, I will likely give her a bonus."

She had meant her words as a caution, but she couldn't have said anything more perfect. I wanted to throw my arms around her, but I restrained myself, only allowing a slight upturn of my lips.

My father responded as I'd hoped he would, unbending even further, and even nodding acknowledgment of Amara's words.

A terrified sort of elation swept through me. This was really happening. I was going to become a mage after all.

"Do we need to have some sort of ceremony or something?" I asked, not wanting to delay in case I lost my nerve.

"Ceremony?" My father stared at me blankly while my mother chuckled.

"To activate me," I said, flushing. I'd never seen an activation before since I didn't have any older siblings to go through it ahead of me.

"I've seen families and mages who like to make an event out of it," Amara said diplomatically, "but it's not at all necessary. The consequences and responsibilities that come from activating someone are significant, but the act itself is easily done."

"Will you do it right now, then?" I asked, gritting my teeth. I'd never bothered to ask my parents what it felt like, but surely it had to hurt to have a hidden seed inside you cracked open.

"If you're sure?" Amara met my eyes squarely, and I held her gaze.

"I'm ready."

She turned to my parents. "Do you have any objection or any reason for us to wait on the activation? I don't need to be on my way immediately, so there's no great hurry."

I thought of my father's moods and of the unknown fate of my friend and frowned. It would be better for us to be on the road immediately. Now that I'd made my decision, any delay chafed.

"No, no, there's no reason to wait," my mother said, clearly afraid I might change my mind if we didn't take the opportunity immediately.

Amara smiled slightly, as if guessing the reason for her sense of urgency. "Very well, then. I'll activate Delphine now."

# SIX

I waited, expecting her to raise a hand or speak or do something discernible. She neither moved nor spoke.

"Well?" I asked impatiently. "Do I need to do something?"

Amara's smile grew. "It's done."

"What?" I stared at her. "What do you mean? You're saying I've already been activated?" I patted down both arms as if expecting to find something different about my body.

"Take a moment," she said. "Don't think about your own body, focus outward."

I hesitated, confused by her words, but I could sense an earnestness behind them. Although I still couldn't feel a difference, I knew with certainty she was speaking the truth about my activation.

I froze, wondering where the certainty had come from. She had so far proved herself to be a trustworthy person, but it hadn't been that. The certainty was rooted somewhere inside me, a sense that didn't brook any doubt or opposition. Amara had spoken the words, and her body had radiated truthfulness.

Her body? Where had that thought come from? The more I

considered it, however, the more certain I felt. It had been her body itself that had told me the truth of her words.

I turned slowly to look at my parents. As soon as I focused on them, I felt an acute awareness of their presence. I could almost hear the blood flowing through their veins and the breath pumping in their lungs.

A sense of unclouded happiness flowed over me a moment before Rocky bounded around the corner of the house and dashed toward us. I expected him to make for my father's side, but instead he bounded straight to me, panting and wagging his tail. When he reached me, he stopped, leaning against my leg.

His happy contentedness pressed against me as heavily as his physical form. It was like the pain I had sensed from him in the cart the day before, but magnified many times over. Had the earlier sense been a result of my seed? I had always assumed everyone sensed such things, but now that I considered the matter more closely, I hadn't always felt it so clearly. My awareness of Rocky had grown as my seed reached maturity, even before it was activated.

And now that my power had awoken, even that stronger sense of recent months seemed like a whispered echo. It was nothing compared to how aware I was of everyone around me now.

I couldn't possibly doubt any longer. I had clearly been activated.

Amara held her hand out to me, and I stared at it. Was this another part of the process? Was I supposed to bow over it or kiss it or something to pledge my loyalty to her as my influencer and my master for the next two years of my apprenticeship?

She chuckled. "Just take it."

Hesitantly, I reached out and lightly clasped her fingers.

Gasping, I jumped back, breaking the contact. My heart raced and sweat broke out along my hairline as I stared at her.

"I...That was...I..."

"Unlike with my own elements affinity, healers need physical contact to make full use of their power. The fact you're sensing anything without physical contact is a sign of your strength." Her tone remained calm and positive, but her smile had faltered at my reaction.

I gulped in several breaths, slowly nodding as I commanded my body to calm itself. To my surprise, it obeyed, my roiling stomach settling. I blinked, too startled to speak. That had never happened before.

"Be careful," Amara said in a low, urgent voice. "In these initial weeks while you're learning control, you can protect others by avoiding physical contact, but you can't close off your connection with your own body."

"I...How did you know?" My opinion of her rose even further.

"Don't be too impressed." She sounded rueful. "I'm actually demonstrating my inexperience. I've never been involved with training a healer before. I should have warned you to be careful before I activated you."

"Is Delphine in danger?" my mother asked, fear in her voice.

Amara hesitated, her lips twisting. "Again, it's my error for not fully informing you of the dangers. I don't want to deceive you in any way, so I will acknowledge there is a small amount of risk. Some risk exists for all newly activated mages, due to the strength of their power. It's one of the reasons we have such strict rules around apprenticeships and learning control. But that risk is amplified for healers—even those with a weaker seed can make a fatal error."

"Fatal?" my father asked gruffly.

"Only in the rarest of cases," Amara said quickly. "And I can assure you that despite my initial misstep, I'll keep a close eye on Delphine going forward. I won't let anything happen to her."

My parents exchanged a long look before my mother

nodded. But it wasn't as if they could do anything at this point. Amara had activated me now, and the law was clear on that point. Whether we liked it or not, she was my master for the next two years.

During the entire exchange between Amara and my parents I had remained frozen in place, terrified of doing something dangerous unintentionally. My fear must have shown because Amara turned to me.

"Don't you worry either, Delphine," she said in a soft, calming voice. "The fact you're older than the average apprentice will help you here. You have more experience and natural control, and that will aid you in bringing your ability into line."

"I don't understand what I did." The words came out in a tight, unfamiliar tone.

"Please relax," Amara said, smiling this time. "You won't accidentally use your ability by moving your body or speaking."

I nodded but couldn't bring myself to make any more substantial motion.

Amara hesitated, looking toward my parents. My mother seemed to pick up on her message first, taking my father's arm.

"There is plenty to be done on the farm still, so we'll be about our work. But you should make yourself at home inside." She gestured toward the open door of the farmhouse. "I'll make some tea and see if I can dig out some leftover cake. This is a moment to be celebrated."

My father stiffened at her words, obviously not at the point of celebrating my apprenticeship to a mage. But at least he didn't say anything aloud.

Amara thanked them both and guided me across the yard and inside the house. Seating me in an armchair, she pulled over a second chair so she could sit right by me.

"Now that your seed has been activated, you have full access to your power. You don't need to summon it or use any words or actions to access it. The power is part of you now, the same way your limbs or your eyes are part of you. If you want to pick up a cup, or kick a ball, you can do so with a single thought. Your mind instructs, and your body obeys. It's the same with your power. Our aim in our training will be to make your use of power as controlled and instinctive as the use of your limbs."

An amused chuckle preceded my mother's arrival with a plate full of slices of lemon cake.

"I wish you luck, Master Amara," she said. "Our Delphine didn't master walking until she was nearly two. She was determined not to fall, so she preferred not to take a step at all rather than practice walking and fall over constantly."

"Makes sense to me," I muttered.

Amara hid her smile behind her hand. "We can move slowly at the beginning, but it will be necessary to practice with your ability."

"But how can I risk *falling* if I'm operating inside someone else's body?" I asked, fear washing over me.

"It's good to have an appropriate level of caution," Amara said. "There are other aspects of your power we can focus on for now. When we find a healer with enough experience and strength, you'll be able to work alongside them and observe without putting anyone's life at risk."

I drew a shaky breath, liking the sound of working on other aspects of my power. I had no desire to start messing around with anyone's insides.

"The important thing for now," Amara said as my mother disappeared back to the kitchen, still chuckling, "is not to put your own body at risk. You've just gained a connection with all breathing creatures, and it's like you've just gained an extra arm. Except this limb is clumsy and poorly connected to your brain, so if you have a fleeting thought about hitting someone in the face, it just might reach out and try to do it."

I considered what had happened earlier. I had commanded my churning stomach to settle, and it had obeyed, as if my will had gained new control over my body. It turned out that was exactly what had happened.

"Is that how those other apprentices died?" I asked in a shaky voice. "They thought about their heart stopping or something similar, and their power obeyed their thoughts?"

"That's right, but you really don't need to be too concerned. We haven't had a death like that in Tartora in over a generation. Just exercise caution for now, and you'll gain the control you need in no time. The first thing we'll work on is awareness of your ability and when you're using it. Once you're clear on that, you won't accidentally make use of your power."

My mother returned with cups of tea, and I forced myself to focus on the cup in my hands and the warm liquid moving down my throat, refusing to let my thoughts wander. She kept up a stream of conversation with Amara which helped, telling her about my preferences and quirks in the embarrassing way only mothers do.

I held onto the discomfort, using it to distract myself as I let her sweep me away to pack my bags. Amara said she had plenty of room in the back of the cart, so I ended up packing two large bags, even slipping in several favorite books, and my larger writing kit. My mother would want regular updates on our travels, and I looked forward to being able to tell her about the parts of the kingdom she had never had a chance to visit.

When we finally came back downstairs, I had calmed, no longer hyper-focused on every thought and action. Amara had joined my father in our absence, the two of them inspecting the small collection of horses in our stables.

"Delphine will soon surpass me in this area," Amara said as they walked back inside together. "I can only sense a problem in the vaguest way, and I can't fix it. She'll soon be able to pinpoint exactly where the problem is and fix anything that isn't too complex. Eventually, given her strength, she'll be able to heal almost anything at all."

I grimaced, sudden discomfort assailing me. I'd been so focused on my fight with the stranger, and then on getting permission from my father, that I'd never stopped to wonder if I was being dishonest by not revealing my squeamishness to Amara. She thought she had taken on an apprentice who had the potential to be one of the kingdom's strongest healers. Would she still have taken me on if she knew the truth?

Before I could get too twisted up in the thought, my mother appeared, bearing a tray of delicacies. Apparently lemon cake hadn't been sufficiently celebratory.

My father rubbed his hands together at the sight of his favorite smoked sausage. He seemed to have softened toward Amara significantly during their time in the stables—perhaps as a result of her willingness to get her hands dirty on a small and inconsequential farm. He must have seen the same thing I had—Amara wasn't like the Guild mages of the capital, the ones he hated.

Making an appreciative noise, he raided the platter. But just as he popped a round of sausage in his mouth, Rocky raced through the open door with a particularly loud bark. The dog must have smelled the sausages, which were also a favorite of his.

My father jerked in surprise, twisting to peer at the animal. I just rolled my eyes, reaching toward the tray myself. Father would no doubt soon be feeding Rocky sausage, although he always told me off for hand-feeding the dog.

But my father didn't bend down, and a sharp cry from my mother made me startle. She leaped to my father's side, taking my gaze with her. Horror filled me as I took in his appearance. Fear twisted his face and his body spasmed, although he wasn't making a sound.

"He's choking!" Amara said sharply.

She whacked him on the back, but although his whole body

shook, he still didn't make a sound, his hands pressed against his throat.

Amara spun to me. "Delphine! Quick! You can save him!"

"What?" I gasped, fear making me shake. But even as my mind stuttered, my legs were already carrying me toward him.

He dropped to his knees, and I knelt beside him. But my hands gripped together, squeezing tightly as I remembered the sickening rush when I made contact with Amara. Even now, I couldn't quite bring myself to touch him.

"Quickly," Amara instructed. "I'm sorry, Delphine, but there's no time for caution now. If you want your father to live, you're going to need to do the best you can."

"But what if I..." My words trailed off as my father reached out himself and gripped my bare arm.

Immediately I was overwhelmed with a jumbled awareness of every part of his body. I could sense every vein and all the blood pulsing through them. His heart still pumped, but his lungs were no longer contracting. His other organs jumbled together in my mind, although I couldn't name them all. I didn't have the knowledge to bring order to the parts I could sense. Instead they all pressed on me at once, clamoring for attention.

My stomach responded immediately, my senses swimming and my gut churning. Any second I was going to be sick.

Instinctively, my mind cried out for everything to stop, trying to find enough space to think clearly. I didn't speak aloud, but instantly I felt a change. I could still sense all the parts of him just as clearly, my mind just as overwhelmed, but the sense of pulsing movement had disappeared.

My father's body went limp, his hand slipping off my arm. Instantly the connection between us was severed.

I dived forward, my own body's reaction forgotten as I reached for his arm myself this time. Both of my hands clung onto him as a distant, wordless scream tore from my own throat.

*No, no, no, no!* my mind silently recited, desperately willing his systems to return to normal, and his blood to start flowing again.

The returning rush of movement in his veins hit my senses with relief this time instead of overwhelm, but the momentary relief from intense fear unlocked the tight clamp on my stomach and I retched, my stomach starting to spasm.

"Delphine!" Amara's commanding voice cut through the chaos in my body and senses, her hand landing heavily on my shoulders and her fingers digging in to the point of pain. "Settle your stomach now. Focus! Your father's life depends on it."

Desperately, I pushed aside my confusion and fear and commanded my stomach to settle, just as I had earlier. The spasming muscles immediately subsided, the burning in my throat receding as my stomach's contents resettled into place. I coughed, trying to suck in air, but I couldn't afford to waste any more time on my own body.

"Can you sense something out of place?" Amara asked urgently in my ear. "Something in his body that doesn't belong there?"

As soon as she said it, I could feel it. How had I not noticed it earlier? His body was rebelling against the foreign substance, trying desperately to expel it, although he couldn't suck in the air needed to cough.

"I can feel it," I said, not sure how else to explain it. It wasn't actually the sense of touch, any more than it was sight. But the inside of his body was as clear to my mind as if I could see his throat with my eyes or touch his heart with my hand.

"Contract the muscles of his throat just below the sausage," she instructed. "Follow its progress up until you push it all the way out."

Trembling from head to toe, I tried to focus on his throat. I didn't know how to identify his muscles from the other internal parts of him, but I hadn't needed to know the details to soothe my own stomach.

"Squeeze," I whispered, speaking aloud in an attempt to focus my thoughts as I silently instructed his throat to contract.

His muscles tightened, and the foreign substance moved, inching upward. Elated, I focused even harder, contracting his throat all the way up until the substance popped free. Every part of his body sagged in relief as he sucked in a huge gulp of air.

I collapsed, our contact breaking again and the mess of confusion in my mind fading. My father was coughing, but weakly, both hands at his throat. As he pulled them slowly away, I paled. His skin was red and swollen and would clearly soon be mottled with bruising.

"Your neck! I—" I burst into tears without completing the sentence.

He tried to speak, but his voice was too rough and hoarse to be understood. Reaching out instead, he pulled me into a hug. My mother wrapped her arms around both of us, her tears falling on my ear.

"He's alive, Delphie," she wept, "that's all that matters. The bruising will heal."

I looked to Amara for confirmation, and she met my gaze steadily, her face serious.

"You're the healer here," she said. "You tell us."

My eyes widened. I was trying my best to ignore the jumbled sensations coming from my parents' bodies due to their embrace. The last thing I wanted was to purposely dive back into my connection with my father's insides.

"Don't try to heal him," Amara instructed. "You're not advanced enough for that. Just have a look."

I drew a deep breath and reluctantly focused my attention. I was so terrified of accidentally sending my power an unintentional command that I was barely letting myself think at all.

To my surprise, his throat already felt familiar, though. My mind latched back onto the part I had earlier manipulated, and I could feel the bruising. Nothing seemed permanently crushed, however. As far as I could tell, there was no damage that wouldn't heal on its own.

With a sigh of relief, I extracted myself from my parents' arms. The peace that descended once we were out of contact felt more comforting than the contact had.

The thought made my heart squeeze painfully. Would I never be able to comfortably embrace anyone again?

"Don't worry," Amara said at my side, once again seeming to read my mind. "You'll get used to it, and then you won't even notice—unless you want to."

I gave her a tremulous smile, wanting to believe her words were true although it felt unlikely.

I cleared my throat and focused back on my father. "Your throat should get better. Although it might hurt for a while."

"Thank you, Delphine," my mother said, tears in her eyes as she reached for me, only to stop and let her hand drop. "You were activated just in time."

Delayed shock hit me, my whole body trembling uncontrollably. My father had just died, if only momentarily. If I hadn't asked Amara to activate me today, he probably would have stayed dead. Delaying my activation for so long suddenly seemed foolhardy in the extreme. What had I been thinking?

Memory of my earlier sickening awareness of his internal organs swept over me, reminding me exactly why I had never desired this life. Saving my father had brought home the value of learning more healing, but every part of me rebelled at the idea of spending more time connected to the bodies of others.

How many hundreds of hours of practice would it take to achieve the necessary mastery?

I sank down to sit on the floor, putting my head in my hands. The will might be there but my body and mind were traitors, working against me. What if I couldn't do it?

CHAPTER

# SEVEN

I tried to convince my father to travel into Tarin to go to the healing clinic, but he refused, unwilling to spend money on something that would heal naturally, especially when the injury didn't stop him working.

"What if I'm wrong, though?" I asked Amara after my father grew tired of listening to my worries and stalked away toward the stables. "I have no idea what I'm doing." My volume dipped. "I nearly killed him! I stopped his heart beating."

Even Amara looked a little shaken by the revelation, but after a moment, she fixed me with a determined look.

"But you got it started again. You don't understand yet, but that speaks to your strength. You have more awareness and control than a weaker seed would have at this point. You need to trust yourself. If your sense was that he'll heal fine, then I believe it's true. My healer friends tell me that anatomical education and knowledge help, but a lot of it is still instinctual.

"And the stronger someone's seed, the more they instinctively understand how bodies work. It's why many of the strongest healers end up focusing on research instead of running healing clinics. If they can make breakthroughs in understanding and healing techniques, then weaker healers can put that increased knowledge into practice. In the long run, that means more people can be helped. Much of your medical training will be about learning prevention, early intervention, and healing techniques that use less power. For someone as strong as you, there will always be the option of brute forcing your way through a single complex working."

I let her words wash over me, focusing on the impromptu lesson to quiet my racing thoughts and frantic heartbeat. For a moment I even imagined myself as a researcher before I abruptly remembered that my future was already set. I wouldn't spend it at a healing clinic in the capital, but right here on my family farm outside Tarin.

At least Amara had succeeded in calming me down. And preparing the evening meal with my mother calmed me further. The familiar action brought a much-needed sense of normality to my final evening at home.

I slept in my bed, and Amara slept in our guest room—a more comfortable night for both of us than the previous one in the stables. I suspected I would be wise to savor every night spent on a soft mattress from here on. The next two years looked likely to bring all sorts of different sleeping envi-ronments.

I was reluctant to leave while my father was still injured, but both my parents were insistent that we start on our way the next morning.

Now that the decision was irrevocably made, my father seemed eager to have us both gone. And while my mother was grieved over the farewell, she was no less encouraging of our departure. From the surreptitious looks she kept directing at my father, I could guess why.

Who knew how bad his mood would be in the wake of my activation and departure? And it would surely only grow worse the longer he had to restrain himself due to the presence of a mage in his house. At this rate he might withdraw into himself for days.

Amara hadn't pressed for our departure, but she didn't fight it either. She even waited patiently while I bid a lengthy and tear-filled farewell to my parents. My mother risked a single, brief hug, pulling back quickly at my intake of breath when we made contact. My father, by contrast, was restrained, speaking very little. But tears sprang to my eyes when he gruffly told me to take Rocky with me.

"I couldn't separate him from you!" I told him. "Rocky would be miserable without you."

Rocky himself tried to make a lie of my words by pressing himself against my leg. Two days ago, I would have sworn the animal would never choose to be separated from my father, but since my activation, he had been following me like a shadow.

I knelt down and buried my face in his neck, ignoring the discomfort that came with the contact. Commanding him to stay, I whispered that he needed to watch over Father. I was afraid of his reaction and how it might hurt my father, but he seemed to take my words to heart. Thumping his tail against the ground, he licked me once before trotting over to stand at alert at my father's feet.

With a teary smile, I rose and climbed into the cart. After a final round of waves, we started down the road that led away from the farmhouse.

"Are you all right?" Amara asked after several minutes of silence. "With the physical contact, I mean."

I tried to surreptitiously wipe away my tears. "I tried to build a wall, like you said."

"A wall?" She stared at me curiously. "I said that?"

"Didn't you?" I frowned, trying to remember. Now that she was questioning me, I couldn't actually remember her speaking those exact words. "I guess not. Isn't that what you meant, though? That I need to separate my consciousness from my new awareness?"

"Did it work?" She looked at me sideways, her eyes alight with curiosity.

"It helped a bit." I sighed. "Not as much as I'd hoped."

"What I actually meant is that you'd grow accustomed to it," she said. "So that over time, you wouldn't notice it consciously anymore. Like with the sky. If we're outside, it's always there in our vision—blue or gray, cloudy or clear—and if we have a reason to think about the weather, we'll take note of it. But most of the time we have no active awareness of it."

"Oh." I felt like an idiot.

"I'll be interested to hear how it goes, though," she said. "If you partially succeeded in building your wall today, then practice should make it stronger."

My eyes flew to her face. "You want me to keep working on it?"

"Of course! This sort of thing is exactly why we need to vary how we handle activation and training in Tartora. Just like there's much to be learned from cross-influencing, there is always insight to be gained from fresh perspectives and approaches. We lose that when we gather everyone at the Guild and train them in the same way. I want to encourage you to think differently, Delphine, not force you to be like every other healer apprentice."

Her words eased a lingering tightness in my chest. I had only agreed to apprentice with Amara because she seemed different, but after the fiasco of my activation, I had forgotten that fact in the wave of fear.

I managed to produce a smile, although it was a little shaky.

"Thank you. I'll continue practicing it, then."

"Excellent. And make sure you keep me apprised of your progress. I want you to explore your own path, but as your influencer, I'm also responsible for you. I may not be a healer, but I am an experienced mage, and it's my role to keep you safe and ensure you learn the necessary control."

"Yes." I shivered, remembering the moment my father's heart had stopped beating at my command.

"Like right now," Amara said.

"Now?" I asked, startled.

She nodded. "I don't intend to introduce formal lessons to our daily schedule—we won't be sitting down at a desk and studying each day. I believe there is far more to be learned from experience. But some reading will be required, as well as some direct lessons from me. Travel days like today provide an excellent opportunity for such activities."

I murmured agreement, pleased to hear I wouldn't be confined to lessons like a child again. Was that what mages did to their apprentices at the Guild? I was doubly glad I'd refused to go there if so.

"As I told you yesterday, our first focus needs to be on helping you acquire the necessary level of control to prevent any damage to your own body. That's something we can practice while traveling."

She looked sideways at me. "I don't need to tell you how much clearer your senses are now. You can experience that for yourself. I'm relying on what I've been told by healer friends, but I understand you're now able to sense all those parts of your body that operated subconsciously before. I'm glad it doesn't seem to be overwhelming to you like physical touch is."

"What?" I frowned, trying to understand her words. "What can I sense?" I looked down at my body. I didn't feel any different.

The horse pulling the cart—a calm mare named Acorn whose presence radiated contentment—faltered, as if in response to a tightening of the reins. I looked up to find Amara staring at me.

"You don't sense your own body?" Her sharp tone scared me.

"Should I?" Panic rose up, making my voice shake. Was something wrong with my power? Or worse—with my body?

Acorn resumed her steady pace, a calm mask descending over Amara's features as well.

"Please don't be alarmed," she said. "Remember that I have no experience training a healer, let alone one as strong as you. I'm sure there is some obvious explanation I've overlooked."

A crease appeared between her brows. "Have you noticed it at any point? I'm talking about things like the beat of your heart. Is your strength allowing you to instinctually push it into the background, like we were talking about earlier?"

She gave me another sharp look. "You had a strong reaction when I first talked about using your power on yourself. Had you already done that?"

I bit my lip as I tried to remember the exact order of the various distressing events of the previous afternoon.

"Yes, I—" I hesitated, cutting myself off and then rushing to continue with different words. "It was after the activation when you had me touch your hand. I touched you for the first time and felt your...insides." I gulped. "I instinctively calmed myself after that. And then again when I needed to heal my father."

I knew I wasn't being entirely accurate in my description of what I'd done—hiding behind the word calming—but I wasn't ready to admit the full truth to anyone, let alone a master mage.

"It sounds like your awareness of your own body only awoke after making contact with someone else and feeling theirs," Amara said thoughtfully. "That seems reasonable enough. Your power was still in the process of awakening. But now you say you're not sensing anything at all?"

I shook my head, gathering the courage to speak. "Not in a constant way. But I could try to see what happens when I focus on it if you like?"

She considered. "It was certainly an unusually traumatic activation. So perhaps small deviations are to be expected. If you could make the attempt, I would be interested in what you find."

I nodded, my attention too focused to allow for words. Amara had warned me against tampering with my own body in these early weeks. I had done it in order to heal my father, but that had been an extreme situation. I should avoid doing it again if I could. I just needed to sense my body without interfering with it.

But would I cope even with that much? I had barely made it through every instance of physical contact since my activation. Could I focus on my insides without setting off my most hated reflexes?

Slowly, reluctantly, I tried to think about the blood pulsing through my veins and the rise and fall of my lungs. A queasy feeling in my stomach accompanied the thoughts, but it was a familiar feeling, not born out of my ability. I could sense nothing else.

"I..." My lips twisted, worry filling me again. "I'm sorry, I can't feel anything unusual."

"Hmmm..." Amara seemed to have left behind any trace of concern, consumed by professional curiosity instead. "Your reaction to contact with others is intense, and your first interaction with your own body was bound up in that reaction. Why don't you try touching me?"

"On purpose?" I asked, wide-eyed. "And actually focus on your body without a wall? But you said I should avoid that for now—that it could be dangerous."

"I trust you," she said calmly. "You won't attempt to change anything inside me, I'm sure."

My head started vigorously shaking of its own accord. "But what if I make a mistake?"

"I trust you," she repeated, something implacable in her

tone.

She was my influencer and my master for two years of training. Refusing to cooperate with her lessons wasn't an option. I could see myself dragged before the Triumvirate at that rate.

I stretched out a hand toward her arm, but just before it made contact, it froze, trembling slightly. Amara spoke again, her voice warmer, the words wrapping around me and soothing my anxieties.

"As soon as you make contact, you'll be able to sense every part of my body. Do your best to ignore that. Those sensations are just a jumping point to allow you to feel yourself. Focus inward."

I drew a deep breath, but Amara spoke quickly before I could make contact.

"But don't change anything about yourself, remember. All we want today is awareness."

I nodded, and before I could change my mind, thrust my hand the rest of the way forward to wrap around her wrist.

Instantly I was overwhelmed with awareness of Amara's internal systems. I threw up a wall as I had done earlier, although I couldn't explain how I was doing it. It was like my mind's eye could see the red bricks stacking on top of each other one by one.

I wasn't fast enough, though, and the wall had cracks and holes, limiting its effectiveness. My stomach churned, and I had to use all my willpower not to use my power to calm it.

Instead I tried to expand my awareness of myself beyond my belly, searching for veins and heart and lungs. My head swam, saliva filling my mouth.

"Stop, stop!" I managed to gasp, and Amara pulled back on the reins.

Acorn slowed to a halt, and I almost fell out of the cart, I managed to make it to the side of the road before the contents of my stomach came up. My belly retracted and spasmed as it expelled my breakfast, only calming once it was fully emptied.

Amara leaped down to join me, one hand rubbing circles on my back while the other handed me a water skin. I took it gratefully. Rinsing my mouth, I spat out a mouthful before taking a large drink.

"I'm sorry," I said when I could speak again. "It seems like some of that celebration food must have disagreed with me."

Amara's circling hand froze before resuming its previous pace.

"You poor thing," she said. "I know I told you not to use your power on yourself for now, but if you need to settle your stomach, that should be safe enough." She hesitated as if she wanted to say more but didn't speak.

"Thank you," I said, feeling a flush mounting up my cheeks. It was only the first morning of my training, and I'd already disgraced myself.

Amara's kindness as she helped me into the cart only further exacerbated my guilt and embarrassment. I should tell her the full truth of what had just happened. But no matter how many times I decided to speak up, I couldn't bring my mouth to actually form the words. What sort of healer felt sick at the mere mention of a wound, let alone at the sight of actual blood? Knowing what was coming, I should have refrained from eating the food my mother had prepared.

In the aftershock of my run-in with the stranger, my anger and the sour taste of my fear had overcome my normal caution. But now it was hard to recall the intensity of those emotions. What had I been thinking allowing Amara to activate me? I could clearly never be a healer.

"It's all right," Amara said softly as she directed Acorn to resume walking. "You'll soon get the knack of how to heal yourself—and others too."

I pressed a hand to my head, wishing a healing ability included the power to erase unpleasant memories.

"How did you go, though?" Amara asked after a brief moment of silence. "Did you sense anything before we had to stop?"

"I could sense you clearly," I said slowly. "I tried putting up a wall to block it out, but it was only partially successful. It was enough to calm my mind somewhat, though, so I did try to focus on myself like you said."

"And?" she prompted when I faltered.

"I got nothing, beyond a sudden awareness I was about to be sick."

"Nothing?"

I shrugged, not sure what to say.

"Let me think about it some more," she said. "In the meantime, we'll try something different. The positive side to this situation is that you don't seem to be an imminent danger to yourself. So we can work on building up your control in general. I'm confident we'll work out what's going on eventually, and when we do, you'll find it a lot easier to handle if you've already learned some general control."

I nodded, trying not to show my uneasiness. What was she going to ask me to do?

"I had the impression yesterday that you can sense people and animals around you without needing physical contact," she continued, and I released a shaky breath.

This part of my power didn't scare me. This was the part I liked.

I sat up straighter. "Yes, I can. I realized I could sense it before as well, but it was so faint in comparison that I didn't think anything of it. It's not like when I make contact—it's not all blood and internal organs. I would describe it more as a general sense of their presence. With people, if I'm close like we are right now, I can sense the most basic body functions, like

96

your breathing, but with animals, it's more a general sense of their current state—whether they're in pain or afraid or happy. I can tell that Acorn is mildly pleased to be plodding along in such pleasant weather."

Amara chuckled. "Suddenly you're all words. Clearly I just need to find the right topic."

I flushed and slumped back on the hard wooden seat.

"Don't stop," she said with a smile. "That wasn't a criticism. It helps me if you talk. I want to understand what's going on in your mind. It will help me be a better teacher."

"All right, I'll try," I said, feeling awkward and wishing I didn't have anything to hide.

"Those external senses you're talking about are because of your strength," she explained. "Healers below mage level generally have little to no ability to sense anything without physical contact. Even someone as strong as Halmir would only have the vaguest external awareness."

"Really?" I frowned at her. "But you were able to sense Rocky from as far away as the road, and you don't even have a healing affinity. I know you have a healing influence, but I thought that only gave you echoes of your cross affinity, not advanced abilities."

"No, you're right," she said. "While I have an unusual sense of connection with both humans and animals for an elements mage, I can't actually heal at all. The only conclusion I can come to is that the awareness you're feeling—which I also have to a lesser extent—isn't actually an advanced ability. Rather it is a basic ability that is accessed only by those with greater sensitivity."

"You mean that it's the overall strength of your power that allows you to share that part of the healing ability?" I asked.

"Exactly." She sounded pleased. "And it makes it a good place for you to start. It's not only an external ability, but one that shouldn't require great skill, control, or effort from you. You won't even need to be nervous since it's non-invasive."

I sat up straight, my eyes fixed eagerly on her face. Did I really get to start with such a pleasant part of my ability?

"What do you want me to do?" I asked.

"I'm curious to see your range," she said. "Try to relax and reach out with your mind. Tell me what animals you can sense around us."

"Reach out with my mind?" I tried not to sound nervous. I didn't want to fail at my first proper lesson.

"Why don't you close your eyes this first time?" she suggested. "It isn't necessary, but it might help to remove distractions until you're used to it. Essentially it's the same as looking into the distance or listening for sounds from far away. You're just reaching with a new sense you didn't have before. It should be just as instinctive. You just need to learn how to recognize it."

I drew a deep breath and closed my eyes, trying not to scrunch them tightly. To my surprise, the moment I concentrated on reaching outward and feeling for life around me, my sense expanded. Amara had been telling the truth when she said this new sense was as embedded in my mind as my sight or hearing.

"There are birds overhead," I said.

"How many? And what type of birds? How far away are they?"

I scrunched up my face, trying to concentrate. "There are two in the skies above us, both birds of prey, looking for their next meal in the fields below. And there's a group of more than ten birds in that clump of trees on our left."

"More than ten? You can't be specific?"

I grimaced, my eyes still clamped shut. "They're moving, darting around and among each other, so it's hard to tell. But they're all the same type."

"Can you tell which type?"

The more I tried to focus on the small, quick-moving animals, the more confused I got. I let out a long breath and relaxed. Amara kept talking about instinct—maybe I was trying too hard.

As soon as I stopped concentrating so intensely on the birds, the answer came to me.

"They're sparrows."

"How do you know?"

"I...I'm not sure. I can just tell."

Was that the wrong answer? Was there something specific about the birds that I should have been able to identify?

"Good." Amara's response made me relax, and I reminded myself that this wasn't an audition. I already had the position as Amara's apprentice, and she couldn't legally get rid of me. I didn't have to know everything from the beginning. The whole point of my training was for me to learn.

"What about on the ground?" she asked. "Is there anything living at ground level among the trees?"

I didn't reply as I directed my awareness below the birds.

"I can sense five squirrels, a large family of rabbits, and..." I frowned. "Too many mice to count."

"I feel sorry for the closest farm," she said with a chuckle, and I winced in sympathy.

"Hopefully they have good cats—or even better, someone with a healing affinity."

Amara nodded. "There's no affinity that isn't helpful on a farm. The earth and growing things, the weather, and animals are all central to farm life." She carefully kept her eyes on the road ahead. "I know you would have preferred a weaker, plants seed, but I feel like there's more to your reluctance to be activated. I don't suppose you want to tell me the other reason?"

"Other...other reason?" I stammered, unable to hide my shock.

"If you're still not ready to tell me, it can wait." She still didn't look at me, her voice calm and even.

"I don't..." I cleared my throat. "That is, I'm not sure what you mean."

She chuckled softly. "Really? Don't concern yourself then." I began to relax, only for her to add, "We can talk about it another time."

I tried to think of a response but couldn't come up with one.

"How far away do you think those trees are?" she said as if the previous conversation hadn't happened.

I looked to my left automatically, but I'd never been good at estimating distances.

"I have no idea, sorry."

"I would guess two miles," she said thoughtfully.

"That far?" I peered at the trees, acknowledging that they appeared smaller and further away than I'd remembered. I was surprised I'd even noticed them at all.

"That's an impressive range already," she said. "Especially for creatures as small as a mouse. But I'm curious if you can go further. Try reaching ahead of us along the road. This stretch of road is straight, so we can see a long way, but can you sense beyond your line of sight? There's a small hamlet ahead. Can you feel the people there?"

I squinted at the empty road ahead of us. My family's rare trips away from our farm had always been in the other direction, toward Tarin. I'd never come this far on this road, so I had no idea how much further the hamlet was. I was as curious as Amara about my ability, though.

I shut my eyes and concentrated, reaching along the road. At first there was nothing, just a vast blankness as if I was trying to stare into a pitch-black room. But just as I was about to give up, I felt something brushing the edges of my awareness. Straining, I latched onto the rhythmic feeling of breathing. People.

"There are people," I said breathlessly. "But they're far away."

"How many?" Amara asked.

I counted, moving slowly so as not to miss anyone.

"Nine," I said at last. "Three children and six adults."

I opened my eyes and looked up at her. "I almost gave up before I reached them. How far is the hamlet?"

"While your eyes were closed, we passed a road marker indicating ten miles." For the first time during the morning, Amara's voice held a slight tension beneath her usual calm.

"Ten miles?" I asked, awed. "Is that far?"

For a moment, Amara hesitated before slowly nodding. "Very far. To be honest, I wouldn't have suggested the exercise if I'd realized we were still so far out. I don't know any healers who can reach that far."

"But..." I gaped at her. How could that be true? Amara was a Guild mage and a master. Surely she knew all the kingdom's master mages, even the healers.

Slowly she began to chuckle. "For the first time I'm questioning my own rashness. I can only imagine what Hayes would have to say about my stealing you."

"Hayes?" I asked, completely confused.

She laughed again. "Sorry, I was talking to myself mostly. Hayes is an old friend and—more importantly—a healer. He would berate me for locking you into a traveling apprenticeship with an elements mage when I didn't know the full extent of your strength. The situation in Tartora is starting to change at last, and our strength is growing again after many years of gradual decline. But strong mages are still in short supply."

"You don't need to worry about that," I said, "since there was no way I was going to the Guild and apprenticing under this Hayes, or anyone else. You didn't steal me away from a healing mage."

She grinned at me. "Do you promise to tell him as much?"

"Of course." I smiled back. "You're my master now. I'll always have your back."

"I'm starting to wonder why I didn't take an apprentice earlier," she said. "It's nice not to be alone."

I looked back at the road as my cheeks grew rosy. It was hard to grasp what she was saying about my strength—surely I couldn't be anything so very special—but it felt nice to have my presence appreciated. Despite my fears, the more I learned about Amara, the more certain I became that I wasn't going to regret my rash decision to become her apprentice.

"It's too late for recriminations anyway," Amara said cheerfully. "For now, we should continue the lesson. I want you to alternate between reaching for the hamlet and monitoring the animal life around us. The more you practice, the easier it should become to use this ability. And I want to know when the hamlet stops being a stretch to reach. Let me know when you can feel the people comfortably."

I nodded and immediately swept the area, sensing a number of small ground animals as well as a few new birds in the sky. It was surprisingly relaxing reaching out of myself and focusing on the world around me. The animals were all intent on their normal business, unbothered about things like affinities and seeds and apprenticeships.

As I reached down the road again, a jarring note disrupted my peace. I leaned forward, my eyes closing as I tried to focus.

"What is it?" Amara asked sharply.

"Pain," I gasped out, shuddering. "So much pain. I think something is dying."

# EIGHT

"Dying?" Amara's voice anchored me in the cart, reminding me that the pain I was sensing wasn't my own. "You said something, not someone? It's not a person?"

I shook my head, trying to push past the overwhelming strength of the pain to identify the animal behind it. I failed, once again submerged in the animal's distress. The intensity of the sensation even overwhelmed my usual nausea.

Before I realized my own intention, I had scrambled to my feet. Without waiting for Acorn to stop, I flung myself down from the cart. Staggering, I only just managed to keep my feet under me, setting off at a sprint down the road.

"Delphine!" Amara shouted after me, but I could barely hear her through the intensity of my focus.

My breath was soon coming hard and fast as my legs protested the unusual level of exertion. I didn't slow, though, veering off the road as I reached a spot level with the animal.

A few trees lined the road, wild grass growing beneath them. A flash of sickening red caught my attention at the base of one of the trunks. Something had brushed against the bark and left a streak of blood. My stomach turned over, but the spike of panicked energy suppressed the reaction, as if my body was already too overloaded to process its usual reaction.

Following more drops of red, I ran to the last of the trees. Slumped in the grass against the trunk was a small bundle of red and orange. Dropping to my knees, I reached out both hands and pressed them to the rough, sticky fur.

Relief filled me at the sense of movement and life inside the fox. It was still alive, although its heartbeat was weak and getting weaker by the moment. I had no way to tell what predator had attacked it, but its gashes were deep, and it was losing far too much blood. Without the intervention of an animal healer, it had only minutes left to live.

Familiar fear filled me. But this time it wasn't at my weakness but at my lack of experience and knowledge. I was the only possible healer in range, but I had no idea how to heal such deep gouges.

A hand landed on my shoulder, and a soft voice spoke.

"This is the way of things in the animal world," Amara said sympathetically. "You're not responsible for this."

I shook my head stubbornly. "I don't care how natural it is, I can't just leave her to die without even trying."

Amara paused. "If you're sure you want to, you can try. I don't see how it could do any harm, as long as you accept that you might not be successful."

I scrubbed at the tears on my cheeks and nodded. "But what do I do? I have no idea how to..."

"You didn't know how to expel that food from your father's throat, either." Amara's voice steadied my erratic emotions. "Until you get further training, you'll have to rely on instinct. And brute force," she added. "You have the advantage of strength which most people don't."

The fox now lay frighteningly still beneath my gentle grip, so I focused on the connection between us, urgency driving me forward. My power was still an unfamiliar part of me, but I directed it to the torn and damaged parts of the fox. Commanding it to restore the animal's body, I tried not to think too closely about what that meant, instead allowing my mind to float along the veins, muscles, tendons, and bones in the damaged areas.

Although I knew nothing about fox anatomy, my ability knew which parts felt healthy and which broken. Sweat broke out across my forehead as I willed the damaged, wrong-feeling parts to fix themselves.

I felt it as it happened—the skin closing back over, the muscles knitting back together, and the veins reforming, using the fire of my power as their fuel.

Fire? I frowned at the instinctive description. Was I burning her?

I nearly pulled my hands away but stopped myself just in time. I couldn't feel any burn damage. It wasn't that sort of heat. My power just felt like fire and wind, sweeping through the fox's insides.

At last, I could find no remaining spots of wrongness or damage inside her. I slumped backward onto the ground, my head sinking into my now bloodied hands.

My whole body shook with aftereffects from both the exertion and the emotions. The peace radiating from the fox in place of the earlier pain was calming, but I could still feel myself hovering on the edge of shock.

Amara gave a soft sigh. "That's a lot less noisy."

I looked up, her voice grounding me and helping fight back the confusion and dizziness.

"You could feel her pain as well?"

Amara nodded. "But only as an echo compared to what you must have felt. I couldn't feel it at all until I got closer."

"But is she really healthy now?" I asked, struggling to believe I'd really managed the healing without making any mistakes. "She was so close to death."

Amara's lips twisted apologetically. "I have no idea, sorry. But if there's anything wrong, she doesn't seem to be feeling it. When we reach the next town, we can have their animal healer check her over."

"We can bring her with us?" My hands tightened around the warm body still resting in my lap. "Really?"

Amara looked down at me and the fox and chuckled. "Was there an option where we left her behind? You both look pretty attached at this point."

I flushed, not wanting to admit that I hadn't expected a master mage to make any special accommodations for an apprentice. I had once again misjudged Amara, and it was time I stopped doing that. She was obviously nothing like the mages at the Guild who lived self-centered, indulgent lives.

Unaware of my thoughts, she took one of my arms and helped haul me to my feet, my own arms full of the fox.

"I think we'd better get both of you cleaned up," she said ruefully. "Unless we want to scare the townsfolk."

I looked down at myself, and my eyes widened. I'd been too distracted earlier to worry about how much blood was being smeared across my clothes. And the poor fox looked even worse, her fur matted with sticky red.

But now that the crisis was passed, sight of the bright red made me sway, the blood rushing from my head and a roaring filling my ears. I tore my eyes away and gulped, trying to clear my mind of all thoughts.

"There's a stream not too far down the road," Amara continued, unaware of my sudden reaction. "We can make early camp there for the night and get you both cleaned up and this lady fed and settled. I know I'm always ravenous after a healing. If we stop there, we'll be able to reach Ostaria comfortably before nightfall tomorrow."

I gulped, my stomach heaving dangerously. I'd just successfully completed a proper healing. I couldn't disgrace myself now by vomiting.

But when I reached with my power, intending to just settle my stomach, nothing happened. Like earlier, I couldn't sense my own body at all.

I frowned and glanced at Amara. Should I say anything?

But she'd already climbed back up into the cart and was beckoning me to follow. The surprise of my failure had distracted me just enough to settle the immediate danger, so I hurried over to join her. As long as I kept my eyes on the horizon, and my mind blank, I should make it to the stream.

We reached it without issue. A tributary of the western Celadon River, it wasn't wide, but it flowed briskly. Within minutes, all the red had washed away, making me grateful for the water, however icy.

The fox proved more recalcitrant, but I ruthlessly dunked and scrubbed her. And even the cold soaking didn't entirely shake her out of her shock. I suspected if she'd been in a normal frame of mind, I never would have succeeded with the bath at all.

With the last traces of her injuries gone, I was able to breathe easily again. As long as I kept my mind from wandering back to the scene beneath the trees, I shouldn't have any more trouble.

"Don't worry," Amara told me when she caught me sending worried glances toward the resting animal as we prepared the evening meal. "It's normal enough to be sleepy after suffering such significant injuries and then a major healing as well. I saw it often in the animals my old master healed. Some would require a full day to come back to a normal state of awareness."

I looked at the fox again. "Did we do the right thing in bringing her? Maybe she has a den of kits somewhere."

"I don't think she would have left them if so," Amara said. "Not at this point of the year. But you should be able to tell."

I looked from the mage to the animal. "I should?"

"Connect with her and ask yourself whether she's recently given birth. You should be able to sense the answer. According to my old master, the traces left on the body are very obvious." She shrugged, clearly apologetic not to be able to give me more direct help.

Crossing slowly over to where the fox rested by the fire, I knelt down cautiously, not wanting to alarm her. She merely flicked her tail, however, waving it once in a gesture of communication I didn't recognize. I glanced back at Amara who was watching us.

"I think she's quite a young fox," she said. "And she seems to have taken to you." She sounded amused.

"I would hope so after my effort on her behalf," I muttered, but my heart wasn't in the complaint. I couldn't help smiling at the sight of her, curled by the fire, plump and healthy.

Now that she was clean, I could see she was an elegant vixen with a fiery orange coat, mottled black on her tail and legs, and contrasted by the white that ran from the underside of her chin all the way down her belly. She would have looked like a small dog, if not for the indefinable air of a wild animal that hung about her, even while she accepted our ministrations.

Reaching out a gentle hand, I settled it on her thick coat. She raised her head to look at me but merely lowered it again after a moment's gaze.

As expected, just the sensation of her insides was enough to send my own roiling. Without the shock and urgency of our earlier interaction, there was nothing to suppress my normal squeamishness. I tried to push past it, glad we hadn't yet eaten our meal.

I focused my mind on the question of whether the fox bore signs in her body of a recent litter. But as the seconds stretched, my mind grew fuzzy. Gasping, I pulled my hand free but stayed in my crouched position, letting my head hang low as I struggled to push back the lightheadedness. Hopefully Amara hadn't noticed anything.

I finally pushed back to my feet, moving slowly. Joining Amara, I took over the job of spooning out the simple stew she had prepared.

"I think you're right," I said once we both had a bowl full. "I can't explain why, but I feel certain she's only newly grown into adulthood and hasn't had any kits yet."

"Well done." Amara gave me a smile I didn't deserve, making me shrink inside.

At least my stomach had calmed enough for me to enjoy the warm dinner. As my belly filled, my enthusiasm slowly returned.

"We should give her a name." I scraped clean the last of my stew.

"She looks like part of the fire sitting there," Amara said. "Is a fire name too obvious for a fox?"

I laughed. "No, why should it be? I don't even know any other foxes with names. What about...Ember?"

"I like it." Amara looked at the fox. "What do you think, girl?"

She opened one eye and looked between us before closing it again. We both laughed.

"I'm taking that as a yes," I said. "Ember it is." I hesitated. "But do you think she'll leave once the shock of the healing wears off?"

Amara frowned. "It's hard to say. She is a wild animal. But it's possible she'll feel bonded to you now. The power in your healing ability already calls to animals—you saw it with Rocky and even with Acorn."

"Acorn?" I directed an astonished look toward the tethered mare just inside the circle of our firelight. "I haven't noticed her directing any particular affection my way."

Amara laughed. "She's normally extremely cantankerous

and greatly dislikes everyone but me. I've never seen her so docile in my life. I don't think I could have taken on an elements or plants apprentice. She would have ended up biting them."

"Acorn?" I asked again, still unable to believe it.

"I swear it's true," Amara said through a laugh. "The fact you can't believe me just shows how much of a transformation she undergoes in your presence."

I was still marveling at Amara's claims as I harnessed the horse to the cart the next morning. She gave me no trouble, pressing her head against my side in what appeared to be affection.

"Is it my power making her do this?" I asked Amara as she put our tightly rolled bedrolls into the back of the cart.

"Well, that and the sugar cubes in your pocket." She grinned and went back for our packs.

Acorn let out a whuffing breath as if in agreement with Amara. Shaking my head, I retrieved two cubes and held them out in my flat palm, grinning as she eagerly gobbled them up.

Ember strolled over and leaned against my leg. I picked her up, cradling her in my arms. Her furry warmth already felt familiar, and a pang shot through me at the idea that she might disappear by the end of the day.

Climbing carefully into the cart, I settled her in my lap, reminding myself that she was a wild animal, and I couldn't hold onto her if she didn't want to stay.

The day passed quickly, the weather beautiful and the road smooth. It was a well-maintained thoroughfare since the western half of Tartora was blanketed in farmlands and most of the produce was transported north or south via one of the rivers. Tarin was in the southwestern part of the kingdom, so we sent most of our crops further west to the Celadon, which formed Tartora's western border. I had often heard townsfolk talk of making this journey northwest to Ostaria on the Celadon River, but I had never made the trip myself.

"What's it like?" I asked, unable to suppress my curiosity.

"Your parents never took you to Ostaria?" Amara asked. "I know Tarin is much closer to your farm, but Ostaria is considerably bigger and hosts a lot more travelers."

I sighed. "I would have liked to, but we couldn't leave the farm. There's never been anyone we could trust it to in our stead, and neither Father nor Mother wanted to leave the other to manage the farm alone. Not when it would have been a multi-day trip. They never even took me south to see the ocean, since that's just beyond reach of a day trip."

It was all true, if not the full truth. I was certain Mother would have found a way to get us to both the beach and Ostaria if it hadn't been for Father. Any mention of a trip provoked one of his bouts of silent moodiness. Just the idea of traveling reminded him of what had happened last time someone left the farm, as well as the fact that he had expected to be managing it alongside his brother. If I had grown up alongside my uncle—and hopefully an aunt and cousins as well—how different my life would have been.

If Amara picked up on the undercurrent in my tone, she didn't comment on it.

"I'm sorry you won't get a chance to see the ocean anytime soon, given we're heading generally northward, but I hope you like Ostaria. I've always had a fondness for it, and in particular for one of its inns. It has an especially excellent washroom." She sighed with remembered pleasure.

"Washroom? Is that significant?" I asked, confused. The only inn I'd ever visited was the small one in Tarin, and even then only a couple of times. I didn't think I'd ever made use of their washroom.

Amara nodded fervently. "It all comes down to how many bathtubs they have and who manages them. If they only have one tub, you have to hurry in and out because there's always someone waiting, and if the attendant isn't skilled enough, they might only be able to keep the water warm. Bath attendants always have an elements affinity, but they vary in both strength and skill." She hummed to herself in remembered pleasure. "The attendant at the inn in Ostaria can keep the bath at the perfect temperature for each patron, no matter how long you stay in. I once soaked for over an hour, and the water never cooled."

I blinked, unsure how to ask my question without sounding rude. "But you're an elements master. Why do you need the attendant to keep your bath warm?"

She laughed. "Of course, I *could* do it myself, but the whole point of soaking in a tub is relaxation. I don't *want* to do it myself."

"Oh." I considered the point. "I suppose that makes sense."

Since we didn't have anyone with an elements affinity in our household, baths were something to be hurried through, everyone rushing to take their turn before the lukewarm water cooled. I had never been one for long soaks.

I sighed. "Every farm should have someone with each of the affinities. It would be a big help."

Amara raised an eyebrow, looking down at me with a hint of amusement in her expression. "This is a change of sentiment."

I flushed. "I never thought a healing affinity was bad for a farm. I just think a plants affinity is more helpful. My parents won't always be around to keep the crops growing healthily."

I bit my tongue, wishing I had the courage to confess my other reason for wanting a different affinity, but a rider approached from behind, moving fast to overtake us, and the moment passed. More and more traffic appeared as we neared Ostaria, and we ended up traveling behind a closed carriage, carrying passengers who must have been more wealthy than either of us.

I glanced several times at Amara, wondering if she might know them—perhaps they were even mages—but she showed no special interest in the carriage. If I hadn't seen her power for myself, I would doubt her claims of mastery. She seemed in every way like a normal traveler.

Ostaria was big enough to qualify as a small city, having a wall all the way around and guards at the gate. The guards showed little interest in us, although they kept us waiting for some time while they spoke to the occupants of the carriage and bowed them through the gates. When it came to our turn, they merely waved us through.

Amara caught me frowning after the carriage and laughed.

"Avoiding that sort of thing is part of the reason I travel with just this cart," she said. "Believe me, it gets old very fast."

"Do you think you might know whoever is in there?" I asked.

"I hope not," she said lightly, not elaborating.

I was too interested in our surroundings to push her harder. The cobblestone streets were broad and clean, bustling with people in the late afternoon sun. All types of vehicles could be seen, along with plenty of foot traffic.

The stone houses themselves were neat and well kept, many suggesting occupants of comfortable circumstances. I could immediately see why Amara had thought Ostaria of greater interest than Tarin. The city was much larger, more prosperous, and busier than the town I'd grown up near. Even the colors seemed brighter and more vivid, flowers growing everywhere in window boxes or small, well tended plots, and the shops boasting awnings in varied shades.

When I finally finished staring around open-mouthed, I realized Amara had been watching me with the amusement back in her eyes.

"I thought you would like it," she said, and I grinned back at her unabashedly.

"It's the most interesting place I've ever seen."

"Just wait until we reach the inn." She urged Acorn to pick up her pace, despite the congestion of the street.

"Until we reach the baths, you mean?" I asked, making her chuckle.

"When you live your life traveling, you learn to appreciate what familiar comforts you can find."

Her words made my insides contract. How long would it be before I enjoyed the familiar comforts of home again?

But I couldn't take my decision back now. If I wanted to run my family farm one day, I first needed to complete my apprenticeship, which meant I was better off focusing on what was before me now rather than getting lost in home-sickness.

"Here we are," Amara called triumphantly, turning Acorn into the courtyard of a large inn.

A groom appeared within seconds, running to Acorn's head. He looked concerned, the worry only disappearing slowly when Acorn accepted his presence calmly. When he sent Amara a questioning look, she burst out laughing.

"See, I told you Acorn acts differently with you around, Delphine. Even the grooms here remember what she's normally like."

She stepped down, helping me to alight without disrupting Ember who was looking around with great uncertainty. By the time we were both safely down and able to move toward the inn's doors, a stout man had appeared, his manner and dress declaring him the innkeeper.

Before he could do more than welcome Amara, however, a woman pushed forward to take his place. Clearly his wife, she was full of effusive welcome for Amara. The traveling master was obviously a well-known and liked guest.

When her eyes fell on me, however, her expression stiffened, her smile disappearing as her eyes fastened on Ember.

"Is that a *wild animal?*" she asked, her voice too loud. Her expression made it clear she would have liked to say something more disparaging but was held back by Amara's status.

"She is a patient," Amara said, unshaken by the woman's transformation.

"A patient?" The innkeeper and his wife exchanged a look. "Your patient, Master Amara?" he asked cautiously.

She smiled, although her expression seemed a little too calm, more like a mask than true emotion.

"Goodness, no. I haven't changed affinities since my last visit."

Both the innkeeper and his wife chuckled awkwardly at this impossible suggestion.

"The fox is the patient of my new apprentice, Delphine. Delphine has a healing affinity."

"Apprentice?" The innkeeper's wife stared at me, more astonished at this news than she had been by Ember's presence. "I've never known you to have an apprentice, Master Amara!"

"There is a first time for everything," Amara said lightly, although there was a hint of impatience behind her words, suggesting she was bored of the conversation and ready to be ushered inside.

I couldn't help marveling at the perfect blend of authority and civility in her manner. I had never seen this side of her before, and I suddenly found it impossible to think of her as a regular traveler. When needed, she knew how to carry the weight of her true status.

"You're most welcome, Apprentice Delphine," the innkeeper said.

"Most welcome," his wife affirmed, even bobbing a curtsy. "But I'm afraid you can't bring a wild animal into our inn. What will the other patrons think? The fox will do well enough in the stables, I'm sure."

Despite her general deference, the steel in her voice made it clear she didn't intend to budge on the issue. Amara must have come to the same assessment because after only the smallest of pauses, she nodded.

"Delphine, you take Ember over there." She pointed to the side of the inn where a separate building stood, also fully enclosed within the inn's outer wall.

As I glanced over, the groom from earlier led Acorn inside the second building, which had to be the stables.

Amara gave me a significant look. "I'll see you up in our room."

I frowned, having no idea what she was trying to silently communicate. After an awkward moment, I nodded and hurried away, looking over my shoulder in the hope of some final sign.

But Amara was already stepping through the inn's doors, accompanied by both the innkeeper and his wife. Whatever she wanted me to do, I was going to have to work it out on my own.

CHAPTER

# NINE

I walked along the front of the inn toward the stables, trying to look like I knew what I was doing. No one paid me any notice thanks to the arrival of a carriage full of new customers. When I reached the corner of the inn and rounded it, I found myself in front of the stables.

A groom came hurrying out, bumping past me with a barely muttered apology, his eyes focused on the team harnessed to the carriage. The glancing blow of his shoulder didn't hurt, but it spun me slightly, facing me toward the side of the inn. My eyes latched onto a plain wooden door.

A daring thought popped into my mind. Amara had said only two things. That I should come over here, and that she would see me in our room. But she must have known I wouldn't abandon Ember to be alone in the stables, especially while the fox was still in a state of shock. Had Amara intended me to smuggle Ember into the inn?

I put my hand over my mouth, stopping the giggle that was trying to bubble up. Was a master mage really encouraging me to sneak a wild animal into an inn over the protests of the innkeeper?

Once the idea had taken root, I couldn't shake it, however. I had taken on responsibility for Ember's healing, thus making me responsible for her until she regained full alertness. Amara might not be a healer herself, but her influencer had been, so she understood that. She also knew we wouldn't let Ember destroy the room or bother the other guests. Was this her way of avoiding an unnecessary fight with the innkeeper and his wife?

A flurry of activity approached, and I pressed myself back against the stone of the inn wall. A parade of grooms trooped past, leading the four-horse team from the carriage into the stables. None of them paid me any notice, so I shuffled along until I was next to the side door.

As soon as the last of them had disappeared, I darted a glance around the courtyard. It was empty now, the guests having entered the inn with the innkeeper. Spinning, I grasped the door handle and pulled, hoping I wasn't going to find it locked.

I released a breath as it swung open. The inn's servants must use the door for access to the courtyards and stables. Ducking inside, I pulled it closed behind me as quickly as I could without making any noise.

Peering around me, I waited for my eyes to adjust. No lanterns or candles had yet been lit in this section of the inn, making the air around me murky in the semi-darkness of dusk.

As soon as my vision improved, I hurried down the long, straight corridor that led into the depths of the inn. From the little I knew of inns, guest rooms wouldn't be in this section of the building. My best bet was to find some stairs and get up to the next level.

Wrapping my cloak around Ember, I slowed my pace at the sound of voices. The background hum suggested several people were talking at once, so I was likely hearing either customers in the main room or staff in the kitchens. Either way, I wanted to avoid them.

I was about to turn back and start trying doors when I reached a staircase so narrow I hadn't noticed it before. Gripping Ember more tightly, I dashed up the stairs.

My haste was nearly my undoing since my feet outpaced me, and I slipped half way up. My free hand flew out, barely managing to steady myself on the stone wall. I froze in position, my heart beating rapidly, and Ember stirring in my other arm.

She gave a soft yap that set me into motion again.

"Quiet!" I said, and she instantly subsided, bowing her head.

"Sorry," I pressed my free hand on her head, instantly contrite. "I just don't want anyone to find you, girl."

When no one appeared at the top or bottom of the stairs to challenge me, I started upward again, moving more cautiously this time. I reached the top without further incident.

The staircase opened onto a much wider corridor, this one carpeted. I stepped out, confident I'd found the domain of the guests. But once in the hallway, I stopped, unsure how to proceed. I couldn't knock on every door looking for Amara.

While I was still hesitating, unsure how to proceed, a door opened, and a familiar figure stepped out. Amara looked the other way first before turning in my direction and spotting me.

"Ah, Delphine, there you are," she said calmly.

I hurried over to her, relieved.

"Sorry to keep you waiting," I said breathlessly. "I wasn't sure—"

"Inside." She gestured toward the open door behind her.

I ducked around her and scurried inside, only breathing easily once she'd followed me and closed the door behind us.

"I hope I was right about what you meant me to do." I pushed my cloak aside, revealing Ember curled in my arm.

Amara smiled. "I can see you and I are going to deal well together."

"Won't we get in trouble?" I looked doubtfully around the lavish room.

The carpet underfoot was thicker than I had expected, and the curtains were heavy brocade. It must have been one of the inn's best rooms.

"Don't worry," she said. "I didn't want to make a fuss in front of other customers, but both the innkeeper and his wife have a soft spot for me."

"You helped them in the past, didn't you," I guessed.

She smiled slightly. "It was a minor matter, but they've been more than gracious ever since."

I considered the possibilities. "Did you keep the inn safe from a serious storm? Or maybe prevent it burning down?"

She turned a laugh into a cough. "The latter."

I shook my head. "No wonder they like you."

"I try not to take advantage of it, so we do need to keep Ember out of sight of other guests." She pointed at a large wooden box sitting by the fireplace, a rough woolen blanket at its bottom and a small dish of water at its side. "As you can see the innkeeper has already provided."

I gaped at it while she made no attempt to hide her amusement.

"The innkeeper doesn't have standards that are quite as strict as his wife's," she said. "And if we're fortunate, he'll have talked her around by tomorrow, so we won't need to be quite so surreptitious in the future."

Relieved, I deposited Ember in her new temporary home. She sniffed all around the box in a dainty fashion before settling herself on the blanket and closing her eyes.

"She seems to approve." I surveyed the room again, taking in the two heavy wooden beds, pushed up against opposite walls, and the matching dark wood of the furniture. "So do I. I've never stayed in such a fancy place."

Amara's eyes crinkled. "I should warn you that not all our nights will be spent in such pleasant surrounds."

"Of course not," I said absently, wandering over to the bed that had my pack on it. "We slept on the ground last night, after all."

"I applaud your adaptability," Amara said.

I turned, looking suspiciously for any sign I was being mocked, but she had already crossed to her own pack.

"Should we go downstairs to eat?" I asked, remembering the smells that had accompanied the chatter of voices from earlier.

"No." Amara shook her head firmly. "First the washroom."

I laughed. "I should have known."

"Come on," she said. "You're going to enjoy this."

She was soon proven correct. Given the hour, all three of the wooden tubs in the female washroom were available, and we happily claimed two. A quietly spoken assistant appeared as soon as we sank into the water, adjusting the water temperature at our request. I asked for mine as hot as I could bear, ready to enjoy every moment of the luxury.

In the end, only our rumbling bellies chased us out, and the attendant teased us about our wrinkled state as she handed over dry towels for our use. Amara laughed back, clearly recognizing the girl from previous visits. Her praise for the girl's skill with the bathwater turned the attendant's cheeks fiery red, and she bowed us both out of the room much more deeply than Amara's status required. She'd probably be boasting to her friends within hours over receiving such a compliment from a master mage.

Given the lateness of the hour, we headed straight for the dining room, gorging ourselves on a perfectly cooked meal. As I leaned back from my empty plate, I groaned.

"I can see why you like this place. You might have to roll me back up the stairs."

Amara grinned and hauled me to my feet. "Come on, lazy-bones. You can manage a single staircase."

Grumbling but smiling, I followed her back to our rooms, a napkin wrapped bundle weighing down my pocket. I had selected the rarest looking bits of meat to bring up for Ember, the best I could manage until she was well enough to hunt for herself again.

But when we entered the room, the box by the fire was empty.

"Ember?" I spun to examine the large room. "Where are you hiding?"

I knelt, peering under first one bed and then the other. When there was still no sign of her, I looked toward Amara in concern.

"You're sure she's not under there?" Amara's brow creased. "Maybe she was scared by some sounds from the corridor?"

I shook my head. "She's definitely not. And I can't see anywhere else in here for her to hide."

I hurried over to the window, realizing for the first time that it wasn't actually a window but a door leading onto a narrow balcony. And it was ajar.

"Oh no," I whispered, stepping outside and peering down toward the back of the inn and a small, well tended garden.

"She's gone?" Amara's voice was gentle. "She must have recovered then."

"She was probably hungry." Tears pricked at my eyes. "I shouldn't have left her for so long. I should have brought food up more quickly."

Amara's hand rested on my shoulder. "We always knew there was a chance she wouldn't stay."

I nodded, not trusting myself to speak. The emotions were surprisingly overwhelming. The fox was the first animal I had healed, and I couldn't help but feel I'd failed her. We hadn't even had her checked by the local animal healer.

"I'm going to go after her," I said, not meeting Amara's eyes.

"Delphine," she said softly, but I shook my head stubbornly.

"My healing hasn't been checked by an actual qualified healer yet. I can't just let her run off. With my ability, I should be able to sense her location if I can just get close enough to her."

Amara hesitated for a moment before nodding. "Very well, then. But don't stay out too late." She must have recognized that I wasn't going to give in easily.

Murmuring my thanks, I grabbed my cloak from where I had left it on the bed and hurried down the corridor to the main stairs. I forced myself to slow down enough not to trip as I had on the way into the inn, but within moments I was outside in the courtyard.

I didn't waste time circling the building. The garden was small enough that I had been able to examine the whole thing from the balcony. There hadn't been any sign of Ember.

Pulling up the hood of my cloak against the chill in the evening spring air, I hurried through the inn's gates and onto the streets of the city. The crowds had largely dispersed, most people heading home for the evening meal, I assumed. There was still enough traffic for me to feel safe, however, and I threw my full attention into the search for Ember.

As soon as I reached out with my ability, as Amara had shown me, I was overwhelmed with heartbeats and the pulsing sense of flowing blood. There were too many people in close proximity, and their presence overwhelmed everything else.

I groaned. I was going to have to search the old-fashioned way, after all.

Striding forward as quickly as possible, I began to patrol the streets closest to the inn, looking down alleyways and keeping my eye out for gardens of any size.

My eyes were soon tired from flicking this way and that, straining for any sign of red fur. Assuming the fox would avoid crowds, I moved further and further away from the well-traveled area around the inn and into the backstreets.

Only when I heard furtive voices did I realize the background noise of the streets had decreased significantly as the people thinned. I had been trying too hard to ignore the sense of so many bodies around me and hadn't noticed when they disappeared.

I could still feel people in the houses on either side, but it felt quiet enough that I might have some hope of identifying smaller animals as well. I sent out my awareness, searching for the now-familiar sensation of Ember's internal systems.

I had passed over five dogs and seven cats, and had just latched onto something that might be a fox, when a name caught my ears, shattering my concentration. Grey.

Looking up, the emptiness of the street struck me again but with different import this time. I was alone in the backstreets of an unfamiliar city.

My heart took off, racing at a frantic beat that was strong enough to break through to my new senses. Without thinking, I instructed my heart to calm down, and the beats instantly dropped so substantially that my head spun and I nearly collapsed. Gasping, I corrected myself, only breathing freely when the lightheadedness passed. As soon as my heart returned to its regular rhythm, I reinforced the wall protecting my body.

The second I did so, I noticed the voices again. They were coming from a nearby alley, the speakers just out of sight. I edged closer, trying not to make any noise with my steps. My heart had sped up again, but I determinedly ignored it, keeping my focus on the speakers.

When I reached the alleyway, I cautiously peered around the corner. Two men were facing each other, paying no particular attention to their surroundings. They were standing in front of a wooden door that gave access to the side of a large building. It appeared to be a shuttered warehouse that would have looked abandoned if not for the two men.

One of them shifted slightly, making me gasp and draw back. It was definitely Grey—the taller of the men I'd seen in Tarin. His image was imprinted on my mind given how many times I had gone over the memory of Miranda being dragged away.

Halmir had been convinced Grey and the others were heading north to Calista, but here they were in Ostaria. Was it just a stop on the way to the northern kingdom? Did that mean they were still gathering more recruits before returning home?

I squeezed my eyes shut, thinking of the door. Had Miranda, Serena, and the others been sent ahead to Calista already, or was it possible they were right here, behind that door?

I reached out with my power, suppressing a gasp when I sensed more people inside the warehouse. Part of me wanted to storm straight inside, but there were so many of them. And I didn't even have a way to confirm if Miranda was among them. For all I knew, they could all be Grey's henchmen.

I slowly inched to the side and peered around the corner again. This time I focused on their words instead of their appearance.

"We need to do better here than we did in Tarin," Grey said, his tone annoyed.

"We will," the other man assured him. "Ostaria is much bigger, so it will be easier to go unnoticed by the authorities. I've already found a few youths who are showing interest. I've told them you won't appear unless they can gather a crowd, so they've promised to spread the word."

I sucked in a breath. They were planning to abduct more youths here in Ostaria?

But even as I had the thought, I rubbed the back of my neck, uneasy. If I was honest, it didn't sound like they were talking about abducting people. If they were taking the time to charm and sway the Ostarian locals, maybe I really had been mistaken about Miranda.

I peered into the growing darkness. Whatever had happened that night in Tarin, I didn't intend to give up my search for my friend. Even if she'd made a rash decision in the heat of the moment, I didn't doubt she was regretting it by now. She wouldn't abandon her father like that—not when she was all he had.

Their voices dropped in volume, and I edged further around the corner, straining to hear. If Grey confirmed the youths were inside the building, I could take that information to the authorities of Ostaria. Even though it wasn't their own people in question—yet—they might be willing to act, for the sake of the neighboring town and their lost children.

I had nearly rounded the corner completely when a heavy hand landed on my shoulder, making me shriek. Twisting, I tried to peer up at the new arrival, but the hand tightened, holding me in place. I managed only the general impression of a tall, muscled man.

He moved his hold down to the top of my arm, taking the other one as well and hustling me into the alley, pushing me from behind. Both Grey and his companion had turned at the commotion and were watching me with wide eyes.

I struggled to break free, digging my heels into the ground when I couldn't shake myself loose. The man merely tightened his hold, lifting me completely off the ground.

I screamed, as much in frustration as fear, and tried to kick back at him. My blows seemed to have no effect, however, and within moments I was deposited in front of Grey.

I made one last attempt to writhe free, but the hands holding me in place only tightened even further. Sighing, I gave up momentarily, instead meeting Grey's gaze defiantly.

"You have an eavesdropper," the man behind me said matter-of-factly. "What do you want done with her?"

"Let me go at once," I said immediately. "What can you be thinking? The streets belong to everyone."

"My words do not, however." Grey examined me with a calculated gaze. Behind it was something else, though, and my insides clenched in fear at the sight of the concern on his face.

I knew well that there was nothing intimidating about my appearance. If Grey was worried at the idea of my having overheard his conversation, then he must have said something sensitive before my arrival. What had he said, and how was I going to convince him that I hadn't heard it?

I cleared my throat. "I don't know who you are, or why you're lurking back here, but glancing down an alley hardly makes me a criminal. I'll be returning on my way now."

Despite my bold words, my captor made no move to release me.

Grey stepped forward. "Who are you?"

He stooped slightly to put his eyes on the level of mine, his mesmerizing green gaze pinning me in place as effectively as the hold of his henchman. This was a man used to commanding obedience. Somehow I knew that whatever he ordered, the two men with him would obey without question.

"Maybe she's heard about us," Grey's companion said, sounding smug. "She looks about the right age."

A flash of interest leaped in Grey's eyes as he assessed my face.

"A new recruit, you think? She certainly looks seventeen." He grinned at me. "Shall we take a look and see if you meet my requirements?"

Something in his gaze made me shrink back, but I couldn't go far given the human mountain holding me in place.

"You're going to test her?" Grey's companion sounded shocked.

Grey threw him a lazy smile. "Why not? There's no one here to go telling tales."

He looked back at me, something crackling in his gaze. Despite myself, I could feel the magnetism of this man. No wonder he managed to entrance youths in every town he visited.

His expression slowly transformed, however, his brows pulling together and his mouth turning down.

"What's her affinity?" his companion asked. "Does she have any strength?"

Grey's unhappy gaze tightened, burning with something disturbingly like curiosity.

"You can't tell?" His companion was clearly even more shocked by Grey's failure than by his decision to test me in the first place. "What do you mean you can't tell? That's impossible."

"And yet..." Grey smiled, the effect chilling as his eyes held mine. "You've suddenly become very intriguing, young lady. Let me get a hold of you."

He reached out a hand for one of my bare wrists, and I jerked backward so violently that I took my captor by surprise, sending us both staggering back several steps.

If Grey wanted physical contact, did that mean he was a healer like me?

*Healer or assassin,* whispered a terrible voice in the back of my mind, making me break into wild thrashing. Already off balance, my captor's hold loosened slightly, further galvanizing my efforts.

But Grey stepped closer, unfazed by my desperate resistance. His hand loomed toward me, his fingers assuming a terrifying aspect I had never attributed to a hand before.

Tears squeezed from the corner of my eyes, running down my cheeks. I didn't know what was going to happen when Grey touched me, but I didn't want to find out.

A streak of movement distracted us both just as he was about to make contact. I looked sideways in time to see an orange blur launch itself at Grey's arm, sinking sharp, pointed teeth into his wrist.

Grey shouted in pain, whipping his arm back and forth until the fox attached to it went flying through the air and hit the wall of the warehouse.

"Ember!" I screamed, struggling anew.

Grey turned back to me, an ugly look in his eyes. His good hand gripped the puncture marks on his other wrist, red drips welling between his fingers and slowly dripping to the ground.

"Bring her here," he said, but I was too distracted by my terror for Ember to feel fear on my own behalf.

She lay still at the base of the wall, although my power told me she was still breathing—for now. Without touching her, I couldn't tell the extent of the damage.

I struggled against my captor, trying to get free to go to Ember, but it was no more effective now than it had been earlier. The man pushed me toward Grey, and despite my resistance, I moved closer.

Before we reached him, however, a deep growl emerged from the depths of the alley. We all turned in time to see a fifth person appear from the darkness.

Moving too fast for my eye to easily track, he struck Grey's companion in the back of the head, sending him to the ground. I shouted a warning as Grey lunged toward the attacker, bare hand outstretched, but the assailant seemed aware of the danger.

He was already covered from head to toe, a scarf concealing all of his face except his eyes, and he remained a constant blur of motion, denying Grey the opportunity to pull at his clothing. Deftly avoiding his grasp, he approached me, a blade appearing from somewhere to spear toward me.

I screamed and cowered down, allowing the steel to flash past me and bury itself in my captor's shoulder. The man grunted, finally letting me go.

As soon as I was free, I ran toward Ember, nearly falling in my haste. I slid to a stop, stooping to press my hands against her fur. Every sense was heightened, my blood thrumming through my veins, and I had no time to think of being sick. Faster than I would have thought possible, I pushed my healing power into her, mending the broken ribs and making one damaged lung whole again.

A curse sounded behind me, and then the breathless voice of my rescuer spoke in my ear.

"Come on!"

A gloved hand grabbed my wrist, tugging me so hard I barely had time to scoop up Ember. Stumbling, I tried to get my feet under me as I let him pull me out of the alley.

Grey was only steps behind us, his hands outstretched as if he meant to grab at the exposed skin of my face.

I threw myself sideways as we rounded the corner onto the main street, just evading him. A wagon rumbled in our direction, and I heard Grey's soft curse as he stopped his pursuit, fading back into the alley.

My rescuer didn't slow, however, tugging me along the street and round turn after turn. Only when we reached a more populated area did he finally slow, stepping into the first alley we passed and shoving me against a wall.

I gulped down air, trying to catch my breath as I peered around him out onto the street.

"They didn't follow us?" My words died as I turned back to him and found piercing blue eyes boring into me.

Unforgettable eyes.

"It...it's you," I stammered.

The stranger from Tarin unwound the scarf from his face, revealing an expression of disgust. "That should be my line. Here I thought my luck had been startling when I stumbled on Grey again so quickly. I should have known better. My luck was never that good."

"I...You were there watching him?"

"I think he has his converts in that warehouse. Not for much longer, though—thanks to you. They'll all be off to some new hideout long before morning. And now Grey knows about me as well. I'd managed to stay out of sight before this."

He sounded furious, but I was too distracted by his earlier words.

"You mean Miranda *was* back there?" I turned toward the street, consumed by a futile desire for action. "I thought you said she'd be sent somewhere else by the time Grey surfaced in a new town?"

"That's his usual mode of operation. For some reason he's doing things differently this time." He didn't sound like he thought that was a good thing, but I was delighted at the idea Miranda might be here in Ostaria with me.

"We have to tell someone before they have a chance to move."

He raised an eyebrow. "Who exactly would we be telling?"

I faltered, my face slowly falling.

"They'll already be on the move anyway," he said. "Grey doesn't hesitate."

He fell silent, watching me. I gulped, unnerved by his scrutiny. Abruptly, he stepped forward, trapping me against the wall. His tall frame took up my whole vision, only the warmth of Ember forming a barrier between us.

My body quivered at his nearness, although I tried to keep it from showing in my expression.

His eyes roamed over my face. "Something about you fascinated him," he breathed. "I've never seen him react to someone like that. It's rare for him to use his power to test someone, but it's never failed when he did." His gaze tightened. "I've never heard of that particular test failing for anyone with enough strength to perform it."

"What—" I swallowed, trying to moisten my dry mouth. "What do you mean *test*? Like the healers do with children's seeds? I've guessed Grey is a healer, but healers need contact to test someone's seed."

He frowned. "Exactly how ignorant are you?"

Defiance rose up in me, but I forced it down. I needed answers more than I needed to assuage my pride.

"Assume very," I said shortly.

He sighed. "Master mages are permitted to probe the power level of another person. It requires great strength, which limits how many can do it, but the Triumvirate felt the need to limit its use even further. Officially, only those who've passed the mastery exam are permitted to test others."

"Why?"

His mouth twisted slightly. "It's considered a highly offensive thing to do. Supposedly, if you've reached mastery level, you've demonstrated sufficient control and sense to only use the test when absolutely necessary." His derisive tones suggested he doubted that assumption.

"Grey is a master mage?" I gasped.

He rolled his eyes. "Not officially. He certainly hasn't passed the mastery exam. I don't think he's even officially a mage. But I suspect he has the strength of a master."

"How is that possible?" I asked slowly, trying to make sense of it.

To be so strong, Grey must have had a powerful influencer. But everyone with that level of power was a member of the Mage's Guild, and completing an apprenticeship under one of them would make Grey a mage as well. Grey couldn't have master mage level power without having a master mage as influencer. Which meant he must be an official mage of the Guild.

My head hurt thinking around in circles.

"Not everyone completes their apprenticeship," my rescuer said, reading my confusion.

I frowned up at him, but I couldn't read the thoughts behind his guarded expression. Did he mean Grey had been activated by a master mage but had abandoned his apprenticeship and thus never qualified as a mage himself?

"I have no idea how you're in Ostaria at all," my rescuer suddenly burst out, "but what in the kingdoms were you doing in that alley? You not only got in my way *again,* you've now attracted Grey's attention in a dangerous way. You should get out of town immediately."

I bristled. There was no way I was running if Miranda might be here in Ostaria.

But it didn't seem like the right moment to say as much.

"I was looking for her." I held Ember out slightly, and he glanced down at her, his face softening slightly for a moment.

Despite myself, my attitude toward him softened an equal amount. I couldn't help but like others who liked animals. In fact, now that I thought about it, he hadn't emerged to challenge Grey until Ember needed protecting.

For some reason, the thought sent a giggle bubbling up out

of me. This man had been unmoved by my struggles but had been helpless to resist coming to the defense of one small fox.

"Her name is Ember," I said, when he looked at me with a wary expression, as if he feared I might have fallen into hysterics.

Ember lifted her head, regarding him with a steady gaze before raising her tail in the air.

"She approves of you," I giggled, again before clapping my free hand across my mouth. Maybe I really was in danger of hysterics after the unexpected events of the evening.

My rescuer looked at me again, and that slight softening still lingered. I gulped, my pulse speeding up as I became aware of our proximity, the two of us pressed against the wall of the dark alley.

But his expression hardened again, his eyes becoming diamonds, sharp enough to cut. I shrank back against the stone behind me, but I still couldn't forget his earlier look.

"My name is Delphine," I said softly.

He blinked once, my introduction apparently taking him by surprise. After a moment, he leaned back slightly, easing the atmosphere between us.

"I'm Nik," he said gruffly.

I smiled, surprisingly pleased to know his name.

"Thank you for rescuing me and Ember back there."

"Are you sure she's all right?" He glanced down at the fox.

I nodded. "She wasn't initially, of course, but I'm a healer. I healed her before I picked her up."

"A healer?" His eyebrows rose. "A healer strong enough to complete a healing that quickly and then speak of it so flippantly—despite still being an apprentice, which you must be from the look of you." His eyes narrowed, his gaze turning introspective as if he was talking more to himself than me. "Exactly what sort of power do you have, I wonder? I think I'd like to see what interested Grey so much."

"What does that mean?" I asked sharply.

He grinned at me, the expression half-amused, half-menacing. "Grey isn't the only one with the strength to probe a mage."

My mouth fell open. "You're a master mage?" My voice dripped with skepticism. "There's no way you're old enough to have sat the mastery tests."

"Passing the mastery tests is only an *official* requirement," he said with a hooded gaze I couldn't interpret. "Grey's words apply in this alley as much as the other. There's no one here to tell on us." He paused. "Unless you're planning to report all this?" There was definitely a mocking note to his final question.

"I—" I tried to think of something intelligent and cutting to say and failed.

What would the authorities of Ostaria make of this outlandish story? I couldn't even imagine trying to explain it all to them.

There was Amara, of course. I could tell her, but what could she do to bring this man to account?

"Exactly," he said with the same satisfied amusement.

I expected him to make some further boasting comment or even a further request, but he remained silent. A slight stiffening of his muscles told me he was doing something, but I felt nothing.

After a moment, he pulled back, clearly surprised.

"My power can't connect with yours at all. It's like there's...a wall there, or something."

"A wall?" I stared at him, my mind whirling.

I'd built a wall by mistake when I'd misunderstood Amara's words. She'd encouraged me to strengthen it at the time, so I hadn't thought there was any harm in it. But then, later, when I'd tried to connect with my own body, I'd failed. I hadn't understood why at the time, but could it be because of the wall I'd put in place?

The more I thought about it, the more sense it made. Earlier that night, I'd accidentally slowed my heart, but I'd been so distracted, I hadn't noticed the significance of being able to connect with my body again. If it had been my wall blocking my access earlier, I could only assume I had let it drop after time passed without any incidents, unwittingly allowing myself access again.

And yet, the first time I used that access, I had again responded on instinct and put the wall back in place, reinforcing it in the process. My fear at having access to my own body had taken practical expression. And that instinct had protected me from Grey's testing. But I'd shown I could take the wall down and put it up at will. If I could do it on instinct, surely I could do it on purpose.

"Just give me a second," I said.

Nik frowned but didn't interrupt as I slowed my breathing and brought my ability to the front of my awareness. Ember and Nik's heartbeats sounded loudly, their bodies pressing against me, but I pushed past them, turning my focus inward. Now that I knew what I was looking for, I could sense the wall.

Forcing myself to work against my instincts, I dismantled it brick by brick, willing myself to open up. Immediately I felt every system in my body thrumming and alive. Panting, I tried to push the awareness away before I lost the contents of my stomach all over Nik.

"Quickly," I gasped out. "Test me again."

This time I was so connected with my body that I felt the presence of an outside force. But it had no sooner made contact than it pulled away again.

Nik staggered back two steps, his eyes growing wide.

"You're strong!" he said as I slammed the wall back into place, sagging against the stone behind me with trembling legs.

He stepped forward again, grabbing my upper arms roughly, his eyes burning into mine.

"You're mage strong," he said. "More than that. You could

be a master one day. How is that possible? Why aren't you at the Guild? *How are you not at the Guild?*"

"I..." My words stumbled over themselves at his intensity. "I...I've only just been activated. My influencer is a traveling master. Wh...Why?"

"This isn't good." Nik finally let me go, stepping back and allowing me to breathe again. "This is very bad. You've already intrigued Grey enough that he's going to be looking for you. And once he makes skin-to-skin contact, he'll be able to find a way past that wall of yours."

"And that would be bad?" I asked hesitantly.

"Of course it would be." He raked a hand through his dark hair. "As soon as he discovers your strength, he'll be determined to have you."

"Have me?" I squeaked, wishing I didn't sound so terrified.

"Grey focuses on seventeen- and eighteen-year-olds—those whose power is activated, or ready to be, but who are still young and susceptible. But he hasn't been fool enough to tackle the capital, let alone the Guild. Which means he hasn't been able to get his hands on youngsters anywhere near as powerful as you. Children with seeds like yours go to the capital sooner rather than later. You represent an unusual opportunity—one he won't want to let slip by."

"You're saying Grey will want to abduct me too?" My hold on Ember tightened enough to make her squirm, and I forced myself to relax my grip.

I glared up at Nik, although none of it was his fault. "He won't find me such an easy target."

A reluctant smile tugged at Nik's lips, making me lose my breath again. I hadn't seen him smile before. And this had only been a half-smile, so I could only imagine how devastating a full smile would be.

"Unfortunately you said you've just started your apprenticeship," he said. "Despite your power, you won't be a match for Grey."

"My master is, though," I said, confident my faith in Amara wasn't misplaced.

"Your master?" Nik raised an eyebrow, considering my words. "Yes, you'll have to let them know immediately. They can take you far away from here."

My mouth snapped closed, unease filling me. Amara didn't know Miranda, but she did have a responsibility—both moral and legal—to me as her apprentice. If I told her what had happened, would she act to protect me, whisking me straight out of Ostaria and leaving Miranda and the others in Grey's clutches?

Nik's eyes narrowed as he watched my face, as if he could read my thought process. He had told me to leave Ostaria—did that mean he would tell Amara himself if given the chance? I spoke at random, hoping to distract him.

"Why do you care? Don't tell me you're worried about me?"

He drew back even further, scoffing. "Worried about you? Hardly. You've been nothing but a menace since you first appeared. But running into you just might be the best luck Grey's had so far, and I'm against anything that helps Grey."

"Why do you care so much?" I asked, genuinely curious despite my initial intention of distracting him. "Do you know someone in that warehouse like I do?"

"Me?" He turned away slightly, laughing scornfully. "You think it would still be standing if that was the case?"

I shivered slightly at the threat in his tone, even though it wasn't directed at me. I couldn't help feeling a slight thrill at the idea of being loved by a man like this—someone willing to overcome any obstacle to help me.

"Why, then?" I asked, desperate to drive out the foolish thoughts. "You don't seem old enough to be an official."

"An official?" While his laugh held some actual amusement

this time, it still had a dark edge. "Hardly. But that doesn't mean I'll let Grey tear this kingdom apart."

"Tear the kingdom apart?" I frowned at the dramatic overstatement.

When he stayed silent, I prompted him again. "What do you mean?"

He still didn't speak, however, and when he turned back to me, his calculating eyes told me he was thinking of something else.

"Shall I see you safely back to your accommodation?"

I was instantly on alert, remembering my earlier fear. There was no way Nik was worried about my safety. Was his offer a ploy to find Amara so he could convince her to take me out of Ostaria? Amara had both the means and the right to make me obey if she decided we were changing plans and moving on immediately.

"That's unnecessary," I said quickly. "I can find my own way."

"Can you?" His face told me he doubted it but wasn't going to push the matter.

"I suppose you'll go back to the warehouse now, just in case," I said. "If you find any clues, will you let me know? I have a friend there, remember."

"Do you intend to leave me your address?" he asked with a hint of amusement.

"I..." I bit my lip. "I'm sure we'll run into each other on the streets again at some point."

Nik stepped forward, leaning over Ember so his mouth was beside my ear. His lips brushed against the wisps of hair there, making my breathing stutter and stop.

"I sincerely hope not, Delphine the healer," he whispered, his words chasing out the thrill of his nearness.

Abruptly pulling back, he gave me a look laced with amusement, as if he knew the effect he had on me. Before I could think of anything to say, he strode out of the alley and was lost in the evening traffic of the main road.

I gaped after him, trying to pull myself together. Eventually I balled my hand into a fist and hit it against my leg.

"Why can I never think of the right thing to say to him?" I asked Ember.

The fox didn't reply.

# CHAPTER
# ELEVEN

By the time I reached the room at the inn, my nerves were shredded. I'd been as jumpy looking over my shoulder for Nik as I had been looking for Grey and his men. But no one on the streets had shown the least interest in me.

As soon as the door closed behind me, I slumped against it with a sigh of relief.

"You didn't find her?" Amara's sympathetic voice snapped me out of my distraction, reminding me I wasn't alone.

"Actually..." I pulled my cloak aside to reveal Ember.

Hoping to head off any further questions, I busied myself settling the fox in her crate and providing her with the package of food that was still in my pocket. But when my flurry of activity finally ended with me preparing to climb into bed, Amara spoke again.

"What happened? You looked shaken."

I stopped, my back to her, one hand on my blankets.

"I ran into Grey—that man who was in Tarin and might have taken my friend."

"Miranda was her name, wasn't it?" Amara sounded happy. "So she's here in Ostaria? That's wonderful news. You can clear the whole situation up, and we can see her back on her way to her father."

I turned around slowly. "I didn't see Miranda or either of the other two from Tarin, just Grey and a couple of his followers. I don't know for sure if Miranda is here."

"Did you ask this Grey?" She was watching my face a little too closely for comfort, so I tried to smile.

"I didn't get the chance to ask."

"That's too bad." Her eyes suggested she knew there was something I was holding back. "We can only hope we run into him again."

Her words reminded me of my own to Nik, as well as his response, and I almost leaped into bed, pulling the blankets up to half cover my face. There was at least one person on the streets of Ostaria who I wasn't likely to run into by chance. He would clearly be avoiding me like the plague in the future.

"Do you want to leave Ostaria? We could move on sooner than planned if you like," Amara said, showing she understood more than I'd shared.

It was kind of her to refrain from prying and to offer me a way out. But I couldn't accept the escape she offered.

I replied quickly and firmly. "No, indeed. I haven't even had Ember checked over yet. There's no reason to hurry off—especially if Miranda might be here. We told her father we'd keep an eye out for her."

"Very well." Amara climbed into her own bed but paused just before extinguishing the one remaining lantern. "But I hope you know you can come to me with anything that's bothering you."

"Thank you," I whispered into the darkness as the lantern light disappeared.

I slept fitfully, Grey chasing me through my nightmares, sometimes with Nik at his side, and sometimes with Nik standing against him.

Nik had said that if Grey managed to touch me, he would find a way around my wall. So every time I saw him, I added bricks to it, building it higher and thicker, locking myself away.

I woke in the morning, panting and more exhausted than when I'd gone to sleep. Amara had already disappeared, and I wasn't surprised to find her in one of the bathtubs. I was grateful for a soak after my long night and didn't comment that we'd already washed the night before.

The breakfast provided by the inn was as delicious as the evening meal had been, and we were both full and sparkling clean by the time we took to the streets of Ostaria. Amara didn't hesitate as she led me only a few streets over to a cheerful stone building with a large, enclosed yard.

"I thought you said animal healers are normally on the outskirts of towns," I said as I examined the clinic with interest.

"Ostaria is large enough to have many healers," she explained as she rapped loudly on the large wooden door. "Along with a small hospital staffed with healers from the capital, it has more than one animal healing clinic. There's one on both the northern and southern sides of the city to cater to farm animals. And this clinic mainly sees animals from within the city itself."

"For pets, then," I said, secretly impressed at the luxury of it. "Are you offended, girl?" I crooned at the animal in my arms. "You're not a pet, are you?"

Amara raised an eyebrow as Ember stirred sleepily before resettling.

"Do you think it's a bad sign that she's sleepier than yesterday?" I asked. "I can't feel anything wrong inside her."

"Don't forget that foxes are mostly nocturnal," Amara

replied. "Yesterday she was dazed but awake—this is more like her normal state during the day."

"Oh, of course." I felt like a fool. I should have realized that for myself.

"Don't worry," Amara said. "That's why apprentice healers study so much, despite their instinctive understanding of healing. It helps to know about anatomy and behavior since your ability can only take you so far on its own."

I nodded, but the door opened, cutting off further conversation.

A smiling, older woman greeted us, ushering us inside with only the faintest flicker of surprise when she saw what type of animal we'd brought with us. She had on a plain gray gown in serviceable wool with a crisp white apron over the top, everything about her screaming competence. I didn't doubt that every nook of the clinic was sorted and organized.

"The healer is with another patient now," she said, ushering us to a waiting room and gesturing toward a row of seats against one wall.

She put one hand on Ember's fur, a look of vague surprise crossing her face. She didn't comment, however, beyond a reassurance that the healer would be with us soon.

"Is she not a healer?" I whispered to Amara when the woman disappeared out of the room, leaving us alone. "Why did she make contact with Ember, then?"

"She would have a healing seed, I'm sure. Every employee at a clinic and hospital does. But it's likely a weaker one—well below the level required to qualify as a mage, certainly. So she wouldn't be the one healing pets, but she likely does an initial screening of new arrivals."

"But the main healer here is a mage?"

"I am," a cheerful voice said as a tall man strode into the room, an amused smile on his face. "Would you like my exact qualifications?"

"Oh no...no." I stood up and gave him a half bow. "I didn't mean—"

"Don't tease my apprentice, Clay." Amara strode over to meet him, pressing one of her cheeks against his in greeting.

"Your apprentice?" Clay pulled back to stare at her in astonishment. "You can't mean it."

"Of course I mean it." She gave him a reproving look. "Would I joke about something like that?"

"I'm impressed!" He shook his head. "And here I was thinking you were getting too old to ever change your ways."

"Amara isn't old," I said defensively, pulling the man's attention back to me.

He inclined his head courteously. "I'm most grateful to hear you say so since I'm several years older again. I'm Clay."

"I'm Delphine. And this is Ember." I held her out, and he looked at her with curiosity.

"Do I dare ask how your apprentice comes to have a fox for a pet, Amara? Or what manner of ailment she suffers? I'm not exactly an expert on foxes, I'm afraid, but she looks like a fine specimen from what I can see."

"She isn't exactly a pet," Amara said. "And we're not exactly here for a healing."

"Not exactly, hey?" He grinned. "Sounds like a story that needs tea." He raised his voice and bellowed, "Tara!"

He'd barely finished the name when the lady from earlier reappeared with a tray in her hands holding a teapot and several cups.

"Excellent." Clay's smile grew even broader. "I remain convinced that you possess a yet-undiscovered affinity for always knowing what's needed and when."

She scoffed, although she couldn't quite hide her smile as she placed the tray on a small table between two of the chairs. "It's called age, wisdom, and experience—something none of you youngsters would know anything about."

"See?" I couldn't help smiling myself. "I told you Amara isn't old."

"Old? That young thing?" Tara winked at me before sailing back out of the room.

Clay chuckled. "Tara is a true gem. Runs this clinic like clockwork and keeps everything shipshape. It was a mess before I hired her."

"I can only imagine," Amara said dryly. "I'm glad I never visited in those days."

"Didn't you hear what she said?" Clay asked with a wicked twinkle. "You were probably a baby back then."

Amara laughed and moved toward the tea tray, while Clay turned to me, his eyes going to Ember.

"She's clearly not in any distress," he said.

"No," Amara agreed. "As I said, we didn't come for a healing. She was badly injured by a larger animal, but Delphine has already healed her. We just came for you to check the healing."

Clay's eyes flew up to my face. "Your apprentice is a healer?"

"She is," Amara said calmly. "Unfortunately it means I can't check the healing myself. That's where you come in."

Clay threw back his head and laughed. "Amara finally gets herself an apprentice, and she has a healing affinity. I don't know why I'm surprised. You'd never take someone with an elements seed, would you?"

"Naturally not." Amara's eyes twinkled at him over a steaming cup of tea.

"May I hold her?" Clay asked, holding out his hands toward Ember.

I handed her over, surprised at my reluctance. Would Ember protest? But she barely stirred, and I reminded myself Clay was a healing mage with the same connection with animals that I shared.

He was silent for only a moment before his smile returned.

"I can see no sign of injury, although she has the feel of one newly healed. Well done, child."

A smile spread over my face as my shoulders sagged in relief. I hadn't realized how tense I'd been waiting for his verdict.

"What was the nature of her injury?" he asked. "Amara said it was significant?"

Some of my relief faded, replaced by embarrassment. "I'm sorry, I don't know what was wrong. Only that she had several large gashes which had damaged half her body, including some organs. I...I'm not sure which ones," I admitted.

His eyebrows rose so high they almost disappeared into his hair. He looked across at Amara.

"You aren't teaching her anatomy? I know you have different ideas, but that's too much. You can't take on a healing apprentice and not provide basic education. She can learn it from a book if you don't know enough to give lessons."

Amara merely looked amused by his stern lecture. "Calm yourself. Of course she'll need to learn anatomy, although I shan't attempt any lectures on the subject myself. I'm not withholding education, we simply haven't had the chance to begin yet. I only activated her three days ago. In fact, I was hoping you might be willing to give her a guiding hand to get started for as long as we're in Ostaria?"

"Three days ago?" Clay handed Ember back to me, astonishment on his face as he examined me for a second time. "And you healed her yesterday? From injuries that severe? On your own?"

"Of course not," I said hesitantly. "Amara helped me."

"Amara...Amara helped you?" He stared at me before suddenly looking across at Amara and bursting into laughter. "I know you put great stock in cross influencing, old friend, but don't tell me you claim to be able to heal now?"

"No, of course not," Amara said with a sour note. "Delphine

merely means that I provided her verbal guidance. Very general guidance."

Clay shook his head as his chuckles subsided. "Remarkable. Truly remarkable." He gave me a cautious look, loaded with curiosity. "I don't suppose you'd consider allowing me to…"

"Of course you can test me," I said quickly, eager to cooperate with Amara's friend and the first healing mage I'd ever met. "I don't mind."

I tried to dismantle my wall to allow him access, as I had done for Nik. It resisted, however, and I barely managed the necessary crack before I felt the brush of foreign power touching mine.

The opening I had created might have been small, but it set me shivering at the sudden rush of awareness. First Ember's body in my arms and then the more distant thrum of Clay and Amara washed over me, making my stomach rebel.

It only lasted seconds, however, before my wall sprang back into place. I took several calming breaths as Clay turned from me to Amara with a raised eyebrow.

"You found her on a farm somewhere? I'm no longer surprised you changed your ways and finally took an apprentice, but why wasn't she already at the Guild? I know some of the smaller towns have to make do with weak healers, but don't try and tell me any tester could have missed strength like that."

"I didn't want to go to the Guild," I said firmly, hoping he wasn't going to take offense.

He merely grinned—a response that seemed as natural to him as breathing.

"You're well matched, then." He glanced between us.

When his and Amara's eyes met, something unspoken was exchanged, a communication I couldn't even guess at. Whatever history they had went much deeper than the one I shared with my influencer.

150

"So do you intend to specialize in human healing or animal healing?" he asked, focusing back on me.

"I haven't even considered the question," I admitted. "Everything happened in a bit of a rush."

"I'm planning to take her to the hospital next," Amara said. "Since she's never been out of Tarin before, she's never seen one."

"Well, I'll be most happy to offer what instruction I can during your stay," Clay said. "I have to put my best foot forward if I'm going to win such a powerful future healer to the side of the animals." He winked at me, and I blushed at the implication that I was someone mages would want as an ally.

"Very proper," Amara said with a nod. "The healers at the hospital can do the same. But you should all remember that Delphine doesn't have to be locked into one or the other. She does have other options."

I couldn't think what she meant for a minute until I remembered her own master had specialized in both. Was that what she meant?

"Of course you would say that." Clay chuckled. "But in the interests of objectivity, I hope you're going to tell Delphine that there are advantages to specializing in one of the main branches —and choosing which one early. Especially since you'll have limited access to healing mage teachers."

He sent an inquiring look at Amara. "At least, I assume you're planning to continue with your traveling ways?"

"Of course," she said. "I believe the variety of experience will make up for anything Delphine misses in consistency. And I'm not going to pressure her into making a decision before she's ready."

"Fine, fine!" Clay held up his hands in laughing surrender, turning the conversation in other directions.

The two of them chatted for a while longer, catching up on the doings of friends and acquaintances I didn't know. I was happy to stay out of the conversation, drinking the cup of tea Amara offered and taking comfort in Ember's solid warmth.

Clay wanted me to pick a specialty, and Amara wanted me to visit clinics and hospitals and begin my training, but I still hadn't told anyone about my embarrassing reaction to blood. I hadn't even told Amara about my wall growing out of control. Now that I heard her talking to Clay and making plans for my training, it felt like a betrayal on my part. I hadn't been a good apprentice so far.

It was time for me to do better. I would confess the truth as soon as we left the animal clinic.

# TWELVE

Despite my resolution to tell her about the wall as soon as we left, we'd barely made it back onto the street before she was pointing across at a larger, taller building made of imposing white marble.

"That's the hospital?" I gasped.

Amara chuckled. "Ostentatious, isn't it? But they have good reason. All the hospitals in Tartora are built that way since it makes them visible and memorable. People need to know where to go in an emergency, and many people who aren't familiar with Ostaria come here just for the hospital."

I nodded. I had known a couple of families from Tarin who had made the journey with a sick or injured family member who needed more complex care than the local healer could provide.

I stopped in front of the broad double doors, gazing up at the building. It was larger than I'd expected and must employ many healers of varying strength levels. Was that why Clay had been so sure there would be someone here with the time and willingness to train me?

I glanced back to the animal clinic, speaking hesitantly. "It's fortunate you have a friend like Master Clay here."

"Fortunate?" Amara followed my gaze before looking back at me. "It's true he has both skill and experience which is ideal. And he has strength, too, since Ostaria is large and lively enough to attract a few master mages. Being on the river with easy access to the capital helps in that regard. But while there aren't masters in all towns and villages, I still have friends everywhere I go. Don't get the wrong impression. I might travel alone, but I'm not lonely. And I won't have any trouble finding you healing instructors across the kingdom."

"Sorry," I said quickly.

She shook her head, smiling at me. "You don't need to apologize. I'm as new to being an influencer as you are to being an apprentice. If you're lacking relevant information, it's because I failed to impart it to you. I'm the master here—it's my job to know what you need to know and when."

She inclined her head toward the imposing building. "On which note, your master is saying it's time to visit your first hospital."

I nodded, looking away and hoping my cheeks didn't look as pale as they felt. If she noticed, she didn't say anything, leading the way through the doors without hesitation.

I followed much more slowly, my dragging feet wanting to turn and run. I was already terrified, and I hadn't even made it inside. But when she ordered me inside as my training master, I couldn't refuse—especially not when I hadn't explained my reluctance yet.

A stark white hallway, free of any decoration, led into the depths of the building. Doors opened off both sides, many of them open. Rooms of varying sizes could be seen, the larger ones filled with rows of beds, while the smaller ones held a single bed each, along with a desk and chairs.

"Those are treatment rooms." Amara pointed through an open door at one of the smaller rooms. "The larger ones are for patients who need to stay for longer periods of time."

"Stay?" That explained the size of the building. I'd been wondering why it needed to be so large when it was surely staffed with strong healers, unlike the clinic back in Tarin. "I thought they had mage healers here. Can't they heal the patients within minutes?"

"They do have mages," Amara said. "But that doesn't mean anything and everything can be instantly healed. The most complex healings can take even powerful healers an hour or more, and there are never enough strong healers to go around. Many people have to be satisfied with partial healings, leaving it to time and their body's own effort to finish the job. Some of those patients are able to go home to recuperate, but some stay here under observation by healing assistants."

"Assistants?" I asked. "Are they regular people with weaker healing seeds like at the clinic back home?"

"Yes, that's right. There's a whole team of them working here."

"I see." So even in this impressive building, not everyone could be healed of everything. I frowned, gripped by a sudden concern. "If they don't have the strength to heal everyone..."

"Don't worry," Amara said with a knowing smile. "Those in greatest danger are treated first, regardless of their ability to pay. The crown funds all the kingdom's hospitals, as well as the clinics in smaller towns like Tarin. Strong healers are expected to serve for some time in one of them before they're permitted to open a private clinic to cater to wealthier clients."

I bit my lip. I'd vaguely known that the clinic at Tarin was funded by the crown, but I hadn't considered the issue more broadly. The picture she painted didn't align with the one I had grown up with—a picture of arrogant mages living lives of luxury and indulgence. I had thought Amara must be an exception, but what if that wasn't true?

I shifted uneasily, pushing the thought away. Just being

here was uncomfortable enough without adding further unease.

"So everyone in here has a complicated issue that can't be easily healed?" I asked, glancing into a room that had over ten occupied beds.

Amara shook her head. "It isn't as simple as that."

"A lot of them are just old," said a cheeky voice from inside the room. "They've grown resistant to healing, as we all do eventually."

A girl appeared, looking too young for the crisp white apron she wore.

Amara greeted her with familiarity. "You've finally been activated, then?" She nodded at the girl's outfit.

The girl smiled proudly. "Last week."

Amara turned to me. "This is Hazel. She's been hanging around the hospital, getting underfoot, for as long as I've known her."

"It isn't fair our seeds aren't ready for activation until we're *seventeen*." She gave me a conspiratorial look as if she expected me to agree with her sentiment, and I managed to scrape together a slightly astonished smile. She must have taken it as agreement because she continued breezily on. "Thankfully there's plenty to be done around a hospital that only requires a pair of strong hands. I've been observing the healings and helping out in the wards for years. But it's much more interesting now I can use my ability. Don't you think so?"

She fixed me with a wide-eyed look, her pause stretching long enough to make it clear she actually expected an answer this time.

"Oh, well..." I couldn't quite think of anything more intelligent to say, given how terrified I was of this building.

Hazel laughed, a high, bright sound that made several of the patients smile.

"I can tell you're an apprentice, like me, because you have

that dazed, slightly nauseous look most of them have when their masters first drag them along here.”

I started, giving her a closer look. Was my nausea really showing on my face?

“I suppose you have an elements affinity like Amara?” she continued. “You’d be surprised how many elements mages go funny at the sight of blood. Most of the ordinary folk think it’s foolish of mages to require their apprentices to have a basic knowledge of the other affinities, but I think it’s sensible. Most of the elements and plants apprentices look like you when they first arrive—but most of them have gotten over their nerves by the time they leave. There’s nothing as frightening as the unknown.”

She beamed at me, showing no hint of judgment for my perceived weakness.

“Actually, Delphine is a healer like you,” Amara sounded amused.

“A healer?” Hazel turned enormous eyes on me.

Despite the fact she was even younger than me and had barely started her apprenticeship, I still squirmed under her scrutiny. She’d already shown she saw too much.

“You don’t look like a healer apprentice at all,” she said frankly, making Amara laugh again.

“Do you think there’s a particular appearance required to be a healer, Hazel?” Amara reached out and pinched a strand of the girl’s hair. “You’ve always been a rascal, but that’s a bit much, even for you.”

“I don’t mean her physical appearance.” Hazel cocked her head to the side examining me. “It’s her manner, her...” She waved her hand around vaguely, as if unable to find words to express her meaning. “You’ve known me for years, Master Amara. You’ve seen what I was like since I was small. Usually healer apprentices are like me—they’ve spent years itching to be inside the hospital, healing people. By the time they finally arrive, they're full of excitement, not dread."

I cleared my throat. The speed and cadence of Hazel's speech made her sound flighty, but she was startlingly perceptive.

"I think Delphine is probably in shock, poor thing." Amara patted me on the arm. "It's a big leap from life on a farm to the hospital in Ostaria."

"Did you come from a farm?" Hazel sounded genuinely interested. "I grew up here in Ostaria, so I can't imagine an isolated life like that. Did you like it?" She continued on without giving me time to answer. "I guess Ostaria must seem as large and impressive to you as I imagine Tarona must be." She sighed wistfully. "I've always wanted to go to the capital. I hear the main hospital there makes this one look tiny."

"Once you've completed your apprenticeship, you can apply to work there," Amara said, and Hazel brightened immediately.

"That's the plan." She looked at me. "So you've never been to Tarona either? I suppose you'll be going soon now you're a Guild apprentice." She sighed again. "I was so disappointed when I got tested. I only got as far into the hospital as the testing room, but even that was enough to know I never wanted to leave. So it was no surprise I had a healing seed. But I was so hopeful I might have surpassed my parents and been strong enough for a guild apprenticeship."

"You weren't far off," Amara said kindly. "Which means you'll always be welcomed in the hospitals of Tarona. You know better than me that there's more than enough work for everyone."

"That's true!" Hazel brightened quickly, giving me the impression she wasn't the sort of person to stay down for long. "But still, you're lucky, Delphine." She smiled at me without any trace of ill will.

I smiled back, afraid the expression looked pained. The

familiar feeling of being an impostor swept over me. A proper healer should be drawn to healing, like Hazel. Wasn't that the work of the seed inside them?

So what had gone wrong with me?

"I'll get one of the masters," Hazel said, stepping further into the corridor. "They'll want to greet you, Master Amara—and meet the new healing apprentice, of course." She laughed. "I'll try to find one of the more amiable masters for you—one who won't give you a scolding for stealing a powerful healer away to your cross-influencing cause."

She had only taken a few steps away when I spoke, my voice sounding a little desperate. As much as I didn't want to speak up around Hazel, I wanted to expose my weakness to an unknown master healer even less.

"Everyone keeps telling me I'm so strong, but if that's the case, shouldn't I be able to get some sense of those people?" I gestured at the row of beds inside the closest room.

Hazel whirled back, a confused look on her face. Amara also stepped forward, a frown creasing her brow.

"What do you mean? You can't sense them?" Amara gripped my arm. "Not at all? But you could feel the people in that hamlet from ten miles away."

"Ten miles?" Hazel gaped at me. "You could get a healing sense of people ten miles away? But you can't feel the people in that ward?" Her eyes lit, clearly intrigued by the mystery. "That makes no sense."

My stomach swirled. I didn't want to be any stranger than I already was.

"Can you tell anything about them at all?" Amara asked. "Give it a try."

I reached out, as I had on the road, but there was nothing. Why hadn't I noticed how peaceful it was inside my head? It had been the same earlier at the animal healing clinic, but I'd been so focused on Clay's assessment of Ember's health that I hadn't noticed.

"I can't sense anything at all," I said, the beginnings of panic sounding in my voice. "Has my ability disappeared? Is that possible?"

"No, it's not possible," Amara said firmly. "Give me a minute to think."

I tried to recall the last time I'd used my ability or felt anything in relation to it. It had been at the animal clinic, but only for a brief moment when Clay wanted to test me, and I'd lowered my wall to allow him in.

"My wall!" I gasped.

I tried to turn my attention inward, but I was just as shut off from my own body as I was from the people and animals around me. I couldn't even feel Ember in my arms, and I had physical contact with her. No wonder I'd been coping with my squeamishness so well.

"Your wall?" Amara frowned. "What do you mean?"

"Sorry, I meant to tell you earlier, but I didn't get the chance. Last night I worked out why I couldn't sense my own body on the road. I'd completely walled it off."

"Walled it off?" Hazel moved closer, eyes alight with curiosity. "What does that mean? Is it something I could do?"

I ignored her, focusing on Amara. "At first the wall was just protecting my body. But it protected against more than just my own power. I had to lower it to be tested." I swallowed. "I think...I think I was working on it in my sleep last night. I had terrible dreams all night, and I remember trying to make my wall stronger. I thought it was just a dream, but my subconscious must have actually been doing it. It was harder to lower the barrier for Master Clay than it had been the evening before. And now my sense of other people is blocked off as well as my sense of myself. I've accidentally made it too strong."

"Fascinating," Amara breathed, the worry in her eyes

replaced with interest. "Who knew such a thing was possible? I'll have to consult with Master Colton as soon as I get the chance."

"Master Colton?" I stared at her.

"He's the Master of Healing," Hazel said, almost bouncing in her excitement. "The head of the healing affinity."

I barely restrained from snapping back at her that I knew who he was. I wasn't totally ignorant. I was just highly uncomfortable at the idea of anyone having a conversation with him about *me*.

"Don't worry," Hazel said, once again seeming to pick up on my emotions. "All the stories say he's the least intimidating of the affinity heads."

But as terrifying as the idea of Master Colton was, I had more pressing concerns.

"How can I continue my apprenticeship if I can't access my power?" I asked, gripped by the new fear.

"I'm sure it's not that drastic," Amara said in what was clearly meant to be a soothing voice. "Why don't you try taking down the wall now? You said it was harder to do with Clay than it had been earlier, but not that it was impossible."

Her slight emphasis on *earlier* probably went unnoticed by Hazel, but I caught it with a sinking feeling. I'd spoken without thinking and all but told her I'd been tested the night before while I was out looking for Ember. While we were apart. She wasn't asking me questions now, but that didn't mean she wouldn't later.

"All right," I said, too distracted to quibble. "I'll try."

Focusing with difficulty, I tore at the wall, ripping a much bigger hole than I'd done for Clay.

Instantly I was slammed with sensation. My awareness of Ember—the only one I had physical contact with—was by far the strongest, but every person in the hospital was easily within my range. And almost all of them had something wrong with them, a taint in my awareness that pressed at me. Illnesses and injuries bombarded me from every side.

My eyes jerked to the closest patient, fastening on a bandage around his arm. It had to be an old dressing because red had seeped all the way through the white layers. My stomach lurched.

I tried to reach for my power to settle my nausea, but already roaring filled my ears. It blocked out the alarmed voices of Amara and Hazel as spots of black grew across my vision, filling my head with cotton wool. I forgot all about my power and instead put out my arms, reaching blindly for something solid.

My hand found nothing but empty air, and I collapsed, darkness closing around me completely.

# THIRTEEN

I came back to consciousness slowly, keeping my eyes closed. The first thing I noticed was the blessed quiet. Nothing was assaulting my senses anymore. Slowly, I cracked open my eyelids, nervous about what I would find.

My surroundings were unfamiliar. I wasn't back at the inn.

Looking around the room, I saw white walls and a wooden desk. I groaned. I was still in the hospital. Given the quiet, that had to mean my wall was back in place.

"You're awake?" a familiar voice asked, and I finally noticed Amara sitting on a chair in a corner of the room.

"What happened?" I cleared my throat, trying to get rid of the croaky rasp that had sounded in my words.

"You collapsed." She pulled her chair forward, placing a cool hand against my forehead. "Although you were briefly unconscious, Hazel assured me you didn't need a more senior healer." Amara cocked her head to one side, watching me with a concerned gaze. "I hope my trust in her wasn't misplaced?"

"I..." I paused as I considered checking myself and remembered that would involve opening my wall. "I feel all right?" I finally said.

Amara sat back with a calculating look. "I know you've been

keeping something from me. But the beginning of this apprenticeship was so sudden. I didn't want to press you until we had a chance to get to know each other better. I was hoping you would decide to confide in me yourself. But it's clear the issue is a bigger one than I realized. I think it's time you told me exactly what's going on."

I winced and pushed myself into a sitting position.

"I was going to tell you. I'd already realized I needed to, and I was actually going to say something on the walk to the hospital, only then it was so close." I shook my head at the silly reason for my failure to speak up.

"Well, now seems like a good opportunity," she said with a wry smile.

I took a fortifying breath, feeling as foolish as I had the first time I'd been overtaken by the symptoms as a young girl.

"I'm squeamish," I said in a rush. "I can't see blood or injuries without getting sick and faint. Even just talking about an illness or how our insides work makes me feel lightheaded. And no, it's not just all in my head," I said defensively, although Amara hadn't said anything. "They're physical symptoms, as you saw. If it's sudden, or if I try to ignore the symptoms, I end up fainting."

Amara stared at me. When the silence grew too long, I laughed awkwardly.

"Have you ever heard anything so ridiculous as a squeamish healer? Now you can see why I think my affinity is some sort of mistake. I'm not a healer. You heard what Hazel said. Healers are excited to heal. They want to be around illness and injury so they can fix it. I'd love to be able to fix it, of course, but that would require me not turning into a second patient within seconds of my arrival." I gestured around the treatment room. "I'm worse than useless."

"So that's why you constructed the wall," Amara said

thoughtfully. "I was wondering why an idle comment had taken such root. It turns out it was fueled by desperate need."

I sighed. "I might as well not have any power at all."

"Nonsense," said a cheerful voice from the door.

We both turned to see the smiling face of Clay.

Part of me wanted to slide under the blankets to avoid the humiliation I'd brought on myself, but the other part of me was too interested in his words to run away.

"There's no need for you to look so pained, Apprentice." He came into the room, standing beside Amara's chair and looking down at me. "This is merely a minor inconvenience."

"Minor?" I shook my head. "If I access my power, I lose consciousness. That doesn't seem minor to me."

He looked sideways at Amara, putting on a stern expression that seemed out of place on his face.

"This is the problem with your much vaunted cross-influencing. If you'd been a healer yourself, you would have known how to help your apprentice through this. Even as an elements mage, if you'd been at the Guild, her symptoms would have been recognized."

I sat bolt upright, my hands clenching around the blankets. "You mean I'm not the first? This happens to other healing apprentices?"

Clay chuckled. "Of course! Did you think you were special?" He winked at me.

"It's not common or anything," Hazel said, popping into the room from where she'd clearly been listening in the corridor. "It hasn't happened to anyone apprenticing here at the hospital—at least not in the years since I was tested for my affinity. But I did once hear it mentioned by one of the master healers. He had a previous apprentice who had the problem."

"And what happened to them?" I focused in on her, not even caring that she had inserted herself into the conversation.

"The master didn't go into detail, but it sounded like a

minor problem that was dealt with in the first months of the apprenticeship. Master Clay will probably know more." The smile she gave him was slightly strained.

"Yes," Clay said, sounding amused at the apprentice's discomfort. "Even I, a lowly animal healer, know enough to deal with something like this."

Hazel's eyes widened slightly at having her prejudice called out, although Clay was clearly unbothered by it. When I looked back and forth between them, Clay caught my confusion and grinned.

"I never had any hope of luring Hazel into specializing with animals. She had her heart set on the hospital from the beginning."

"Of course," Hazel said promptly. "Why would I want to focus on animals when there are *people* needing healing?"

"I thought all healers loved animals?" Amara sounded amused. "Because of your connection with them."

"Of course I love animals," Hazel said. "It's not that I want them to suffer. It's just that people are so much more—"

"Precisely," Clay said, neatly cutting her off. "Which is why I, for one, am grateful so many healers want to specialize in healing people. It allows me to focus on animals without guilt. Just like I'm sure you're grateful there are other healers wanting to specialize with animals."

Hazel nodded, looking suitably chastened.

"See, this is why you shouldn't push your rivalry so hard," Amara told Clay disapprovingly. "Young people always take this kind of thing too seriously. Both specializations should be working together. I'm sure you have things you can learn from each other."

Clay looked at me. "I hope you, at least, mean to offer me some sympathy! Here I am, beset on every side, after rushing over here at the first word you were having difficulties."

"Oh! You came for me?" I gulped. "I'm so sorry for causing you so much inconvenience. I didn't mean—"

"Stop, stop!" He held up his hands to silence me. "I was only joking, Apprentice Delphine. Of course I came. I've already promised my old friend that I would help with her new healing apprentice, after all. And you shouldn't listen to either of these two. There's no real rift within the healing affinity—merely a friendly rivalry. We need something to keep us occupied in this small town."

He winked at me again, and I fiddled with the blankets. After a lifetime spent between my farm and Tarin, it was impossible to think of Ostaria as a small or boring town.

"Delphine has had a rough enough day without any further teasing," Amara said sternly. "I will even acknowledge my own deficiency in this matter. Please explain what is needed, or if you cannot, find me a healer who can."

"Ouch, Amara, you wound me." He was still smiling at her, though, so he didn't seem to have taken any real offense. I'd never met anyone who joked like he did, and I found myself wondering what it would be like to be his apprentice.

It didn't seem like a bad picture. Would specializing with animals be easier than healing people? I could imagine spending my life working with people like Clay, bringing peace and wellness to people's animal friends.

I tucked away the appealing image for later. For now, I couldn't even consider specializing in anything until I could actually use my power.

"Squeamishness is really something other healing apprentices have encountered?" I asked, struggling to accept the incredible news.

"Really, truly," Clay said in a voice that was somehow both serious and warmly reassuring. "It's a rare condition, but it's familiar in the Guild, at least among the healers. For some reason, it's more prevalent among those with a seed of mage strength than among the ordinary population."

"How interesting!" Hazel exclaimed. "I wonder why? Is it the strength of the seed that sets off some sort of opposite reaction?"

Clay threw her a smile. "Perhaps? It hasn't been properly researched since it's a condition that's easy for the apprentice to overcome themselves."

Wild, unbelievable, heady relief swept over me, followed by a hopefulness I hadn't felt since I was a small child. I wasn't irreparably broken. I could be fixed. I could learn to use my power. I could be useful, just like I'd always dreamed.

If only my father was here so I could tell him the good news.

As soon as the thought occurred to me, a horrible chill lanced down my spine. It would be news to my father... wouldn't it?

For a horrifying moment, I considered the possibility that my father had known all along that my squeamishness was a known condition for healer apprentices and could be cured once I came into my power. Had he deliberately lied to me to keep me crippled and chained to his side?

I quickly rejected the thought. My father had a plants affinity, as did my uncle, and their parents before them. He had never had much to do with healers of any strength, and Clay had said squeamishness was an uncommon affliction. There was no reason to think my father would ever have encountered it or heard of its cure before.

But he could have found out. There was no denying that reality. From Clay's comments, it was a well-enough known condition that surely either Halmir or one of the string of healers at Tarin's healing clinic would have heard of it. And if they hadn't, I was sure Halmir, at least, would have contacted the Guild to ask about it. He had been trying to convince me to agree to an apprenticeship for years.

My father might not have deliberately covered up the solution, but he had kept me from discovering it. He had used my affliction for his own purposes.

I slumped back against the bed, overwhelmed. Now that I had opened the gate to such thoughts, they came flooding into my mind. How long had there been an element of uncertainty lurking inside me, ruthlessly suppressed and ignored? It seemed obvious now that I should have questioned my father's perspectives, but I also understood why I hadn't. I had been terrified of overturning the only world I knew.

But the cracks had already begun to show before now, hairline fractures appearing soon after I met Amara—a mage entirely unlike his portrayal of them. I still hadn't properly questioned his teachings, though—the habit of years too strong to break.

Until now. Once the thoughts had begun, they wouldn't stop, tumbling out one after another and building a picture I wished I didn't have to face.

My father had latched onto my squeamishness, blowing it out of proportion as a tool to keep me chained to the farm. As long as I believed I had no hope of ever using my power, I would have no temptation to run away to the Guild.

My stomach churned, a familiar feeling, although a new cause. Lying in this hospital bed, I was seeing my father through a whole different lens.

How much pain had I suffered—both physical and mental —due to the unfortunate combination of my squeamishness and my healing seed? And instead of bringing me relief, my father had encouraged that pain. He had allowed his own hurt and prejudice to poison my life. He had deliberately kept me weak in order to control me.

That wasn't love. It wasn't the role of a parent as my mother had explained it.

Tears dripped unheeded down my cheeks as I realized my

mistake. If only I had told my mother the truth. Unlike my father, she would have left no stone unturned in seeking a solution.

Fresh pain gripped me as I realized my father had known that. He had known my ability was the one issue my mother would never bend on, and so he had driven a wedge between the two of us, telling me my affliction was a shame I needed to keep hidden, a burden that would cause her grief.

Because of my father, I had never been truly open with my mother.

My head swam, and I closed my eyes. Through all the years of frustration and anger over my joke of a seed, one constant had been certain. My parents loved me, and they would always be my safe home and my support. My insides clenched as that foundation cracked, the silent roar of it reverberating through me.

I had never once doubted that my goal was to qualify as a mage and return to my family to run our farm. But just the thought of facing my father made sweat break out on my palms. Had he ever loved me at all? I felt too betrayed and angry to think clearly, and all I wanted was for my mother to wrap her arms around me and tell me everything was going to be alright, as she had so often done when I was a child.

But even the thought of her had lost its soothing effect. Instead guilt gripped me. My mother had never done anything to earn my mistrust. I should have seen through my father's deception and told her the truth from the beginning.

A hand took mine, lightly squeezing. I opened my eyes to find Amara looking at me, a concerned crease between her eyes.

"I wish I'd known from the beginning, and I'm sorry I couldn't tell you were suffering in silence. But you heard Clay. We can fix this, and you will become a great healer."

I swallowed, consumed in equal parts by a desire to pull my hand out of hers and to throw my arms around her. I wanted to believe that she would look after me—that she would help me fix all my problems—but I had once believed my father knew all the answers as well.

"Of course you'll be a great healer!" Clay said. "Especially since you have Amara to guide you. Who knows what great contributions you'll make to the healing affinity. In fact, I'm already curious to hear more about this wall of yours. It explains how you were holding Ember so casually earlier."

"Is there something significant about that?" I looked from him to Amara who looked just as blank as me.

Clay laughed. "Between your holding her and the way you'd healed her, I thought you were the most advanced apprentice I'd ever encountered. I was almost ready to throw my support behind Amara and speak up at the Guild on the benefits of cross-influencing."

"What do you mean?" Amara asked. "Was there something strange about Delphine carrying Ember?"

"Wait," I gasped, feeling terrible for not noticing earlier. "Where is Ember?" I looked wildly around the room, but she failed to appear.

"Is that the fox?" Hazel asked. "She took off like a shot when you collapsed. I hadn't even noticed her under your cloak until then, or I might have made some effort to catch her."

"She's probably back in her box by the fire by now," Amara said. "There's no need to look so concerned, Delphine. She's a wild animal and knows how to look after herself. It isn't even her first time wandering around the streets."

I hesitated before sighing and nodding. I still didn't feel entirely comfortable about her disappearance, but there wasn't anything I could do about it right now. I was just glad I hadn't landed on top of her when I fainted.

"But why is it significant that Delphine was holding Ember?" Hazel asked Clay. "Don't you animal healer types always have animals hanging off you?"

"Delphine was only activated three days ago," he said.

"Three days?" Hazel gaped at me. "And you're carrying a pet around with you?"

"She's not a pet," I said automatically, but my focus was on Clay. "I still don't understand..."

"You look older than me," Hazel said, "so I assumed you'd been an apprentice longer. I wouldn't dare touch anyone—human or animal—without my master with me. There are always new apprentices at the hospital, and it usually takes months before they're confident enough about their control to risk it."

"Oh," I said foolishly, their surprise now making sense. "Yes, of course. I had some trouble like that myself before I made the wall."

"Wall?" Hazel asked. "What does that mean?"

"Delphine has blocked off her ability." Amara spoke for me, her attention on Clay. "It was a defensive measure at first, because of her nausea, and it's worked—but a little too effectively. It seems to be growing in strength and getting harder for her to dismantle."

Clay rubbed his chin. "I can't say I've heard of anyone doing that before. It sounds like it could be a useful tool for new healing apprentices, though. I assume you at least knew enough to warn her when you activated her? Those first few weeks are a dangerous time for new healers."

Amara nodded. "Of course. I think I inadvertently pushed her toward creating the wall. But what do you usually do to keep your apprentices safe instead?"

"Terrify us into being more cautious than we've ever been in our lives," Hazel said promptly. "I can't even think about my own body without having a panic attack."

Clay looked at her with a raised eyebrow. "You've never had a panic attack in your life, troublemaker. We'd all sleep more easily if you had a bone of caution in your body."

She laughed. "I don't know what you're talking about." She turned to me. "Actually, I recite multiplication. It was my hardest subject in school and brings back terrible memories. It never fails to distract me."

Clay nodded, looking back at Amara. "Distraction is the usual technique. Train their minds to be disciplined. Keeping your thoughts under tight control while healing is a useful skill, so the training achieves multiple purposes. Even experienced healers need to be cautious when they're operating inside someone else's body."

He surveyed me with narrowed eyes. "If you could put that wall up and down at will, it would actually be an ideal solution for squeamish healers in those first weeks while they're still learning basic control. Those who suffer nausea like you usually have a hard time until they can be trusted to heal themselves."

"Can't their masters heal them for that first period?" Amara asked. "I know I can't do it for Delphine, but surely you..."

He shook his head. "We can help during an actual healing, and we do help new apprentices while they're training. But once their seed is activated, the new sensations are so intense that they're usually suffering almost constantly. Since the symptoms have a mental cause rather than a physical one, we can't just permanently fix them. They would need constant masking."

Amara frowned. "Are you sure it can't just be fixed? Healers can treat illnesses of the mind."

He sighed. "Only some of them. The best and strongest healers can treat problems in the brain, but some mental conditions aren't created by damage or imbalances."

"Sometimes people's brains are making them sad," Hazel continued for him, "and sometimes their life is what's making them sad. In the second case, all we can do is mask the symptoms for a short while to provide some relief. The patient has to use that space to find their own healing."

"Are you saying I'm doing this to myself?" I asked indignantly. "That it's all in my head? Do you think I'm faking the physical symptoms?"

"Of course not," Clay said. "Your symptoms are real. The brain controls everything, so just because something originates in the brain doesn't mean it stays there. I'm not saying your physical symptoms are fake, I'm saying there isn't a physical malady I can treat—and that includes inside your brain. This isn't strictly an illness at all. Something in your nature makes you more uncomfortable with the idea of injury than the standard person. Your body is merely responding to the discomfort in your brain."

"So what can she do about it?" Amara asked when I stayed silent, processing Clay's words.

"As I said, it's possible to temporarily suppress the physical symptoms," he said. "For us healers, we can choose to suppress our symptoms indefinitely. And the stronger the healer, the more successful we'll be at that task. Usually we don't recommend it as a permanent solution since it ignores the underlying issue. But in the particular case of being squeamish, a temporary solution is almost always enough to solve the problem. Because a healing apprentice has constant exposure to what triggers their squeamishness, they grow used to it over time. Plus they gain a sense of empowerment from being able to heal the ailments they encounter. Combined, those two elements are enough to overcome the original discomfort."

He looked at me. "I can't say how long it will take in any individual's case, but you'll be able to operate as a normal healer as soon as you gain enough control to safely suppress your own symptoms. Some level of the squeamishness may always remain, but it will drop to a manageable level well before your apprenticeship ends."

"Well, that's a relief," Amara said briskly. "I was afraid we had a more serious problem on our hands."

"Um, it sounds serious to me," I said, sliding down to lie on my back and stare up at the ceiling.

I knew Clay's words should spark the earlier wild elation, but it was hard to feel hopeful with the specter of my father's betrayal hanging over me. I had longed for a usable seed so I could ensure the safety and future of my family and our farm. What did it mean to gain that longed for power just as all desire for that safe family haven was ripped away from me?

Two years had seemed long just days ago, but now it felt far too short. I didn't want to face the decision about what I would do once it was over.

"This wall could cause problems," Clay said, pulling my mind away from the spiraling thoughts about my family. "But with most uses of power, practice is all that's needed. As long as the desired activity is within the capacity of someone's seed, then practice is the key."

Hazel groaned. "You sound like the masters here at the hospital. Practice, practice, practice."

Clay ruffled her hair. "Some things are universal. Ask the elements and plants apprentices and they'll tell you the same thing."

She stepped out of his reach, patting her hair back into place with an indignant look.

"I do sympathize," he said with what looked suspiciously more like amusement than empathy. "You make me glad my own youth is behind me."

Amara snorted. "We can all be equally thankful. You were the most obnoxious apprentice."

"Me?" He clapped a hand to his chest. "What are you talking about? I never let the need for endless practice get me down."

"Exactly," she muttered. "No one should be that cheerful all the time."

Hazel and my gazes met, and we both tried, unsuccessfully, to suppress laughter. Amara smiled at me.

"I'm glad to see you looking a bit more cheerful. Do you feel up to getting out of that bed now?"

Guiltily, I sprang up, pausing briefly as all the blood rushed out of my head at the sudden movement.

"Steady there." Clay lightly gripped my elbow. "I think the usual approach for cases of nausea will work well enough for you, despite the complication of the wall." He let go and turned to Amara. "She needs to learn control and how to discipline her thinking. So don't hold off on starting her training—but focus for now on the peripheral areas of the healing ability that don't involve actual healing."

She frowned. "You mean testing children's seeds?"

He nodded. "And truth testing as well. That will give Delphine the opportunity to take down her wall and practice using her ability in environments where everyone is healthy. And, of course, Ember should stay home on those excursions, and physical touch should be avoided as much as possible. Delphine seems to be a fairly extreme case, so just sensing people at all might cause some discomfort, but if they're healthy, then exposure should deal with that fairly quickly."

"Testing people," I said slowly. "That sounds doable."

"I have no doubt you'll take it in your stride." Amara stood. "And since you've recovered for now, I think the first thing I should do is get you out of this building. Clearly the hospital will have to come later."

I couldn't have agreed more, so we hustled outside, bidding our farewells to Clay on the street. He promised to check up on my progress regularly before watching us set off toward the inn.

"I'm sorry I can't take you out of Ostaria altogether," Amara said regretfully.

I stiffened. In all the excitement of the day's activities, I'd temporarily forgotten about Grey and Miranda, but thoughts of the Tarin girl came rushing back at Amara's words. We couldn't leave until I'd tracked her down.

"I don't want to move on," I said quickly, earning a curious look from my influencer.

"Having so many people in one place can't be helpful for your comfort," she said. "But if you're going to train in the side aspects of the healing affinity, you need to be in a larger center like this one. They do much more regular truth and seed testing here than they would somewhere smaller."

"Yes, of course. That makes sense." I nodded enthusiastically.

She narrowed her eyes at me. "Don't think you're off the hook. I know there's more you're not telling me."

I froze, falling behind a couple of steps, but she reached back and tugged me forward.

"Relax." She shook her head. "I think you've been through enough today. I'm not planning to force it out of you."

*Yet.* The unspoken extra word hung heavy in the air between us.

"I'm sorry," I said softly.

She smiled at me. "I've already told you that I expect it to take time between us. I meant that. I want you to learn to trust me as your master and as a person, and I realize that doesn't start with me forcing you to tell me all your secrets."

"I..." I paused, my mind struggling to take in her words and my thoughts pulled back to my father who had wanted my secrets to stay buried forever. I couldn't force myself to make sense of it all. Eventually I spoke again. "Thank you. I appreciate that." I couldn't think of anything else to say.

If Amara picked up on my heavy mood, she gave no sign of it, her smile turning smug. "I should have known I would be an excellent master. I don't know why I waited so long."

I gave her a startled look, and she winked at me. Gratitude washed over me as I realized she was purposely lightening the mood.

"Clay is a bad influence," I said, chuckling, and she laughed back.

"I always enjoy seeing him again."

I gave her a surreptitious look. Did Amara have a deeper interest in Clay than just as a colleague and old friend from her apprentice days?

She showed no self-consciousness, however, and I could hardly ask her after she'd shown such forbearance about my secrets.

"I do want to tell you everything," I said, my words surprising even me. Keeping my secrets had been a mistake in the past. "My mind is just in a bit of a muddle at the moment. Once I have it all straight myself, I'll definitely tell you."

Amara smiled. "Thank you."

She maintained her supportive demeanor that evening when I announced after the meal that I was going out for a walk. I expected her to protest about me going alone, but she seemed to think this was all part of the thinking process and raised no objections.

Ember—who had indeed been safely back in her box— perked up with the arrival of twilight, making it clear she wanted to join me. I scooped her up for the short journey out of the inn, but once we were loose on the streets, I set her down so she could stretch her legs.

She stuck close to my heels, easily losing herself in the night shadows that swirled around my cloak.

I had no particular destination in mind, but I'd been telling the truth when I said my mind was in a muddled state. I needed space and movement to have any hope of untangling it.

On top of the hurt, confusion, and hope, I couldn't shake lingering embarrassment. Amara had given no indication that she found me a deficient apprentice—in front of Clay, she had even taken the blame on herself as my master—but I wanted to be an apprentice who made her proud. She had taken a chance on me, and I hated letting her down so immediately.

Enclosed in the inn room with her, the feelings of inadequacy had grown, but out here in the cool air and the darkness, they began to unravel. Clay had seemed impressed by my strength and my healing of Ember, and Amara continued to be fascinated by the wall I had accidentally created. Even Hazel had been nonchalant about the nausea. I was the only one overthinking the issue.

But how could I not after the years I had spent believing it was an insurmountable problem? Years of anxiety fueled by my father. The father I had thought loved me.

I shook my head and increased my pace, letting the physical activity drive out the poisonous thoughts. Ember brushed against my leg, and her presence steadied me. Even after I'd dropped her earlier, she'd chosen to return to me. Animals didn't lie and manipulate for their own purposes. Their love was as straightforward as it appeared, and I accepted her devotion like a balm for my heart.

The faint stirrings of my initial excitement returned. Soon, I would be able to freely use my ability. I would be able to protect Ember—and other animals like her—from pain and illness.

"Don't get ahead of yourself," I muttered aloud. "For now, you need to keep that wall in place. Which means you're better off focusing on Grey than on healing."

Just the sound of his name sharpened my senses. He was somewhere near, and Miranda might be too. If I could find and rescue her, then Amara and I wouldn't need to be bound to Ostaria anymore.

But I knew almost nothing about the city. I had no idea where to even begin to look. The only thing I could even think to try was retracing my steps from the night before.

Nik had seemed certain Grey and his people would be long gone from the warehouse, but I couldn't help feeling a spike of anxiety as I approached the alley where they had trapped me. I pushed past it, though, entering cautiously.

Ember hung back, as if she also remembered the place, but it seemed as deserted as expected. The door that had been behind Grey and his companion stood unprotected.

I pressed my ear against it. After hearing nothing but silence, I worked up the courage to try opening it. It swung inward without any resistance, nearly sending me staggering. I stepped inside, flinching when the door swung closed, leaving me in near blackness.

I held my breath, but I could still hear nothing. I seemed to be truly alone in the large, empty space.

Shaking myself, I turned back to the door. I needed to find a way to wedge it open so I could get some light in here. Perhaps I could find some clue Grey had left behind.

Even as I thought it, I knew it was foolish. What helpful thing could he possibly have left behind? But I wanted to be doing something, and I couldn't think of anything else.

Before I could reach the door, however, the handle moved. I stiffened and threw myself against the closest wall, hoping to be out of the line of sight of whoever was coming in.

Had Grey or one of his men returned?

The door swung all the way open, and I tensed, ready to run if the new arrival spotted me. But I had barely absorbed the presence of the tall, dark figure before he was moving.

Spinning and leaping too fast for me to escape, he trapped me against the wall, the feel of cold steel against my throat keeping me still.

CHAPTER

# FOURTEEN

The door clanged shut, plunging us back into darkness. For an endless moment, we stood frozen in position, before I remembered I was no longer helpless.

My mind reached for my wall while my hands flew up to grasp my assailant's wrists. All I needed was skin-to-skin contact, and I would become a weapon far more deadly than the blade he wielded.

But my searching fingers found nothing other than the leather of gloves and several layers of material. My assailant's grip tightened just as a growl sounded from close to the ground.

We both froze before a flurry of movement provoked a muttered curse. My attacker stepped abruptly back, swinging his leg up. A muted thump was followed by a high whine.

"Ember!" I screamed, stumbling toward the sound of the whine.

"Ember?" repeated a deep voice.

A light flickered and flared, a lantern illuminating our portion of the empty warehouse. Nik, dressed in his usual black, was staring at me with a horrified expression.

"You! *Again!*" He sounded furious.

When I didn't respond, too frozen with a mix of shock and

relief, his expression turned disgusted. "You're fortunate I didn't kill you."

"As are you!" I snapped back, my temper surging. "Healer, remember?"

He laughed derisively, extending one hand and arm. Between his sleeve and his glove, there wasn't so much as a flash of visible skin.

"Do you think I would go into battle against someone like Grey without armor?"

I bit my lip. So it hadn't been chance that my attempt at skin-to-skin contact had failed.

Another whine sent me rushing toward the bundle of orange fur on the ground, although with my wall down I could already tell she was all right. As I knelt beside her, I glared over my shoulder at Nik. "You kicked her!"

His eyes narrowed. "She bit me." He gestured to his boot which had a visible bite mark in the leather.

"Good girl," I muttered quietly, bending over her.

She was breathing shallowly, something making her uncomfortable, and guilt overtook me. She had behaved in an aggressive manner totally unlike her natural fox instincts, and she had done it to protect me. Again.

Placing a gentle hand against her fur, I forced myself to focus on her injuries. As soon as I made contact, nausea sprang to life in my stomach, the burst of energy that had been holding it back since I pierced my wall no longer sufficient.

My head swam, and I used my power to steady myself, easing my symptoms before reaching into Ember.

"You fractured one of her ribs!" I exclaimed accusingly, even as I strengthened the bone, smoothing it back into wholeness.

Nik shifted uncomfortably. Did he actually feel guilty? Was he capable of such an emotion?

He cleared his throat. "I didn't realize it was her. I thought something rabid was living in here."

I rolled my eyes but stayed silent. Despite my earlier tone, I couldn't exactly fault him for reacting defensively to an attack in the dark.

When I finished the healing, I sat back, relieved to break the contact. As soon as my wall snapped back into place, I sighed.

"Do animals develop a resistance to healing as well?" I tried to count how many times Ember had been healed now. "Ember really needs to stop throwing herself into harm's way for me, or I'm not going to be able to heal her so easily anymore."

"It must be nice to have someone so loyal," Nik muttered, so quietly I almost didn't catch the words.

I twisted to look at him, sadness filling me at the closed expression on his face. Did Nik have no one in his life to show him loyalty? Is that why he spent his time roaming the night-time streets of town after town, passing through like a phantom?

The loneliness of such an existence made me shiver. Ember pressed herself against me, as if sensing my momentary melancholy. I ran a hand over her fur, murmuring my thanks before slowly climbing to my feet.

"I suppose I don't need to ask why you're here." Nik sounded sour.

"Yes, that should be obvious. I'm not sure why you're here, though. Weren't you going to investigate this place last night?"

Nik ignored my accusation. "What were you planning to do if my guess was wrong, and Grey was still here? This is the last place you should be."

"I guess I trusted you," I said with more confidence than I felt.

Why *had* I trusted his words so implicitly? I'd done the same thing earlier when he'd said Miranda would disappear before Grey resurfaced, and yet he'd been wrong on that occasion by his own admission. I knew nothing about this man, so why did I put so much stock in his words?

"Trust me?" Nik laughed darkly. "Don't be a fool."

"Are you not trustworthy, then?" I met his eyes steadily.

For a moment he was silent, staring back at me, an arrested look in his gaze. But with a quick shake of his head, he broke the moment.

"I have it on excellent authority that I can't be trusted at all."

I frowned, saying nothing as I watched him. Nik had been surprised I wasn't at the Guild, but why wasn't he? He was a mage and couldn't have long finished his apprenticeship. Had something happened to turn him against his influencer and send him off on his own?

"Maybe I am a fool, then, because I trust you," I said firmly.

His eyes flashed to mine, not able to hide his surprise.

"At least in regards to this," I added. "I believe you're set against Grey and his theft of Tartora's young people."

Nik relaxed slightly, but my next words made him stiffen again.

"Do you hate the new kingdom? Is that why you're so set against Grey?"

"Hate Calista?" he scoffed. "Save a kingdom and see what thanks you get. Of course I don't hate Calista."

I raised an eyebrow. "Are you trying to say you were the one to save the fallen kingdom? Because you don't look much like Queen Cadence."

He gave a bark of genuine laughter. "I'll take that as a compliment."

I rolled my eyes. "Everyone knows Calista's new queen was the one to restore the fallen kingdom from its cursed state, reintroducing the world to power mages and ushering in a new era of growth in power."

"I see the propaganda has reached even the remotest parts of Tartora," Nik said.

He had denied hating Calista, but his words only reinforced

the impression he was prejudiced against Tartora's northern neighbor—once a wasteland but now restored and in the process of being rebuilt.

"Are you saying it wasn't Queen Cadence who saved Calista?" I asked.

He sighed. "Of course I'm not saying that. Everyone knows it was her." His words had a slight mocking lilt, echoing mine earlier. But he seemed to mean the words. "She just didn't do it alone."

I laughed. "Are you saying that when she ventured into the fallen kingdom, she chose *you* as one of her companions? That was more than a year ago, had you even graduated your apprenticeship then?"

His eyes slid away from mine, and I snorted. Of course he hadn't.

"If you love Calista so much," I added, "I don't know why you're so set against its emissary."

"Grey isn't Calistan," Nik ground out through his teeth.

I put my hands on my hips, pinning him with a skeptical glare. He whirled away from me, striding toward the closed door.

"I don't know why I'm wasting my time on this conversation," he muttered as he walked. "If you want to believe Calista is the problem, go right ahead."

I ran after him, grabbing his arm to hold him back.

"Wait! If you're so sure it's not Calista, explain it to me. Who else wants to steal away our best and brightest young people? Everyone knows the Calistans need people to repopulate their abandoned land. Tarin is way down south, but we still had a family who chose to head north last year."

I shook my head, remembering the buzz their departure had generated in the town.

"Everyone says the Tartoran crown is sympathetic to the new Calistan king and queen," I continued. "I've even heard people claim King Marius shows more care and affection for them than he does for his own children. Otherwise he wouldn't be turning a blind eye to Grey."

Nik ripped his arm from my grip, turning back to me. I drew away, unnerved by the fire in his eyes.

"The Tartoran crown isn't turning a blind eye to Grey! And they certainly wouldn't do so just because he was Calistan!"

"Are you sure?" I asked, gathering together my courage. "I've heard Princess Morgiana is doing a similar thing to Grey— traveling around and gathering young people to send to Calista. Clearly the Tartoran royalty are enamored with the new kingdom."

"You think," his voice dropped low, vibrating with danger, "that the princess is going around abducting children? And that the crown is allowing it to happen?"

"I..." I stumbled back even further. "No, I don't suppose the princess would be *abducting* people. I guess Grey has been a bit overenthusiastic."

Nik drew a deep breath. "Tartora has agreed to allow those with Calistan heritage to return to their homeland if they wish to do so. They're even allowing free immigration by those without Calistan heritage. But they have good reason for it. Tartora is gaining something in the exchange, even if no one bothered to explain it to the villagers of Tarin."

I straightened at the scorn in his voice. "But they explained it to you?"

He shrugged.

My eyes narrowed. "If you know so much, explain to me why the king hasn't stopped Grey, then."

"Because he doesn't know about him," Nik snapped.

"Why haven't you told him, then!"

He turned away from me. "You think the king of Tartora would listen to me? When I have enough evidence, I'll take it to the capital myself."

"Will you?" I asked, genuinely curious. "Are you sure you don't want to solve the problem single-handedly?" I hadn't received the impression he was someone interested in working as part of a team.

His shoulders stiffened slightly, and he didn't respond. I smiled with satisfaction. I'd read him correctly after all.

But a moment later I sighed. Whatever his motives, I had no hope of finding Miranda without Nik.

"You really believe the king is unaware of Grey?" I asked. "How is that possible when he's taking young people from all over?"

Nik turned back to me, the anger on his face replaced with sadness.

"You said Grey was stealing away our best and brightest young people, but it's not the best and brightest he's taking, is it?"

I stared at him, shaken by the question.

"If it was," he continued, "Grey would never have gotten away with it for so long. Instead, he targets the dissatisfied, the malcontents, the troublemakers. The ones who don't fit neatly into their communities and who the authorities could do without—the ones they sometimes privately wish would disappear."

"But that description doesn't fit Miranda at all!" I protested.

"No," he agreed. "Grey isn't as cautious in the villages because he thinks no one there matters. If he was more careful in the countryside, he might have even avoided leaving discontented rumors in his wake. But he caught the people's attention because his dismissal of them presses on an existing nerve. The countryside know they aren't valued equally, and now they think the crown doesn't even care if they all leave for Calista. We can be grateful, though. Grey's attitude shows his overconfidence, and that sort of confidence will eventually lead to a misstep. And that's when we're going to catch him."

"Are we just going to wait, then?" I asked.

He paused partway to the closed door. "We?"

I joined him, Ember at my heels. "Yes, obviously. I have to find Miranda, and even if I could somehow sneak her away, I can't just leave Grey free to continue abducting other people. I want to help gather enough evidence to convince the authorities."

"*We* aren't going to do anything," he growled. "I will be finding the necessary evidence and taking Grey down. The best thing you can do is stay out of my way."

I stalked around him, positioning myself between him and the door and giving him my best glare.

"You tested me yourself, so you know I'm a powerful healer. Are you really saying it wouldn't be helpful to have a healer with you?"

"That depends on the healer." He gave me a contemptuous look. "You can't even look after yourself, let alone anyone else. If I have to keep rescuing you, I won't get anywhere."

"You rescued me one time! The other times we were fighting each other. Think how much more effective we could be if we work together."

He shook his head and tried to brush past me, but I held my ground.

"Fine," I said, trying a different tack. "You might not want me helping you, but I'm not giving up on this. So you can either choose to work with me, or we can keep tripping over each other like we have been so far."

Nik stilled, his expression telling me my words had found their mark. I tried not to smile too broadly. While I did think I could be of help, I couldn't deny I would be gaining more than him in a partnership. Everything I knew about Grey so far had come from Nik, who had been tracking him far longer than me.

"Don't slow me down," he snapped, and I bit my lip, trying

to suppress my excitement. From Nik that was the closest thing I was going to get to enthusiastic agreement.

He held up his lantern and scanned the interior of the warehouse. The light wasn't enough to fully illuminate every corner, but it looked convincingly empty. If it hadn't been for Nik's arrival, my visit here would have been useless.

Nik must have concluded the same thing because he strode the rest of the way to the door and pulled it open. But instead of striding outside, he knelt in the open doorway. The door attempted to swing closed, banging against his hunched back, but he ignored it.

Splaying the fingers of his right hand against the packed dirt beneath us, he closed his eyes.

Seconds ticked by in silence and even Ember stepped forward to sniff at the ground next to his hand as if searching for what was holding his interest. My curiosity grew too great to be contained.

"What are you doing?" I asked, the words abrupt and loud in the empty space.

"I told you not to get in my way," he said through gritted teeth, not opening his eyes.

"You're the one in my way," I muttered. "You do know you're in the doorway, right?"

His eyes sprang open, and he straightened in one fluid movement, suddenly looming over me.

"I don't need or want a partner. If you insist on coming along, at the very least stay *silent.*"

I gulped and nodded, annoyed with my own compliance. But I wanted his cooperation, and I hadn't had the chance to prove myself yet. I should have stayed silent in the first place instead of provoking him.

"Can you explain now?" I asked in my best meek tone.

He eyed me suspiciously before sighing. "I'm tracking them.

When I came back here last night, they were gone, of course. But they hadn't managed to clear out the entire building."

"So they did it during the day?" I looked around the empty space. "Why didn't you watch for them and follow them when they came back for it?"

"I did," Nik growled, hesitating before adding, "But I have to sleep sometime."

"You missed them?" I stared at him, wondering why I was so shocked. Of course he needed to eat and sleep, like anyone else. A smug feeling crept over me. "Are you sure you can do everything by yourself?"

His eyes narrowed. "Naturally I had a backup plan."

"Communing with the dirt?" I quipped, but he cocked his head and gave me an arrogant look that was quickly becoming familiar.

"I know all about your ability," he said, "but you haven't even asked my affinity, have you?"

"I—" I stopped, realizing it was true. I knew he was powerful—his ability to test me had proved that—but in the chaos of our previous interactions, I'd never even considered his affinity.

"You're a plants mage?" I guessed.

His half smile seemed to confirm it, although he didn't say anything.

I frowned down at the dirt beneath us, trying to remember anything about the plants affinity that might be relevant. Both of my parents had it, but they didn't have mage-level strength. My mother's education plan had included more detailed descriptions of each of the affinities, but I couldn't recall anything of relevance.

"I know you're powerful," I said slowly. "So I'm sure you could bring all sorts of wondrous plants springing to life in the middle of this building, but I'm not sure how that would help us right now."

"Do you think that's the only thing plants mages can do?" He sounded contemptuous, but I refused to shrink back this time. He spoke as if I was looking down on his affinity, but nothing could be further than the truth.

I straightened, facing him defiantly. "People with a plants affinity are the backbone of this kingdom! Those plants they grow feed every person in Tartora from the poorest child to the king himself. And, as well as filling our bellies, those plants also clean our air, brighten our days, feed the animals, and preserve the land itself. Ensuring the health and growth of the kingdom's plant life isn't a minor thing."

Nik stared at me, for once bereft of speech. After a moment, he recovered himself enough to raise one eyebrow.

"Don't tell me I've found a healer who doesn't think healing is the pinnacle of the affinities?"

I turned away, pushing past him to exit the warehouse.

"What, nothing to say in defense of healing?" He needled as he followed me, Ember slipping between us.

"The relevant point is finding Grey," I said firmly. "Which leads me back to my original question. What exactly were you doing back there?"

Nik looked as if he didn't want to answer, but after a moment he relented.

"I stayed awake all night and most of the day, but I had to sleep for a few hours in the late afternoon. Your arrival woke me."

"My arrival? But not Grey's people carrying out bags and parcels and who knows what?"

He shrugged. "They must have come while I was in the deepest part of my sleep. The important thing is that they came recently and in a quieter part of the day. They probably timed it for dusk when their activities would be partially obscured. That means I still have a chance of tracking them through the ground."

My mouth dropped open. "Is that possible? I've never heard of such a thing! I know those with a plants affinity also share a connection with the earth itself, not just the things that grow in it, but that's..."

"Obviously the average person with a plants affinity couldn't do so."

"What about the average plants mage?" I raised an eyebrow as I waited for his response.

"I never said I was average." He smirked at me, looking far too pleased with himself.

When I just narrowed my eyes, he sighed again.

"I don't care what's normally done, I only care about getting the results I need. I had to come up with a new strategy after I lost Grey in Tarin thanks to a certain someone..." He gave me a significant look before continuing. "Have you heard of elements mages who can track people through the air—a bit like a dog following a scent?" He looked down at Ember with a half-smile. "Or a fox."

I nodded. I vaguely remembered my mother mentioning it in a long-ago lesson. It had only interested me because of the relation to animals.

"But you're not an elements mage," I said, and he stiffened, the muscles across his arms and shoulders tightening as he clenched his fists. Unsure what I'd said wrong, I hurried on. "Can you do the same thing through the earth?"

"I'm not so much using the earth itself as the network of roots within it," he said after a loaded pause. "I got the idea from...someone I know. He used the root network to send messages, and I worked out how to combine that idea with the tracking ability of an elements mage."

"You mean you came up with that idea yourself in the last few days? So you're the only one who can do it? That's brilliant!" The compliment slipped out before I thought to filter it.

His ego was already unnecessarily inflated without me further flattering him.

"It might only work because I'm plants cross elements," he said, his manner suggesting he was being drawn into speculation in spite of himself.

"You're cross influenced?" I asked, astonished. "And you have master-level power? That's really rare! You need to talk to my master. She would love to meet you. She's elements cross healing."

"She?" He stared down at me. "Your master is a woman? And she's elements cross healing?" He raised an eyebrow. "You're apprenticed to Master Amara?"

My mouth dropped open. "You know her? You know my master?"

Fear rushed through me as I remembered that I had been intending to keep them apart. I'd already been worried he might convince her to whisk me away—and that was before I found out they knew each other.

"Of course. I—" He started to speak before cutting off his words, a closed expression slamming over his face as if he realized he'd said too much. "Never mind. That doesn't matter. You said yourself that what matters is finding Grey. And the longer we stay here yapping, the older the trail gets."

"But..." I sighed and let it go. He was right about the trail and finding Grey. And what was I trying to achieve anyway? It's not like I wanted to push him into meeting Amara.

Nik eyed me suspiciously for a few moments, but when I stayed silent, he knelt once more, pressing his hand against the ground. When he stood again, he didn't speak, merely striding deeper into the alley in the opposite direction to the street.

I kept my curiosity inside, scrambling to follow him as he hurried toward the dead end. When we reached the wall, however, I realized it wasn't a dead end at all. The brick wall was broken by a simple door that gave access to whatever was on the other side.

Nik attempted to open it, but it remained stubbornly in place.

"It's locked," I said, disappointed. "Can we circle the building and find the spot from the other side?"

Nik gave me an amused look, purposely holding my eyes for several seconds before looking back toward the door. I followed his gaze and gasped.

The door no longer looked much like a door. The dead wood of its planks had somehow sprung back into life, the wood around the latch covered in so many green shoots that it resembled a plant more than part of a building. The lock itself had disappeared completely, the metal dropping free of the writhing wood.

"What? How?" I gaped at Nik.

"Plants mage, remember?" he murmured with a satisfied smile.

I nodded shakily, feeling every bit the ignorant apprentice. We'd been investigating together for mere minutes, but it was increasingly obvious why Nik had originally spurned my offer of help.

Pushing the door open, Nik ducked through. He didn't bother to hold it open behind him, and I barely caught it before it whacked me in the face. The small rudeness restored some of my shaken confidence. Seeing his power at work didn't change his annoying, arrogant personality.

Ember and I followed him through the door into a second alley. This one was much shorter than the previous one, however, opening almost immediately onto a broad street. The thoroughfare was well lit but almost deserted at this hour.

Nik stopped just before stepping out of the alley, kneeling again to feel the earth. When he stood, he turned right, and I followed without comment.

He led the way in the same manner through several turns. We were soon on back streets where the buildings crowded close together, in some cases looming over the street itself in a way that made me shiver. One or two of them looked old and decrepit enough that they might collapse on our heads.

Nik was unshaken, however, ignoring our surroundings, except to follow the trail only he could sense in the ground beneath us. And while I wouldn't have admitted it out loud, I took courage from his presence.

We eventually reached a building that might have been another warehouse, although it was smaller and more run-down than the previous one. It was in a much shabbier area of town, backing against the city wall.

Nik held out an arm to stop me. "This is where they went." He spoke quietly but with confidence.

I nodded, afraid to speak in case I attracted attention from someone inside. Scanning our surroundings, I noticed a pile of crates against the neighboring building. They appeared to be empty, most of them too splintered for use, and they would no doubt have been cleared away before now if they'd been left in a nicer area of the city. They would serve us well, though.

I pointed toward them, and Nik nodded. Before either of us could move, however, the door into the run-down warehouse began to open.

# FIFTEEN

Shock held me immobile, but Nik sprung into immediate movement. Grabbing me around the waist, he whisked me with him, pulling me behind the crates so quickly that I couldn't get my feet properly under me. I would have collapsed to the ground if he hadn't kept his arm around me, pressing me firmly to his side.

Ember seemed to understand Nik's intent because she didn't protest his hold this time, staying silent at our feet as Nik peered through the crates. Several people had appeared in the street and were milling in front of the door.

I willed them to move off, but they lingered. I couldn't see all of them clearly through the occasional gaps in the piled crates, but I thought I recognized the brute who had held me captive in my one encounter with Grey, as well as the other man who had been with him.

I twisted slightly within Nik's grasp, trying to get a clearer view. Was Grey himself with them? What about Miranda?

I couldn't see either of them, but my eyes fell on a different familiar face. I gasped at the sight of Serena in the streets of Ostaria, and Nik stiffened, his free hand clamping over my mouth.

I stilled, realizing my mistake. No one was rushing toward us, but several of them were looking in our direction. Their suspicious glances seemed too weighty for one stifled gasp. Had someone caught a glimpse of movement as they emerged onto the street?

"I'm telling you, I think someone's there," one of the men said, confirming my fears. "Can you see something behind those crates?"

Nik and I both froze, not even daring to breathe as we held our positions.

The man who had been beside Grey at our previous encounter peered toward us. From the way the others deferred to him, he appeared to be their leader, and I could see he was torn.

"Grey wants us back quickly, and we won't manage that if you're jumping at every shadow," he told the first speaker.

"It wasn't just a shadow!" the man protested. "And we should smash down those crates anyway. Anyone could be hiding there watching us."

"Still scared of that man from yesterday?" Serena asked in a scoffing voice. "The one in black?" She spoke tauntingly, as if she didn't take any threat seriously, but I caught the nerves in her gaze as she glanced at the crates.

"Who said anything about being scared?" the enormous one asked, weighing in for the first time. "I'm more worried about who's going to be expected to do the work. Are you going to be carting off crates, little girl?"

Serena turned her back in the characteristic, petulant gesture I remembered from Tarin. Thanks to her attitude I had never warmed to her—an attitude born of the relative strength of her seed compared to others in the town. Her sense of superiority had alienated her from more than just me, and that isolation had turned her into a perfect target for Grey.

I peered at her, noticing the slight shake in her hands, and the way she was trying to hide it. She might have brought her situation on herself, but I still felt stirrings of pity.

The large man was still eyeing the crates with distaste, but the leader seemed torn. He took a hesitant step in our direction, and I felt Nik's muscles tense. Was he preparing to draw his blade, or was he preparing to silently use his ability? Either way, I wanted to help, but I had no idea how.

Nik's hands dropped away from me, but before either of us could take any further action, movement exploded at our feet. Ember leaped into the middle of the pile of crates with a growl, and we could do nothing but duck down out of sight as the whole pile shuddered and shook.

High squeaks and hisses sounded from beneath the wood as several streaks of movement exploded from the bottom, racing past the group in front of the warehouse. They all jumped, obviously more unnerved than they'd been letting on.

After a moment of stunned silence, the leader gave a strained chuckle.

"I'll acknowledge it was more than shadows," he said to the concerned man. "But you must be jumpy if you're mistaking a nest of rats and a stalking cat for people. I imagine those crates provide a nice hunting ground for the local felines."

The whole group relaxed, apparently satisfied with the explanation and eager to return to their original task rather than clearing away abandoned rubbish. Within moments, they had all disappeared, heading toward the more populated part of the city.

"Should we follow them?" I asked once I'd regained my breath.

Nik shook his head. "They'll be on a supply mission, so there's nothing to be gained by that."

"Will they steal supplies?" I asked, wondering if that could be an avenue for gaining official attention.

Nik shook his head. "They won't do anything to draw negative attention to themselves. Not yet. You'll note they even took a couple of the youngsters to make the group less remarkable."

I sighed. "Sorry about making a noise. I recognized one of them from Tarin."

Nik looked down at me with an unreadable expression. "Your friend?"

"Sadly, no. It was another girl—one who appeared to leave willingly. But if Serena's here, that's a good sign that Miranda is too." I looked at the closed door of the warehouse, dropping my voice even lower. "Should we have a look inside?"

Nik hesitated, clearly wanting to say yes. But after a quick glance at me, he gave a decisive shake of his head.

"Didn't you see? One of them went back inside. Grey and whoever else is in there will be on alert now. They may even come out to investigate. We should go immediately. If they can't find any further evidence of our presence, they'll hopefully dismiss their concerns and remain here for now. We can come back tomorrow night."

I hesitated, examining his face. I had the distinct impression he would have considered going in anyway if I wasn't here. But he was right to be cautious. Apparently my presence was already doing him good—even if he didn't appreciate it.

I couldn't resist throwing him a cheeky grin as we hurried off in the opposite direction to that taken by Grey's people. "If you'd been on your own back there, they might have come investigating behind those crates and found you. Are you glad you have a partner now?"

Nik stalked forward, not even looking at me. "If I hadn't had to reveal my presence last time—thanks to you—they wouldn't have been on such high alert. And besides," he glanced down at Ember who trotted at my feet, "it wasn't you who saved us. I will concede that the fox, at least, is helpful."

I huffed, but his words distracted me.

"Do you think she went after those rats on purpose?" I asked. "Was she trying to distract those men and shield us?"

Nik frowned, his eyes lingering on her elegant form as she kept pace with us. "Foxes are intelligent, but I've never known one to act like she does. She seems devoted to you."

I bit my lip. "I've already had to do major healings on her several times. It's worrying me, actually. Her behavior is very unusual for a wild animal."

"Animals are always drawn to healers," he said. "Even before their power is activated, although the effect increases afterward. Healers' pets are always unusually devoted. It seems like your power has created a connection between the two of you. At the very least, it seems to have raised a strong protective instinct in her."

I reached down and scooped her up, holding her small body close in my arms.

"I just hope it doesn't get her killed."

"You're a healer, aren't you?" he said callously. "So don't let her die."

"It's not always that simple," I muttered, but I let the point drop since we'd reached familiar streets near the inn.

I stopped abruptly, making Ember look up.

"I know the way from here," I said to Nik.

He looked like he was going to protest, but after a moment he just shook his head and turned to stride away. I blinked after him in surprise before recovering enough to call after him.

"Farewell to you too."

He didn't even break stride.

"I'll see you tomorrow night," I added, and that made him falter.

After a moment he continued, however, not having turned back to me.

"Rude," I muttered as I watched him disappear into the night. "Even if it was you, Ember, and not me, we did still save him back there. If he can't manage a thank you, he could at least say goodbye."

Sighing, I hurried the rest of the way to the inn, not wanting to be scolded by Amara for staying out too late. Nik was no doubt hoping I wouldn't appear again, but I'd taken careful note of the route to the second warehouse and had every intention of returning.

---

I woke with my mind full of Nik and Grey and the brief glimpse I'd had of Serena. I had no interest in the day except to hope it passed quickly so night would fall again.

Amara, however, had other ideas. She dragged me out of bed with far too cheerful an expression.

"Don't worry," she said, misinterpreting my reluctance. "I meant what I said yesterday. I'm not going to drag you back to the hospital. We're going to try something different today. No illness or injury involved."

Despite my earlier disinterest, my curiosity rose at her words. The idea of using my power without the specter of the nausea was more appealing than I'd anticipated.

We ate a hearty breakfast in the main room of the inn, and to my surprise, Amara had Ember join us. The fox sat calmly on a cushion by my chair, accepting the admiring glances and comments of passersby, and even accepting choice scraps from the hands of her admirers.

"See," Amara said with an amused look. "The innkeeper's wife came around eventually—once she saw Ember isn't going to cause any trouble. She's more softhearted than she looks."

I wouldn't have believed it possible if I hadn't seen the woman sneaking Ember morsels of breakfast from her own hand, but I was relieved not to have to hide the fox in my cloak anymore.

When we ventured out into the streets, Ember stayed behind, happily curled in her box by the fire. The innkeeper had even promised to send someone up to check on her while we were gone.

True to Amara's word, we bypassed both the hospital and Clay's animal healing clinic. As we passed the latter, Amara spoke.

"You'll need to start studying anatomy soon, like Clay said. Thankfully you can learn it from books well enough, so you won't need a regular tutor. But I'll try to ensure we make regular visits to places like Ostaria that have experienced healers available."

"Do I need to start today?" I asked reluctantly. Just the thought of the books' contents made my stomach churn.

She shook her head. "No, I haven't even purchased the books yet. Clay will help me with that while we're here, since Ostaria is large enough to have a dedicated bookstore. But I want to wait before handing them over to you. Once you have the necessary control to keep your physical responses suppressed, you can start the reading. Otherwise I'm guessing you'll have the same problems you had in the hospital."

She gave me a questioning look, and I nodded fervently, full of relief. Once again, Amara had proven she had my best interests at heart.

"So where are we going today?" I asked, looking around with curiosity.

We'd reached the center of the city, an area I hadn't visited yet since my nighttime wanderings had taken me to the fringes.

"In small towns like Tarin, parents take their children to the local healing clinic for testing," she said. "Most such towns have only one healer of any significant power, and he or she is responsible for testing seeds as well as healing. But Ostaria has many healers, and they want to limit the number of children traipsing in and out of the hospital just for testing. So healers are rostered to make regular visits to the schools and offer testing there."

"Schools?" I asked. "Is Ostaria big enough to have more than one?"

Amara nodded. "I know in villages like Tarin, many children are taught by their parents, as you were. It's a practical option when many families live out on farms. But in the cities and even the larger towns, all children attend school. They aren't actually tested in class, of course, since their parents want to be present. Instead they put aside a room for the healers to use on the specified day and parents can book a time."

"Let me guess," I said. "One of the schools has a testing day today?"

Amara grinned. "As luck would have it, yes. It's a fairly junior healer rostered on today, so I don't know him, but he was more than happy to have an apprentice visit."

I suspected it was Amara herself he was more interested in meeting, but I kept quiet. He was willing for us to be present and that was all that mattered.

CHAPTER

# SIXTEEN

The school turned out to be a neat stone building, larger than the average house but smaller than the hospital. It had an enclosed yard full of children, most of whom were running in all directions.

As we approached, a woman stepped outside the building and rang a large bell. The children immediately stopped their play and raced over to form a ragged line, chattering loudly the whole time. The woman beamed at them, her motherly vibe making me smile. I would have enjoyed coming to a place like this every day.

A pang made my smile fall away. Every decision my father had made to keep me on the farm had taken on a new light now. Had he been afraid that if I spent more time in Tarin, I might find a solution to my problem?

We hung back as the children streamed inside, standing near a couple who pressed close together, looking anxious. When the end of the line passed them, they called to one of the children, and he broke off from the others to join them.

"Mother! Father! Is it nearly time?" He looked more excited than nervous, and the woman mustered a smile for him.

"As soon as the other children are settled, we'll go inside," she said. "I'm sure you'll get an excellent result."

They had to be the first family on the list for the day's testing. I turned to confirm it with Amara and noticed someone at the very end of the line of children. The boy was gazing wistfully at the small family grouping, looking reluctant to go inside and leave his friend.

When the child due for testing caught sight of him, he smiled broadly and waved for the other boy to go inside with the others.

"I'll come to class as soon as I've been tested," he called to his friend, thrusting his chest forward proudly. "And I'll tell you all about my awesome seed."

The other boy grinned and hurried toward the doors, but the father grabbed at his son's arm, frowning.

"Why are you talking to him?" he asked. "I thought we told you not to have anything to do with him. A good-for-nothing like that—without even parents to set him straight—will just drag you down. You'll see once you've been tested. You're worth far more than a street child like that."

I stiffened, my eyes flying back to the other boy, hoping he hadn't heard. He was just disappearing inside the building, but from the rigid set of his back, I suspected he'd caught every word.

My heart sank as I thought of how happy he'd been for his friend only a moment ago. Had the second boy already been tested and found to have a weak seed? Was that why the other father despised him so much? Surely it couldn't purely be because the lad was an orphan?

Amara sighed quietly, drawing my eye. She looked as sad as I felt.

"The crown ensures every Tartoran gets an education," she said softly, "but there's only so much they can do to combat prejudice."

Anger welled inside me. "Everyone talks about our seeds like they're a great leveling force, allowing those born to poverty and obscurity to rise as high as the Triumvirate itself. But our seeds are still just an accident of birth. It's no more that child's fault that he has a weak seed than that he has no parents."

Amara nodded. "Why do you think I choose to be a traveling master rather than living in luxury in the capital? Those of us with powerful seeds owe a debt of service to the rest of the kingdom. We were given more at birth, so we must give more back as well."

Tears sprung to my eyes, fueled by an unexpected rush of gratitude. My own father had kept me trapped, but Amara—a stranger to me—had chosen to seek me out and set me free. She was the opposite of the mages he had taught me about—spending her life helping those who lived far from the glamour of the capital.

I couldn't even blame my father's attitude on his poverty and disadvantage. My mother had lived the same life as him, but she had still chosen to love me selflessly—even if that meant letting me go. My uncle might have been the one to commit the first wrong, but my father had chosen to let those wounds fester until they stunted us both. That decision hadn't harmed my uncle, who knew nothing about it—it had harmed my father and ultimately me, someone he claimed to love.

I blinked furiously to fight back the tears. My anger with my father was still fresh, and it was hard to reconcile with the images of my childhood that kept resurfacing. I could feel my father, sturdy and solid beneath me, as he hoisted five-year-old me onto his shoulders. I could hear his voice telling me that everything I could see was mine, even the sky itself—that here, on this dependable land, I would always have a home.

I wanted to lash out at the father in front of me. To tell him that his love for his own child wasn't enough to justify his attitude toward the boy's friend. Did he want to poison his son with his own narrow-mindedness? Couldn't he see the damage he was doing?

The words remained inside, barely restrained. Regardless of this stranger's behavior, he wasn't the real target of my anger, and it wasn't my place to harangue him.

"Come on," Amara said softly, not mentioning the moisture in my eyes. "Whatever we think of those parents, that boy still deserves to be tested just like every other child. We can't let our feelings get in the way of the job we're here to do."

"Wait, *we're* here to do?" I asked, shock replacing the messier emotions swirling through me. "I thought we were just here to watch the local healer?"

"We're here for you to learn, and what better way is there than by doing?" Amara asked in a suspiciously prim tone.

I groaned, my earlier indignation entirely swallowed by my anxiety. "What if my wall gets in the way?"

"You'll find a way around it," Amara said calmly. "I'm sure of it."

I swallowed, trying not to look as terrified as I felt. I only hoped she was right.

"Oh, you're already here!" A young man rushed into the school yard, stopping beside us and bowing to Amara. "I'm running a bit late."

I hid a smile at his distracted air. He had the feel of someone who was late a lot.

"I'm Bjorn." He stuck out his hand toward me, before noticeably starting and pulling it back. "Oh, sorry! I nearly forgot you're a new apprentice. You won't want to touch anyone."

"I'm Delphine," I managed while Amara grinned openly at us.

"And you must be Master Amara, of course." Bjorn bowed to

her again. "It's an honor to meet you. I've heard a lot about you."

"Not from Clay, I hope," she said with a laugh, and Bjorn laughed as well, ushering us ahead of him into the school.

As we stepped inside, I glanced back and saw the small family still lingering outside, their curious gazes fastened on the three of us. The interested look in their eyes made me wonder if Bjorn's greeting had been more calculated than it appeared. After his respectful, almost awed, reception of Amara, I doubted they would object to our presence at their child's testing. Whether they would be equally calm about a new apprentice doing the actual testing remained to be seen.

The room set aside for our use was small but painted in a bright, cheerful yellow and with a small vase of flowers on the large windowsill. Bjorn busied himself bringing in two more chairs so that six chairs stood in a rough circle.

"The testing itself is a simple matter, of course," he said. "But many parents are anxious and full of questions before and after. We leave plenty of time for each testing so that we don't have to hurry anyone along."

"A nice day off for you healers." Amara winked.

He laughed. "That entirely depends on how many disappointed parents we get. Last time I was here, one of the children had a different affinity from both of her parents and a lower strength than they'd expected as well. Her mother burst into tears as soon as I announced the results, and her father kept insisting I'd made a mistake and demanding I call for a more experienced healer to retest her."

I winced, although he seemed to find the memory more amusing than traumatic. If a parent responded to a fully quali-fied healer that way, what would they say to a mere apprentice?

Bjorn caught my expression. "Don't worry, Delphine. If anyone causes trouble with you, we'll just dazzle them with Master Amara's qualifications."

She grinned. "I may have an elements seed, but I'd like to see any parent tell me they need a more experienced mage in my place."

Bjorn chuckled. "I'd enjoy seeing them try. But thankfully the vast majority of parents are reasonable, and most children test according to expectations."

"Is it really so unusual to get a surprise?" I asked, remembering my own testing. The healer had been shocked by my seed, but I had always imagined it was a result of his inexperience.

"It's unusual for strength, at least," Bjorn said. "Affinities are harder to predict from parentage since everyone has all three in their family background somewhere. But even so, there's still a strong correlation between parents and children. And even for those who diverge, it's not usually a surprise to their families since they'll have seen hints of it already. Even the youngest healer children are usually good nurses, for instance, and they're always drawn to animals. And elements toddlers love to wander out into storms. It gives their poor parents heart attacks if they're not elements themselves." He chuckled. "My younger sister was like that. Most of us in my family are healers, but she's elements."

Amara smiled reminiscently. "I remember being fascinated by storms as a youngster. The bigger, the better."

I shivered. "That sounds horrible. I like to be curled up safely inside when it starts thundering."

Amara tilted her head, looking at me closely. "*Does* it sound so horrible? Take a moment to really think about it."

I frowned. My initial instinct was to insist that I knew myself, but it was clear Amara was giving a lesson of some sort, so I obeyed. To my surprise, I couldn't seem to remember what had sent me scurrying inside in the past. Just thinking about the crackle of electricity in the air was exhilarating. Why had I always hidden from storms in the past?

Bjorn looked from my arrested expression to Amara's amused one, and then back again, curiosity in his gaze.

"We've had a rather action-packed beginning to Delphine's apprenticeship," Amara told him. "She hasn't had a chance to think about what it means to have an elements influencer." She turned to me. "You still have a healing seed—nothing can change that. But you're not just a straight healer now. You're healing cross elements, and as you grow in your ability, you'll discover all sorts of ways in which the lingering effect of my power has influenced yours."

"Like a plants mage who can track someone through the ground," I whispered to myself.

"What?" Amara's brow creased, and I bit my lip. I hadn't meant to speak aloud.

Thankfully a knock at the door saved me from having to answer. As Bjorn stood up to usher in the boy and his parents, I mentally kicked myself. I needed to be more careful.

The parents responded to Bjorn's introductions with respect, showing Amara the same deference they'd witnessed Bjorn showing her in the yard.

"As you would no doubt be aware," Bjorn said, "we often have apprentices here in the testing rooms. But we're honored today to be joined by the apprentice of Master Amara, who is one of the youngest masters in generations."

I noticed he carefully avoided mentioning her affinity. She didn't correct the omission as she gracefully received a second round of even more deferential greetings from the two parents.

The boy in question looked a lot less interested in our identities, finding it hard to sit still on his assigned seat. As he bounced up and down, I smiled at him. From what I'd seen outside, he was confident in his results and eager to get back to his classroom so he could boast to his friends.

"I'm sure he has an elements affinity like me." The father clapped his son on the back, a proud look in his eye. "My father has one, too, as did his father before him. I'll be inheriting the family smithy soon, and of course I'll take my son on as my apprentice when he reaches age."

"Unless he's even stronger than you," the mother said with a hint of excitement. She turned to Bjorn. "I'm sure he doesn't have a plants seed like me—he's far too attracted to fire." She shuddered dramatically. "But he could be stronger than either of us, couldn't he?"

"It is certainly possible," Bjorn said diplomatically, although I could read on his face he didn't expect it.

"It would, of course, be an honor to send our son off to the Guild to become a mage," the father said with a glance at Amara. "But a son to inherit the forge after me is all I ask for. As long as he's strong enough to discern pure metals from tainted ones, to keep the furnace at the right temperature, and to keep himself safe from burns, I'll be happy."

I got the distinct impression he would prefer his son wasn't too strong. While a mage son would bring honor to the family, he would never run a smithy in Ostaria. Anger flashed through me as I once again saw my own father in this man.

I drew in a slow breath as I fought the feeling down. This man wasn't my father, and he had already stated he would send the boy to the Guild if he was strong enough. It was hardly a crime for him to want to train his son himself, or to want to pass on the family business.

If I could extend understanding to this man, was I being unfair in blaming my father for doing a similar thing? Was he really so unjustified in wanting to keep me around?

Not in wanting, I realized with a swell of sadness. I didn't blame my father for wanting me to stay, I blamed him for taking away my choice. And more than that, for doing it in a way that left me bound and weak. If he had succeeded, I might have lived my whole life without ever having access to a central part of me.

That would not be this boy's fate, regardless of his results today, and that was the essential difference. One way or another, he would have access to his full self, and today was the first step toward that future.

Determination filled me. Everyone thought I could do this testing, so I was going to believe in myself too. I glanced at Bjorn, ready and willing to start but unsure what was actually involved.

"Don't worry," Bjorn said to the boy in a cheerful voice. "It doesn't hurt at all. In fact, you won't feel a thing. You're lucky because you're going to be tested twice. Apprentice Delphine will test you and so will I."

Relief filled me. Despite my sudden confidence, I preferred knowing my findings would be backed up by someone more experienced. And from the expression on her face, the boy's mother felt a similar relief. I smiled at her, and she smiled tentatively back.

Bjorn turned to me with an encouraging nod. "You go first."

I glanced at Amara, still unsure how I should go about the testing.

She leaned close enough to speak quietly into my ear. "Take down your wall first. You're not in physical contact with anyone, and no one here is injured, so it shouldn't be too overwhelming. For the actual testing, you'll need to touch the boy, but when you do, try to focus on his seed and don't get caught up with his other systems."

I gulped, unsure how I was supposed to do that. But the boy was already holding out his arm obediently, so I couldn't delay any further.

Pushing past my natural reluctance, I tore down a section of my wall, bracing for the inundating wave of sensation. It wasn't as bad as I'd feared, however. Amara had been right.

Had I already started to become desensitized from exposure, as Clay had predicted? The six healthy bodies in the room felt less overwhelming than my parents' presence had back on the farm.

Slowly I reached out my hand and placed it lightly on the boy's forearm. Immediately my awareness of everyone else dimmed to almost nothing as my power surged into the boy's body, encompassing every part of him.

The rush of blood through his veins and the pumping of his heart and lungs pulsed through me. But when my stomach clenched in response, my head spinning, I sent part of my power breezing through my own body, blowing the sensations away.

My stomach settled and my mind cleared in the wake of my power. Relieved, I smiled and focused back on the boy. Carefully not thinking about his heart or lungs, I looked instead for something inside him that wasn't linked to a physical organ.

Now that I was free of other distractions, I sensed it almost immediately. Deep inside the boy, something coiled, its sleeping power calling to me. I instinctively recognized the feeling of heat and wind and crackling lightning.

"Elements," I said, surprising myself with my certainty. "He has an elements seed as you predicted."

Both parents and the boy himself smiled, as did Bjorn. His encouraging expression made me look down, noticing for the first time that his hand also rested lightly on the boy's outstretched arm. The healer clearly wasn't waiting for my assessment before doing his own testing, he was just keeping quiet to give me a chance to speak first.

A wave of relief washed over me. Bjorn and Amara must have discussed it ahead of time, and he knew how inexperienced I was. He was already in contact, ready to use his power to protect the boy if my control slipped.

Bolstered by the realization that I had back up, I considered the boy's seed again. It was surprisingly easy to sense his affinity, but how did I measure his strength? And how did I communicate something so unquantifiable to his parents? I tried to remember the wording the Tarin healer had used when testing me, but I couldn't recall the details. He'd been too excited, and I'd been too shocked to take note.

I had no choice but to betray my ignorance in front of the family. I looked across at Bjorn. "How do I tell how strong he is?"

Bjorn rubbed the back of his neck with his free hand. "That's a little difficult to explain. It basically comes down to experience and exposure to enough seeds. That's why apprentices do lots of testing in their two years. After a while you start to get a feel for it."

"That is most unhelpful," Amara said disapprovingly. "Surely you can tell her something."

Bjorn thought for a moment. "You felt the seed easily," he said eventually. "From there it's just a matter of how strongly you sense the affinity coming from it. Once you've felt a few different seeds, you'll be able to judge the difference."

"That's all very well," the father said abruptly. "But what about my son? Surely one of you can tell us his strength?"

"He's of middle strength as a non-mage," Bjorn said with a broad smile. "Likely similar to your own strength, I imagine— and certainly sufficient for the blacksmith tasks you mentioned. You need have no hesitation about activating him yourself when the time comes."

"Middle strength!" his mother exclaimed in delight, pulling him into a hug.

His father beamed, only slightly less enthusiastic at the news.

"I was a little worried he might be weak like me," the mother confessed quietly to Amara and me as the father clapped his boy on the shoulder. "But everything is perfect now."

I smiled back at her, pleased that my first attempt at testing had gone so smoothly. If only every family was as happy with the results their children received.

Unlike the long questioning session Bjorn had described, the family moved out of the room quickly, leaving us to discuss the matter without them. I felt I'd been of no help at all, but both Amara and Bjorn praised my efforts.

"How could you possibly tell the strength when you have nothing to compare it against?" Bjorn asked. "And you can't look at the strength of those already activated for comparison either. Unlike me, you might have the strength for it, but it would be a major breach of etiquette."

"Goodness, yes, don't do anything of the kind, Delphine," Amara commanded. "You'll face enough scrutiny given your unconventional apprenticeship without offending people into the bargain."

"Come now, surely that's an exaggeration," Bjorn protested. "I'll admit news that you've taken an apprentice has generated a fair bit of interest and excitement among the mages in Ostaria. But I haven't heard anyone say anything negative."

Amara smiled. "That's because mages willing to make a home outside the capital are already more broad-minded than their fellows who stay welded to the Guild. Why do you think I prefer to live my life out here?"

Bjorn snorted. "You might be right on that point. But does that mean you're planning to take Delphine to the Guild to undergo official scrutiny?"

I stiffened at the suggestion. Amara hadn't mentioned anything like that.

"Not imminently," she said. "But I imagine our travels will take us through the capital at some point. If Delphine is going to be accepted, then Master Colton will need to examine her, at least."

I gulped. "I really don't care that much about being accepted."

Bjorn and Amara both chuckled.

"Don't let Amara prejudice you," Bjorn said. "The Guild isn't such a terrible place. And it's become even more lively since the exchange with Calista." When I gave him a questioning look, he added, "We're training some of their young mages in preparation for founding a new Calistan Mages' Guild. So our Guild is bursting with young people right now."

"I've heard rumors about that," Amara said. "Maybe I really will find it a changed place."

"Excuse me?" A nervous voice from the open doorway made us all look up.

The next appointment wasn't for some time, but the family had obviously arrived early and noticed we were already alone.

Bjorn ushered them in, and we went through the same process as with the previous child. It was a girl being tested this time, and she looked utterly terrified.

Bjorn was gentle in his manner with her, explaining the process patiently before asking her to hold out her arm. When she finally did, I rested my fingers on it as lightly as possible before sending my power into her.

It was harder to find her seed than it had been with the boy. I had thought experience would make it easier, but apparently my one success had made me cocky. I did eventually manage to locate a sense deep inside her that reminded me of my farm back home—something warm and green and growing.

Bjorn had also connected with her, but this time he didn't wait for me to speak first. Focusing fully on the family, he spoke in a sympathetic tone as he explained that the girl had a very weak plants seed.

Both parents were clearly disappointed but remained subdued, neither of them demanding a retest. The father asked a few questions about what sort of prospects there might be for his daughter while the mother struggled to contain the silent tears streaming down her cheeks.

I focused on the girl, who hadn't lifted her head since her testing.

"Do you like plants?" I asked, using the same voice I used when meeting new farm animals for the first time.

She didn't lift her head but managed a slight nod.

"I'm not surprised," I said. "I'm a healer, and I've always loved animals."

She looked up at that, frowning. "But I thought they said you were strong. I'm weak."

Her head immediately dipped again, as if she was startled by her own voice.

"That's true," I said. "But weak or strong, we both have an affinity. Since yours is with plants, that means you have a connection with the ground and with growing things. I grew up on a farm, you know, and I always wished I had a plants affinity."

She looked up again at that, interest in her eyes.

"Even though I didn't have any plants power at all, I was still able to help my parents a lot," I continued. "There's plenty to be done on a farm, even if all you have are your own two hands. I'm sure you could find work on one, regardless of your strength."

"I'd love to live on a farm," she said wistfully. "There aren't enough living things in the city."

Her mother straightened at her daughter's words, the tears stopping as she gave her husband a defiant look.

"And why shouldn't she! My brother has a farm, and he's always complaining about needing extra hands. Now that we know the truth of her situation, there's no reason to hold out for something better."

The husband threw his wife a look, but on meeting the steely determination in her eyes, he sighed and nodded.

A broad smile immediately transformed the girl's face.

"Really?" she asked. "I can go to uncle's farm?"

Her mother laughed. "Not immediately, child. You've only just started school this year! But when you're older. Your uncle might even take on your apprenticeship himself. I'm sure there's something he could teach you, even if you only have a touch of power like me." She sighed. "If you'd been elements, I would have activated you myself, of course. There are plenty of roles in the city for those with an elements affinity, even if it's not a strong one."

The mother escorted her daughter out of the room, having now launched into a lecture on the need to focus in school, and the father trailed out behind them. I sat back in my chair with a sigh. That had nearly been a disaster.

"Well done, Delphine," Amara said.

I looked up and met her eyes, flushing at her approving look.

"I can see you have a natural knack for connecting with the children," Bjorn agreed. "Some healers don't, and no amount of practice helps. They're the ones who always hate being rostered on for this job."

The next family had a boy whose healing seed was even easier to identify than the first boy's had been. Bjorn declared him to be of high non-mage strength, leading to great excitement from his parents.

They spent nearly the whole allotted hour asking questions of Bjorn and trying to ascertain their son's potential future options. By the time they left, I was exhausted—although I hadn't had to answer any of their questions myself—and more than ready to break for lunch.

# SEVENTEEN

"That one was so much easier," I said as we sat outside in the sun to eat our packed meal of bread and cheese. "I struggled with the girl."

"That's because she had a plants seed," Bjorn said around a large mouthful. "And she was also weak. That's the worst combination for you."

"Why does it matter what her affinity is?" I asked when my own mouth was empty.

"You're healing cross elements." Amara cut Bjorn off before he could speak again with a full mouth. "So you have a connection to both those affinities. But the power connected to plants is totally foreign to you. And since a weak seed is harder to sense in general, a plants seed is doubly so in your case."

"Are you cross-influenced?" I asked Bjorn.

He chuckled. "I'm a good Guild boy, not a rebel like Amara here. I only just had enough strength to qualify as a mage, so I was eager to make the most of it."

"So do you find it hard to identify elements and plants seeds, then?"

He shrugged. "It's harder than with a healing seed, but I've tested enough children now that I can identify anything easily enough. You'll be the same soon."

Excited chatter and laughs rang out as the doors of the school building opened and children flooded into the yard. We stayed in place against the building wall, watching them as they began to eat and play.

I smiled to see the delight they had in the spring sunshine and the company of their friends. Most of them would have been tested in their first year of schooling, but none of them were old enough for activation yet. What seeds hid inside them?

Without consciously meaning to do so, my words sparked my power. Before I realized I was reaching out, I had connected with one of the girls playing hopscotch close by.

Her elements seed sang to me, crackling with lightning. It was stronger and easier to sense than the blacksmith's boy's had been. Was that because of my increase in experience?

My power reached for the girl hopping just behind her. She had a healing seed buried inside, its power calling in kinship to my own. But despite the familiarity of her seed, it was definitely harder to sense than her companion's.

So it hadn't just been an increase in my experience, then. The difference was in the girls' strength. This was what Bjorn had described when he talked about needing comparison to recognize the level of strength.

I was reaching for the next closest child, eager to compare their seed as well, when I realized what I was doing. I gasped, attracting both Bjorn and Amara's attention.

"Is something wrong?" Amara asked.

"I thought healers needed physical contact," I said breathlessly. "So how did I just test those girls over there?" I pointed to them. "I didn't plan to do it, I was just thinking about their seeds, and the next thing I knew, I connected to them."

Bjorn's eyebrows shot up, and Amara turned to him, looking confused.

"Do you know what she's talking about? I also thought healers needed physical contact to test seeds."

He put his bread down. "Actually it's a little more complicated than that." He paused, looking at me. "You really tested them from over here?"

I nodded. "Was that wrong of me? It's not like testing another mage, is it?"

He laughed. "No, don't worry, no one's coming after you with pitchforks. Testing children's seeds is unexceptionable—as long as their parents have already brought them for testing. It might be a little rude to do it to a very young child who hasn't had their seed assessed yet, but those girls would have been tested years ago."

"Did you test them?" I asked. "Does the one on the left have a strong elements seed and the one on the right a weak healing seed?"

Bjorn squinted at them. "It wasn't me. I only joined the roster for this school at the start of the year, so I haven't tested anyone that old. And I rarely remember which seeds belong to which children, anyway."

"Can you check them now, then?" I asked. "I want to know if I got it right."

Bjorn shook his head, although a smile lingered around his mouth. "I can't tell from this distance."

"You can't?" I frowned across the school yard. "But it wasn't hard."

Amara burst into laughter. "Please remember you're my apprentice and anything you say or do will reflect on me. So don't go shaming your elders, please."

Bjorn grinned. "Since the only mages you've really interacted with have been Master Amara and Master Clay, I'll forgive you. But please remember that most of us don't have your strength."

I flushed, stammering out an apology. "I'm so sorry. I wasn't thinking."

"Please always think in the future," Amara said, but her eyes were still laughing.

"In answer to your question about physical contact," Bjorn said, "even the strongest healers need physical contact to actually change anything in someone's body. But as you know, a mage can sense certain things about people and animals from a distance. For the strongest mages, that includes testing children's seeds. But you likely haven't heard of it, Amara, because us healers are creatures of habit. Since we train to use our ability through physical touch, most of us prefer to use it wherever possible, even if it isn't strictly necessary."

I shuddered. I felt the exact opposite. I was most comfortable with those parts of my ability that I could use without physical touch. I had only tested those two girls so instinctively because I hadn't had to touch them to do it.

"Just because something is usually done a certain way is not a reason you have to do it that way, too," Amara told me firmly. "If you can test children without needing physical contact, by all means, do so."

"There's certainly no issue with it," Bjorn said. "Although you may want to experiment with both approaches to see if you notice any difference. It's possible that being in contact will give you more detail."

A loud cry followed by an even louder cheer pulled my attention to a tree on the far side of the yard. The blacksmith's son from earlier had climbed halfway up the trunk, trying to keep pace with his friend. I recognized the other boy as the one who had been labeled an orphan by the blacksmith. Apparently the son had defied his father's orders and was continuing to play with his friend.

"What about that boy?" I pointed at the second boy who had now reached the top branches of the tree. "I don't suppose you know about his seed?"

Bjorn peered in the direction of my pointing finger. "I don't recognize him. Why?"

I shrugged. "I just wondered." I didn't want to go into the conversation I'd overheard that morning, but I couldn't shake a lingering sadness for the boy, who likely had a weak seed.

"The boy we tested this morning was old for testing," Bjorn said. "He must have been late to start school. So his friend's parents probably brought him for testing last year."

I frowned. "But he doesn't have any parents."

Bjorn's face fell. "An orphan, is he? How tragic." He picked his bread back up and resumed eating. "Sometimes guardians aren't as diligent about bringing children in for testing. Eventually a teacher will notice and book him in themselves if necessary."

I stood up, unable to let it go so easily. If this boy lacked conscientious guardians, he was already at a disadvantage. Why should he wait to identify his seed?

I walked to the foot of the tree, trying to peer up through the leaves. I couldn't see much, so I called for the boys to come down. They both slid down so fast, I suspected they weren't supposed to be climbing in the first place.

When they finally stood in front of me, their guilty expressions confirmed it. But a moment later, the expression on the face of the blacksmith's son cleared as he recognized me.

"You're the healer!" He nudged his friend. "The one I told you about. She's a master!"

Both boys stared at me with awed faces, and I laughed. "Actually I'm an apprentice. My master is sitting over there." I pointed back to Amara. "Congratulations on your result," I added to the boy who'd spoken.

He swelled with pride, nudging his friend again, and I turned to the second boy.

"What about you?" I asked. "What's your affinity?"

He had been gazing at me curiously, but at my words he looked down at the ground and scuffed his toe in the dirt.

"He hasn't been tested," his friend said for him. "He never had an appointment."

"Would you like me to test you now?" I asked.

The boy's head sprang back up, his eyes wide. "Would you really? Right here?"

I smiled. "It's an easy thing to do. And it doesn't hurt or anything."

"I'm not worried about that," he said with a confidence that made me believe his words.

I reached out with my power, slipping easily through the cracks I had made earlier in my wall. As soon as I connected with him, I felt his seed. It pulsed in the middle of him, a warm and friendly presence.

I pulled back out, finished with my test, although the boy didn't know anything had happened.

I turned back toward the two I'd left behind. "Bjorn," I called, waving for him to join me. "Could you come over here?"

"Is there something wrong?" the boy asked, alarmed.

I shook my head. "Not at all. You have a healing seed, I'm sure of that much. And I think..." I let my words trail off. "I just want to confirm something before I say any more. I'm only an apprentice, so I'm new at this."

The two boys exchanged wide-eyed looks as Bjorn and Amara both crossed the yard.

"It turns out he hadn't been tested," I said to them both. "So I just had a look, and I think..." I turned to Bjorn. "Can you check for me? I'm sure he has a healing seed, but—"

Bjorn reached out a hand, and the boy obediently placed his

own in it. Bjorn's eyebrows rose and he whistled. "Well, that's unexpected."

"What is it?" his friend asked. "Is there something wrong with him?"

"Far from it," Bjorn said. "Young man, you have a healing seed of medium non-mage strength." He glanced at the other boy. "It's stronger than your friend's here."

"Medium strength?" both boys echoed in unison.

"Wait until Father hears that," the blacksmith's son crowed. "He was so sure you had a weak seed like your parents, but you're stronger than me!" He didn't seem in the least upset about being surpassed by his friend. "I'm always telling him he's wrong about you." He turned to Bjorn. "Does that mean he'll work at the hospital, like you?"

Bjorn looked at the other boy. "Would you like to? You're strong enough that there's every chance you'd be accepted for an apprenticeship at the hospital. We take on people of a variety of strengths."

The boy slowly shook his head, looking dazed. "Actually, I've always wanted to work with animals."

"Finding an animal-focused apprenticeship should be equally feasible," Bjorn said. "You can talk to one of the animal healing clinics, or even one of the larger farms. There's no rush, since you're a long way off seventeen."

I frowned, looking at the boy. He might be a long way from activation, but what was his life like now? Did he need somewhere to call home?

"How do you feel about horses?" I asked.

The boy's eyes lit up. "I sometimes hold the reins for people who need to step into a shop. Some of them will give me a coin for the task, but I do it happily even if they don't."

"What are you thinking?" Amara asked, but I shook my head. I didn't want to speak up in front of the children when nothing was confirmed.

The afternoon flew past as I tested more children—this time trying it first without physical contact and then with. I could see why most mages preferred contact—it made everything sharper and more focused. But that was the exact reason I disliked it.

By the time we returned to the inn, I was exhausted. But when we entered the yard, I swerved toward the stables instead of the main building. I thought Amara would protest or question me, but she just followed silently.

Inside the dim aisle, I greeted those horses who had their heads over the half walls of their stalls. Stopping to rub each nose, I murmured praise, understanding the young student's interest in the animals. They were intelligent, affectionate, and useful. Seeing the horses here made me miss the faithful ones I had left behind on my parents' farm.

But conscious of Amara's silent presence, I limited my time with each horse, making my way toward the tack room halfway down the length of the stables. Sticking my head inside, I found an older man polishing a saddle.

He nodded his head but offered no other greeting and made no attempt to rise. I smiled at this sign that he didn't care about rank or station.

"I don't suppose you have need of any youngsters to fetch and carry for you?" I asked.

He stopped polishing and leaned back in his seat, looking at me speculatively. "Fetch and carry? I can't imagine you're interested in such a thing, miss."

I laughed. "No, not me. I mean a much younger child. Maybe seven or so?"

The man scratched his chin. "That depends."

"He has a healing seed of medium to high strength and a strong affection for horses." I hesitated. "And he's an orphan."

"Ah." The man sat forward again and resumed his polishing. "So that's the way of it."

My heart sank.

"Tell him to come see me, and I'll size him up."

"Really?" I stared at him, wondering if I'd somehow misunderstood.

He looked up and raised an eyebrow. "Send him round. I'll make up me mind once I see him."

"Thank you!" I wanted to say more, but I didn't think it would be welcome, so I beat a hasty retreat instead.

Amara was waiting for me with raised eyebrows.

"I know." I gave her a guilty look. "I'm interfering."

"Don't expect a reprimand from me for that." She chuckled. "You'll soon learn I have a terrible reputation as a busybody."

"I find that hard to believe. Everyone seems to love you."

"Not everyone." She grinned. "And, of course, most people don't use the term *busybody* for a master mage. But one or two may have told me I like to stick my nose where it doesn't belong."

I laughed. "Did those people live at the Guild?"

"Maybe." She put an arm around my shoulders and guided me toward the inn door. "Come on. Let's get something warm in your belly. You did a good job on your first proper day, apprentice of mine. A very good job."

# EIGHTEEN

I would have liked to fall straight into bed after the evening meal, but I knew Nik would happily investigate Grey without me. And knowing him, he wouldn't tell me what he'd found either. If I missed my chance to meet him tonight, I might not be able to find him again at all.

At least Ember had the energy I lacked, dancing by the door in her eagerness to be gone. Amara smiled at sight of her and didn't question my departure, probably thinking I was taking the fox out to stretch her legs.

As I exited the inn, I couldn't shake my guilt at not telling Amara what I was doing. But hopefully Nik and I would find the evidence we needed that night, and then I could tell Amara everything and ask her to take me to the relevant authorities.

My worry over finding my way back to the abandoned warehouse proved groundless. I remembered the route more easily than I'd expected. And even Ember seemed to know where we were going, growing more and more restless the closer we got, as if she had no desire to return.

Eventually I scooped her up, afraid she might run off and be lost in the night. As soon as I felt her solid warmth against my chest, I realized I had picked her up for my sake as much as hers. I was nervous and her presence was reassuring, even if she was just one small fox.

When I neared the warehouse, I slowed, eventually sliding along the wall of the closest building, doing my best to keep to the shadows. There didn't appear to be anyone around to see me, however, and the door was firmly closed.

I reached out with my power, thinking to count how many people were inside and to check whether any of them were near the door.

I counted one in close proximity to the front of the warehouse and pushed further on, looking for the others. I found nothing, however. I frowned. Had something happened to affect my range? Why couldn't I sense them?

And where was Nik? Had he come earlier—during the day even? Was he trying to avoid me? Panic rose inside me, a fizzy feeling that made it hard to keep still.

How long should I wait for him? If Grey had gone out leaving only one guard behind, it was an unexpected opportunity. Did I need to take a look inside the warehouse on my own?

My arms tightened around Ember, and she squirmed in protest. I forced myself to take a deep breath, pushing the panic down. This wasn't the time to do anything rash.

While I was still reassuring myself, the door swung open so violently it smashed against the wall. I jumped, nearly colliding with the pile of crates. I managed to save myself before making contact, but a small squeak slipped out.

Footsteps sounded, and Nik appeared. The two of us stood for a moment, staring at each other before he sighed.

"I should have known it was you," he said.

"Was the person in the warehouse you?" I gasped, suddenly hit with a foolish fear. Had I misjudged the whole situation? Was it all a set up, and Nik was actually working with Grey?

Nik's eyes narrowed, and he held up a hand. "Stop."

"Stop what?" I eyed him warily.

"Stop whatever nonsense is going on in your head right now."

I flushed, hoping the meager moonlight wasn't bright enough to reveal my embarrassment.

"I don't know what you're talking about. Although I would like to know what you found in there. Where are Grey and his followers?"

"They're gone."

"All of them?" I frowned. "Well, shouldn't we—" I broke off abruptly. "Wait. What do you mean by *gone*? As in, gone out to one of Grey's meetings? Or gone to a new warehouse?"

"As in, gone from Ostaria. I already tracked them as far as the city wall, but I lost their trail there." He turned suddenly and slammed his fist into the wall of the warehouse. "I missed them again!" He punched the unforgiving stone a second time.

When he drew back his fist again, I dropped Ember and grabbed his elbow with both hands.

"You're going to injure yourself if you keep that up."

He shook me off violently, pulling away, but he didn't throw any more punches.

"If you already tracked them out of Ostaria," I said slowly, "what are you doing back here?"

He stilled, his back to me. "I came back to check for anything they might have left behind. I don't think they were originally planning to move on so quickly. They were still scouting the local youths. Grey hadn't even started winning over any followers yet."

"That's a good thing, at least," I said tentatively, trying to draw him out of his black mood. "We didn't rescue anyone, but at least there aren't any more victims."

Nik didn't move, so I stepped closer again, circling him so I could see his face.

"Do you think they left Ostaria so quickly because of us?" I asked.

"It's likely," he said in clipped tones. "But I don't like it. It doesn't fit Grey's pattern, and..." He trailed off, looking at me with an intense expression.

"You still think Grey's after me, and you don't understand why he's run off like this," I said slowly. "But coming after me is a serious risk, given my apprenticeship to a master mage. You must be mistaken about the risks he's willing to take."

"Perhaps." Nik didn't sound like he believed it.

My eyes focused on his right hand. He wasn't wearing his usual gloves, and his knuckles were bright with red.

My hands reached out of their own accord, taking his injured hand in both of mine. The sudden skin-to-skin contact was shockingly intimate in the moonlight. A gesture that had once meant little had gained new meaning since the activation of my power.

"You've hurt yourself," I said softly.

His muscles clenched, but he didn't pull away. When I looked up, he was watching my face intensely. My breath caught in my throat.

"I can heal this for you, if you like," I whispered.

He didn't move or speak, and I took his silence as permission. Cracking open my wall, I let my power slide into his hand, soothing and healing the broken, bruised parts.

It was a minor injury, and the healing only took seconds. But I didn't let go of his hand.

Reaching for my handkerchief, I wiped at the blood that now stained smooth, unblemished skin. But the silence was like a heavy weight, so I blurted out the first words that came into my mind.

"Did you really come back to look for evidence? Or did you come because you knew I would be waiting for you?"

He ripped his hand away, snatching the handkerchief from my grasp and rubbing it roughly over his stained skin. As soon as he was finished, he dropped it in the dirt at our feet.

Despite his sudden burst of activity, neither of us stepped back. Instead, he leaned in, closing the distance between us even further.

"Don't get the wrong idea, healer. I'm here for Grey, not you. The best thing you can do is run far, far away."

But his dismissive, intimidating manner didn't have its usual effect. I could still feel the lingering sensation of my power connecting us. Instead of shrinking away, I leaned in as well.

Keeping eye contact, I reached out and took back his hand, gripping it in both of mine as I had before.

"I could kill you right now, and there's nothing you could do to stop me," I whispered.

He held utterly still, his eyes boring into mine in the semi-darkness.

"I'm not useless, and even Grey knows that, apparently," I continued, still not flinching from his gaze. "Stop telling me to leave—I'm not going anywhere."

I swayed even closer, and I thought, for a moment, that I read capitulation in his eyes. He took a breath, but whatever he'd been about to say or do, I would never know.

A voice cracked across the night like a whip, making us spring apart.

"What exactly is going on here? What are you doing in this part of the city, Delphine?"

I stared at Amara, horrified. Had she followed me here?

It seemed the only possible explanation.

"Who exactly are..." Amara's terse words faded as she looked more closely at Nik. Both of her eyebrows slowly rose toward her hairline as she fell into silence.

After a loaded pause, she spoke again. "Nikolas. This is indeed a surprise."

"Amara." The slight bow of his head seemed more insolent than respectful, making my brows knit together. When he'd mentioned her previously, he'd used her title and seemed at least neutral toward her, if not actually respectful.

"You've certainly grown up." Amara's eyes flicked from him to me, but I couldn't read their expression.

"And you look exactly the same." He stood with his back straight and stance rigid.

My eyes flew between them, trying to make sense of the interaction. What history did they have, and what did Amara know about Nik?

"What exactly have you been doing on these night walks of yours, Delphine?" Amara asked, making me forget all about my own curiosity.

Remembering the position she'd found us in, I flushed and hurried into speech.

"We've been tracking Grey—looking for Miranda and for evidence we can use to have him arrested."

"Grey?" Amara's eyebrows shot up again. Whatever she'd been expecting me to say, that hadn't been it. "Say that again. Grey is here in Ostaria?"

"Not anymore," I said regretfully. "They must have left sometime during the day today which means we just missed Miranda. Nik was able to—" I cut off abruptly when I caught the slight shake of his head.

Did he not want me to mention his tracking ability in front of Amara?

"Were you healing him when I arrived?" Amara asked. "Is that why you were holding his hand?" She looked like she wasn't sure if that was better or worse than her first assumption. "Just how dangerous is this Grey person?"

"I..." I wasn't sure how to answer.

I had healed Nik, but not because of any danger from Grey. But somehow I didn't think it would help either of us to tell Amara that Nik had injured himself in a fit of fury. Unfortunately, that left me floundering, and Amara turned to Nik.

"I don't know who Grey really is yet," he said. "But I intend to find out. And I intend to stop him before he tears Tartora apart."

Amara's brows creased. "Tears the kingdom apart? You think he's a real danger, then?"

"I know he is." Nik met her gaze firmly, conviction on his face.

Amara's frown deepened. "And you thought it was a good idea to involve my newly activated apprentice in this mission of yours?"

"It wasn't exactly his idea," I rushed to say. "I'm the one who insisted on helping. Because of Miranda. I promised Halmir I'd rescue her."

Amara ignored me, keeping her focus on Nik.

"You may have chosen to throw your life away, Nikolas, but that doesn't mean you can treat the lives of others cheaply."

He stiffened, his face darkening. "I told her she should leave. In fact, I told her Grey—"

From where I stood off to the side, I shook my head vigorously, and he cut off whatever he'd been about to say. My shock at his compliance was so great I went still—just in time to avoid being caught by Amara who threw me a suspicious look.

Earlier in the evening, I'd resolved to tell her everything, but given her current anger, it didn't seem like a good time for Nik to mention his totally unfounded theory that Grey had some special interest in me. Especially since Grey's latest behavior didn't support the idea at all.

Amara drew herself up, her eyes turning icy. "I had intended for Delphine and me to make an extended stay in Ostaria. Leaving now will be inconvenient. But I clearly need to get my new apprentice away from your influence."

Nik took a swift step forward, his face furious. "You elements mages have always looked down on the rest of us, but—"

He broke off as Amara grew in front of our eyes. Tiny threads of lightning crackled up and down her arms as she transformed from my kindly mentor into a figure of terrifying power. I stumbled back a step, and even Nik stopped, his face tensing. He was also cross elements, so he had to be sensing the energy crackling over her as easily as I could.

"I don't think I'm superior because of my affinity," she said in a voice that was menacing despite its low volume. "I am superior because I'm a master mage while you are nothing but a reneger."

The word crackled across the space between them, hitting Nik like a physical blow, although I'd never heard of a reneger before.

Both his hands balled into fists, but he said nothing. When the silence grew too painful, I hurried to fill it.

"I like Ostaria, but I'm also happy to leave since Miranda's no longer here. Grey will have headed north toward Calista, so we should go north as well. We might be able to catch up to them."

Amara spun to face me, looking displeased. Nik flinched slightly in response, a subtle gesture I nearly missed.

"Why would he have gone north?" he asked in his most scoffing tone. "Haven't I already told you to forget about Calista?"

"Are you saying you tracked him south?" I asked disbelievingly.

"I'll be leaving by the south gate at dawn," he replied.

"If I could believe that, we wouldn't have to leave at all," Amara muttered.

Nik gave her a challenging look. "Are you calling me a liar?" His eyes flicked briefly to me at the end of his sentence, but I couldn't read the expression in them.

Amara also looked at me, taking in my confused face before turning back to Nik.

238

"Before today, the thought would never have occurred to me. But finding you here like this..." She trailed off, her eyes narrowing before she began a new sentence. "North does seem a more logical direction for Grey to go."

"Are you saying you believe this nonsense about Grey abducting Tartorans on behalf of Calista? If so, by all means, assume he's fleeing north to his home." He sounded both disgusted and unsurprised.

Amara drew in a long breath, settling back to her usual self, although her face was still steely and her eyes sharp.

"If Grey is truly abducting people, then of course I don't think Calista is behind it."

I frowned, surprised by the strength of their conviction on the matter. Who else could Grey be working for?

"You can stay here or go south, whichever you prefer," Amara continued. "It's no business of ours. We will go north as soon as possible."

I bit my lip. If Nik had really tracked Grey south, then that's the direction we should be moving. But what if Grey had gone south temporarily just to throw off any observers? Regardless of his kingdom of origin, it still made most sense for him to be moving north. What was there south except the endless ocean?

Amara looked at my face and sighed. "If you really want to find Grey and your friend, this is for the best anyway. Nikolas can check south, and we'll look for Grey on the northern road. If we see any sign of him, we can report it immediately."

I wanted to protest. If the matter could be resolved just by reporting Grey, we would have done it already. But I could tell it wasn't the moment for objections. Amara had clearly made up her mind, and I was already in a shaky position given my secret nighttime activities.

"Do as you wish," Nik said tightly.

He looked from Amara to me, and I wondered if I was imagining a softening in his expression. The fingers of his left hand brushed across the knuckles of his right, touching the place where his injury had been.

"Thank you," he muttered, and I blinked twice, wondering if I'd misheard.

"You're...welcome," I finally managed to say, and he nodded once.

"Take care, healer."

Again I was too astonished to properly reply until he'd already wheeled around, the moment passing. He stalked away, not bothering to offer a farewell to Amara.

I watched him go, trying to understand what had just happened. It certainly didn't seem the right time to ask Amara for her impressions.

Ember gave a sharp bark, and Amara nodded.

"I agree. It's time we were home in the safety and comfort of the inn."

"I don't think that's what she was...I mean, yes, I agree," I corrected myself hurriedly.

Amara gave a tired laugh. "Oh relax, child, I don't intend to bite you—however displeased with you I currently am."

I nodded vigorously and fell in silently behind her as she led the way back toward the inn. Several times she looked back at me, sighing and opening her mouth as if to speak. But each time she decided against it, waiting to begin until we were both wrapped up in front of the fire with a cup of hot tea.

I expected a lecture, but instead she just looked at me.

"I suppose you have questions," she said. "I have some too."

"What's a reneger?" I asked, the query bursting out of me and taking us both by surprise.

"Of everything that happened, that's what you're most curious about?" She sounded amused, and I was glad to recover a more familiar atmosphere between us.

"I don't think I've ever heard the word before."

"It isn't needed often, I'm glad to say." She sighed heavily.

"A reneger is someone who abandoned their apprenticeship, never completing their training. There are mechanisms in place for replacing a master in the case of injury, illness, or neglect of duties, but to abandon an apprenticeship completely..." She shook her head. "Reneging on your apprenticeship is utterly forbidden, and being a reneger means being an outcast from both the law and society."

I stared at her, a number of things about Nik making more sense in light of her words. A shiver ran over me at the thought of what it would be like to be so completely cast out.

"Is that why he's so determined to catch Grey?" I asked, mostly to myself. "Does he hope to win back a place in society by completing a great service to the kingdom?"

Amara shook her head. "I'm sure he knows better. A reneger can't come back just by accomplishing good deeds. The law has imposed the harshest of penalties for reneging in order to act as a deterrent. Otherwise young people would be abandoning unfavorable apprenticeships all the time. And that would be dangerous for everyone. Without proper training, a person's power becomes a threat to themselves and to others. And this is one case where the privilege of the strong is no assistance. The more powerful someone is, the greater the possibility of danger."

I remembered the power Nik had demonstrated and blanched. He must have been activated by a master mage—so how had he come to leave such a prestigious apprenticeship? Was the reason he hadn't reported Grey to the authorities that the authorities were after him too?

Amara sighed again. "I would like to think Nikolas was interested in redemption, but there's only one way to regain your previous status after becoming a reneger. You must return to your abandoned master and complete your apprenticeship." She looked at me. "Do you really think the man you met has the necessary humility for such an undertaking?"

I grimaced, not needing to answer what was clearly a rhetorical question.

"So why is he so determined to catch Grey if he'll remain an outcast afterward?" I asked.

Amara shrugged. "I have no idea. We were never close given he's fifteen years my junior."

"But you know him." I watched her face closely.

She kept her gaze on the dancing flames. "He wasn't studying at the Guild while I was there, of course. He was a young child in my student days. But even then, he was considered one of the kingdom's most promising future mages."

"Then why—" I began, but she cut me off.

"What I'm more interested in is you, Delphine. Since you're my responsibility."

I gulped, effectively distracted from my question.

"Why didn't you tell me what was going on?" she asked, and I winced at the disappointment in her tone. It hurt far more than any lecture could have.

"I was going to tell you. In fact, I was planning to tell you tonight." I paused, aware of how weak the excuse sounded. Especially since I'd used it before. With a deep breath, I hurried on. "The truth is that I thought you'd do exactly what you are doing and hurry us out of Ostaria if I told you. And I didn't want to leave while Miranda was still here."

I expected her to reprimand me, but instead she looked guilty which only had the effect of making me feel worse.

"I know you're just thinking of my safety," I added. "And I know it's your job to watch over me for as long as I'm your apprentice. But for me, rescuing my friend is worth taking some risks."

Amara sighed. "The sentiment does your heart credit—if not your good sense. I'm sorry that we can't think alike in this, but at the end of the day, I'm the master and you're the apprentice. It's up to me to make the decisions."

She rubbed the back of her neck, her lips compressing into a thin line. "If both Nikolas and Grey have left Ostaria, we could stay after all."

I made a small noise of protest, and she met my gaze.

"Despite what Nikolas said, you still think Grey's gone north?"

"I think it's a real possibility."

She shook her head. "Fine, then. We'll compromise. We'll head north which is away from Nikolas, at least. The last thing you need is to get tangled up with a reneger. And on the way we can look for signs of Grey." She gave me a stern look. "Not that I want you investigating him on your own."

I nodded enthusiastically. "I can agree to that. I swear I won't go out looking for him alone."

Amara's suspicious gaze went to Ember who was pacing the length of the room, clearly unsettled.

"Ember doesn't count," she said, and I laughed.

"Foxes and all other animals do not count," I agreed, and we finished the evening with shared laughter—the last thing I'd expected when she dragged me home.

CHAPTER

# NINETEEN

In the end it took us several days to leave Ostaria. During that time, Amara appeared to have genuinely forgiven my deception. When I had agreed to my activation, I had known I was putting myself under her authority for two years, and she had confirmed her position in the hierarchy. But she had also been reasonable, consultative, and forgiving—treating me like a member of her team rather than a mindless inferior. And, as always, I couldn't help comparing her to my father.

I had been a child in his care, but I had also been a person, and he had denied me the right to have a voice in my own life. The comparison made me angry, but it also made me feel guilty. When I had deceived Amara, she had forgiven me—shown me kindness even. Was I going to take her gracious example and spurn it?

But no matter how many times I resolved to forgive my father and let the past go, I couldn't shake the bitterness of his betrayal. In the same way that the good memories of his love and care stopped me from seeing him as a monster, the enormity of his betrayal stopped me from embracing the future I had once imagined for myself.

All I could do was hope that time would help—or at least that it would reveal a different, better future.

We visited Clay several times. He was dismayed at our early departure and was clearly aware there was a reason behind it. He didn't push Amara to explain, however, instead clearing his schedule for us. At the bookstore, he chose anatomy books for my future studies, and at his clinic, he helped me practice basic control exercises.

Thankfully Amara was true to her word and the books were stored with our luggage, all our immediate focus remaining on the development of my control. As well as working with Clay, she took me along to a second testing day at a different school, and by the end of it I could identify the feel of a seed's strength without needing to refer to the official tester.

I even managed to find the orphan boy from the first school and conduct a hurried introduction with the stablemaster at the inn. The man's words were gruff, but the boy didn't seem in the least daunted, instead appearing delighted to be surrounded by horses. Neither of them noticed when I slipped away, and I took it as a hopeful sign.

Whenever we walked the streets of the city, coming and going from lessons or errands, I caught myself watching for Nik out of the corner of my eye. It was foolish, since he was long gone from Ostaria, but I couldn't shake the instinct.

In the end, I was grateful when we finally rode out on Amara's small cart. I would likely never see Nik again, and I needed to leave thoughts of him behind and focus on my studies instead. When I next encountered Grey, I wasn't going to be weak and helpless.

Ember perked up when we left the city walls and entered the countryside. Seeing the change in her made me nervous. I'd grown used to her warmth by my side, but I couldn't stop her from returning to her natural habitat if she wished to do so.

I slept restlessly the first night on the road, but when I woke in the morning, Ember was still curled at my side, her nose toward the dying fire.

"I think she's too attached to you to leave at this point," Amara said as we packed up camp and climbed back into the cart, the sleeping fox curled among the bags.

"Is it wrong of me to keep her?" I asked, plagued with guilt now that I'd gotten my wish.

"It would be if you tried to keep her by force. But if she chooses to stay, there's no reason for you to feel guilty."

I frowned at the horizon. Her words sounded good, but was it as simple as that?

I tried to put my worries into words. "I've healed her several times now—and most of those were injuries she received because of me. If I accidentally bound her to me with my power, is that really her free choice?"

Amara frowned sideways at me, clearly considering her answer.

"It does you credit that you're concerned about it. But remember the state she was in when we first found her. She would have died without your intervention."

"Are you saying she owes me her life?"

Amara shook her head. "Not that, exactly. I'm saying that her only options were death or a connection with you. Surely you don't think the former would be a better option?" She smiled down at me, and I reluctantly smiled back.

"No, I guess not."

Amara paused, looking at me again. "Maybe it's time for the speech."

"Speech?" I stared at her.

She grimaced. "Apparently I should have given it to you in our first lesson—yet another of the ways I'm deficient as the master of a healing apprentice, as Clay pointed out to me."

"I'd rather be your apprentice than anyone else's—even

Master Clay," I said, earning a smile from Amara. "So what's this speech given to all healing apprentices?"

"I'll probably get the exact words wrong," she said ruefully, "but it boils down to the fact that the power inside you has the ability to both heal and destroy in equal measure."

"We're called healers," I said in a subdued tone, "but people with my affinity also make the best assassins."

Amara's lips pressed together. "Exactly. You wield the power of life and death more directly than the other affinities. Apparently that ability can go to some people's heads."

"You mean they become dangerous?" I asked.

She frowned. "It's more complex than that. Many healers spend their whole adulthood saving lives, and it's an admirable pursuit. But it's admirable because every life is unique and valuable. Saving lives doesn't give you a right to those lives— and it doesn't give you credit in some invisible ledger."

"Invisible ledger?" I blinked at her.

She laughed. "That bit was confusing to me, too. But I gather there have been cases the healing affinity doesn't like to talk about publicly. Cases where healers felt that the lives they had saved gave them the right to take other lives—as if they were exchangeable, a life for a life."

I sucked in a breath. "That's horrible! You don't need to worry about that. I'm definitely not about to go on a killing spree—no matter how many people I may one day save."

"I'm glad to hear it," Amara said in a tone that was a little too serious. "It would reflect badly on me as your influencer."

I snorted. "Yes, the one and only problem with that scenario."

She smiled, but after a moment, grew more somber. "In all seriousness, though, I think it applies in this case as well since the principle goes both ways. When you heal someone, it's a gift given in the moment. Just as you don't have any claim to the rest of that person's life—or anyone else's in exchange—

you also aren't responsible for anything they may choose to do afterward. You didn't impose a burden on Ember, you gave a gift, and she chose her response. Don't take away the value of her choice by trying to take responsibility for it."

I considered her words in silence.

"Well," I said at last, "consider me suitably humbled."

Amara chuckled. "Oh no, you're much too young for that. I'm sure it will take at least another ten years before you can make such a claim. Maybe twenty."

I laughed back. "So I need to be roughly your age to achieve true humility?"

She winked. "Naturally. Whatever age I am at the time, of course. When you reach my current age, you'll find you still need another ten or so years."

"I can only be grateful I have such an example to aspire to," I said with enough gravity that we both laughed again.

"With that out of the way," she said when our mirth subsided, "I want you to spend our travel time focusing on identifying people and animals around us. It isn't something healers usually do because most aren't strong enough for it, but it will help you develop your control and hone your senses."

I happily agreed to such a reasonable request and spent the next weeks doing exactly as she'd asked. We traveled northeast along the road that ran beside the Celadon, sleeping in the open or in hay barns we found along the way.

Our progress was slow since we stopped in every hamlet or village even vaguely close to the road. None of them were large enough to have an inn, but most of them were familiar with Amara and had requests to make of her.

She used her elements power freely when asked to do so, accepting whatever gifts of food and provisions were offered in exchange. But I noticed that she spent more of her time training the villagers than performing acts beyond their ability. Although she was powerful herself, she seemed to have mastered many of the ways that someone with a weaker elements seed could maximize the use of what power they had.

"If I can help in the moment, of course I'm happy to do so," she told me when I finally asked her about it. We were packing up camp in the morning, and she continued working as she spoke. "There are plenty of things that can only be done by a stronger ability. But I can't be in every village on every day. My dream is to always leave a community more capable than when I arrived."

"It's an admirable dream." I thrust away the inevitable thoughts of a father who'd wanted to cripple rather than empower me. "But shouldn't the villagers be learning those skills from their activators? Isn't that the point of the apprentice system?"

"That's the theory behind it," she said. "And it works well in the bigger population centers. But in the more remote regions, there are many people who never travel at all—sometimes whole communities of people have never been further than the closest trading center. So their knowledge pool never grows. They miss new developments and often have a limited knowledge pool to begin with."

I climbed onto the cart, musing on her words. The picture she painted was a familiar one since my own family had never traveled beyond our small town. If there was something that could be accomplished by my parents' abilities that was unknown to the farmers of Tarin, how would they ever learn of it?

"That was the life I was choosing," I murmured. "I might have lived my whole life without traveling beyond Tarin."

"But you didn't." Amara settled beside me and signaled to Acorn to get moving.

The horse lumbered into a slow walk, and I spoke quietly, almost under my breath.

"Because you came. I didn't live that life because you came."

"No." She looked across at me. "Because you chose something different."

"But also because you came."

"But also because I came," she conceded, a distant look in her eyes. "And that's why I do it. That's why I'm a traveling master. Because sometimes, someone has to come."

She turned and looked at me, and something passed between us—something heavy that I didn't yet have the courage to name. Shaking my head slightly, I reminded myself that I still had almost two years of being an apprentice, and that Amara herself was still young. She wouldn't be retiring any time soon, so there was no reason to get maudlin and start thinking about passing of torches and other such foolishness.

The day was a sunny one, and it was no hardship to turn my mind to my training. The time passed quickly as I identified the various animals around us. Not being near any larger villages, we barely passed any other travelers, but we found a stream in the late afternoon and made camp beside it.

I prepared the fire pit, proudly coaxing a flame into life. Once it had taken hold of the branches, I sat back and smiled at the friendly warmth. I might not be able to control fire, as Amara could, but the impact of her influence left it feeling like a pleasant and welcome companion.

At first I had complained that it was pointless for me to learn how to start a fire when Amara could produce flames from her fingers. But she had rightly pointed out that I wouldn't always be with her. She seemed to think she would be remiss in her training if I didn't learn how to properly prepare, start, maintain, and douse a campfire—a different skill from managing the fire in the fireplace at home.

"Look at you, ready to set off on your own." Amara sank down beside me with a weary sigh.

I snorted. "Hardly that. But you were right—I'm glad to know how to manage a fire. Just like I'm glad to be immune to minor burns thanks to your cross influence." I looked ruefully down at the hand I had absentmindedly used to adjust a burning branch.

"Make sure you say that to Clay next time you see him," she said smugly.

I sighed, thoughts of Clay bringing a reminder of all the comforts of Ostaria. They seemed a long time ago now. "I wonder if I'll ever see him again."

"Of course you will!" Amara pulled out the ingredients for the evening meal. "I have a fondness for Ostaria, so we'll definitely be back. You still have nearly two years of your apprenticeship, remember."

I looked at her out the corner of my eye. Was it the city or the master healing mage she had a fondness for? As usual, her face gave me no clue as to whether any warmer feelings lay beneath her words.

I yawned widely, although I'd done little in the way of physical activity all day. When I yawned again, even more widely, both the ground beneath me and the air around me seemed to tremble slightly in time with my body.

But when I stilled, the rumbling continued.

I turned to Amara to find her staring upstream, her body and face frozen. The sound grew and intensified, cracking and rushing as if we were camped next to a raging river instead of a sleepy stream.

"Amara?" I said just as the trees along the stream were hit by a wave that appeared to be made more of dirt and logs than water.

"Amara!" I screamed as the debris-filled water rushed toward us.

I jumped to my feet, but the flood had already crossed most of the remaining distance. Within seconds, it would crash over us, Acorn, and even our cart.

I gasped, scooping up Ember from next to the fire and

leaping the short distance to Acorn. Throwing my arms around her neck, I braced my legs wide. Shielding Ember between us, I waited as a second passed and then another. Nothing hit us.

Breathing raggedly, I turned around.

Amara still sat where I had left her, her brow furrowed and her hands in her lap. The water and debris had shifted, however.

Instead of bearing toward us in a wide wave, the flood had narrowed, its level rising to tower over me but its edges confined to the stream bed. My mouth fell open as I watched the unnatural phenomenon of a tower of dirty water raging past me.

I stretched out one arm, ready to dip my fingers into the passing water.

"Don't!" Amara snapped, making me snatch my arm back.

She finally moved, giving me an exasperated look. "Can't you see how much debris is in there? Do you want one of your fingers broken from a passing branch? I've had to channel a lot of force into that flow. It's moving quickly."

"You did this?" I asked, although the answer was obvious.

Amara didn't answer, her gaze growing distant. I slowly sank back into my previous position beside the fire, marveling at the power Amara had to be using to divert an entire flood.

Gradually the height of the towering river rushing past us lessened, indicating less water was being channeled along the bed of the stream.

Amara spoke again, sounding less strained. "It's reached the river and is dissipating. The Celadon is large enough here to absorb it, but I need to guide it some way downriver, just to make sure it doesn't cause unforeseen problems."

I held my breath, not wanting to disturb her in any way. Elements mages meddled with the natural environment, and they had to be as careful of unforeseen consequences as healers had to be of accidentally stopping someone's heart with a stray thought.

Eventually the color of the passing water began to clear, the height of the stream returning to only twice its usual flow. Amara gave a sigh and relaxed, her shoulders slumping.

I gulped, trying to find my voice. "Did we nearly just die?"

Amara rolled her shoulders, stretching herself slowly.

"Hardly. I'm an elements mage, remember. If I hadn't been distracted talking to you and preparing the meal, I would have sensed the water coming even sooner. As it was, we were never in any danger."

I pressed my hand to my racing heart. Apparently my body hadn't quite absorbed that message yet.

Slowly my calm returned, however, and I noticed that the animals were entirely unalarmed. Apparently I was the only one who had given in to terror.

"I think your healing cross influence has rubbed off on Acorn or something," I said. "She doesn't seem like an ordinary horse. Aren't horses supposed to have excellent senses? But she didn't even seem to notice the flood. She wasn't bothered by it at all."

"We've always gotten on well." Amara smiled at the horse affectionately. "But she's changed since your arrival. I've noticed animals are much less likely to panic in the presence of a healing mage. Did you even notice that your instinct was to run to the animals?"

I blinked. Wasn't that the natural thing to do?

"Let me guess." Amara grinned at me. "You're thinking that anyone would do the same? I can promise that's not the case. Our seeds affect us from birth—to the point where it's hard to even imagine seeing life through a different lens from the one given by our affinity."

"Oh." I considered her words. "But in this case, a little concern wouldn't have been out of place. We got lucky. If you weren't an elements mage, we could all be dead right now. Where did the flood even come from? It hasn't rained for two days."

"That is a very good question." Amara turned stern eyes upstream.

"What do we do now?" I asked. "Surely we can't just make camp as if nothing happened?"

"No." Amara sounded slightly dangerous, her words carrying some of the lingering power that had diverted a flood. "We need to find out exactly what is going on here."

CHAPTER

# TWENTY

It didn't take us long to douse the fledgling fire and repack our belongings. We had camped between the stream and a dirt track that branched off from the main road and disappeared uphill. It seemed the logical path to take, but we couldn't follow it for long. Beyond our campsite, it had been washed away by the flood, leaving only muddy ground littered with branches and rocks.

Amara stopped to survey the sodden earth ahead, her hand resting lightly on Acorn's mane. She had chosen to walk beside the horse's head rather than take her usual place in the cart, and I felt awkward holding the reins in her stead.

Glad for the excuse, I clambered down and joined her in front of the cart. "A plants mage would be helpful about now. There's no way Acorn can pull the cart through that. The wheels would get bogged almost immediately."

"Are you sure a plants mage is what's needed?" Amara asked in a light tone that seemed out of place in the situation.

I frowned at her. She had to be tired after her earlier feat—was she getting lightheaded? Should I suggest she sit down?

She met my concerned look with an amused smile, nodding toward the wheels of the cart. I looked down and gasped.

Instead of resting on the ground, as they usually did, all four wheels were floating about an inch above the dirt.

"What...is that?" I asked in a strangled voice.

Amara laughed. "Elements mage, remember?"

I had a sudden memory of Nik accusing Amara of being a typical elements mage who thought her affinity was the greatest of the three. It had seemed unfair at the time, but her grin told me even Amara couldn't escape traces of the infamous elements arrogance. I rolled my eyes.

Amara continued to smile. "Consider this another impromptu lesson. Your power is useless to connect with anything outside the bounds of your affinity, but that doesn't make you powerless. It just means you need to find a different way to achieve your ends. Here, it may have been logical to wish for a plants mage to harden the mud, but it's not the only possible solution. I've put a small cushion of air under each wheel which should allow them to skate across the top of the muck. The flood moved through quickly enough that the bog shouldn't be too deep. As long as Acorn can make it, we'll be fine." She looked at the mud ahead, and her expression turned rueful. "I hope you don't mind walking through that, though. We probably shouldn't add to the cart's weight unnecessarily."

"Never mind me! Amara, even the strongest mages have limits. Your power isn't endless, and you just stopped a flood. You're going to collapse if you try too much."

She laughed. "Thank you for your concern, but I'll be fine. I was a master long before you were even ready for activation. I know my own limits well enough."

I examined her, looking for any hidden signs of exhaustion, but she looked as relaxed and confident as ever.

"Well...if you're sure," I said hesitantly.

She shook her head. "Anyone would think you were the master and I the apprentice. Come on, let's get moving. It's only getting darker."

She patted Acorn on her flank, and she lurched into movement. The cart slid easily behind her, Ember perched on the seat, ears up and tail high, as if she were the driver.

I smothered a laugh, unable to properly process the surreal scene. After a moment I hurried forward myself, though, not wanting to be left behind.

The mud was sticky, making each step difficult, and I had to pay attention to the ground in the gathering gloom, trying to avoid obstacles that might trip me up and send me face first into the muck. My calves and thighs were soon burning, and by the time we saw lights ahead, my eyes ached from squinting in the near darkness.

"Aha!" Amara's voice floated back to my position at the rear of the cart.

I mustered the energy to increase my pace enough to join her by Acorn's head. As soon as I reached her, the questions died on my lips.

Before us was the obvious cause of the flood.

We had been moving slowly uphill, but here the land sloped more steeply upward, and at the top was the remnants of what had once been a dam. A poorly constructed one from the looks of it.

"The villagers are fortunate their houses are on the high ground above the dam," Amara said in a neutral voice. "Otherwise they would all have been swept away when it burst."

"But we weren't so fortunate!" I cried, not as capable of taking an objective view of the situation. "We only survived because of you. If it had been any other travelers instead of us ..."

"Yes." Her tone hinted at emotion behind the calm after all. "And that's why we'll be having an urgent conversation with the villagers before the night is over."

I winced, my sympathy taking an abrupt swing toward the

unknown villagers. Their bad night was about to get a lot worse.

It took us a while to pick our way up the final slope and around the edges of the dam and what remained of the lake behind it. But as soon as were past, the path appeared again. A soft thump told me Amara had released the air cushions on the wheels, and I gave her another surreptitious examination, trying to work out how close she was to the edge.

She still gave no sign of being any more tired than usual, however. There was no hint of hesitation in her stride as she marched into the middle of the village.

We were spotted immediately. The villagers were all outside already, standing huddled around lanterns, their faces full of fear, confusion, and anxiety.

"Who's in charge here?" Amara called in a loud voice, and the people exchanged panicked looks.

After a long moment, a young man stepped forward.

"Our village is too small to have a mayor or official leader. Whatever you have to say you can say to all of us."

Amara took her time, letting her eyes roam over the crowd.

"Then I assume you'll all be taking responsibility for what just happened? I've seen the dam you built, and I feel certain the proper construction permissions were skipped."

Murmurs swept the group at her words, and several people broke off the fringes of the small crowd to disappear into the nearby homes. The young man who had spoken earlier looked undaunted, however, and I couldn't help admiring his courage.

"You can see the size of our village for yourself," he said. "Construction permission from the crown requires consultation with a plants mage. Do we look like we could afford that?"

Amara's eyes roamed over the crowd again, this time moving further to examine their houses and the livestock fenced nearby.

"It's a small village, certainly, but you look prosperous

enough." She tilted her head, her gaze piercing and attitude authoritative, and I saw the man flinch.

But he quickly rallied. "Only because we built the dam! Before it, we were struggling to survive. To afford the funds for proper construction, we first needed the wealth the dam brought. It was an impossible situation. What were we to do?"

Amara didn't soften. "Seek consultation with a plants mage post construction, of course."

"But that would be admitting what we did!" a woman called in protest. "And why should we do that when we're so out of the way here that no representatives of the crown ever pass through?"

"The king isn't uncaring toward his people," Amara said sternly. "He doesn't require mage consultation because he wishes to drain the coffers of his people. Mages need to be involved in such large-scale construction projects because a poorly built dam is a danger to more than just its creators. You were fortunate that it burst when there was an elements mage downstream, or you would have had deaths on your conscience as well as illegal construction."

"A mage?" The cry rang out from several lips. "You're a mage?"

Everyone moved back, the ring of empty space around us growing until the young man was the only one still facing us. He no longer looked confident now, his face equal parts guilty and fearful.

"We truly meant no harm," he said.

Amara sighed, her straight posture softening. "That, at least, I believe. I've already examined what remains of your dam, and for now there is no further danger."

"You did?" I whispered from just behind her. "But how can you tell? You're not—"

"A plants mage? No." She glanced back at me. "I have no special insight into the rock of the dam wall, but I can sense the water it's supposed to be holding back. It's telling me there are no further cracks that will let anything through. What remains in the lake will stay there for now. We can safely sleep for the night and look more closely in the morning."

"You intend to stay here for the night?" the young man asked cautiously, having overheard her words.

"Naturally." Amara raised an eyebrow, daring him to object. He didn't.

"Was there anyone downstream when it burst?" she asked after a moment of silence. "If you have anyone dangerously ill or injured, my apprentice is a healer. She's inexperienced but strong, and she'll do her best if the situation is urgent."

I gulped, fixing my eyes on his face as I waited for what I hoped was a negative response. It took him a moment to reply, however, looking between us in confusion.

"She's your apprentice? And she's a healer?"

"Yes, yes," Amara said, weariness showing for the first time. "She's cross influenced. That is hardly the most noteworthy thing happening here. Do you have need of her services?"

The man focused on me, sounding a little dazed. "Not immediately, no. I don't know of any urgent need."

"Good." Amara echoed my own sentiment completely. "In that case, we'll sleep."

I moved a step closer, being as surreptitious as I could. I didn't want to get my head snapped off for hovering, but when Amara stumbled slightly over a stone, I couldn't help bracing her under her elbow. Sure enough, it earned me a reproving look.

"I'm not about to collapse, Delphine. You don't need to look so worried."

"Sorry, Master Amara." I grinned, unrepentant. "I can't help it."

The young man bowed. "Master Amara? And Apprentice

Delphine? I'm sorry we didn't do proper introductions. My name is Sarn."

"I wish I could say it was nice to meet you," Amara said, "but that doesn't seem quite appropriate in the circumstances."

He flinched, and I took pity on him. "Is there somewhere we can sleep tonight? And somewhere we can put our horse?"

"Of course!" Sarn leaped into action, seeming much more comfortable with something to do.

Whether because of Amara's status, or because they were trying to win us over, the villagers decided we should have a house to ourselves. The residents vacated it before we arrived, leaving a clean home with two bedrooms for our sole use. I expected Amara to protest since she didn't usually stand on ceremony, no matter who she was dealing with. But she accepted the empty house without comment, even allowing Sarn to care for and feed Acorn in her stead.

As soon as we were alone, I put my hands on my hips and stared her down. "Admit it—you're tired."

She laughed and sat down in front of the hot meal that had been left on the table for us.

"You're persistent, I'll give you that."

"Why are we here in this empty house, playing at being grand, important mages, unless it's because you're exhausted?" I sat down across from her, fixing her with an accusing look.

She sighed, chewing slowly before responding. "I have no interest in pomp and formality if the point is to make me feel superior. But this situation is different. These villagers are living such a remote life, they've lost all respect for the crown. But as you've seen today, there's a very important reason why mages have to be involved in all major public construction. As well as a plants mage to help with the dam's construction, there should have been an elements mage to assess the impact of a dam in this location. The reason the Triumvirate is given an almost equal footing in governance as the king is because the services the Guild renders the kingdom are so essential. Guild mages might be hidebound and self-important—but that's because they *are* important, and they know it."

I blinked. "Was that a compliment or criticism? I'm not sure."

Amara took another large bite, a smile tugging at the corners of her mouth. "The Mages' Guild can't be all bad. I'm a member, after all."

I snorted but left her in peace to eat, keeping a close eye on her while she did so. She might be claiming she had no excessive fatigue, but her actions told a different story. After eating slowly, she announced she was going straight to bed, despite the early hour. I followed her lead, and we both slept solidly, glad for the proper beds.

In the morning I woke to an older lady delivering a breakfast feast. Amara slept through the noise, so I ate quickly and slipped outside into the morning sun with only Ember for company.

No one was waiting to greet me, so I wandered through the village alone. It was more of a hamlet than a village, considerably smaller than Tarin. But the buildings were well-maintained and, most importantly, the animals all looked well cared for and plump.

I greeted several donkeys, half a dozen horses, five cows, and an untold number of chickens as I strolled from pen to pen. The birds reacted to my presence with alarm, despite my ability, presumably because of the fox padding silently beside me. The larger animals were unbothered by Ember, though, coming forward to nudge at me or sniff me.

A particularly proud looking stallion put his head on my shoulder, making me laugh.

"I approve of you, too, fine sir." I patted his long neck.

While I was still standing, mostly obscured by the horse, three villagers walked up to the next pen over.

"What terrible luck that a Guild mage was passing by just when the dam burst," one of them said glumly.

"Hush!" another snapped. "If it had been anyone else, they'd be dead right now, and then we'd really be in trouble. We should be grateful for our good luck that she's an elements mage."

"The important thing is that King Marius is going to find out about us," the third said. "And then his pet mages will no doubt extort every last coin we have."

"Hush!" the second speaker snapped again. "Do you want to get us in worse trouble if someone overhears you? It's bad enough there'll be more mages coming. We should send Callum up to the far pastures to watch the sheep until they're gone."

I frowned, trying to peer around the horse without being seen. Who was Callum and why did he need to be sent away? Was he a criminal they were concealing from the law?

The first speaker sucked in her breath sharply. "Goodness, yes! We need to keep him out of sight completely. I'll speak to his mother today. She's already anxious enough, poor thing. He'll have to go to the Mages' Guild for training eventually, and that's far enough away. She'd be heartbroken if the crown let Calista steal him away forever. How that man can call himself our king when he favors foreigners over his own people, I don't know."

"How many times do I have to tell you not to talk like that?" the second speaker scolded. "At least restrain yourself until the strangers are gone."

I bit my lip. Callum was a youngster, then? One with a strong seed from the sound of it.

Ember growled quietly at my feet, and I looked down to find her staring at the three villagers. I shushed her, afraid she'd draw attention to us, but the trio was already moving off.

I left as soon as they disappeared from sight, returning to the house where I'd left Amara. Concern over what I'd heard sped my gait, and it didn't take long to get there. I found her waiting for me outside, with Sarn in tow, so I had to put the matter aside for the moment. I didn't want to bring it up with any of the villagers around.

Amara surveyed the suspiciously empty village around us with a raised eyebrow. "Scared, are they?" she asked Sarn, but she sounded more amused than offended.

The long sleep had softened her attitude—yet another confirmation that she had been more tired the night before than she'd let on.

"You wanted to examine the dam more closely?" Sarn asked, wisely ignoring her question.

Amara confirmed it, but Sarn didn't move immediately, his uneasy gaze on Ember.

"Don't worry about her," I said. "It's her bedtime anyway."

Almost as if she'd understood my words, Ember brushed against my leg before trotting straight for the door. Amara had left it partially open, so the fox disappeared out of sight inside. Sarn watched her go with a crease in his brow, but he shook it off without speaking and gestured for us to follow him.

It was only a short walk to the artificial lake and the half-destroyed dam wall.

"Did you say the water *told* you the dam was secure?" I asked Amara when we reached it.

Amara chuckled. "Not in so many words, of course. But I pressed the water against the remaining part of the wall with considerable force and not a drop passed through." She got a faraway look in her eyes before nodding once. "It's holding firm today as well. That's good news."

"What do you intend to do?" Sarn asked fearfully.

"I'll inform the Guild, of course." She gave him a compassionate look. "There's no other choice at this point. I'm not a plants mage, and you need one to give this structure a more thorough examination." She hesitated, gazing downstream. "I can include my assessment as an elements mage, at least, so you shouldn't need a second one of those. As the dam stood previously, you were diverting too much of the natural flow. You won't be able to build it as high again. But a smaller dam should be safe for this location."

Sarn's eyes brightened. "You think they'll let us keep a dam of some sort?"

"I can't guarantee it, but I'll speak for you in my report." She looked at the muddy swathe of ground that was still strewn with all sorts of debris. "If I were you, I would clean up the path before anyone arrives from the capital—there's no need to give a bad impression before they even reach the village."

Sarn eagerly agreed, guiding us back to the village where we discovered Acorn already harnessed to our cart. Ember was perched in the back, looking displeased but unharmed.

"You seem in a hurry to get rid of us," I said, making Sarn fall over himself with explanations.

He finished the speech by saying, "Of course if you want to stay, you'd be most welcome," all the while sounding terrified we might actually take him at his word.

I snorted. "Don't worry, we don't want to stay."

"We've added a bag of food to the back in thanks," he said hurriedly, trying to hide his relief.

Once we were back across the mud and on the main road again, I couldn't hold in the chuckles.

"Did you see his face?" I asked Amara. "He couldn't get rid of us quickly enough." Indignation rose inside me, driving away the laughter. "Hardly the gratitude you'd expect given you've promised to help them."

Amara sighed. "There will be consequences from the crown, I'm sure. I can't blame them for being worried and distracted."

I frowned, biting at my lip. "Did you hear them talking about King Marius at all?"

She looked across at me. "Did you? You shouldn't take it too seriously, if so. As I said, it's only human nature to be resentful when you're scared about your future."

I shook my head slowly. "I could understand negative comments about the construction policy, but that wasn't what concerned me. It sounded like the village has someone under seventeen who has tested with a mage level seed. They seemed to think that if the crown sent someone official to the village, that person would steal this child away and send them to Calista."

"What?" Amara stared at me. "Why would the crown or the Guild do such a thing?"

I shrugged. "It was an overheard conversation, and the villagers didn't go into detail. But I'm afraid Grey might have been through this hamlet at some point."

"You think he's been there?" Amara gazed doubtfully back toward the dirt track that led to the hamlet.

I grimaced. It did seem unlikely. "I suppose if he'd been through personally, they would know he's not affiliated with the Guild or its mages. But Grey must have taken this route at some point and visited some of the larger villages nearby. I suppose it's normal that rumors get distorted as they spread."

"So the locals know youths are disappearing, and they think they're going to Calista," Amara said slowly. "Just like you thought back in Ostaria."

I shrugged, feeling awkward. "I don't know if they're going to Calista for sure. I'm just worried they might be. You heard what Halmir said back in Tarin."

"Yes, I heard him." Amara sounded grim. "And now they're saying the same thing in this hamlet."

She fell into silence, and the expression on her face was so dark I didn't dare interrupt whatever thoughts were putting her in such a mood.

## CHAPTER
# TWENTY-ONE

Neither of us mentioned the rumors again, keeping more silent than usual for the remaining two days before we reached Caltor. But my spirits lifted at the sight of the city walls, and Amara straightened beside me, as if experiencing a similar effect. We would both welcome a comfortable stay at a large inn.

Caltor was a similar size to Ostaria, and like the more southern city, it also sat on the eastern shore of the Celadon River. However, Caltor was located well above the place where the two northern branches of the river joined into a single flow. And since it was on the western branch, it was more centrally located than Ostaria. Given its proximity to the capital, its streets were even busier than its sister city.

According to Amara, it had seen considerable growth since the restoration of northern Calista, given it lay on one of the popular routes between Tarona and Calista's capital of Cali-nara. But I couldn't help wondering if its proximity to Calista also put it in more danger from Grey? I could only imagine he'd already visited the city—probably more than once.

The guards at the gate were more diligent than the Ostarian ones had been, eyeing us both suspiciously and examining the back of the cart. The sight of Ember, curled up and sleeping between two bags, made them raise their eyebrows, but neither protested her presence.

When we were finally waved into the city, I looked sideways at Amara. "Have they always been like that?"

She twisted to frown back at the gates. "Not from what I remember. That was a first."

We both lapsed back into silence, and my unease was quickly forgotten as I looked around me, eagerly taking in the sights of my second city. In many ways it reminded me of Ostaria. The houses had a similar design, and the cobblestoned streets were almost identical. But the stone used for construction was several shades darker than in Ostaria, giving the whole city a grimmer feel, and the awnings of the shops were all a uniform forest green.

Amara caught me looking at them and smiled.

"I have to admit, I prefer the cheerful chaos of Ostaria," she said. "Caltor has strict regulations on many things. The city officials like to keep a uniform appearance throughout the city."

"It looks grand," I said slowly, eyeing the gold trim on the closest awning, "and elegant. But I think I prefer all the bright colors of Ostaria as well."

"There are plenty of good people here, though," Amara said. "And even more master mages than in Ostaria since we're closer to the capital. I shouldn't have any trouble finding a healer to help with your learning while we're here."

"Will we be staying long?" I asked, my tone eager given the appearance of an inn of substantial size.

Amara grinned as she directed Acorn into the inn yard. "I've been missing proper beds and hot baths, too. I think we can manage an extended stay."

As in Ostaria, the innkeeper and his wife clearly knew Amara, showing her respect and deference, although they lacked the warmth and enthusiasm of the previous inn's owners.

"Let me guess," I said out the side of my mouth. "You haven't saved this inn from a fire yet."

Her mouth twitched, although she kept her eyes on the landlord. "Not yet," she whispered back.

When the innkeeper's wife bustled away to greet another new arrival, I heard her using the title Master. I twisted to look at the older man but could see nothing remarkable about his appearance beyond the quality of his clothing. Amara had just told me there were more master mages in Caltor, and her words were already being proved true. Their presence made Amara's status stand out less which had to be another factor in the attitude of the innkeeper.

We were still shown to a comfortable room, however, and a box was provided for Ember without protest. When we discussed our next movements, Amara mentioned several mages she knew in the city.

"We should visit the healers at some point," she said, "but I'm not taking you to the hospital yet. Or even to an animal clinic. I know you've been practicing a lot while we've been traveling, but I'm still not sure you're ready for it. For now, we can start with another non-medical aspect of your ability. That should give us a chance to check your progress."

"Another non-medical ability?" I tried to think what it could be.

"Truth telling." Amara didn't look up from where she was unpacking items of clothing from her personal bag.

"Oh yes, of course!" I sat up straighter. "How could I forget about that? It's the one aspect of our ability that even regular healers don't use physical contact for. A useful ability too." I frowned. "I can't say I've noticed it particularly, though. Should I have picked up some sense of it on my own? Everything else has bombarded me, whether I wanted it or not."

Amara glanced over at me, a smile spreading over her face. "I'll take that as a compliment."

I gave her a questioning look.

"If you haven't had any sense of it, it must be because I haven't been speaking any untruths. Don't you think you would have noticed if I was telling you lies?"

A warm feeling crept over me as I considered her words. I hadn't noticed any lies—which meant it wasn't only Amara who had been telling me the truth since our meeting. I shook my head, trying to suppress the pleasure. If Nik had been telling me the truth, that meant he was far away now, and irrelevant to my future. And regardless of his current location, it was pure foolishness to care about whether he'd been honest with me or not. Did it please me to know he had been honest when telling me to stay away from him?

"So how am I going to train in truth telling?" I asked, trying to stay on topic.

Amara turned from her bags, her side of the room neat and orderly. "I've been waiting for us to reach a city again so we could visit a law keeping hall. Smaller towns don't have halls but instead rely on their regular healers for urgent matters. But the cities and larger towns have their own law keeping facilities since they service not only their own area but also adjudicate any official cases brought in from the smaller towns. The law keeping hall of Caltor keeps more than one healer on staff just to truth tell. It's a good job for those with a lower level of power, since it doesn't require mage level strength."

"If strength isn't relevant, does that mean anyone who has the healing affinity can truth tell, no matter how weak they are?" I asked, trying to remember if I'd ever heard anyone talking about it on one of our infrequent trips into Tarin.

"To some extent they can." Amara rubbed the back of her neck. "But it's not entirely true that strength is irrelevant. I haven't experienced it myself, of course, but I'm told that the stronger the healer, the more clearly they can read the truth. It's not always a straightforward process, since the truth is rarely a simple, black and white thing."

I nodded, well able to imagine the sort of situations the law keeping hall might encounter. And even more complicated were the personal issues that would arise in a population where a third of the people had a healing affinity.

Unable to help myself, I wondered what I would have sensed from my father if I had been activated earlier. Did his ignorance about how healers managed squeamishness mean his words would have registered as truth?

"Of course, law keeping can't be achieved only by truth telling, unfortunately," Amara said, bringing my mind back to the present. "For one thing, healers can only detect if a person believes the truth of their own words, not if the words are actually true. Plus you have to know the right questions to ask the right people."

"It sounds like interesting work," I said thoughtfully.

Amara's words made it clear a powerful healing seed like mine would be wasted in the role. It was a pity the things I was more interested in doing—testing seeds and truth telling—were able to be done by those with weaker seeds.

"We'll go to the law keeping hall in the morning," Amara said, breaking through my thoughts. "So get a good sleep tonight."

Of course, since she'd instructed me to sleep well, deep rest eluded me. I tossed and turned for most of the night, my thoughts a jumble of the new town, the promised lesson, and guilt that I still hadn't located Miranda.

The villagers from the hamlet seemed to fear Grey, but did that actually mean he'd passed their way? Nik had tracked Grey south on this occasion, at least, so shouldn't I have found a way to convince Amara to go south as well? Had I placed too much reliance on my own certainty he was moving north?

When morning finally arrived, I got up eagerly, ready for any distraction to chase the fruitless thoughts from my mind. Amara took credit for my enthusiasm and obligingly finished her breakfast and morning routine quickly. In the end, we made such good time that the law keeping hall was only just opening as we arrived.

We entered a spacious marble entrance hall and were greeted by the bored-looking clerk reigning over the lone counter.

"Are you here regarding an existing case or a new one?" he asked, keeping his attention on Amara.

"Neither," she said, making him frown.

"Fines apply for wasting law keepers' time." He spoke in a bored voice, as if reciting from a rule book. "Law keepers may not be used to resolve personal quarrels and are not available to answer questions unrelated to a new or existing case. Unless a crime has been committed, you cannot—"

"Does Anka still work here?" Amara asked, cutting off his monologue.

A gleam of interest entered the clerk's eyes for the first time. He re-examined Amara before turning to me, as if I might hold a clue to our identity.

"You're here to see the head of the hall? Do you have an appointment with Master Anka?" he asked.

"No, we've only just arrived in Caltor." Amara sounded as relaxed as always. "But if you could let her know Amara is here to see her, I'm sure she'll make time for us."

"*Master* Amara?" The clerk's eyebrows shot up to his hairline. "*The* Master Amara?"

She smiled broadly. "I'm not aware of another one."

"If you'll wait right here, I'll be back in just a moment." The man gave us a respectful bow and hurried down a nearby corridor.

I turned to Amara, regarding her silently. It was being borne in on me that I had apprenticed with someone much more important and well-connected than I'd initially realized.

"Don't look at me like that," Amara said without turning. "Anka just happens to be my aunt."

"Your aunt?" My mouth fell open. "Why didn't you say anything?"

"It wasn't relevant before now. Were you expecting me to provide my apprentice with a litany of all my living relatives and their respective positions and affinities?"

"No, of course not. I just didn't realize…"

"That I'd have any important personages in my family tree?" She chuckled. "It does seem surprising given how weak and low ranked I am."

Her words drew out a laugh despite my surprise. "I wouldn't dare think anything so obviously untrue—as you well know. I suppose I hadn't thought about the possibility at all since I only have distant relatives myself. I've never met any of them, so I'm used to it just being Mother, Father, and me."

The clerk reappeared, so we let the conversation drop and obediently followed him into the bowels of the law keeping hall. I had been imagining it as an enormous dungeon, gray and dank, complete with chains hanging off the walls, but it was completely the opposite.

Light and airy, most of the walls were the same white marble as the reception hall, and none of the doors or windows I saw had bars. The long hallway was lined with small rooms, and the whole effect reminded me forcibly of Ostaria's hospital.

I threw Amara a questioning look and found her regarding me with amusement.

"You're thinking it looks like the hospital, aren't you?"

"Of course it does," said the clerk stiffly. "Both are public buildings."

"I haven't decided if reusing the styling and plans was a purposeful choice or merely a cheap one," Amara said. "But the current hospitals and law keeping halls across the kingdom were all built in the same period by King Marius's great-grandfather."

The clerk ignored her words, stopping in front of a thick door with an elaborate handle. With a slight bow, he gestured for Amara to knock. When she did so, a muffled voice bid us enter.

The office behind the door was large but decorated sparsely, the only hint of opulence in the deep red of the carpet and curtains. The older woman behind the dark wood desk stood when she saw us.

"Amara, this is an unexpected pleasure."

Amara swept forward to embrace her. "Aunt. It's good to see you again."

Anka pulled back from the hug and gave me an appraising look that seemed to strip me of every protective layer and pretense. "And who's this youngster?"

I shrank back instinctively, making Amara laugh. "Leave her be, Aunt! She's not one of your criminals."

Anka smiled at me. "Apologies, child. Old habits are hard to shake."

I bowed. "It's a pleasure to meet one of Amara's relatives."

"She's well behaved, at least." Anka bustled over to a low table surrounded by comfortable, padded chairs. As she picked up the teapot from the tea service laid out on the table's surface, she looked back to Amara. "But who is she?"

"My apprentice."

"Your what?" Anka nearly dropped the teapot, succeeding in clanking it noisily against one of the teacups.

"My apprentice," Amara repeated calmly, gesturing for me to approach the tea area at her side.

When I just stood beside the table uncertainly, she sighed. Putting a hand on each of my shoulders, she pushed me into a chair.

"Well, well, well." Anka gave me an even closer look than she had done earlier, making me squirm and wonder what I'd done that might need confessing. "Never did I think I'd see the day Amara would take an apprentice." She looked up at her niece. "But don't tell me you're still roaming here, there, and everywhere, dragging this poor girl with you! Isn't it time you settled down at the Guild?"

"Delphine is as uninterested in *settling* at the Guild as I am." Amara accepted a teacup and saucer from her aunt.

Anka handed one to me next, and I could barely keep my hands steady. I'd been looking forward to coming to the law keeping hall, but perhaps I should have anticipated that law keepers would be intimidating.

"It was proper of you to bring her to me for an introduction," Anka said to Amara, "but if you're looking for my approval, you won't get it. You're getting far too old for this roaming lifestyle. How in the blazes are you going to find—"

"Aunt," Amara cut her off with a warning look, making me instantly curious as to what Anka had been about to say.

After a look at Amara's face, Anka subsided, however.

"I didn't bring her here because of our connection," Amara said. "I brought her here in the hope you'd be willing to give her some training."

"Training? Me?" Anka sat down, a teacup of her own gripped in one hand. "I've always had a fondness for you, Amara, you know that. But I've no use for elements mages in my hall. You should know that, too."

Amara hid a smile behind her cup. "Really, Aunt! Don't you know me better than that?"

Anka frowned, her brows knitting together as she examined Amara's face, trying to make sense of her words. I could see the moment realization hit her.

She sat back, turning wide eyes to me.

"Don't tell me you've apprenticed a healer!" She didn't wait for our confirmation. "Of all the nonsensical things! And with you flitting about hither and thither, too."

"I don't see the harm in that," Amara said. "She's getting a tour of the kingdom's best healers and teachers. She's already met Clay, and now I've brought her to you."

Anka tried to maintain her stern look, but I could see it was a struggle. Her eyes already indicated she had relented in the face of Amara's flattery.

"You always did know how to make pretty to your elders," she told her niece with a shake of her head.

"Would you like to test me?" I asked. "I can lower my wall, if you'd like to."

Anka leaned forward, raising an eyebrow. "There's plenty to be unpacked in that statement. Have you found an exceptionally humble and polite youngster, Amara, that she would offer such a thing without prompting?" She chuckled. "Or is it actually extreme confidence speaking?" She didn't wait for a reply before continuing. "As to lowering your wall...I have no idea what you're talking about there." Her eyes narrowed slightly. "But it sounds fascinating."

I flushed. "My apologies. It's just my inexperience talking. Everyone of master level strength that I've met so far has wanted to test me, so I forgot it's something that's usually considered rude."

Anka turned to Amara with a look of surprise. "Everyone? What exactly has been going on with your apprentice, Amara?"

Amara took her time answering, her eyes narrowing as she looked at me. My flush deepened as I remembered that Clay was the only one who had tested me in her presence.

I cleared my throat. "Master Clay was curious, and I had no reason to deny him. I had no experience of mages before meeting Master Amara, so I don't have any prejudice against it."

"Clearly Amara has found you in some remote hole somewhere," Anka said. "It's the sort of thing she would do. But it's

278

equally clear you're more powerful than you have any right to be, given that background."

My face tightened, and I was about to protest that anyone could be born with a powerful seed when she hurried on.

"Oh, I don't dispute that even those from small towns have a chance of being born with a powerful seed. They are not, however, usually still hanging around those small towns once they reach an age to be activated."

I bit my lip, forced to acknowledge she was right. But I wasn't willing to go into my father's history with this stranger—even if she was Amara's aunt. "Why does my willingness to be tested have anything to do with my strength?" I asked instead.

"That's just basic human nature." She gave a self-satisfied smile. "Something I have a great deal of experience with. If those who tested you had subsequently looked down on your strength, you would have rapidly developed the antipathy to the process that most of us feel."

"Oh." I thought it through and was once again forced to concede she was right.

"It is worth pointing out," Amara said, "that my dear aunt is a senior law keeper and therefore has a great deal of experience with the *worst* of human nature. Not everyone is as prideful and ambitious as your standard Guild mage."

Anka chuckled, undaunted by Amara's criticism. "I see your feelings for the Guild haven't softened. It's a pity, especially since you aren't the only one unexpectedly in town."

Amara stiffened, making no move to ask the obvious question as to who else had recently arrived. Anka chuckled, seeming amused by Amara's cold response, but didn't push the matter further. Instead she looked back to me.

"If you're so willing to be tested, child, I won't say no. I may have more insight than most, but I've no less curiosity." She gave me an expectant look.

I rushed to pull down my wall. I'd become so practiced in the last weeks that it barely required a thought to dismantle the whole thing. A sense of her beating heart and steady breathing hit me, as well as Amara's, but my stomach churned only lightly since both of them were in excellent health.

After a moment, Anka sat back in her chair, a contemplative look on her face, and I took that as a signal to put my wall back in place.

"Yes..." she said slowly. "I can see why you took her on, Amara."

"It would have been a waste to allow someone in her own town to activate her," Amara replied, her normal calm returned.

"Who would have thought such an opportunity would fall into your lap?" Anka said slowly. "A strong seed who shares your aversion for the Guild—and a different affinity from you into the bargain. How could you resist?"

"How, indeed?" Amara asked lightly.

"How experienced is she?" Anka asked, turning businesslike.

"Hardly at all. I activated her only weeks ago."

"Weeks?" Anka raised her eyebrows. "And you're already bringing her to me? Law keeping is usually an afterthought for most healing apprentices."

"Unfortunately she's squeamish," Amara said. "So we're starting with testing and truth telling while she develops control."

"Ah. A pity." Anka gave me a considering look. "It's rare we get someone with your potential with a true interest in law keeping."

I sat forward. "I thought weak abilities were sufficient for most truth telling?"

Anka nodded. "Most of my people are of moderate to high non-mage strength, with the occasional weaker mage. But someone of higher strength, such as myself, is needed to run the hall, and I like to have one or two under me with at least moderate mage strength.”

“For what purpose?” I asked, too curious to hold in my questions.

“There’s more to a law keeper’s role than just truth telling,” Anka replied. “In extreme cases, where a death has occurred, we have to examine the body for time and cause of death. And, where possible, we like to heal the victims of violence ourselves. That way we can accurately assess the extent of the damage, as well as the likely cause. When we’re called in at a later stage— after natural or assisted healing has already occurred—the assessment becomes more difficult.”

“But still possible?” I asked. “Even after full healing, you can tell what the damage was and how it was likely given?”

“Some can—those with sufficient strength and skill. Thus why every law keeping hall needs at least one higher strength mage.”

“Aunt is the strongest law keeping mage the crown has,” Amara said matter-of-factly. “They’d love to have her in Tarona, but for some reason, she insists on working here rather than in the capital. I can only guess she has more sympathy for my dislike of Guild life than she claims.”

“Nonsense,” Anka said. “This is a retirement, of sorts. Capital life would tire anyone of my age.”

Amara snorted. “Nice and slow here, is it?”

Anka sipped her tea with a dignified expression, prompting Amara to turn to me.

“She’s famous in law keeping circles. In her first week here, she faced off against a rioting crowd alone. She didn’t know any of the inhabitants back then, but she was able to sense and identify the troublemakers who had riled up the sincere townsfolk.”

“There was nothing to that,” Anka said. “They reeked of deception, the lot of them.”

Amara smiled. "No, nothing to it at all. Which is why Master Colton, the Head of Healing, said he couldn't have done such a thing himself—not in the middle of a rioting crowd like that."

"That's hardly surprising," Anka said coolly. "Colton has specialized his whole career in healing people. He'd make a terrible law keeper."

Amara laughed, looking at me. "Clay warned that you'd have human and animal healers competing over your specialization—but there are more than two for you to choose between."

Anka looked up, an eager spark in her eye. "Have you not chosen a specialization? If you're not interested in a settled life, you couldn't ask for a more exciting option than law keeping. You see all sorts of things in this profession."

"Thank you," I said, taken aback, "but I'm not sure—"

"Leave her be, Aunt," Amara interjected. "It's too soon for her to be boxing herself in. We have to deal with her squeamishness first, and then she needs the chance to experience all the different facets of healing before making a decision. Besides, her dislike seems to be of the Guild itself and not of a settled life. She intends to return to her parents' farm after her apprenticeship."

Anka settled back, looking disappointed, while I blinked at Amara.

She was right, of course—that had been my initial intention when I accepted Amara's offer of an apprenticeship. But hearing her say it now felt jarring. Could I really return to my farm as if that life hadn't been a lie?

And even if I put aside the issue of my father, did I even want that life anymore? He had taught me to cling to it so fiercely, fearing anything that might rip me away. But had it ever been more than *his* desire? What did I want for myself?

"Of course I'll be happy to show her the basics anyway," Anka said, cutting through my introspection. "We can avoid the actual healing aspects for now and just focus on the truth telling. I'm busy today, but if you bring her back—"

Angry voices outside made her stop. She stood, turning toward the closed door of her office.

It swung open, banging against the opposite wall as an incensed man strode inside.

## CHAPTER
# TWENTY-TWO

A mara rose swiftly, hurrying to her relative's side.

I scrambled up as well, not sure how much help I could be, but ready to assist in providing a united front.

The man, who looked like a prosperous merchant from his clothing, was red-faced with anger. He didn't hesitate at sight of the mages confronting him, striding forward to stand nose-to-nose with Anka.

"Don't try to fob me off this time! I don't care if I don't have an appointment! I want to know what you're doing about this troublemaker—and I'm not the only one. Calista has gone too far, and if the capital doesn't intend to stop them, then Caltor will take matters into its own hands."

"That is enough!" Anka's voice sliced through the tension like a whip crack. "I've told you once, and I'll tell you again. Neither the king nor the Triumvirate are colluding with Calista to steal your precious sons and daughters."

"Then why don't you stop them from leaving?" the man demanded with no abatement in his anger.

Anka sighed heavily. "I can understand your concern, but you know better than this. If our youngsters choose to leave, there is nothing we can legally do to stop them. They may not be fully of age until nineteen, but the law permits a new apprentice to choose their own activator, and once they have been activated, authority over them moves from the parents to the master. If an apprenticeship is offered, law keepers are no more permitted to block a young person's acceptance than family members are."

"Choose for themselves?" the man roared, spit flying. "My son never expressed the slightest wish to leave Caltor until that snake came along and lured him with false promises. I'm telling you, if you won't get rid of him, I will!"

Anka grew taller, the lines of her face somehow becoming even sterner. "If you act against the law, you will be held accountable."

The man finally seemed to remember who he was facing, slowly deflating before our eyes. Anka, clearly extremely experienced in dealing with angry townsfolk, softened her voice to match the change in his posture.

"All accusations are investigated. If Calista is indeed working against Tartora's best interests, it will be brought to light. And you may rest assured that King Marius will not remain idle in that case. But you of all people know the benefit Caltor has reaped from the new trade lanes opened with Calista. If we move hastily, many will suffer."

The remaining bravado seeped out of the man, replaced with an arrested look. I could almost see him weighing his prosperity against the potential danger to his child.

"Naturally we cannot punish before guilt has been proved," he said gruffly. He glanced toward the door, eager to escape now that the fire of his anger had been extinguished. But something held him back. He looked at Anka again. "If anything happens to my son..."

"The safety of Caltor's young people has always been—and will always be—my top priority," she told him gravely.

He hesitated again before giving a perfunctory bow and hurrying from the room.

There was a long moment of silence before Anka let out a slow breath.

"Well, that was interesting," Amara said.

"Feel free to deal with it yourself if you find it so interesting," Anka said sourly.

Amara raised an eyebrow. "The townsfolk have been giving you serious trouble, have they?"

Anka sighed and sat back down. "A subset of them. Basically all the parents of youths nearing or just past activation. They claim some newcomer is riling up the kingdom's children with false promises. Since they all seem convinced Calista is behind it, I thought it was more of the usual nonsense that circulates in any town. But now they're claiming he's actually here..."

She closed her eyes, rubbing the bridge of her nose. "As you've seen, it's not a situation that can safely be ignored any longer. In fact—" She halted suddenly, shooting us a look. "Well, never mind that. Suffice it to say, a law keeper acts as a peacekeeper as often as anything else. Proactive action is better than assigning blame once things go south."

"Very wise," Amara said. "And naturally we shan't pry into the affairs of the law keeping hall."

I was fairly certain I read curiosity in her eyes—it was certainly blazing in me—but I could hardly insist Anka tell us confidential information.

As we rose and exchanged farewells with Anka, my thoughts turned to Nik and what he'd once told me about the youths Grey chose to take with him. If he was right, this merchant had no need to fear for his son. However fascinated the boy was, Grey would never accept a youth from such an influential family.

An uncomfortable feeling filled me as I considered the way

the man had given way just at the mention of financial loss. If he wasn't willing to cause trouble for the sake of his own son, did I really think he would continue to make a fuss when his son remained behind and other, unknown, children were taken in his place?

Seeing the man's behavior only confirmed Nik's words. Grey was getting louder and attracting official attention he'd managed to avoid before. It was a good thing, as far as I was concerned, but I was no longer confident it would lead to any actual action.

As soon as we were ushered outside by the clerk from earlier, I turned to Amara.

"Was that merchant talking about Grey? Is he here in Caltor? Should we have said something to Master Anka about him?"

"What would you like to say?" Amara asked. "We can certainly go back if you have anything of value to report." She gave me a challenging look.

My shoulders slumped. She was right, of course. If I'd had anything concrete to report, I would have gone to the authorities before now.

After an extended pause, Amara spoke again. "I hope you may now lay down your sense of responsibility for Grey's behavior. If he has ties to Calista, I don't doubt my aunt will find them."

I muttered something inaudible, not quite ready to agree. I was glad Anka was aware of Grey's existence, but that didn't lessen my sense of personal responsibility toward Miranda. I had told her father I would try to find her, and I'd achieved nothing helpful so far. It was only chance that I'd ended up back in the same town as Grey.

Amara watched me closely throughout the rest of the day, and when evening arrived, she didn't look happy at my request to go out into the streets with Ember. But one look at the unsettled fox made her relent.

"The poor thing clearly needs to get outside to relieve herself and stretch her legs. But I hope that's your only reason for wanting to go," she finished sternly.

"I'm also curious to see more of the town," I said. "It has quite a different feel from Ostaria."

Amara regarded me with narrowed eyes. "You're not going out to search for Grey again?"

I shook my head. "I promised you I wouldn't do that anymore, and I meant it. But poor Ember can't stay cooped up in here all night after already being here all day."

Amara sighed and nodded. "Don't be long."

I escaped with almost as much relief as Ember. The fox pranced down the street with her tail high, sniffing everything she came across. I felt like the human equivalent, my eyes dancing back and forth as I took in the sights of Caltor at dusk. After weeks on the road and in small towns and villages, I was surprised how much I had missed the bustle of a city. There was an excitement in the air that was missing in smaller places.

"Would I get sick of it if we stayed?" I asked Ember as we meandered along without any particular purpose. "Maybe if we're in a city for long enough, I'll start to miss the empty fields and clear sky of home. Is that why Amara likes to always be on the move?"

At first it had seemed natural that she wanted to be as far from the capital and Guild as possible. But meeting Anka had finally forced me to confront my prejudice about mages. An isolated example like Clay was easily brushed off, but none of the mages I was meeting were anything like my expectations of them.

At this point, I didn't even know why I was surprised. My previous impression of the Guild had come from my father, just like my ideas about my own power. He had held up a mirror to show me the world, and I was finally realizing how distorted the reflection had been.

Mages weren't universally self-centered, egotistical beings who lived lives of luxury. All the ones I'd met so far were hard working people, using their strength to benefit their communities as much as any farmer or blacksmith did.

But that didn't mean my father's impression of the Guild was entirely wrong either. Amara avoided it, clearly at odds with its ethos, and she had said Anka chose not to live in the capital as well. So what was it really like? Would I hate it, as I had always believed, or would I find its charms were more than the empty allure I had been raised to expect?

Would the capital have all the life and vigor of Ostaria and Caltor but heightened by its larger size and greater importance? Would I feel the same buzz in the air that I felt here? Part of me longed to find out but the other part wished I could avoid Tarona and the Guild forever.

I shook myself, trying to dislodge a sensation that felt too close to fear. I had once believed myself strong against the wiles of the capital, but now I was afraid to discover not only the true nature of the Guild but the truth of my own heart as well. Far better to stay out here, away from the seat of power, where I could surround myself with mages who were more interested in being useful than important.

Someone brushed past me, catching my attention. They didn't stop, however, busy about their own business. The people in Caltor moved with more purpose than those in Ostaria, walking more quickly and not stopping to chat on the sides of the road. It fit with the more regimented look of the town, but it made me feel more of an outsider given my purposeless wanderings.

I looked up and down the street, seeking a goal. Did they have night markets here? The city was big enough, and I would love to explore one if it existed.

Although I caught no sign of a market venue, my eyes locked onto two youths who walked with their heads together, buzzing with suppressed excitement. I recognized their manner easily—they might come from a city, but at heart they were the same as the youths back home. They were on their way to somewhere or something of great interest.

Acting on instinct, I fell into step beside them. If there was a market, or something similar, they seemed the most likely to lead me there. And if there was some other reason the youths of the city were gathering at nighttime...

I suppressed the thought, feeling guilty. I had promised Amara I wouldn't go looking for Grey, and that wasn't what I was doing. I was equally interested in the girls' destination, regardless of what it ended up being. And if they were on their way to one of Grey's gatherings, then I would leave immediately and go straight back to tell Amara. Surely she couldn't find fault in that?

Before long, the buzz of voices reached my ears. The girls had led me to a square, but I could see no sign of stalls or vendors. Instead, there was a small crowd of young people.

I took several steps into the throng, checking that Ember was close to my side. The many lanterns dotting the crowd cast flickering shadows, and I didn't want her stepped on in the half-light.

I looked back up to see a figure that towered over the rest of the group. The mountain of a man was clearly not a youth, and his eyes roamed over the crowd, as if keeping an eye out for trouble.

I gasped, stumbling back as I recognized one of Grey's companions. He had been the one to grab and hold me during our confrontation, and the sight of him brought back the fear of those moments. It was a small sound, lost in the sea of chatter around me, but somehow it attracted his attention.

For a second we were both frozen, eyes locked. Then we

both surged into movement. He pushed people aside, moving toward me, while I spun and dashed back out of the square.

Since I was already on the fringes of the group, I moved more easily than he did, but my lead was small. And I was at a disadvantage given my lack of familiarity with my surroundings.

Running and panicked, I couldn't remember the route I had come, and I was soon lost in unfamiliar streets. I pushed on anyway, aware of pounding feet behind me. But beyond the sound of his footfalls, my pursuer remained eerily silent, not calling out or doing anything else that might attract attention.

Should I call for help? Grey clearly had enemies in the town, so I might find someone willing to aid me. But I was out of breath from the running, and I couldn't shake the fear that I would only come across as a madwoman if I suddenly started shrieking.

Surely I would elude him soon. A man of that size had to be getting tired, given the pace we were moving.

I risked a glance back, and my heart contracted. My original pursuer had gained two companions, both fitter and faster than him. Maybe I needed to call for help after all.

I sucked in a deep breath, but before I could let it out, a fourth person emerged from a side street, barreling into my side. I went flying, the ground knocking my breath violently from my lungs.

For a minute my mind was overwhelmed with panic as I struggled to suck in a breath. Instinctively, I swept away my wall, letting my power surge through my body and force open my airway and lungs.

I panted as the sweet night air flowed into me again. For once I was grateful for the sensations that bombarded me as my four pursuers closed in. Without my wall up, I could use my power against them. But I needed skin contact to achieve that, and all of them were pulling on gloves as they circled me.

I slowly pushed myself onto my knees and then up to my feet, not wanting to precipitate an attack by sudden movement.

"Grey's been looking for you," one of the men said with a grin. "He's going to be mighty pleased with us when we bring you in."

I swallowed. "I'm not going anywhere with you. I'm not interested in Grey's cause or his new land or whatever story he's selling."

All of them except the enormous brute laughed.

"That's no problem. We have our ways with those who are reluctant—if they're valuable enough. And Grey thinks you might be worth the effort."

"I...I don't know why," I said desperately. "There isn't anything special about me."

The speaker laughed again, a nasty sound. "Grey will be the decider of that. And he thinks you're plenty interesting."

I shrunk back but gloved hands were reaching for me from all sides. Ember pressed against my leg, and I silently begged her not to move. She couldn't protect me from four attackers at once, and if she was hurt, they might not give me a chance to heal her.

"Why don't you come along quietly?" the man said again. "Grey's very good at convincing people. You might find you're not so reluctant once you hear what he's got to say."

"Grey isn't touching her." The cold voice cut through the tension around me. Suddenly I could breathe again.

Tears of relief sprang to my eyes as a tall figure stalked down the backstreet toward us. Somehow, impossibly, Nik was here.

"You again!" the large man said, speaking for the first time.

"Me." Nik looked him up and down, clearly unafraid, despite the other man's size and companions.

"This is no business of yours," the first man said, clearly unsure of Nik's identity.

Nik strode through their circle and took a firm grip on my upper arm.

"She's mine," he said.

My heart stuttered and sped up at the confidence in his tone. I knew he was putting on an act for my assailants, but it didn't matter. Everything had changed now that he was by my side.

I straightened, my lips tightening. Examining the two closest men, I looked for cracks in their armor—spots where a reaching hand might find skin.

At some unknown signal, all four of them drew swords and leaped forward at once.

I reached for the closest one, but Nik moved faster, pulling me behind him. He didn't draw a blade of his own, though. Instead he simply stood still, his body blocking their access to me.

I winced, flinching in sympathetic anticipation of the expected blows. But none of the men reached him.

Instead, shouts of protest filled the night as all four of them writhed wildly. I peered around Nik.

Thorny vines had sprouted from the ground and were working their way up the legs of the men, holding them in place and biting into their skin. I turned wide eyes on Nik to find him steely faced, watching the thrashing men.

"I said, *she's mine*," he repeated. "You can run back and tell your master."

One of the men made a strangled sound as a vine wrapped around his middle.

"Oh yes." Nik made a lazy gesture with his hand, and the vines pulled free.

They didn't fall to the ground, however, but remained upright, waving from side to side slightly, as if ready to pounce again at any moment.

The men hesitated, looking at one another.

Nik laughed harshly. "Whichever of you is trying to take control of the vines right now, don't even bother. I can promise you aren't strong enough to take me on."

Confidence seeped from every line of his body, and I shivered. If I were one of them, I would have already run.

Perhaps sensing the same thing I did, the closest man sheathed his sword and dashed off down the street. The others followed quickly, only the large one throwing a reluctant look over his shoulder, as if he would have preferred to take us on.

The vines remained upright until the last of the men disappeared. Only when we were alone did they collapse to the ground and lie unmoving.

I drew in a shaky breath. "I was going to protect myself, you know." I held out a hand. "Deadly assassin, remember?" I paused and then added, "But thank you."

Nik smiled slightly, his gaze roving over my body. "Are you all right? You're not hurt?"

My breath caught at the expression in his eyes. But as soon as our gazes locked, his face hardened, a veil dropping over his emotion.

"Do you think they bought it?" he asked.

"B...bought it?" I asked.

"That act?" He stared into the distance where the men had disappeared. "That we're allies."

"Allies?" I wished I could come up with something more intelligent to say, but I was struggling to follow the abrupt twists in his conversation. "You want them to think we're allies?"

"I want to divert Grey's attention to me." He gave a feral smile. "He'll find me a more difficult opponent."

I frowned. "I thought you purposely didn't use your power in our last clash with Grey because you were trying to keep yourself hidden from him."

Nik looked down at me. The amused expression lurking around the corners of his mouth took me by surprise.

"You have a way of interfering with that plan. Would you have preferred I let those men drag you off to Grey?"

"Of course not," I said hurriedly. "I'm very grateful. I was planning to fight, but they'd clearly come prepared to face a healer." I glared down the dark street.

Ember growled as if echoing the sentiment, and Nik dropped to one knee to offer her a hand, as if she were a dog. She sniffed it elegantly, giving him what looked suspiciously like a gaze of approval.

He glanced up at me. "I've already told you that we don't want Grey getting his hands on you. You're a target, but I'm an opponent. Better for him to be focused on me."

My brows drew together, my eyes narrowing at the implied insult, but could I really dispute his words? He had stopped four men without the least strain, whereas I had been nearly frozen with fear.

"Come on." He straightened, looking up and down the street. "It's best we don't linger here."

I nodded, falling into step beside him as he led me unerringly through the streets. My mind was distracted, though, going over my own actions during the confrontation.

When injured and scared, I'd taken down my wall without thinking and healed myself. It had been easy, and I'd never once felt out of control. Even the awareness of people close around me had hardly been a distraction.

Had I felt nauseous? I couldn't remember it. If the feeling had been there, I must have suppressed it instantly. Or perhaps the fear had done that for me.

I stared at the cobblestones passing beneath my feet, thinking of the difference between how I had faced the men and how Nik had. It was true that my ability required physical contact, but it had been more than that.

I didn't know how to use my ability properly because I was still hiding from it. The night's activities had made one thing clear—I had enough control that I was no longer a danger to myself. How long had that been the case? Why hadn't I said anything to Amara?

I squirmed uncomfortably. I'd been avoiding the whole issue because I didn't want to move on to the next phase of my training. I was afraid, just as I'd been afraid to face the reality of my seed in the first place. But my fear had only made me vulnerable and weak—the very thing I had determined I wouldn't be any longer.

It was time for the wall to go. It was time for me to learn to use my ability properly.

I reached for the wall and realized with a start of surprise that I'd never put it back in place. Cautiously, I focused on Nik beside me and Ember at my feet. Once I was paying attention, a dizzy feeling filled my head. Instinct wanted me to reach for the wall again, but I held back, instead pushing back the nausea.

Within seconds, my head was clear, the night crisp around me. My stomach was settled as well. In fact, my whole body felt light. I imagined the worst farm injury I'd ever heard my mother describe. Her words had once been enough to make me so lightheaded I nearly fainted, but remembering them now, I didn't react at all. Or rather, my ability entirely suppressed my physical response. I imagined the whole scenario in gory detail and without the physical symptoms, I felt only mild curiosity as to how I might approach healing it.

I gave a delighted laugh, earning a confused look from Nik. I shook my head, not wanting to explain, and his brows lowered. He didn't push, however, just watching me with a tightened gaze, as if he suspected me of being affected by the attack.

Perhaps I was since my giddy excitement quickly faded. All this time I had been angry at my father for blocking my power and keeping me weak, but I had been doing the same thing to myself. I thought I had thrown off the fear and timidity he had sown in me, but I had merely peeled back the first layer. How many more still lay undiscovered?

The thought made me shiver, and Nik responded to the subtle movement, his eyes tightening. I met his gaze only to quickly look away. The intensity of his focus on me set my pulse racing in a way that drove out all my earlier musings.

"I thought you were going south?" I blurted out.

He looked away for a moment before looking back, his expression transformed. Gone was the intensity, replaced with a hooded smile. "Did I say that?"

I frowned, trying to remember the conversation back in Ostaria. "I'm sure you did! I remember it clearly."

Amusement played around his mouth. "I believe my words were that I would be leaving by the south gate. Which I did. Before circling the city and heading north. I've been in Caltor for some time."

I turned to face him, my mouth dropping open. "But... why?"

He kept his eyes forward. "I was taught better than to tell a lie to a healing mage."

Both my eyebrows shot up, and I remembered Amara and Anka's words about the complexity of truth telling. It had never occurred to me that Nik might be carefully guarding his words around me, manipulating his spoken truths to conceal a deeper deception.

"But why?" I repeated.

He glanced at me, his brows quirking down. "Didn't you want to keep tracking Grey?"

I nodded, and he shrugged, turning forward again.

"It seemed clear Amara would force you in the opposite direction to me, and it conveniently happened that Grey had practiced the same deception. I tracked him out of the south gate, as I said, and I followed his trail long enough to see it turning north. So I sent you north and also came north myself, keeping behind Grey but ahead of you."

"You did that for me?" I asked, unsure what to make of his confession.

He looked down at me. "As I remember it, you were the one who said a healer might be helpful."

I nodded quickly. "Yes." I spoke as firmly as I could. "I know I didn't show it today, but I will be helpful, I'm sure of it."

The earlier smile twitched at the corners of Nik's lips, and I snuck another glance at him. Was it my imagination or did he seem more relaxed than on our previous interactions? Almost... almost as if he was glad to see me.

I shook my head, shaking the thought loose. I was letting my imagination run away with me. Nik had made it clear I was a nuisance, and I could hardly blame him. On my first night in Caltor, he had once again been forced to reveal himself to Grey because of me.

When we reached the gate of the inn, Nik stopped. I scooped up Ember, ready to carry her inside, only to linger awkwardly, not sure what to say.

"Will you be all right?" I finally blurted out.

"Me?" Nik stared at me.

"Will Grey come looking for you now?" I clarified.

He gave a chuckle. "Let him try."

I nodded, the awkwardness still lingering. I didn't want Nik to end up in danger because of me, but what could I possibly do to protect him?

"Sleep well," he said, turning and striding away so that I had to call my farewell at his back.

Grumbling to myself, I padded up the inn stairs. Would it have pained him so much to give a proper goodbye to my face?

Only at the door of our room did I remember that I had to tell Amara what had happened. It had seemed a simple prospect when I was following the two girls to the meeting place, but the subsequent events of the evening made a less easy story.

She was never going to let me walk Ember again.

Taking a deep breath, I quietly opened the door, easing inside and shutting it behind me. When I surveyed the silent room, I found Amara already asleep in one of the beds.

Breathing a sigh of relief, I put Ember into her box by the fire and hurried into the bed against the opposite wall. I'd still have to talk to Amara, but at least I had a stay of execution until morning.

# TWENTY-THREE

I thought I would be tossing and turning all night again, but to my surprise I fell quickly into a deep sleep. I must have been exhausted by the evening's events because I slept late the next morning as well.

I awoke slowly, stretching and opening my eyes to morning sun streaming through the window. Remembering the events of the day before, I sat up quickly, looking across at Amara's bed. It was empty.

Taking my time, I got up and prepared for the day, waiting for her to return from the washroom. But as time ticked on, there was no sign of her.

I finally crossed over to her side of the room, only to find a note resting on her pillow. Scooping it up, I read that she was already gone for the day—off on private business—and that I had the day off.

I blinked and read it again. A day off? I hadn't had a day off since I started my apprenticeship, although my tasks had rarely been onerous. What would I even do with a day off?

Ember was no use to me, having already curled up for her day's sleep. And I knew no one in Caltor yet except Anka, who I definitely wasn't going to disturb.

*You know one other person,* a small voice whispered in the back of my mind, but I firmly dismissed it. Even if I wanted to spend the day with Nik, I had no idea where he might be found.

I ate a solitary breakfast in the inn's dining room, and then wandered out to the streets, unsure what else to do with myself. As I meandered around, taking in the sights of the small city, I once again caught myself watching out of the corner of my eye for a tall, dark-haired figure, just as I'd done in Ostoria.

No matter how many times I reprimanded myself, I couldn't seem to shake the instinct—or the hope that leaped up every time I thought I saw him, only to find myself mistaken.

I returned to the inn for the midday meal, pleased I was able to find the way without assistance this time. I planned to return to the streets again in the afternoon but wanted to check on Ember first.

I found the fox still sleeping and decided to lie down for a few minutes on my own bed. Amara hadn't said how long her business would take her, and it was possible she might return at any moment.

Despite my good sleep the night before, I woke to the dim glow of the late afternoon sun. There was still no sign of Amara, but Ember had woken and was demanding attention.

I took the opportunity to hold her, examining her internal systems to make sure there were no lingering issues from her several healings. As I did so, I marveled at my ability to connect with her without any problems. Given the ease with which I'd transitioned, I'd clearly been ready to remove my wall for some time.

My thoughts of the night before had clearly been true. I had left my father physically, but his influence still lingered. Even without his direction, I had been holding myself back.

But now I was free. The ability that I had thought would be a crushing burden was instead an integral part of me. Cutting it off had been unnatural—a constant tension rubbing against my subconscious.

Ember burrowed into my lap. Her warm presence, free from any hint of judgment, soothed my turbulent emotions. For some time I just held her, patting her soft fur, until the aromas of cooking roused me.

Amara still hadn't returned so I once again ventured downstairs alone and ate a solitary meal. Afterward, I returned to the streets, unable to face more time in the inn room. I still hadn't had the chance to tell Amara what had happened the night before, but this time I would stay closer to the inn and away from anywhere I might run into Grey or his people. As long as I stayed on the main roads, I should be safe.

My intention not to look for Grey was sincere, but I still found myself scanning the crowd and peering into every shadow. At first I thought I was motivated by anxiety and told myself to relax, but it didn't make any difference.

Only when my heart leaped in response to the sight of a tall, dark-haired stranger did I realize I was looking for someone else entirely. It wasn't anxiety driving my search at all.

Embarrassed, I sped up, feeling my cheeks redden, although there was no audience to witness my foolishness. Nik might have saved me the day before, but he wouldn't be here on the streets near the inn keeping watch for me. He had no doubt only found me last time because he was keeping watch over Grey's gathering and saw the men run after me.

But even as I thought it, I still kept looking. And every time I saw a flash of a similar build or coloring, I turned to look, my hopes rising and then falling. If only my ability could help me find a specific person in a crowd, but it was useless for such a task.

Turning away from the latest such disappointment, I re-entered the flow of traffic only to catch sight of someone out of the corner of my eye. I turned back to peer down the side street at the person I had glimpsed.

Sucking in a breath, I stepped forward. It was actually him.

But when I reached the mouth of the side street, I stopped. He wasn't alone.

Had Grey discovered him? Was that one of his men? A rush of fear sent me onto the balls of my feet, ready to race to his aid. But something made me pause. The two men were engaged in a conversation, with no sign of any struggle. They were just out of earshot, and Nik was clearly unhappy with whatever the other man was saying, but there was nothing overtly threatening in the stranger's posture.

He couldn't match Nik's height, although he appeared to have a couple decades on him in age. But despite the physical disadvantage, the stranger didn't look in the least intimidated by what appeared to be Nik's increasing irritation. If anything, his manner seemed earnest as he spoke on, all while Nik's hands clenched into tighter and tighter fists.

I was tempted to intervene, afraid Nik might lash out at the older man. But I couldn't bring myself to step closer. I didn't want them to think I was eavesdropping on what was clearly a private conversation.

At last the other man stopped speaking, waiting for Nik to respond. He remained silent, however, the moment stretching out awkwardly. Eventually the stranger gave a visible sigh and spoke again.

Nik snapped something in reply and stalked around him, making the man sigh again. He didn't try to stop Nik, though, instead moving off in the opposite direction, further down the street.

Nik strode swiftly toward me, his head down and his face dark. He had almost reached the end of the street before he finally looked up, finding himself face to face with me.

He froze, his eyes widening slightly as he recognized me.

"Sorry," I said. "I saw you there, and..."

Slowly, as if forcing himself to do so, he unclenched his hands.

"Who was that?" I asked, curiosity getting the better of me.

Nik muttered something under his breath. The words were too rushed and quiet for me to pick up anything but his irritation.

"Sorry," I repeated, "I didn't mean to pry."

I expected Nik to ask me what I was doing there, as he had on previous occasions when we'd met, but he remained silent.

"What were you doing here?" I eventually asked, peering around him down the rapidly darkening side street. "Has Grey been in this area? It seems too near the middle of the city for him."

Nik started slightly, a suspicious red tinging his cheeks. I stared at him in disbelief. Was he flushing?

Slowly it occurred to me that perhaps I was the reason Nik was in this part of the city. Had he been watching for me at the inn and following me ever since? Was that why I kept thinking I saw flashes of him wherever I went?

"Were you looking for me?" I blurted out, making him flinch again.

When he didn't reply, I put my hands on my hips. "Well? You must want something if you left your surveillance of Grey to come find me."

He still looked reluctant to answer, having to force the words out.

"I've found where Grey is keeping them this time. And from the number of youths with him, he still hasn't sent the latest batch away."

"Miranda's here?" I stepped closer, excitement coursing through me. "Can we rescue her?"

He hesitated again before reluctantly speaking.

"That's why I came to find you. I think there might be a chance, but it requires two people."

A different sort of thrill ran through me. Nik really had been looking for me. He needed assistance, and he trusted me for the job.

"What are we standing here talking for, then?" I asked. "Let's go!"

As soon as I said the words, hesitation gripped me. Could I really do this? Hadn't I promised Amara I wouldn't?

I considered my promise. I had told her I wouldn't go looking for Grey alone. I had even joked about how animals didn't count. But Nik was a human—a highly skilled one, at that. So I wasn't actually going back on my word.

It would have been better to talk to her beforehand, of course. But she'd been missing all day, and I had no idea where to find her. I couldn't miss this opportunity. Last time Grey had moved on too quickly, and I couldn't risk that happening again.

"Are you sure?" Nik asked. "It could be dangerous."

"Miranda has been facing that danger this whole time," I said. "I won't turn my back on her now."

Nik examined my face, as if testing my determination, before nodding and leading the way out onto the main street.

He walked quickly, so I had to hurry to keep up, several times glancing back to check Ember was still with us. As I had expected, he led us away from the more populated area of town, eventually stopping at yet another rectangular building with the look of a warehouse. This one wasn't quite against the wall of the city, but it was close.

"They're in there?" I whispered, and he nodded.

"So what do we need to do?" A thought struck me, and my brow creased. My enthusiasm had led me to overlook the obvious question. "I'm all for rescuing Miranda, but why the sudden change in plan? Weren't we just looking for evidence?"

"We're out of time," he said in a grim tone. "Haven't you noticed the mood of the city? The law keepers won't act without proper evidence, but I'm afraid the citizens might take matters into their own hands. And if they do, they won't distinguish between Grey's people and those children. We need to get them out first, and then Grey can face whatever comes for him without a human screen."

I frowned, but memory of the morning before in Anka's office kept me from disputing his words. This was my first visit to Caltor, so I couldn't compare the current tone of the city with its usual air, but Amara had noticed a difference in the guards at the gate. It was quite possible tensions were even more inflamed than I'd realized. It might even be the reason why everyone hurried about their business, not lingering in the streets.

Finally I nodded. Anka clearly knew about Grey, but she and her law keepers hadn't acted. If Nik and I had a chance to rescue Miranda now, I was going to take it.

"What do you need me to do?" I asked.

"The only reason we have a chance at pulling off a rescue is the particular layout of this building," he said. "Grey and his most loyal followers—the ones he lets come and go freely—have been using the main section of the warehouse. They've got the youngsters they lured away in a much smaller office in the back part of the building. It doesn't have a door, but it does have a large window. That's where you come in."

"You want me to get them all out the window?" I eyed him doubtfully. "What will you be doing?"

"I'll be providing a distraction at the front door." His eyes gleamed, as if he was looking forward to it, but I shook my head violently.

"You mean you're going to take all of them on alone? Even Grey? Isn't he a powerful healer? That must mean he's dangerous."

Nik smiled broadly, his hand drifting to his sword hilt. "Only if he can touch me."

I examined him, trying to gauge his mood. I couldn't help but worry he was overconfident, but at the same time, I'd seen him use his ability to take down four men last night with ease. And he was right that his plants affinity had a significant advantage over Grey when it came to a fight, since he could attack from a distance.

"So I smash the window, and I get everyone out," I said.

"You shouldn't have to smash it. I already loosened the wood of the frame. You should be able to knock it out without much more than a tap."

"That's helpful." I looked at him, waiting for him to say more since his manner made it clear there was something else.

"There's usually one of Grey's people in there." He sounded apologetic. "You'll need to climb inside quietly and deal with them before you can start sending people to safety."

I bit my lip, looking down at my hand. It was one thing to try to defend myself in the heat of an attack, but could I really turn my ability against someone in cold blood like that?

"If you don't want to do it..." Nik said, making me look up.

"I'm not abandoning Miranda."

His eyes stayed glued to my face. "Are you sure you're up to it?"

I nodded, resolute. "I'll do it. It's not as if I have to kill them. You can leave it to me."

My confidence had ebbed, however, by the time I found myself standing just to one side of the back window. Light streamed out, indicating the curtains were open, so I kept carefully out of sight.

"You need to stay here," I whispered to Ember, giving her an intent look and hoping she understood my meaning. "You'll just be in the way inside."

She sat, looking off into the night like a sentry, and I hoped that signaled assent.

The seconds ticked by interminably as I strained for any unusual sound. Nik had repeated several times that I needed to wait for his signal, telling me I would know it when I heard it.

A loud shout cut through the silence, making me straighten. It was followed by another and another. Definitely my signal.

Leaping forward, I pushed against the window. Mistrusting Nik's suggestion that a tap would be enough, I put too much strength in. The pane of glass went flying into the room.

Several people shouted as it crashed against a table, breaking into several shards. I scrambled over the windowsill behind it, trying to take in the room and its occupants as I moved.

Most of the young people inside were sitting on a ring of tired looking sofas that sagged with age. Many of them jumped to their feet at my explosive arrival, but it was still easy to iden-tify the older woman guarding them. She stood by the door, clearly having been in position there before my unexpected entrance.

She spun around to face me at the sound of breaking glass, her expression distracted and confused. She had clearly been torn as to whether she should go investigate the shouts from the main warehouse, and her attention was divided. The distraction proved invaluable, just as Nik had hoped, giving me precious extra seconds to find my feet.

By the time she had started toward me, I was ready.

Not bothering to waste time, I launched myself straight into her clutches, my reaching hands latching onto her face. She shrieked, but the sound was muffled beneath my fingers as I pushed my power into her.

I didn't have enough experience to aim for finesse, so I poured my power into her brain, letting my instinct lead the way as I commanded her to sleep. She swayed for a moment beneath my hands and then crumpled to the ground.

I stepped back, panting.

"She's dead!" a girl screamed.

Another girl slapped her across the face, silencing her frenzied cries.

"She's not dead." A young man met my eyes. "You must be a healer too."

I nodded, glad he was strong enough to sense her heartbeat from across the room. His words would be more reassuring to the group than anything I said.

"I'm here to rescue you."

Sudden uncertainty gripped me. I had come this far on faith, but what if these people didn't want rescue? I didn't think I could put them all to sleep before they managed to subdue me.

My eyes searched the silent crowd, looking for a familiar face. I couldn't see any sign of Stefan, the blacksmith's son. Did that mean he had been accepted enough to join the trusted ones in the main warehouse? There was no sign of Miranda, either, although I refused to believe the same could be true of her.

Eventually I spotted Serena on one side of the group. Back in Tarin, my heart always sank at the sight of her, but now it lifted. I opened my mouth to call to her, but before I could say her name, she spoke.

"Delphine?" She stepped forward, staring intently at me. "Is that you?"

I nodded. "Where's Miranda?"

"You're the healer Grey's so worked up about?" she asked, ignoring my question.

I shrugged, uncomfortable, and the boy from earlier spoke again.

"Miranda isn't here. She's the strongest of us healers, so

Grey keeps a close eye on her. Especially now, since that friend of yours got them all...jumpy."

"Friend?" I asked, realizing a moment later he meant Nik.

A loud bang, followed by a high-pitched scream, made us all look toward the closed door that led to the rest of the warehouse.

"He's out there, isn't he?" a girl asked, shrinking toward the window.

"He's here to help." I gestured at the empty rectangle where the glass had been. "He's keeping Grey and his people distracted so that anyone who wants to leave has the chance to get away. Caltor is in turmoil and bad things might be coming soon."

They exchanged looks while I held my breath. Serena was the first to step forward, the outspoken boy only a second behind.

"We want out," he said, and the others all began to nod.

"Good." I hurried toward the window. "Climb out one by one, and I'll come last." I looked at the boy. "Once you're outside, lead everyone around the building and all the way down the street. We'll meet in the square at the end."

The boy nodded once and vaulted through the window opening. From the other side, he reached back to help the next person scramble through. Pleased I'd picked the right person to put in charge, I looked around for a chair to help the process.

There were no ordinary chairs in the room, so I had to pull an entire sofa into position. At first it barely scraped across the floor, but a sudden lurch sent it moving and when I looked up, I saw Serena had joined my efforts and was pushing from the other end.

With the two of us, we quickly had it in position beneath the window. Aided by the sofa, the evacuation sped up, the remaining captives easily clambering onto it and then through the window.

"Hurry," I called quietly into the night. "Don't linger here. Get to the square."

There was a hurried conversation and then the sound of retreating steps. But the boy still remained in place, beckoning for Serena and me to come through. We were the only two remaining, apart from the unconscious woman, so I murmured for Serena to go first.

She hesitated. "What about you?"

"Don't worry about me. I need to find Miranda."

"But she's with Grey!" Serena stared at me, eyes wide. "You can't go after her on your own."

"I have to try."

Serena still hesitated, clearly torn.

"Come on," the boy whispered. "Someone could come at any moment."

As if in response to his words, the door creaked, the knob turning. Serena and I both froze, staring at it.

"Come on!" the boy hissed, but we still didn't move.

Swinging open, the door revealed Miranda. She stumbled into the room, as if pushed from behind, and for a single second I couldn't believe our luck.

But a second person followed her, his attention momentarily diverted as he looked back over his shoulder. Grey.

Miranda stifled a gasp when she saw us, but it was enough to alert Grey. He spun around, taking in the situation with one glance and swearing loudly.

"Miranda!" I cried, and she leaped toward us, her hands reaching for Serena and my outstretched ones.

But Grey was faster. He grabbed her from behind, pulling her back toward him so hard that she stumbled and nearly fell.

"Let her go!" I shouted.

Grey slung an arm around her, resting his hand lightly against her bare neck. He held my gaze as he spoke.

"Why should I relinquish my prize?" His eyes ran up and down me. "Are you offering me a bigger one?"

Before I realized what was happening, a foreign power brushed against mine, and I remembered my wall was dismantled. My eyes flew to Grey's, the pleased smile on his face making my stomach turn.

"I thought there must be something impressive behind defenses like that." His eyes grew hungry. "And then there's the defenses themselves. You'll have to teach me how you did that."

I shook my head soundlessly, backing up until I hit the empty window frame.

"Didn't you come all this way for her?" He tightened his hold around Miranda's neck, making her whimper. "Don't tell me you're just going to leave."

I swallowed, not able to tear my eyes away from them. Miranda was looking at me with desperation on her face, and I couldn't bring myself to abandon her and flee.

Grey smiled at my hesitation. "Come over here, and I'll let her go."

I knew what he wanted. Once he had contact with my bare skin, I would be at his mercy. He was a much more experienced healer than me. I would have no hope in a duel between our abilities.

But when I looked at Miranda's face again, my feet stepped forward. At least I had a better chance than Miranda, who hadn't even been activated yet.

"Delphine!" Serena hissed, but I didn't turn.

"Get ready to grab Miranda and go," I whispered, ignoring her wordless protest.

My steps slowed even further as I neared Grey, every part of me protesting against his nearness. But his hand on Miranda's neck left me no other option.

As soon as I was in reach, Grey's hand snapped out and grabbed my bare arm, yanking me toward him.

He didn't let go of Miranda as he'd promised, but I was prepared for that. As Grey pulled me near, I seized her with my free arm and tore her away from him.

Off balance from attempting to hold us both, he released her. Choosing to focus on me, he used his now free hand to get a firmer hold, pinning both my arms.

But Miranda was free.

"Run!" I gasped out, and she stumbled toward the window, looking back at me with horrified eyes but not stopping.

Serena caught her when she nearly collapsed against her, whispering something I couldn't hear.

"I didn't expect you to be such an obedient little thing," Grey murmured to me, making my skin crawl. "That ability of yours is going to be very useful, indeed."

"I won't help you," I said, my voice cracking on the words.

"Are you sure about that?" His power pushed into me again, and I knew, without knowing how I knew, that it was heading for the bones of my right hand. He intended to break one of my fingers to remind me of the power he held over me.

Without thought, I threw up the wall I had been sheltering behind since my activation. It sprang instantly into place, my long practice making it second nature.

Grey's grip on my arms tightened, his face growing stormy as my wall expelled his power, thrusting it out of my body completely.

"What did you do?" he ground out. "How did you do that?"

I glared at him defiantly. He might be more skilled than me, but that didn't mean I was helpless. The skin contact between us worked both ways. Turning the tables, I sent my power into him.

I had vague thoughts of putting him to sleep as I had done to the woman, but the moment he felt the brush of my power, he let me go, dropping his hands and stepping rapidly back.

Before I could regain my balance enough to follow, he

dodged around me. Rushing for the window, he reached for Miranda, who was already halfway through the opening, apparently wanting to reclaim his previous hostage.

Serena screamed and threw herself into his path. He barely slowed, his hand clamping around her wrist, and his power shredding through her. She didn't make a sound, dropping limply to the floor as he reached again for Miranda.

This time he managed to grab her arm, pulling her back into the room. She fell backward, and he caught her in his arms. I rushed toward them, but he slung her over his shoulder, one hand wrapped firmly around her wrist.

I slid to a halt as he met my eyes.

"Don't come any closer," he said. "Or she dies. You're a healer. You can read the truth of my words on me."

I froze as I sensed his steely determination. If he was going down, he would take her with him without hesitation.

He stepped forward, his eyes on me as he slowly advanced across the room. I stood in front of the door, but when he reached me, I had no choice but to step slowly aside, Miranda's terrified sobs echoing in my ears.

I didn't move far, and as Grey passed, he paused, turning as if he meant to say something to me. Instead of speaking, however, his hand flashed forward, the concealed dagger in his grasp sinking into my stomach.

# CHAPTER
# TWENTY-FOUR

Pain and fire flared inside me, overtaking all my senses as my hands flew to the hilt of the weapon. Dimly I was aware of Grey striding out the door, and I stumbled mindlessly after him.

On the other side, a large space opened out, its shadowy depths hidden by the night. Grey was already heading toward the far side of the warehouse, ignoring the debris, vines, stones, and scattered bodies that littered the floor.

None of the bodies were moving.

Before horror could take hold, a figure loomed out of the darkness, running toward Grey. Nik. He was still alive. My relief was instantly swallowed by a new fear. He couldn't stop Grey or Miranda would die.

"No!" I screamed, but my voice wasn't as loud as I had intended. My diaphragm couldn't seem to contract properly, limiting my breath.

Nik heard me anyway, though, his gaze swinging around to find me in the brightly lit doorway. His eyes dropped to my hands, still clasped around the dagger's hilt, blood oozing between my fingers.

Even across the distance, I saw him falter, saw the horror on his face as he absorbed my state. Changing direction, he ran toward me instead.

Scooping me into his arms, he burst through into the office. Glancing around the room, now deserted except for the two prone forms, he strode over to the closest sofa and laid me down.

Kneeling at my side, his hands reached for the hilt. I batted them away.

"Leave it be," I panted out. "Help her." I gestured toward Serena, my arms strangely weak.

Nik hesitated, but I pushed him away, my strength only just sufficient to make him rock backward.

Grabbing the hilt myself, I pulled it out in one swift motion, screaming with the pain. A healing ability could numb pain, but I didn't have any experience with using my power that way, and I had neither time nor energy to waste. I wasn't the only one needing healing.

Nik leaned forward again at my cry, his face ashen. I ignored him, sending my power racing toward my middle. It burned through me freely, re-knitting the torn places and refreshing the lost blood.

As soon as it was finished, I sat up, gasping at the relief from pain. Nik tried to push me back down, but I glared at him.

"What are you doing? I'm a healer, remember! I'm fine now. We need to help Serena."

He stood, clearly still reluctant, and looked uncertainly between the female guard and the girl lying near the window. Both of them lay still, appearing untouched from the outside.

Exasperated, I brushed past him, falling to my knees beside Serena. As if in response to my presence, she stirred and coughed. Blood sprayed across my dress.

Terrified, I put my hand on her arm and pushed my power inside her. My eyes widened, and I fell back, groaning as I pulled my hand away.

"What is it?" Nik was right behind me. "Did you heal her?"

I shook my head, tears springing to my eyes. "He's literally shredded her insides. I don't know how she's still alive. Everything needs healing. And it doesn't feel...right. My power doesn't know what to do."

Nik looked from me to Serena, determination overtaking his features. "Then we find someone who does."

Leaning down, he picked her up as easily as if she were a child.

"I don't think she'll last long enough," I said, stumbling over the words.

He fixed me with a steely glare. "Then you keep her alive. Keep her alive just as long as it takes."

His words bolstered me, steadying my panicked thoughts. Rushing forward, I put my hand against her and sent my power beneath her skin.

Not knowing what else to do, I focused on her heart and lungs. If her body couldn't keep them going, I would do it for her. As long as her heart kept beating and her breath kept flowing, she had a chance.

I bumped against the windowsill, barely aware of what was happening as Nik passed Serena out to the boy still waiting on the other side. I reached after her, leaning out the gap as I maintained the contact.

I tipped, nearly losing balance, and my feet were swept out from under me as Nik picked me up unceremoniously and lifted me through the window. When he put me down on the ground outside, I stepped closer to Serena, still not having lost our connection.

The boy who was holding her staggered, nearly dropping her. Nik pulled her back into his own arms, giving the boy a contemptuous look. I shook my head, but I was concentrating too hard to find the words to explain what had made him falter. The boy was a healer, and as soon as he took Serena, he must have felt the state of her insides. It was no wonder he had responded with shock.

Nik hurried around the building, and I followed at his side, pouring my power into Serena, although it seemed to make little difference to her state.

"You're doing well," Nik murmured. "She's still breathing."

As before his words steadied me.

"The others are at the square." The boy hurried past us, moving faster since he wasn't encumbered like we were. "I'll gather the other healers and send someone for help."

He disappeared down the street, running at full speed.

"I don't know if she's going to make it." I felt warm tears on my cheeks, but I didn't have the energy to wipe them away. "The square is too far."

A loud, familiar bark made us both stagger to a stop. Ember raced toward us down a side street, Amara on her heels.

I nearly collapsed in my relief. My master had arrived, and everything would be all right now.

But the relief only lasted a moment before I remembered Amara wasn't a healer. She might be powerful, but she couldn't do anything for Serena.

But more footsteps were coming behind her, two more people appearing on the scene at full speed. It took a moment for my confused brain to recognize the man as the one who had been talking to Nik on the street, and I didn't recognize the much younger girl with him at all.

Nik groaned with relief as soon as he saw the two, however, almost collapsing as he lowered Serena to the ground. I sank down beside them, still maintaining my contact.

Neither of the newcomers paused as they sprinted to Serena's side, both of them dropping to their knees and placing one hand on her.

Instantly I felt her insides change, and I pulled my own hand away, relief filling me. They were healers.

Ember had brought Amara, and Amara had brought healers. I didn't know how she'd known, but she'd brought healers—and powerful ones given the speed with which their power had latched onto Serena's wounds.

Slowly I rose to my feet. Exhaustion filled me, although I wasn't sure if it was from my own healing or the power I'd poured into Serena. If I'd been in a better state, I would have liked to stay connected to her so I could observe what the other healers were doing. But given my current state, I didn't want to risk getting in their way.

Amara glanced at me, but she must have assumed the blood down the front of my gown was Serena's because she immediately turned to the prone girl, concern on her face.

I tried to walk to her side, but a hand gripped my wrist. Unafraid of my bare skin, my captor dragged me down a narrow alley.

Mustering my strength yet again, I was about to send my power into my new assailant when he stopped, spinning me around so we stood face to face.

"Oh, it's you," I said with relief, smiling up at Nik.

He didn't smile back. Instead he dropped my wrist and ran his hands up and down my arms, as if searching for an undisclosed injury.

His breathing was harsh, his eyes strained as they bore into me. "Are you sure you're all right? You don't have other injuries?"

"Don't be silly." I smiled at him, some of my energy starting to return in his presence. "How many times do I have to remind you I'm a healer? I'm fine."

"You nearly died." His face was haunted as his eyes roamed over my face.

I shook my head. "No, that's Serena. We should go and check on her. She's the one who was in real danger."

His only movement was to bring both hands up to cradle my face. My breath caught as his eyes held mine.

"I took you there." His voice was ragged. "I asked for your help, and you nearly died. I nearly killed you."

"I'm really all right," I breathed. "I promise. As a healer, I was never in any real danger from a wound like that. Grey was just being spiteful."

"Spiteful? How can you say. He stabbed you!"

His breathing sounded harsh in the following silence, his eyes burning as they held me locked in place, his hands dropping to grip my upper arms. I swallowed, trying to think of further reassurances, but he swayed forward, and I forgot how to form words. For one breath, we stayed suspended there, and then he pushed me backward two steps, pressing my back against the stone wall and his mouth against mine.

A new kind of fire spread through me as his lips devoured mine, one of his hands returning to my face while the other wrapped around my waist.

I kissed him back, providing the reassurance my words hadn't given. I never wanted to let go.

But somewhere, distantly, a voice was calling my name. He broke off, panting, and our eyes met, both of our gazes slightly wild.

"Delphine!" The call came again, and this time Nik dropped his hold completely, stepping away from me just as Amara appeared at the entrance to the alley.

She looked from Nik to me, her gaze heavy with suspicion.

"What are you two doing in here? What's going on?"

Somehow I found my legs and hurried forward, forcing myself to ignore Nik, although I had never been so burningly aware of his presence.

"How's Serena? Is she healed?"

I burst out into the street, looking around for the other girl. I found her still stretched flat on the ground, her eyes closed, and my heart sank.

Had I been off being kissed while she was dying?

"Don't worry," a man's voice said, his tone warm. "She's fine."

I turned to face the man Amara had brought. Now that I'd stopped panicking, I could sense the truth of his words for myself. Serena's body thrummed with its normal, healthy rhythms.

"We thought it would be best to put her to sleep for a bit," the girl at his side added with a friendly smile. "I've never done such an extensive healing. Her body will need time to regain its energy."

I trembled, remembering how Serena's insides had felt before their arrival.

"Why was it like that?" I asked. "My power usually knows what to do, at least partially, but it was chaos in there."

"That was the effect of healing power." The man sounded grim. "Those weren't ordinary injuries, but ones caused by a healer."

I nodded, my body starting to tremble again. "His name is Grey, and he got away with Miranda."

"Your friend from Tarin?" Amara exchanged a worried look with the man.

The look seemed to convey much more than I could grasp, and it occurred to me suddenly that here was the reason for Amara's absence during the day. She hadn't known to bring a healer, she had already been with him when Ember came looking for her. Or perhaps the three of them had already been looking for me after finding me absent from the inn.

"This is Hayes, by the way," Amara said. "He's a master healer visiting from the capital. And this is his apprentice, Luna."

The girl smiled at me again. "It's a pleasure to meet you,

although I would have preferred to do it under less dramatic circumstances. Amara has told us all about you, and I'm excited to get a classmate."

Her warm words confirmed my speculation about Amara's day, although they let loose a host of other questions. Foremost was what she meant by classmate, but Anka's words at the law keepers' hall also flashed through my mind. She had said Amara wasn't the only unexpected visitor to Caltor, and she had seemed to be referring to someone of importance to Amara. Had she meant this man, Hayes? Were Anka's words the reason for Amara seeking him out the next day?

I looked at him speculatively, noting they appeared to be a similar age. Had they studied at the Guild together back during their own apprenticeships?

Hayes himself was looking at something over my shoulder. Before I could question him, he gave a slight bow, his gaze unreadable.

"Your Highness."

I stiffened. *Your Highness?* When had one of the royal family arrived, and what could they possibly be doing here? Surely Hayes and Amara hadn't brought them.

I turned slowly, preparing to drop into a curtsy, but the street was empty of any new arrivals. Only Nik stood there, his gaze fixed on Hayes, his eyes angry.

As I stared at him, he slowly looked from Hayes to me, his expression torn between defiance and apology.

I gasped.

No, it was impossible. Nik—my Nik—couldn't possibly be Prince Nikolas, Princess Morgiana's younger brother.

I had seen a royal portrait many years ago, painted when the twins were children. I struggled with my memory, failing to bring up a clear image of the prince's features. But the one thing I remembered was the startling contrast between the princess's dark brown curls and her brother's straight, fair hair.

"I told you the dark hair looked good on him," Amara said to Hayes, sounding amused.

I couldn't find anything humorous in the situation, however. I felt like a fool. I had sought him out, had trusted him with my life, had *kissed* him—but apparently I was the only one who didn't know his true identity. His *royal* identity.

What was he doing roaming the kingdom? Was this all just some game to him? A temporary escape from the boredom of court life?

I wanted to deny his title, but the look in his eyes and his silence confirmed Hayes's words. And now that I thought about it, I could see how the pieces fit. He had seemed defiant toward authority from the beginning, and yet my criticism of the king —and especially the princess—had enraged him.

I swallowed as I realized I had spoken against the royal family to one of their own. Was he going to return home and report what I'd said?

"Delphine," Nik whispered, but I shook my head savagely, and he fell silent.

Whatever bond had just forged between us in the warehouse and the alley had already been shattered.

# TWENTY-FIVE

"So it really is you," Luna said cheerfully, oblivious to Nik's mood. "Their Majesties will be very pleased to know where you are."

His eyes finally left mine, flashing to her face. His own expression set into a threatening glare.

"Don't you dare tell them I'm here."

Hayes sighed. "I already told you that we can't possibly—"

"And I told you that if you send word, I'll be gone before they can send anyone back for me." Nik turned his glare on Hayes. "I've been gone for over a year. I'm not the prince you used to know. I'm far more familiar with the streets than you'll ever be."

Hayes sighed again. "Is this all really necessary, Nikolas? Your parents and sister miss you."

"Do they?" Nik's face didn't soften at all at mention of his family. "I can't imagine why. They never had any use for me when I was with them."

"That's not fair," Hayes said softly, compassion on his face, but the emotion only seemed to stir Nik further.

"Isn't it? I suppose next you're going to tell me the Triumvirate miss me too?"

I didn't understand the significance of his words, but something in them made Hayes back down. He broke their locked gazes, looking helplessly toward Amara. She looked equally burdened, but she shook her head slightly, as if letting him know to let it go.

Nik looked back at me, but a groan from Serena made me hurry to her side.

"How do you feel?" I supported her arm as she struggled to her feet.

"Like I ran into a wall and then stumbled off the roof of a building." She groaned again.

Luna hurried to join us, her hand reaching for Serena's. "You have pain somewhere? You shouldn't have pain."

Serena evaded her grasp, grinning at her. "That might have been a slight exaggeration. It's more like extreme exhaustion."

"That's unavoidable after an attack like that from such a powerful healer." Hayes sounded apologetic, as if he bore some responsibility as a member of the same affinity.

"Grey!" Serena spat out an insult that made Luna gasp and cover her ears, although her eyes danced.

"He was always threatening to do something like that," Serena added, "but I was never quite sure if he really meant it." She grimaced. "Apparently he did. So I guess I was right to take him seriously and not make an escape attempt myself."

"You were wanting to leave for a while?" I asked. "I thought you went with them willingly."

"I did." Serena gave me a guilty look. "Life in Tarin was so dull, and Grey offered an adventure. You know how I used to be. I was convinced I was too strong for a backwater like Tarin, but my seed wasn't quite strong enough to get me a ticket out—not even to a city, let alone the Guild."

"What about Miranda?" I asked. "Did she want to go with him initially?"

Serena shook her head. "No, she didn't want to leave her father. Grey forced her to come."

"But why?" I frowned, unable to understand it. "I know she has a relatively strong seed for a non-mage, but she won't be ready for activation for a while yet. I get the impression Grey is taking youths who are already activated—or about to be, at least."

Serena's face twisted. "That's our fault. We'd all talked up her strength, and no one ever mentioned her age. Grey didn't bother to actually check how far she was from activation until he'd already dragged her along with us. He might have abandoned her at that point, but since he'd forced her to come, he couldn't let her free to report him to the authorities. Plus, she was a healer, and he seems particularly interested in strong healers. He must have decided she was worth the wait because he kept a closer eye on her than the rest of us."

I could feel Nik's eyes burning into the side of my face, a silent reminder of all his warnings about Grey's interest in me. I kept my focus on Serena, though.

"What happened with Miranda was the first sign something was off," she said. "I tried to ignore it, but then he threatened that if she escaped, he would kill her father."

I gasped. "Surely that was an empty threat!"

"Miranda decided it was, but then Grey got a report from the person he'd left in Tarin. The report included enough information to prove Grey really did have a person loyal to him there, so he had the means to carry out his threat. Plus the man reported that Halmir had disowned Miranda after her disappearance, saying she was no daughter of his. Poor Miranda was heartbroken and lost the will to escape after that."

"That's all lies!" I cried. "I spoke with Halmir myself, and he never said anything of the sort."

"Really?" Serena looked hopeful. "Does that mean the whole thing was a ruse, and he never had anyone in Tarin?

Miranda hasn't been activated yet, and the other healers are weaker, but they all agreed he was telling the truth."

"It was likely a trick," Nik said, finally joining the conversation. "Grey doesn't have the resources to leave people in every town he visits. And, as you know, he's an expert at making anything he says sound convincing. He could talk his way around a healer easily."

"After what happened with Miranda, I wanted to leave," Serena said. "But it wasn't an option. I wasn't the only one, either. Most of us wanted to go home after he revealed the truth behind his promises. But he made it clear he would hold us to the commitment we'd made, and everyone was scared of him."

Amara leaned forward. "And what, exactly, is the truth behind his promises? How were you deceived?"

"He was always talking about the new land, and we all thought he meant Calista," she said slowly. "I'm sure he said as much, but looking back he can't have said it outright, or the healers would have sensed the lie. Going there sounded like an adventure. But he wasn't talking about Calista at all."

"Of course he wasn't," Nik muttered. "That's what I keep saying."

"He claims he's found an entirely new land off the eastern coast," Serena explained. "We've been moving north, gathering others on the way, heading for Grey's base. I haven't seen it myself, of course, but I heard some of his people talking, and I think it's located somewhere in the desert that runs along the eastern coast of Calista. He set himself up there because it's the only spot you can launch from to reach the island safely. Apparently no one sails that coast due to the treacherous shore and the desert, so Grey is the only one who knows about this new land and the route to get there."

She shook her head. "Going to Calista was one thing, but setting sail for some unknown land? Who knows what we'll really find there. And what if we can't come back to visit our families? Are we just supposed to leave our homeland forever?"

"I can understand your hesitation." Hayes voice was gentle and free of judgment. "But there must have been some who still wanted to go?"

"Stefan," Serena spit out the name.

"He wasn't in the back room," I said. "Was he with Grey and his people in the main warehouse?"

"Yes," she said simply, but I could see her seething emotions. She clearly felt betrayed by her fellow townsman.

I looked to Nik, suddenly remembering my one glimpse of the warehouse.

"Is he still alive, then?"

He met my questioning gaze, his own heavy, as if I had disappointed him. "Of course. They're all alive."

Running feet sounded from the direction of the warehouse, and we all straightened, spinning toward the approaching group. But our concern was unnecessary since the figures that appeared wore the uniform of law keepers, several of the young people we'd rescued at their head.

"Serena!" one of the girls screamed, running forward to throw her arms around her friend's neck. "I thought you were dead!" She started crying into Serena's shoulder.

Serena patted her awkwardly on the arm. "Don't worry, I'm fine."

"Are you the wounded girl?" one of the law keepers asked. "Our healer is just…"

"I'm here." A trailing law keeper arrived, pushing through the small crowd of people to stand at the front. "Where is the injured…" His words trailed off as he noticed Hayes. "Master Hayes! Thank goodness. The girl was saved, then?"

"Yes," Hayes agreed. "But it sounds like our services might be needed back in that warehouse." He threw an exasperated glance at Nik, who didn't respond.

"Of course." The law keeping healer gestured for Hayes to lead the way.

Hayes stepped forward, only to hesitate and turn back.

"Don't go anywhere, Your Highness. We still have matters to discuss."

"Your Highness?" The new healer did a double take, staring at Nik. "Goodness, I didn't recognize you at first, Prince Nikolas. Please excuse me." He bowed deeply while Nik threw a poisonous look at Hayes.

Inclining his head slightly, Nik acknowledged the man's greeting, his movements stiff.

The healer looked like he wanted to ask questions, but Hayes bustled him away, Luna herding the rest of the law keepers in their wake.

"They'll take care of the mess you left behind," Amara said to Nik once they were gone.

She looked at Serena and discovered the entire group of rescued young people had followed the law keepers to find us. They were hanging back watching us, uncertainty on most of their faces.

"I know it's late, but I suppose you'd all better come with me to the law keeping hall. Anka will be furious with me if I do anything else."

"And who is going after Grey?" Nik asked. "For every minute we talk, he gets further away."

Amara sighed. "I'm as eager to see him pay for his crimes as anyone, but what do you intend to do if you catch him? You already let him go once because of the threat to his hostage. It sounds like he has need of her, so as long as we stay away, she'll be safe enough. Right now, the most dangerous thing for Miranda would be for us to confront Grey."

Nik stepped forward, his expression incredulous. "You just want to let him go? After what he did?" His eyes flicked back to me.

"I don't *want* to," Amara said, "but I don't see any other choice for the moment. Once these witnesses have recorded official statements, we'll have the evidence we need to mobilize the law keepers. Grey just lost many of his followers, and he won't move as quickly with a hostage in tow. We'll find him eventually."

"Maybe," Nik snapped. "Or maybe he'll go to ground and be lost to us. If he makes it across the border, he's really gone. Even you can't pretend that Tartoran law keepers will scour every inch of the Calistan desert to find him." He turned to me. "Are you really going to let Miranda go like that? I thought you cared about what happens to her."

"I do!" I looked from him to Amara. "Can't we go after him and free her now?"

"If I had no one to think of but myself, I'd leave now," she said. "But Grey himself isn't the biggest danger. You know that, Nikolas—you've said it yourself. You're just too worked up right now to acknowledge it."

"What do you mean?" I asked.

"The real danger to Tartora is what we've seen on the road and here in Caltor," she said. "It's the poisonous seeds Grey has been leaving to cover his tracks. Many Tartorans now believe that their own king is colluding with Calista to steal our young people. It's an outrageous claim, but Grey's been systematically working his way around the kingdom, his words and actions seeming to provide proof. At this point, Tartora is becoming a powder keg. And Serena and her friends are the ones who can defuse the situation. They're what matters most right now."

"Are we really that important?" Serena asked, sounding small for the first time since I'd known her.

"Yes, you are." Amara met her eyes calmly. "Thanks to you, we have the chance to calm the tensions in Caltor immediately, and Anka can then send word out to the rest of the kingdom. That has to be Hayes' and my priority."

"And what about you?" Nik spun to face me. "Is that your decision as well, or are you going to come with me and save your friend?"

His eyes were hard, his face tight, but I read something else behind his icy determination. A hidden note of vulnerability. He'd seen my reaction to his true identity, and now he was asking me to put everything aside and go with him. He was reaching out his hand and waiting to see if I would take it.

I stood, frozen with indecision, my eyes locked on his.

"What are you saying?" Amara snapped, finally losing her cool. "Delphine is my apprentice! Of course she must stay here with me. Do you want her to become a reneger, like you?"

Nik pulled back as if struck, but a moment later he recovered.

"Better to be a reneger and do the right thing, than remain an apprentice and abandon someone you care about."

"Don't twist the situation," Amara said, her calm returning. "Delphine will stay here and help me save the entire kingdom. Staying is how she can do the right thing."

"We have to find Grey," Nik snapped. "If we don't, he'll continue poisoning this kingdom and any other he wanders into. You haven't seen his silver tongue at work or seen the way he charms and manipulates people. We have to go now!"

Amara stared him down silently. For several moments, he met her look for look, but eventually he let out an explosive breath and swung to face me.

"Delphine?" He actually held out his hand this time, and I stared at it.

I had been furious at him after Hayes's revelation, but now I felt only pain and sadness at what I had to do.

"I'm sorry," I whispered. "I can't leave Amara. I have to stay and help Serena and the others tell everyone the truth about Grey."

For a breathless moment, Nik held my gaze, fire leaping

across the distance between us. And then he spun on his heels and stormed down the street, disappearing all too quickly into the darkness.

I gasped, swaying on my feet. Serena steadied me, slipping an arm around my waist.

"I'm sorry," she murmured. "I should never have gone with Grey in the first place."

"No, you shouldn't have," Amara agreed, making me wince at her coldness. But she continued on in the same steady tone. "But it has turned out to be fortunate you did. Your testimony, combined with the evidence of your body, will be enough to have Grey declared a criminal across both Tartora and Calista. We'll find him eventually, don't worry."

She stepped closer and took my arm, taking my weight from Serena. Leading me away from the others, she patted my hand comfortingly.

"I'm sorry, Delphine. I don't properly understand—or condone—what's been going on between you and Nik, but I'm sorry I didn't tell you the truth about his identity back in Ostaria. Maybe I could have prevented some of this from happening."

I drew back, reminded of all that had previously passed between her and Nik—and between me and her about him.

"How could you not tell me?" I demanded.

She winced. "As things have turned out, it appears I should have. But I didn't have the benefit of hindsight, then, and the fact that the prince has gone rogue is a royal secret. Those of us entrusted with it have been sternly commanded not to talk about it."

"Are you expected to keep secrets even from your own apprentice?" I asked sadly, but I didn't need an answer. Of course the crown wouldn't think an unknown apprentice should be entrusted with their secrets.

I looked at Amara, suddenly needing to know something. "Would you have told me if it was your own secret?"

I caught the slightest hesitation in her expression and narrowed my eyes as a possibility struck me. "What? Did you think that telling me the truth about his identity would only make him more fascinating to me?"

Amara's eyes shifted, revealing there was at least a kernel of truth in my guess, but when she spoke it was to refute my words.

"I want our relationship to be built on trust, Delphine. If one of my own secrets becomes relevant to you, I will certainly entrust you with it."

"Do you really have that much faith in me?" I asked, my tone conveying my wounded disbelief.

She took my hand again. "If I didn't before, I will in the future. What you did here was incredible given your level of training. I could see Hayes was deeply impressed. He's actually already agreed to help with your training—at least for a while. And I can see you're ready to start that training. It's clear you've completely overcome your squeamishness."

I nodded. "I was going to tell you about it. And about meeting Grey's men and Nik here in Caltor, but you were gone all day."

Amara winced. "I'm sorry about that. I let myself get distracted by...Well, I shouldn't have let myself get distracted. We've only been together for weeks, and we've both failed each other in various ways. But like it or not, we're bound together. Do you think we can start afresh?"

Looking at her earnest face, my frustration with her melted away. My father had tried to control me through secrets and ignorance, but Amara had just declared her desire for openness between us. She didn't even need to use underhanded tactics to manipulate me since she had the authority to control me without such methods. But she chose to walk a different path—

to build me up and empower me instead of controlling me. I had been fortunate indeed in my choice of influencer.

"There's no need for starting again on my side," I said in a voice tinged with tears. "You've treated me far better than I expected. Even now, you're treating me like we're part of a team. Thank you, Amara. I hope you know you have my loyalty for far longer than the two years that the law binds us."

Amara looked at me for a long moment before glancing down the dark street in the direction where Nik had disappeared. Turning suddenly back, she swept me into an uncharacteristic hug.

"I've already seen that loyalty for myself. Thank you for gifting it to me, Delphine. I hope that you and I can do great things together in the coming years."

"Starting with getting Grey off the streets of Tartora," I said, squeezing her back.

She pulled away, her dangerous smile making me glad I wasn't Grey. "Starting with that."

# BONUS CHAPTER - NIK

READ THE END OF THE BOOK FROM NIK'S
PERSPECTIVE IN THIS BONUS CHAPTER

There was something freeing about letting my power loose. After so long tracking Grey from the shadows, it felt good to step into the open. Defending Delphine from her would-be abductors had given me a taste, but this was even better.

I sent my power reaching into the ground and snaking up into the rafters, continuing on higher into the stone overhead. I held the floor and the roof in my hands, and I didn't intend to let anyone escape.

A man tried to slip out of the main warehouse through the door that led to the children and Delphine. I sent a snaking vine to twist around his ankle, yanking him backward. He tripped and fell, his head hitting the frame of the door as he went down. He didn't get back up.

I smiled viciously and looked for the next person still moving. The first few had come for me in a rush, but when the others saw what happened to them, they'd gone to ground. I didn't mind. I was happy to hunt them down slowly since I was only here to be a distraction.

Grey was the one I really wanted, but he'd disappeared—out of sight from the moment I smashed through the front doors. I was going to find him, though. Grey thought some people mattered more than others, and now he'd set his sights on Delphine. I had no intention of letting him leave this warehouse.

I stepped over a chunk of stone torn from one of the walls and then over the dazed body of the young man it had felled. He looked vaguely familiar, and I thought he might have come from Delphine's village. I hoped she hadn't been fond of him.

Just the idea of it made my chest tight, but I pushed the feeling aside. I needed to stay alert.

Movement in the shadows made me spin around, light on the balls of my feet, ready for action. The largest of Grey's followers—the brute who had once grabbed Delphine—lunged toward me, his blade drawn.

But the attack was only a distraction. The sideways flicker of his eyes revealed the real threat on my left. A dagger flew toward me, carried on a thin, controlled stream of air.

So he had an elements affinity. It figured.

I pretended to be oblivious, keeping my eyes on the approaching man and the blade in his hand. But as the dagger drew close, I sent my power reaching for a small stone that had fallen from the roof as I tore a larger chunk away.

Whipping it through the air, I launched it at the dagger, knocking the weapon out of the thin wind. It fell to the ground with a clatter. Vines sprang from the dirt, wrapping around it and tying it to the ground.

That dagger wouldn't be flying again any time soon.

The man grunted and threw himself the remaining distance toward me. His previous approach had been slow, his attention divided between his movement and his use of his power. But unlike him, I used my power with ease, leaving the majority of my attention on preparing for his physical attack.

Bringing up my own blade, I knocked his aside, sidestepping his attempt at a riposte. He didn't have great skill with a sword, but his height gave him enormous reach, and the confrontation was moving me away from the door I needed to guard. It was time to end it.

Once again pulling my blade up in defense, I kept my eyes trained on the man. But my power reached for the roof, seeking a stone that was already loose from my previous efforts. Wrenching it free, I sent it falling directly onto my opponent.

He sensed it coming at the last moment and sidestepped, but it still caught him on the shoulder. His arm locked up, his sword dropping from his slack grasp. A moment later, he staggered and fell.

A sound distracted me, and I looked toward the internal door just in time to see it swing closed. Someone had gone through to Delphine while I was distracted.

Leaving my dazed opponent, I raced across the warehouse, leaping the fallen stones and vines without looking at them, letting my power guide me. Just before I reached the door, however, a woman appeared, leaping from my right and colliding with me.

We both went sprawling, a grunt escaping me as my breath was knocked from my lungs. For a second, I couldn't move, too winded by the fall. But the moment my body recovered, I leaped up, raising my blade and looking for my new attacker. She had made it to her feet first, retreating far enough to be out of reach but close enough to launch another attack if I tried to head through the door again.

I dropped into a crouch, considering the best way to deal with her. Before I had decided, the brute reappeared, swaying slightly but back on his feet. He joined her, and a sudden wind picked up the dust kicked loose from the floor, sending it into a whirlwind between us that obscured them from view.

I reached for the ground in their general vicinity, sending countless seedlings sprouting across it. The greenery was short and harmless, unlike the thorny vines I'd exploded from the ground elsewhere, but they brushed against the feet and legs of my opponents, letting me know their location.

A shout of warning from the woman suggested she'd realized their purpose, but she was too late. Reaching for one of the seeds I'd scattered earlier, I pushed my power down to create temporary roots and then up into two thorny vines, each reaching for one of Grey's followers.

Another yell echoed through the space, and the dusty whirlwind between us stilled, the dirt falling back to the ground. The woman was completely trapped, but the man still had his hands free and was trying to hack at the vine with a dagger. I sent new branches snaking out, wrapping around both his arms and pinning them to his sides.

With a wordless bellow of protest, he tipped, falling sideways where more vines sprouted up to tie him to the ground as I had done to his dagger.

Scanning the warehouse, I could see no other moving figures. Had I finally found them all? Either way, I wasn't delaying any longer.

I turned back to the door, but its handle was moving, twisted from the other side. I instantly melted back into the shadows, waiting to see who would come through.

Grey appeared, a girl slung over his shoulder. His hand clamped tightly around her wrist—a threatening gesture in the circumstances. I hesitated for a second while I examined her, making sure it wasn't Delphine he was holding hostage.

It only took a moment to determine it wasn't her, but in that time, Grey had already made it part way across the warehouse, ignoring the mess I had made of both his hideout and his people.

I growled and started after him, ready to end this once and for all.

But while my gaze was focused on Grey, my ears caught a separate sound. Someone had followed him into the warehouse, their gait unsteady.

"No!" The attempted shout sounded breathless and weak, but I recognized the voice anyway.

I whirled toward Delphine, unformed fear tugging at me. She was looking straight at me, and for a moment all I could see were her desperate, horrified eyes. Until my gaze dropped to her middle, and then all I could see was the dagger hilt she was clutching, the red blood flowing around her fingers.

Grey had stabbed her.

Rage filled me, hot and bubbling. But the fear was stronger still.

Abandoning my pursuit of Grey, I sprinted toward Delphine instead. I had sought her out and brought her here. I had asked her to do this, and Grey had stabbed her.

The pain on her face struck me like the blows my opponents had never managed to land, blossoming and twisting inside me. Delphine couldn't die. I wouldn't let that happen.

Reaching her, I scooped her into my arms, barely slowing my momentum. She was light, too light, although I told myself that couldn't be due to her wound.

I barreled straight through the partially open door and took in the empty room in a glance. Spotting a nearby sofa, I laid her down on it and knelt at her side.

I had to get the dagger out and find a way to fix her. I knew I wasn't thinking straight, but it was hard to focus around the white hot rage and ice cold fear warring within me. I couldn't let this girl—somehow fragile and strong at the same time—die because of me. I couldn't let her die at all.

I reached for the hilt of the dagger, still protruding from her middle, but the foolish girl batted my hands away.

"Leave it be." Her words came out on a rough pant, as if she was struggling to breathe. "Help her."

She made a vague gesture toward another girl who lay unmoving near the window. I had noticed her on our arrival, but only to categorize her as a non-threat.

When I stayed in place, Delphine pushed at me, her arms barely strong enough to rock me. I hesitated, trying to understand why she was driving me away.

Before I realized what she was intending, she grabbed the hilt in both her own hands and pulled it out in one smooth motion. Her scream rent the room, her expression twisting with pain.

All the blood drained from my face, my stomach burning as if she had thrust the knife into me after removing it from herself. What did it take to make a healer scream like that?

I leaned forward, but her eyes had lost their focus, her attention on something I couldn't see. For a terrifying second, I thought she was slipping away from me, but instead her color returned, her face relaxing.

Through the fog of my panic, I remembered the way she had healed Ember. Delphine was still a new apprentice, but was it possible her strength was sufficient to handle her own healing?

When she sat up, gasping with relief, the knot inside me started to unravel. Her dress was still a torn and bloody mess, but there was no new red seeping out, and when she twisted, I got a glimpse of smooth, unblemished skin. She really had healed herself.

"What are you doing?" she scolded me. "I'm a healer, remember! I'm fine now. We need to help Serena."

I had no idea who Serena was, and I didn't particularly care, not when I hadn't yet ascertained that Delphine was completely healed and out of danger.

But the stern expression on her face drove me to my feet. I looked between the girl and the older woman, both unconscious on the ground. She must mean the girl, surely?

Clearly out of patience with me, Delphine brushed past me, falling to her knees next to the girl. As soon as she did so, the girl stirred and coughed blood across Delphine's already filthy dress.

I grimaced. I was no healer, but that couldn't be good.

The way Delphine groaned and released her hold on the girl seemed to confirm my suspicion. But perhaps Delphine was merely exhausted.

"What is it?" I asked from over her shoulder. "Did you heal her?"

Delphine shook her head. "He's literally shredded her insides. I don't know how she's still alive. Everything needs healing. And it doesn't feel...right. My power doesn't know what to do."

I had no idea what she meant by that, but I could feel her distress. This girl mattered to Delphine, and I wasn't going to let her watch her friend die.

"Then we find someone who does," I said.

I picked her up as I had earlier done for Delphine.

"I don't think she'll last long enough," Delphine said, sounding distressed.

I gave her a stern look. "Then you keep her alive. Keep her alive just as long as it takes."

I already knew Delphine was stronger than my first estimation. I was certain she was strong enough for this, and I would lend her as much of my strength as she needed on top. I refused to see her spirit broken any more than her body.

She seemed to calm slightly, making contact with the girl again.

A boy waited for us on the other side of the window, and with his assistance, I maneuvered all three of us through. When

Delphine nearly tipped through the opening, too distracted by her patient to consider herself, I wrapped my hands around her waist and lifted her through as easily as I might have lifted a kitten.

After relinquishing the injured girl back to me, the boy ran off, planning to gather the other escaped healers. But if Delphine could do nothing for this girl, then the rest of them would have little hope, even working together.

We needed a proper healer and soon.

A bark made me jerk and stop, scanning the nearest cross street. An orange streak appeared, with a woman close behind.

I had been hoping to avoid Master Amara in Caltor, but Delphine's relief at her appearance was obvious. Not that Amara would be much help with a dying patient.

The two people following her were another matter, however. I groaned at the sight of Hayes. I'd barely gotten rid of him once tonight, and I was afraid I wouldn't be so fortunate a second time. But I couldn't deny he was the person we needed right now.

I lowered the girl to the ground, marveling at how heavy she'd grown in the short walk from the building. Delphine sank to her knees beside her, still working to keep the girl alive. She soon had backup not only from Hayes but from the girl following him. She must be the Calistan apprentice he'd mentioned, but I noticed only the vaguest familiarity to her features.

Delphine finally released her hold and rose to her feet. She moved more slowly than I would have liked, and I watched her closely, looking for any sign she might collapse from exhaustion. Her master—who should have been the one most concerned about her well-being—was more focused on the healing underway than her apprentice.

Seized by an uncontrollable impulse, I took advantage of

her distraction. Grabbing Delphine's wrist, I whisked her into a narrow side alley, out of the line of sight of the others.

She tensed, as if she meant to fight me, but as soon as I spun her around to face me, she relaxed.

"Oh, it's you." She smiled sweetly up at me.

The combination of her smile and her proximity made my heart race faster than it had done during the battle in the warehouse. But I couldn't smile back until I was sure she was fully healed. I ran my hands up and down her arms, half expecting to find some new injury hidden from my sight.

"Are you sure you're all right? You don't have any other injuries?" I kept seeing the dagger sprouting from her middle and needed physical contact to drive the image away.

"Don't be silly." She seemed to think I was foolish, and I dimly registered that would have once infuriated me. But all I could think of now was the memory of the blood flowing from her. "How many times do I have to remind you I'm a healer? I'm fine."

"You nearly died." The words were flat and hard.

She shook her head. "No, that's Serena. We should go and check on her. She's the one who was in real danger."

"I took you there." My hands rose of their own volition, cradling her face. "I asked for your help, and you nearly died. I nearly killed you."

"I'm really all right." She sounded breathless, reminding me of the horrible moments before she healed herself. "I promise. As a healer, I was never in any real danger from a wound like that. Grey was just being spiteful."

"Spiteful?" The word exploded from me, bringing a wave of the earlier fury with it. "How can you say...He stabbed you!"

I let go of her face, only to grasp her arms instead, still craving the contact although I now knew she was fine.

She was so close—too close for my self-control. I swayed toward her. How long had I been fighting this impulse, telling myself it was only a passing fancy? But after feeling her half dead in my arms, I could no longer restrain the impulse.

My control snapped, and I pressed her backward. She collided with the stone wall of the alley, and I collided with her. My lips dropped to hers, tasting their sweetness as fire burned through me.

One of my hands cupped her soft cheek while the other wrapped around her waist, pulling her closer against me but wanting to be even closer still. She kissed me back, matching my desperate passion, and the fire inside me roared higher.

I had been lying to myself when I pretended this girl was nothing but a useful and temporary ally.

She was the only person who had ever sought me out and valued me not for my title or influence, but for me. She had looked at my ability and seen strength—had even lectured me about the importance of the plants affinity despite being a healer herself. And she had approved of what I chose to do with my ability, even trusting me enough to risk her life at my side.

I needed her beside me, where I could keep her safe. I needed to keep her with me and never let her go.

I pressed deeper into the kiss. But in the distance, I heard someone calling for her. Her master.

The thought speared through me, and I broke off, my breath ragged. Delphine wasn't mine. Not yet.

She stared back at me, the brightness in her eyes changing to confusion.

When the call came again, I let her go and stepped back, just in time to keep Amara from seeing our embrace. She still regarded me with suspicion, though, her eyes flicking between us.

"What are you two doing in here? What's going on?"

Delphine hurried toward her, leaving me behind.

"How's Serena?" she asked. "Is she healed?"

My lips tightened. How could she put me and our kiss aside so easily, her mind moving on to other things?

She hurried away from me, and for a moment my feet refused to follow. But as soon as she was out of sight, I felt an itching discomfort. I couldn't just leave things like that. I needed to talk to her properly.

I followed slowly, listening to the introductions going on ahead of me. When I neared the huddled group, Hayes looked up, meeting my eyes over Delphine's shoulder.

He gave a slight bow, more respectful than he'd been at the end of our earlier conversation.

"Your Highness," he said in a flat voice.

Delphine stiffened at the words, and my eyes widened as I realized my mistake. For some reason, Amara had chosen not to reveal my identity to her apprentice, but she obviously hadn't instructed Hayes to do the same.

Delphine turned slowly toward me, her brow furrowed in confusion and her hands gripping her skirts, as if she was preparing to curtsy to my parents. Her eyes landed on me, but I couldn't bring myself to meet her astonished gaze, keeping my glare fixed on Hayes instead.

Delphine couldn't know the details of the rejections that had driven me from the capital—unwelcome among my own family. But she must have heard rumors, at least, of the disgraced prince who had been cast aside. How would she see me now that she knew I was him? Would she regret seeking out someone who had been deemed unworthy?

As the seconds ticked by, my eyes were drawn irresistibly toward her. I remained silent, although inside I willed her to understand why I had kept my identity hidden.

Amara said something to Hayes, but I wasn't listening, my whole focus having narrowed to one girl. She looked horrified and distressed as she stared back at me, and I realized I had been a fool to forget my status in her presence, even for a moment. I was a disgraced prince and a reneger, and a girl like Delphine would never belong with me.

Her expression transformed again, fear creeping into her eyes. What stories had she heard? Was it me she feared? The sight of it was too much for me, and her name escaped my lips. She shook her head savagely in response, though, and I fell silent.

Another voice piped up, slicing obliviously through the tension. "So it really is you." Apparently Hayes's apprentice remembered me better than I remembered her. "Their Majesties will be very pleased to know where you are."

I turned my harshest glare on her, recognizing yet more of the dangers that awaited me. "Don't you dare tell them I'm here."

Hayes sighed. "I already told you that we can't possibly—"

"And I told you that if you send word, I'll be gone before they can send anyone back for me." I stared icily at Hayes.

I had no intention of returning to a place where I was unwanted and unappreciated. If I was always going to live in the shadows, it would be on my own terms.

"I've been gone for over a year," I continued. "I'm not the prince you used to know. I'm far more familiar with the streets than you'll ever be."

If they tried to stop me, I would disappear right now.

Hayes sighed again. "Is this all really necessary, Nikolas? Your parents and sister miss you."

"Do they?" I almost scoffed at the suggestion. "I can't imagine why. They never had any use for me when I was with them."

"That's not fair," Hayes spoke softly, his pity more abrasive than contempt.

"Isn't it? I suppose next you're going to tell me the Triumvirate miss me too?"

Even Hayes couldn't deny the rejection I had faced from his

superiors. He looked away, seeking comfort in Amara's face, as he always did.

I looked back at Delphine, the only person here I wanted to speak to, but her attention was on her friend, Serena. She fussed over the other girl until their conversation turned to Grey and Miranda. I gathered the missing Miranda was the girl Grey had carted off like a sack of potatoes.

When Serena mentioned Grey's interest in strong healers, I stared at Delphine, wondering if she would finally take my warning seriously. I had failed and let Grey escape, and now he would be coming for her more determinedly than ever. I didn't doubt he would want her after seeing the way she liberated all his new acolytes from under his nose.

My insides tightened at the thought of Delphine under Grey's spell. I wouldn't let that happen.

Serena mentioned something about Grey having left a spy in Tarin, and I joined the conversation. I needed to dispel such a ridiculous notion before it took root. Grey was tricky and deceptive, but his reach was limited. If he had been leaving people behind in every town, I would have noticed.

Serena accepted the news of Grey's deception, but when she confirmed his new land had never been Calista, I didn't feel the expected vindication. It was hard to feel anything so victorious when Delphine still hadn't looked at me with anything but betrayal in her eyes.

Serena mentioned the boy from their hometown, saying he had been with Grey in the warehouse, and Delphine looked at me, uncertainty on her face.

"Is he still alive, then?"

Disappointment sunk like a stone in my stomach. Did she think I was a bloodthirsty killer?

"Of course," I said heavily. "They're all alive."

The law keepers arrived before I could engage further, but they didn't stay long. Hayes took the opportunity to betray my identity, ensuring I would have to leave Caltor immediately. I would have resented him for it, but there was no way Grey would linger around the city anyway, so it made no difference.

We would have to move quickly if we meant to catch him. But to my shock, Amara spoke not of pursuit but of taking all the rescued youths to the law keeping hall.

"And who is going after Grey?" I asked, incredulous. "For every minute we talk, he gets further away."

Amara sighed. "I'm as eager to see him pay for his crimes as anyone, but what do you intend to do if you catch him? You already let him go once because of the threat to his hostage. It sounds like he has need of her, so as long as we stay away, she'll be safe enough. Right now, the most dangerous thing for Miranda would be for us to confront Grey."

I stepped forward, unable to believe what I was hearing. "You just want to let him go? After what he did?" My eyes flicked to Delphine, once again seeing the dagger emerging from her middle.

"I don't want to," Amara said, "but I don't see any other choice for the moment. Once these witnesses have recorded official statements, we'll have the evidence we need to mobilize the law keepers. Grey just lost many of his followers, and he won't move as quickly with a hostage in tow. We'll find him eventually."

"Maybe," I snapped, my frustration boiling over. She had no idea how difficult Grey was to track. "Or maybe he'll go to ground and be lost to us. If he makes it across the border, he's really gone. Even you can't pretend that Tartoran law keepers will scour every inch of the Calistan desert to find him."

I turned to Delphine, shamelessly appealing to her concern for her friend as I fought to keep her by my side. "Are you really going to let Miranda go like that? I thought you cared about what happens to her."

"I do!" Delphine looked pleadingly at Amara. "Can't we go after him and free her now?"

"If I had no one to think of but myself, I'd leave now," she said. "But Grey himself isn't the biggest danger. You know that, Nikolas—you've said it yourself. You're just too worked up right now to acknowledge it."

I narrowed my eyes at her insult, but her words had given Delphine pause.

"What do you mean?" she asked.

Amara spun an explanation that sounded both smooth and reasonable, swaying both girls. My desperation rose as I saw Delphine's expression change.

I put my whole focus on her, blocking out the others. My desire for her to remain with me surged up, overpowering my earlier acknowledgment that she would never belong at my side.

"And what about you?" I asked. "Is that your decision as well, or are you going to come with me and save your friend?"

She stood still, her eyes on mine, panicked and uncertain. But I had already lost her. I could read it in her hesitation.

"What are you saying?" Amara snapped, breaking through my focus. "Delphine is my apprentice! Of course she must stay here with me. Do you want her to become a reneger, like you?"

Her words hit me like a physical blow, only confirming my earlier realization. I was an outcast—as I had always been in one way or another—and someone like Delphine would never fit that role.

Still, a part of me fought, desperate not to lose her at the very moment I realized how much I wanted her presence. "Better to be a reneger and do the right thing, than remain an apprentice and abandon someone you care about."

"Don't twist the situation," Amara said. "Delphine will stay here and help me save the entire kingdom. Staying is how she can do the right thing."

"We have to find Grey," I snapped, my desperation leaking through. "If we don't, he'll continue poisoning this kingdom and any other he wanders into. You haven't seen his silver tongue at work or seen the way he charms and manipulates people. We have to go now!"

Amara held my gaze, her own rock steady. I stared back, but as the seconds passed, my momentary defiance leaked away. Why would Delphine choose to abandon everything for me?

I let out a breath. "Delphine?" I held out my hand to her, wishing I didn't already know she wasn't going to take it.

"I'm sorry," she whispered. "I can't leave Amara. I have to stay and help Serena and the others tell everyone the truth about Grey."

I held her gaze, letting all my emotions loose, the fire from before leaping briefly inside me again as I tried to remember this moment and what it felt like to stand beside her.

Then I turned and strode down the street, already feeling the looming darkness closing in around me. I had chosen my solitary life, and I would be wise not to forget it. I would always be alone, and this was why. I would never be enough for anyone.

But I still had a purpose.

The fire in my gut shifted, burning brightly again as I thought of Grey. He was out there, his greed set on Delphine, and I would hunt him to the ends of the kingdom if I had to.

I might never be able to keep Delphine with me, but I could still protect her from afar—her and all the other people Grey had touched, the ones discarded by their kingdom.

# NOTE FROM THE AUTHOR

To read what happens next for Delphine, Amara, and Nik, continue their story in book two, Storms of Allegiance.

Or go back and read about the restoration of the fallen kingdom and Nik's history in A Mage's Influence series, starting with Seeds of Glory and Ruin.

To be informed of future releases, as well as A Mage's Apprentice bonus shorts, please sign up to my mailing list at www.melaniecellier.com.

And if you enjoyed Winds of Courage, please spread the word and help other readers find it! You could start by leaving a review on Amazon or Goodreads or Facebook or any other social media site. Your review would be very much appreciated and would make a big difference!

# Acknowledgments

At the end of my Mage's Influence series, I knew Nik's story was really only beginning. And while Delphine gets to be the point of view character in this new adventure, Nik has always been a central part of this story. That's why I decided to include the bonus chapter from his perspective at the end of the book, instead of just on my website like I usually do. I hope you enjoyed getting a glimpse inside his head.

Like so many of us in the wake of 2020, I've been battling burnout, and in particular, creative burnout. Given my need to fill my creative well, I'm grateful for the author friends who pushed me into the (belated) discovery of kdramas, and to my long-suffering husband who carried the household responsibilities while I watched way too many of them.

Although those countless hours let me come to this book with a renewed sense of creative interest, I'm still working on recovering my old productivity, and so I'm excessively grateful to my ever-patient team for helping push me across the finish line.

An enormous thank you to my betas, Rachel, Greg, Priya, and Ber. To my editors, Mary, and Dad, and my new proofreader, James. To my cover designer, Karri, who always shows superhuman patience with me, and my map artist, Rebecca. You are all stars, every one.

Thank you also to Marina for writing sprints and general encouragement, and to the Indie Bunch ladies for always having my back (and front and side) in this crazy publishing world. And, of course, my gracious assistant Lyra who makes a continued valiant effort to keep me from forgetting any important pieces of admin. She's struggling against the tide on that one.

And thank you to God who is the king of turning weaknesses into strengths.

# ABOUT THE AUTHOR

 Melanie Cellier grew up on a staple diet of books, books and more books. And although she got older, she never stopped loving children's and young adult novels.

She always wanted to write one herself, but it took three careers and three different continents before she actually managed it.

She now feels incredibly fortunate to spend her time writing from her home in Adelaide, Australia where she keeps an eye out for koalas in her backyard. Her staple diet hasn't changed much, although she's added choc mint Rooibos tea and Chicken Crimpies to the list.

She writes young adult fantasy including books in her *Spoken Mage* world, her *Mage's Influence* world, and her various *Four Kingdoms* and *Kingdoms of Legacy* series that are made up of linked stand-alone stories that retell classic fairy tales.

www.ingramcontent.com/pod-product-compliance
Lightning Source LLC
Chambersburg PA
CBHW061620210726
48287CB00001B/216